Dear Reader . . .

Have you ever wanted

That is exactly what former actress Eva Eberhart sets out to do when she quits her job as a dance hall entertainer and applies for a housekeeping position at the Trail's End Ranch. All Eva is looking for is a little respect—until she meets her new employer.

Chase Cassidy is a gunman and former felon with a dark past who hires Eva because he believes her to be a prim, proper, down-on-her-luck lady from Philadelphia. From the moment she knocks on his door, Chase has one thing on his mind and there isn't anything respectable about it!

Throw in Chase's headstrong, rebellious nephew, a couple of outlaws dead set on revenge, along with a mysterious mummy case and you'll enjoy what I hope are some very pleasurable hours as you read **AFTER ALL**.

Yours Truly,

Jill Marie Landis

Jill Marie Landis

Turn the page . . . and enter a world of romance and adventure!
Discover all of the critically acclaimed novels
of bestselling author Jill Marie Landis . . .

JADE

Her exotic beauty captured the heart of a rugged rancher. But could he forget the past—and love again?

"Guaranteed to enthrall . . . an unusual, fast-paced love story."
—*Romantic Times*

ROSE

Across the golden frontier, her passionate heart dared to dream . . .

"A gentle romance that will warm your soul."—*Heartland Critiques*

WILDFLOWER

Amidst the untamed beauty of the Rocky Mountains, two daring hearts forged a perilous passion . . .

"A delight from start to finish!"—*Rendezvous*

Jill Marie Landis's stunning debut novel . . .
SUNFLOWER

Winner of the Romance Writers of America's Golden Medallion Award for Best Historical Romance, this sweeping love story astonished critics, earning glowing reviews including a FIVE STAR rating from *Affaire de Coeur*. It was a promise of shining talent that Jill Marie Landis fulfilled countless times over in each of her romantic, sensual novels . . .

A spirited woman of the prairie. A handsome half-breed who stole her heart. A love as wild as the wind . . .

"A truly fabulous read! This story comes vibrantly alive, making you laugh and cry . . ."—*Affaire de Coeur*

AFTER ALL

JILL MARIE LANDIS

JOVE BOOKS, NEW YORK

Spanish quotations taken from *Dichos, Proverbs
and Sayings from the Spanish* by Charles Aranda. Sunstone Press,
Santa Fe, New Mexico. Copyright © 1977 by Charles Aranda.

AFTER ALL

A Jove Book / published by arrangement with
the author

PRINTING HISTORY
Jove edition / January 1995

ISBN: 0-515-11501-0

A JOVE BOOK®
Jove Books are published by The Berkley Publishing Group,
200 Madison Avenue, New York, New York 10016.
JOVE and the "J" design are trademarks
belonging to Jove Publications, Inc.

PRINTED IN THE UNITED STATES OF AMERICA

10 9 8 7 6 5 4 3 2 1

Chapter One

God, I hate this place.

Evangeline Eberhart stood near the steps to the stage at the back of the Palace of Venus Saloon and Dance Hall and watched the crowd of miners, gamblers, and regular drunks cavort in the room below. Most of the latter were already bleary-eyed as they sat hunched over tables placed well out of the way of foot traffic.

She barely heard the tinny sound of the piano and the banjo plunking away in one corner. Nor was it the clink of coins on the felt-covered tabletops, the constant scrape of chairs across the floorboards or the jingle of spurs on the heels of the cowboys' boots that annoyed her. The smoke and the noise did not irritate her either.

But being manhandled was the one thing she had never gotten used to and never would.

After six months of dancing at the Palace, Eva reached the point where she didn't think she could stand one more day.

No sooner had she begun to circulate the room than she was assaulted by a balding, near-toothless miner. Nelson Brewer stood inches away, weaving on his feet, trying to focus bloodshot eyes on her breasts.

"Don't even think about it, old man. Not today." Her hushed undertone was delivered through clenched teeth. She was afraid to think what she might do if he actually attempted to maul her.

1

He staggered a little closer. "How about just a little feel, Evie?" The liquor on his breath was potent enough to light.

"Keep your damn hands off me, Nelson, before I kick your *cajones* up to your Adam's apple." Sure he was old. Yes, he was drunk. But Eva couldn't stop herself as she shoved him backward. He tumbled over one of the empty poker tables at the back of the crowded room. In a drunken stupor, he rolled into a heap beside the legs of one of the gambler's chairs and promptly fell sound asleep.

So furious she could spit, Eva reached down and grasped the top of her raspberry-tinted bone corset where it barely graced the curves of her breasts. She gave the corset a hard yank. Glancing down, she made certain her breasts were covered where they needed to be before she strode on through the fog of cigar smoke.

"Give 'em hell, Evie," one of the regulars hollered.

Eva ignored him and walked on until she cleared the center of the room and stood trembling with suppressed anger beside one of the stained-glass windows set in the front wall.

Hoping to calm down, she allowed herself a minute of contemplation and watched the comings and goings of the townspeople, whose images wavered on the other side of the colorful glass window. It was Saturday afternoon, a day when the farmers and ranchers from the nearby holdings came to town to visit, buy supplies, and congregate for the day. The Palace of Venus was already crowded and bound to become even more congested once twilight fell and the cowboys rode into town ready to celebrate Saturday night with a bath, a bottle, and a woman.

"You all right, Eva?" She glanced up at the sound of compassion in a truly concerned voice. Her cousin, John Hutton, stood beside her. Eva smiled and reached out to straighten his tie.

"I can't take this anymore." She watched his expressive eyes darken in sympathy. The tenderness mirrored there was incongruous with his appearance. He was half the size of a bull and twice as deadly.

He glanced over his shoulder, and then turned around so that he could face the long bar at the back of the room. As bouncer and so-called general promoter at the Palace of Venus, he wasn't paid to stand and chitchat with the dancers while his back was to the action, even if this particular dancer happened to be his cousin.

"You'll get over it, Eva. You always do. 'Sides they don't mean anything by it."

She finger-combed her tousled copper hair into place. "I'm serious. The next man who touches me is going to regret it." She could see by his lack of response that John did not really take her threat seriously.

"This crowd is itching for a fight. I can feel it in the air tonight. You better think before you start anything, Eva. If anything gets busted up, Quincy will take it out of your pay for sure."

She thought of the pitiful savings she had managed to stash away in hopes of making a new start elsewhere. Quincy Powell, gambler, lying two-timer, and owner of the Palace, would indeed go after what little she had if he thought she owed it to him.

The sound of shattering glass drew their attention, and John immediately stepped away, headed toward a duo who had squared off over a spilled glass of whiskey.

"If one more idiot touches me, I swear I'll quit," she mumbled to herself as she watched him work his way easily through the crowd. Tall and broad, impeccably dressed in a starched white shirt and striped wool pants, he had a penchant for neatness that belied his willingness to dive into any brawl. John Hutton kept the local laundry in business almost single-handedly.

She loved him as much as she would a brother, but she knew it was only a matter of time before she would have enough money saved to put her own plan into action and they parted ways. She would have never have stayed at the Palace this long if it hadn't been for John.

Movement directly outside caught her eye, and she drew closer to the window. Through a clear piece in the floral-patterned arrangement of glass and lead, she could see a young man tie the reins of a team of mules to a hitching post just outside the saloon. Casually, he thumbed his wide-brimmed hat back off his forehead and smiled up at a girl perched high on the wagon seat before he reached up to help her down.

Eva felt like a voyeur, staring out at the wholesome pair, watching intently as the young farmer gently helped the girl to the boardwalk. A narrow band of gold on the young woman's hand glinted in the sunlight. Eva's naked left hand curled into a fist. She dropped it to her side.

Unable to help herself, she continued to watch the couple, to take in every detail of their dress and posture. Clothed in a modest calico gown with a handmade shawl tied about her shoulders, the young wife stared up adoringly into her husband's eyes. He gazed down at her just as lovingly, careful to step to the street side of the boardwalk and tuck her hand into the crook of his elbow before they started off down the street.

Longing filled Eva. The emotion was so intense that it brought a biting sting to the back of her eyes. The couple standing a few feet away was separated from her by far more than a stained-glass window. They existed in a world entirely away from her own, a world of polite manners and respectability, of church socials and quilting bees, of vegetable gardens and evenings gathered around a warm stove in a homey kitchen. She bit her lips and turned away, faced the room once more and welcomed the pungent smoke that forced her to blink back tears. Why didn't she deserve to be treated with as much respect as the woman outside the window?

The tenor of the piano music changed as it rolled out and over the room. She recognized the number. It was the one Sam Robins always played to announce the start of the afternoon show. She had three minutes to go backstage and get ready for her featured dance.

Eva glanced down to make certain the pink combination chemise and drawers she wore beneath the frilly, shocking raspberry corset still looked fresh. She took a deep breath and decided to wade through the room on her way backstage, relishing the chance to leave the main floor. Dancing was the only thing she looked forward to anymore. Perhaps it would help her put the disturbingly touching scene beyond the window out of her mind.

The piano and banjo players broke into a rendition of "I'll Take You Home Again, Kathleen," but the melancholy tune did little to quiet the boisterous Saturday crowd. Eva nearly made it to the short flight of stairs that led back stage when a young, ruddy-faced miner stepped in front of her.

"Come on, Evie. I got a bag of gold nuggets with your name on it if you'll only take a turn with me upstairs."

"You know I don't go upstairs with anybody, Jamie. Now move." She thought she'd convinced the carrot-haired youth to let her pass. Instead, he came a step closer.

"Come on, Evie," he drawled, "just for an hour."

"Yeah, come on, Evie," one of Jamie's companions chimed in. "I'll double it if you do us both."

Feeling like a powder keg about to blow, Eva's gaze shot across the room. John was half a room away with his hand on a cowboy's shoulder. He was busy none-too-gently escorting the man toward the door. She was on her own.

"You know all I do here is dance, gentlemen."

Jamie squinted up at her. "I'll bet you've entertained Quincy Powell, haven't ya? Him with his fancy satin vests and high collars. Thinks he's above us hard workin' stiffs, don't he?"

On his feet now, Jamie was pressing too close for comfort. Before she could move on, he grabbed her and jerked her roughly against him. Disgusted, she could feel his arousal beneath his worn wool trousers.

Enough was enough.

"That does it," she whispered as her fingers tightened around the neck of an amber whiskey bottle near the edge of the table beside her.

She swung the empty bottle up and around and watched

with satisfaction as it shattered across Jamie O'Henry's
head and shoulders. He let her go, staggered back, and
knocked over the man behind him.

She dropped the bottle neck, brushed her hands together,
and started to turn away.

"Hey, girlie, you can't do that to my friend!" The miner
standing beside Jamie's crumpled form lunged for her.

A cowboy at the next table leapt to his feet and charged
her attacker. Inches from Eva, the two men crashed onto
the center of the table, which immediately collapsed and
splintered into pieces.

As if on cue, the room erupted into chaos as fist fights
broke out all over. A chair flew toward the long bar at the
side of the room. She saw two bartenders duck in unison.
A section of the wide mirror shattered behind them.

Her cousin was trapped in the middle of the room, a
broad smile on his face, his white teeth flashing beneath
his thick brown moustache. He loved nothing better than a
rousing bar brawl. John grabbed the two men closest to
him, held each by the collar and prepared to bang their
heads together.

Eva walked away, thankful to be ignored, now that the
melee had broken out. She started up the back stairs, relishing the idea of telling Quincy Powell that she quit and
getting out before he learned that she had incited a ruckus
that was building into a very expensive riot in his precious
saloon. All she had to do was pack a few things, ask John
for a loan, and run.

At the top of the stairway, she paused, half-expecting
Quincy to come charging out of his office in response to
the mounting bedlam below. She walked along the upper
balcony, a long narrow walkway that was open to the floor
below on one side. A dozen doors lined the walkway, doors
to the rooms where some of the dancers extended special
favors to the saloon patrons. Obviously no one behind those
locked doors cared a whit about the chaos going on in the
bar downstairs.

She paused outside Quincy's office and knocked, then

quickly decided he wouldn't be able to hear her over the commotion that was growing louder by the minute. Eva tried the knob and found it open, turned it and stepped inside. The tinted oilcloth shades were down, casting the room in an eerie green glow. Enough light remained for her to discover that she had not walked in on Quincy Powell hunched over his account book, but Quincy Powell hunched over the new, brassy redheaded dancer from Abilene, who just happened to be spread out across his account book—and most of the rest of his desk.

If he hadn't already broken Eva's heart and used his snake-charming ways to talk her out of her virginity, the scene might have disturbed her, but Quincy wasn't worth one more minute of misery. It was a relief to learn that her heart had healed and hardened, and she was over him now. Along with everyone else, she was very familiar with Quincy's little indiscretions. Eva took one last look at the too-handsome, yellow-haired man who had once confessed his undying love to her, and noted with satisfaction that the redhead wasn't really a redhead after all.

With her hand still on the doorknob she called out, "Don't bother to get up. I quit," before she slammed the door shut behind her.

She marched the distance of the balcony to her own room, the heels of her high-button shoes clicking on the hardwood floor. Eva reached between her breasts for the key and opened the door, then quickly locked it behind her. From the sound of the incessant crashing and banging accompanied by hoops and hollers below, she was certain she wouldn't be disturbed for a while.

She hurried to an uneven chest of drawers and knelt down. In back of the bottom drawer, hidden beneath a mound of undergarments adorned with ribbons and lace, was a heart-shaped tin. She pulled open the lid and gathered the roll of bills she had hidden there. Inside the coiled money was a ragged-edged advertisement she had ripped out of the local paper.

Unfolding it quickly, Eva stared down at the tersely

worded ad: "Need housekeeper. No experience necessary. Inquire Trail's End Ranch outside Last Chance, Montana Territory." The advertisement was almost a week old. Eva silently prayed the position had not been filled, for she intended to inquire about the job. Of course, she had hoped to write a letter of introduction after she saved enough to outfit herself and buy a train ticket. Now she could apply in person.

The wad of money was woefully thin. If Quincy caught her before she could get away, he would demand payment for damages, and she would be forced to start saving all over again. She had to pack and find John so that she could get away before the real shouting started.

With her hands on her hips, Eva stared at the contents of her room, quickly deciding exactly what to take and what to leave behind. The furnishings were Quincy's. Besides, they were nothing she was partial to—certainly not the loud floral bedspread or the lamp with the fringed shade on the spindle-legged bedside table. Quincy would no doubt charge her triple for anything that turned up missing.

The walls were covered with various posters of woodcuts announcing theater performances she had appeared in over the years. Some advertised the burlesques she had starred in as a child actress. *Aladdin; or the Wonderful Scamp!* was her favorite, for she had greatly enjoyed her role as the puckish Aladdin and still recalled the performance with fond memories. A battered trunk that contained her costumes stood beside the bureau that doubled as a washstand. She decided to leave the posters and trunk behind. John could send them along to her if she ever wanted them.

The armoire door opened with a protesting screech. Eva stared inside and realized she had very few things she could wear as a member of respectable society. In fact, there was nothing at all suitable except for two older pastel dresses: one with pink stripes; the other a sadly rumpled, gray traveling gown that looked like a pigeon among peacocks. She had purchased the gown in Kansas City three years ago while she was still a part of her parents' theater troupe. She pulled out the gown, intent on changing into it and discovered the skirt and one shoulder had been attacked by moths. It wouldn't do at all now, not in such miserable condition. Eva looked over at the money tin and groaned.

Determined to find a way, she hurried to the dresser and pulled out a scarlet corset decorated with dyed feathers. One of the dancers had begged her to sell it to her and, until now, Eva had refused. She ran her hand over the cool satin and blew gently on the feathers to set them dancing. The garment would bring at least eight dollars, and where she was going there was no need for such a showpiece. Her mind made up, she tossed the dress on the bed.

Eva dropped to her knees and reached under the bed for her valise. She pulled it out and smiled at the dilapidated old thing. The bag, like the trunk, had seen most of America in her lifetime of travel from one theater to another. She threw the bag on the bed, opened it, and began cramming a rainbow-tinted selection of underclothes inside. Next she folded the gowns. As she put the last of them into the bag, she noticed the absence of raucous sounds from the saloon below and knew she didn't have much time left.

As she pulled on a red silk robe that reached her thighs and tugged on the sash at her waist, the knock she had expected sounded at the door.

"Who is it?" She hoped it wasn't Quincy. For all she cared, he could stand there and knock until hell froze over. She wasn't about to open the door for him.

"It's John," came the low reply. "You better open up, Eva."

She crossed the room and unlocked the door, stepping back so that he could enter. He stopped just inside the threshold and stared at the jumble of clothes and the valise spread out on the bed. She shoved him forward a step so that she could close the door and lock it again.

"Where's Quincy?" she demanded.

"Downstairs having a fit while he tallies up the damages."

"Was it bad?"

"Let's just say it'll take him a while. What are you doing?" He nodded toward the clothes and valise.

"What does it look like? I just quit, John. I can't take it anymore."

"But, where will you go? How will you get on?" He looked confused, then hurt. "You're the only family I have."

"That's not true. You could go back to my parents and work for the troupe."

He shook his head. "But our plan was to start a theater of our own, to be independent—"

Eva hated to hurt him, but he deserved the truth. "That's what I thought I wanted, John. Owning our own theater was a pretty fantasy, but I've come to realize we'll never be able to afford it on the wages we're getting in places like this. Besides, there's something I've known for a long time; I don't want this life anymore."

"But what'll you do?"

"I deserve more than to be treated like a piece of flesh. I want some dignity, I want to be thought of as more than a bauble with no feelings. I'm going to get a job that's . . . respectable."

Poor John looked more confused than ever. "Give up show business?"

She nodded, hopeful that somehow he would encourage her. Instead, he looked doubtful. "I can't imagine you doing anything else. It's in your blood."

It's in your blood. How many times had she heard her parents say the same thing? Eva shook her head, trying to dismiss the tug of sadness that swept over her. She walked over to the window that fronted Main Street and, as she glanced outside, noted the wagon and the couple she had seen earlier were gone.

"It's in my blood all right, but just now I feel that being a performer is a bad blood disease, like malaria. Let's face it," she said as she walked back over to the bed, shoved aside a heap of lacy underthings, and sat down with one leg folded beneath her, "I'll never be a great actress like

Agnes Booth or Kate Claxton.''

Dreams of appearing in famous New York theaters in highly touted performances like her idols vanished when she was old enough to read her own reviews. "Besides, I'm getting too old. I'm twenty-three for heaven's sake. It's about time I grew up, don't you think? I can't go on doing this forever.''

"Your parents have been begging you to come back since we left," he reminded her.

"Become one of the Entertaining, Energetic Eberharts again?" She blinked back tears and stared down at her hands. "I just can't, John," she whispered as her voice broke. "As much as Mama and Papa want that for me, I just can't. I want more than constantly moving from place to place and living hand to mouth.''

She turned away so that he wouldn't see the tears that filled her eyes. "I want to be settled, I want a home of my own with kids and dogs, and starched tablecloths, and a white picket fence.''

John glanced at the door as if expecting the gambler any minute. "But, Quincy—''

She stood up and shoved her hair back out of her eyes, her fingers caught for a moment in the riotous copper curls that reached her shoulders and she winced. "Quincy nothing. Don't even mention that man's name to me again.''

Whenever Eva thought about the fact that she had squandered her virginity on such a lying, cheating bastard, she saw red. Luckily, her one disastrous affair had been short-lived.

John went on, unmindful of her turmoil. "Things got so busted up downstairs we'll be closed for at least two hours. Quincy's hollerin' about taking the damages out of your pay, Eva. If you walk out now, he's going to be furious.''

The satisfaction she felt knowing the minor riot downstairs had disturbed Quincy's office tête-à-tête made her smile a little. "Tell him I'll roast in hell before I pay him one cent.''

He stared around the room. "What about Chester?''

Eva stood up. The hem of her silk robe fell around her hips. She glanced over at the scarred, paint-chipped mummy case standing in the corner beside the armoire. Once a work of art, decorated with crimson, royal blue, bright yellow and gilt paint, the mummy case held what remained of a molding, dilapidated relic her parents had inherited from her great-grandfather. Her mother, as superstitious as could be, told Eva that her great-grandfather Eberhart claimed it was their good-luck relic. Her mother insisted Eva and John take it with them when they set out on their own.

No one knew whether or not Chester's remains were Egyptian, or even human, wrapped inside the bandages and hidden behind the faded lid of the case. Whoever or whatever Chester was, he must have been a dwarf, that much was clear. The mummy case was only three-and-a-half feet high.

"I can't take him right now," Eva said with a shake of her head. "Put him in storage with my trunk."

She watched John hook his hands in his waistband. His shirt front was spotted with other men's blood, his right shoulder seam had a three-inch split in it. His dark hair was still perfectly combed. She knew a good brawl made him as happy as a bear with a beehive. "I'm worried about not knowing where you're going." He appeared torn when he offered, "Do you want me to go with you?"

Eva went to her heart tin, pulled out the ad and handed it to him. He read it in silence. Then she explained, "I'm going alone, but I need to borrow as much money as you can loan me, and I promise I'll pay you back as soon as I can. I have to buy some clothes and a train ticket."

He looked around the room, his gaze falling on the armoire stuffed with gowns.

"I need a serviceable traveling gown, John," she explained, reading his mind. "That and a matching hat. Something a decent woman would be proud to wear."

John listened in silence, then said, "A respectable getup isn't going to make you a lady."

She took his hand and gave it a squeeze as she tried to smile up at him, knowing she would miss the big galoot. "No, I suppose not. But with any luck at all and a little bit of acting, I can turn myself into anything I please."

"But Evie, you've never been a very *good* actress."

Chase Cassidy reined in his horse and leaned forward, resting his arm against the pommel of his well-worn Denver saddle and waited for his *segundo*, Ramon Alvarado, to catch up to him. His gaze slid over the land, efficiently taking in the surrounding foothills dotted with low brush as he searched for signs of cattle entangled in the brush or mired in a sink hole. He reached up and tugged his faded, oversized bandanna down off the lower half of his face where it protected him from the chilling bite of the wind.

The Mexican foreman drew his sturdy Appaloosa up beside Chase's big bay horse and paused, waiting silently for his boss to speak. Chase scanned the familiar landscape once again while Ramon reached into his vest pocket for a bag of tobacco and cigarette paper.

"We're losin' daylight," Chase said after another minute passed.

Ramon nodded. They had been friends for nearly nine years now and easily communicated with few words. "If there are any cattle left roaming this end of the range, we'd have found them by now," the man admitted.

Chase nodded in agreement. He was bone-tired and getting cold, now that the sun had disappeared over the crest of the nearest hill. He pulled his buff-colored, wide-brimmed Stetson down low on his forehead and shrugged the collar of his heavy, fleece-lined coat up around his neck. It was damn cold for spring, he decided. The bite in the air felt like winter was trying to hang on for as long as possible.

"We'd better head back," he said, but he made no move to leave.

Ramon took a long, slow drag on his cigarette. Deep lines creased the sun-leathered skin around the edges of his eyes. His horse shook its head and set the metal pieces on its bit to jingling. The sound went unnoticed, as familiar to both men as the sound of their breathing.

"Did the boy come home?" Ramon asked.

Chase straightened and nodded. Not unpleasant, the tobacco smoke rode the air between the men.

"Last night. Tore up the kitchen and caused a ruckus, backed Mrs. Robertson up against the wall and started swearing at her."

Ramon shook his head and finished off the cigarette, tossing the butt on the muddy ground. "He carries much bitterness inside him."

Lifting his reins and looping them through his fingers, Chase glanced over at the foreman. "Yeah, well his angry little outburst just cost me another housekeeper. Mrs. Robertson packed up then and there. If it hadn't been dark, she would have walked out last night. As it is, she said she'd be gone by noon." He turned his horse in the direction of the ranch house a few miles away and began walking the big animal. Ramon moved up alongside him.

"The fourth housekeeper in a year, *sí?*"

"*Sí,*" Chase repeated. "The fourth. There's no hope of hiring somebody from Last Chance and now nobody from Unionville's going to want the job, not after Mrs. Robertson gets through spreading the details of how Lane ran her off. I had to overpay her, as it was, to try and keep her. Maybe someone will answer the advertisement I sent into the Helena paper, but as soon as anybody gets wind of my reputation or what Lane has done to their predecessors, I don't hold much hope." He sighed and shook his head as he said half to himself, "Lane's only sixteen and he's had more than his share of trouble, but I'm not going to ignore this behavior. I can't."

Ramon was silent for a long moment, his gaze focused straight ahead. Finally he said, *"Todos nuestra cruz llevamos, unos de plata y otros de palo."*

We all carry our own crosses, some of silver, others of wood.

Chase knew there was no denying his nephew had been forced to carry more than his share of problems. He felt responsible for most of them. He told himself daily that he would have to try harder with Lane, but he didn't hold much hope of success, not when all their conversations of late had ended in shouting matches.

When Ramon kicked his Appaloosa into a canter, Chase followed suit, but even the faster pace couldn't take his mind off his problems. He had thought everything would be so easy once he was back home, but he had been dead wrong. It was impossible to pick up where he had left off twelve years ago. Nothing was going to erase all that had gone wrong in his life. Nothing was going to give back the years he had spent away from Lane and the ranch.

The boy was running wild with a chip on his shoulder the size of the territory, and Chase had lost nearly a quarter of the herd during one of the harshest winters anyone could remember. It had taken nearly all his savings to invest in a few head of new, stronger stock.

Now he was faced with the task of finding a new house-keeper and all he could do was wait to see if someone answered his advertisement.

He wondered if running an ad in the Helena newspaper had been worth the cost.

What woman in her right mind would apply?

Chapter Two

"We're almost there, ma'am."

Eva glanced over at the lanky young man driving the delivery wagon and gave a silent prayer of thanks. For nearly two hours she had braced herself against the roll and lurch of the wagon as it traveled over a trail mired in mud while her barely-out-of-adolescence driver studiously kept his eyes on the road.

She took a deep breath and relished the clear, crisp air, and the open stretches that were a far cry from the smokey interior of a crowded barroom. Although the rolling landscape was still soaked from a recent storm, it seemed to drink up the sunshine that would nourish the budding spring grass and wild flowers. The foothills rose in the distance, wearing a velvety new cloak of emerald. Behind them towered higher peaks still frosted with snow, their mighty, blue-gray presence solid, silent, reassuring.

Eva reached up to straighten her hat, using the moment to carefully tuck a wayward curl back into place, and strained to see the ranch house against the backdrop of the foothills. She leaned forward with one hand upon the seat, careful to avoid accidentally touching the delivery boy, James Carberry. He seemed so terrified of her that Eva feared any contact might send him vaulting over the side of the wagon. Five minutes after they left Last Chance, the town nearest the Trail's End ranch, she gave up trying to draw the shy son of the owners of the general store into conversation.

Fortunately, Eva had stepped off the morning stagecoach

and inquired at Carberry's General Store about a ride out to the ranch just as the boy was leaving to deliver goods. She was still a little puzzled over Mrs. Carberry's shocked expression when the woman heard that she was headed for the Trail's End, but there had been no time to discuss the matter.

She touched her skirt and felt the newspaper ad tucked safely inside her pocket. Her new traveling outfit was a demure, gray, two-piece wool, complete with a hat adorned with pheasant feathers and a silk sparrow tucked into a nest. She guessed the outfit had done the trick, for no one had recognized her from her years with either the Entertaining Eberharts or working at the Palace of Venus.

She could make out the fence now, taut barbed wire stretched between knobby, uneven posts. A low, long ranch house made of split logs blended into a background of trees, outbuildings, and corral fences. As they drew near, she could see that the run-down structure was not the two-story, wood-frame house she had imagined living in. The roof over the porch sagged, the wood shingles were curled with age and the house could use a coat of paint.

Eva knew every last detail of the house she had hoped for: white lace curtains shifting in the breeze, a tendril of welcoming smoke curling out of the chimney, a freshly painted picket fence surrounding a tidy yard. This somber log structure beside a corral and an equally derelict barn definitely had not figured in her dreams.

Eva took a deep breath and called upon the Eberhart fortitude and strong will that had carried her family through good times and bad, opening-night celebrations and midnight escapes from creditors who had come up short at the ticket window. Looking again at the ranch house, she told herself that this might not be the house of her dreams, but it was not all that far from town, and there was still the hope of eventually meeting and mingling with everyday folk. It was unlikely that anyone would recognize her at such an isolated location.

She was made of stern stuff. She could face any chal-

lenge. She had the constitution of a laborer fed by long
hours on the road and short nights in cramped quarters in
shabby hotel rooms. She had a heart of steel forged from
terrible reviews, the rudest of rowdy audiences, and as a
dance hall entertainer, the disdain of more respectable citizens.

It was as good a place as any to start.

The wagon drew nearer. She watched the cowboys corral a number of mixed-breed horses and noted the men
were as different from each other as the colorful herd.
She noticed a tall Mexican man leaning beside an open
gate. Outfitted in a leather vest, with silver buttons that
decorated his shirt cuffs and the side seams of his pants,
he presented quite an exotic picture. His wide sombrero
hid his expression, but not the thick black moustache that
covered his upper lip. She sensed that he was watching
her carefully. So were the others, who kept glancing her
way while deftly performing their tasks on horseback.
The men called out to each other, whistling to direct a
mongrel dog that was helping them cut the horses into
separate corrals.

As she watched the cowhands, James Carberry expertly
maneuvered the team and wagon to the front of the log
structure. The old gray and white speckled hound slipped
beneath the fence rail and left the corral, barking as he ran
to greet them. With his tongue lolling, the dog began to
sniff around the wagon wheels. Eva ignored him as her
palms grew damp beneath her gloves. She couldn't recall
the last time she'd been as nervous. She told herself that
the coming interview could not possibly be as bad as the
night she had tripped during the second act of *Lost Among
the Lilies* and fell headlong into the startled front row of
theater patrons at the Opera House in Cheyenne.

She reminded herself that this was what she wanted and
concentrated on what she planned to say. Her background
story had been an easy one to concoct. She would pose as
a penniless young woman from the East whose mother had
just passed away. Eva sincerely hoped the lady of the house

would not be able to see through her respectable disguise and send her packing.

And what if she did pass muster? She still didn't know if she could do an adequate job even if she did manage to get hired. She thought of her collection of articles carefully clipped from *The Ladies World* and other periodicals and the precious second-hand housekeeping book she had obtained. Would she be allowed to put them to use?

Surveying the building one last time, she found there was not so much as a trace of lace at the windows. Faded Indian blankets were crookedly draped behind the window panes.

"I'll let you off here, ma'am, if you don't mind," young Carberry said, his voice reedy before it cracked. She watched his Adam's apple bob above the tight collar he'd buttoned over his striped shirt. "I generally unload the hardware out by the barn."

"Thank you, Mr. Carberry," she said, hiding a smile when she addressed him as mister and watched him color to the hairline.

He jumped down and hurried to the side of the wagon, his gaze lighting everywhere but never actually meeting hers. He helped her down and let go of her hand immediately, deferring to her as he would to any respectable lady. At least she had fooled him.

She graciously thanked the youth, reached into the drawstring purse at her wrist for a coin and waited silently before the low porch while he unloaded her valise.

"Thank you, ma'am, I can't wait for you ma'am," he told her, pocketing the gratuity before he glanced nervously at the door again. She wondered if she was the cause or if he was always so fidgety.

She continued to smile. "That's quite all right, Mr. Carberry. I'll probably be here a while. I'm sure someone will be kind enough to give me a ride back to town if things don't work out."

He appeared skeptical and shot another swift glance in the direction of the house, cleared his throat, and jumped up on to the high, sprung seat of the wagon. With a flick of the reins, he signaled the team, and the wagon rumbled toward the barn.

The dog stood panting at her heels as Eva dusted off her skirt, straightened her already straight hat, and left her bag sitting at the edge of the porch. After taking a deep breath, she raised her gloved hand to knock at the rough, pine plank door and stepped back.

There was no response.

The hound sat beside her on his haunches, staring soulfully up at her with one brown eye and one marbled blue one.

"Get," she told him, shaking the hem of her traveling suit. Instead of moving, the bag of bones simply stretched out on the rough floor of the porch and laid his head on the toe of her new shoe. Then he whined. Eva looked over her shoulder and found the Mexican still leaning against the fence post watching her. Surely if there was no one inside, he would come over and tell her so. Wouldn't he?

She resolutely turned around and tried the door again, her hand arrested in mid-knock when she became aware of two shouting voices coming from inside the house. Footsteps against a wood floor brought the sounds closer. She thought for a moment the door would open, but the inhabitants of the log house didn't seem to know, or care, that anyone was standing on the porch.

"I don't care how many times you get yourself thrown out of school, and I sure as hell don't care how many times you have to suffer the embarrassment of going back there, but you're not quitting." This first masculine voice, although low and full of measured restraint, was still easily understood.

"What makes you think I give a damn what you want? What gives you the right to tell me what to do? I'm near as old as you were when you had charge of Ma and the ranch." The second voice sounded younger, full of bravado, and yet Eva could sense in his tone just the vaguest hint of uncertainty.

"If I have to hog-tie you to make you mind—"

The second voice was not nearly as loud as before, but was clearly audible and threatening. "You put your hands on me and I'll kill you."

Embarrassed by what she had overheard, Eva pounded on the door loud enough to drown out their next words. When there was no immediate response, she reached down and tried the latch. Just as she touched it, the handle jerked out of her grasp and the door swung open.

Controlled fury.

A shiver ran down her spine as Eva stared up at the tall man framed in the crude doorway. The only way she could describe him in that instant was as controlled fury. She had expected the lady of the house to answer or, at the very least, to be met by someone who looked less like a hired gun and more like a rancher. This man didn't just stand there—he loomed over her like a villain in a melodrama.

A glint of silver on his belt buckle relieved the stark black of his bib-fronted shirt and black trousers. Black boots with the familiar heels cowboys favored made him tower even higher. He had braced his hands on both sides of the door frame, and appeared to hang there as he coolly inspected her with his midnight eyes. His glossy hair was wavy and as black as pitch. A wayward shock of it fell forward over his forehead. In back, the ragged cut covered his shirt collar.

Eva stared back into shuttered black eyes that masked the man's thoughts so completely that she wondered if it was too late to catch a ride back to town with Carberry. *Now or never, Eva.* She drew herself up and met the rancher's cold, hard stare.

"What do you want?"

Chase Cassidy could see that his abrupt tone had startled the beautiful woman standing on his front porch, but he was in no mood to deal with some do-gooder who looked like she was getting primed to talk him into saving his soul from eternal damnation. There was something almost cherubic, something so sparkling about the petite, green-eyed, copper-haired vision, that she appeared to be an angel dropped out of the heavens. For a moment he wondered if she might have done just that until he noticed the valise on the edge of the porch behind her. Chase's frown deepened as he glanced over her shoulder and saw the Carberry boy unloading a roll of barbed wire out by the barn. He turned his attention to the woman once again.

The sight of a such an obviously well-bred lady standing on his porch was a shock, but he had learned long ago to carefully mask his thoughts and emotions. In his previous line of work, veiling his emotions had come as easily to him as breathing.

He didn't take his gaze off her as she stood there staring up at him with eyes as rich a green as a mossy pond in high summer. Nor could he help noticing that her cheeks were the color of ripe peaches.

Somehow while he stood there watching her, the redhead found her voice. "I'm Eva Edwards, and I'm here about the advertisement."

He waited, instinctively on guard as her hand dipped into her pocket. Chase relaxed a bit when he saw her retrieve a much-folded piece of newspaper. She held it out to him, but he didn't reach out to take it. Undaunted by his lack of response, she continued, "I saw this advertisement in a local paper, and I've come to apply for the job of housekeeper—if the position isn't already filled."

Chase could think of plenty of positions he could find her in around the house, but not one of them was decent. Besides, this was a *lady* who had come knocking on his door; a prim, proper, respectable lady, from the looks of her.

"You should have written before you came all the way out here," he said.

"I'm sorry, but I—"

"You won't do," he told her flat outright.

She went straight as a flagpole, coloring from the delicate lace at her ivory throat to the top of her finely shaped forehead.

Still, she seemed determined that he hear her out. "What do you mean, I won't do? How can you say that when you haven't even given me an interview?"

"I can tell. Besides, you don't look like a housekeeper."

She was all wrong for the job. Chase could read it as plain as the pert little turned-up nose on her face. She was garbed like a lady, but her expensive clothes were too fine for a mere housekeeper. A hat covered with feathers and other fancies sat atop her copper curls. Her hands were hidden by cream kid gloves, and he would be willing to bet three head of cattle that the skin beneath them was not chapped or calloused.

"Just what does a housekeeper look like?"

She had him there. Chase frowned, then relaxed as he gave what seemed a perfectly logical explanation. "I was expecting someone older."

"Older? I see. You want an old woman to wear herself out cooking and cleaning."

"It's not all that much work," he admitted.

"Good. Then I should be able to handle it, shouldn't I?"

He was trying to figure out how she had so deftly backed him into a corner when she piped up again. "Excuse me, mister, but I don't see a line of applicants here. Would you mind telling me why not?"

He hesitated, knowing full well she might be the only one who *did* want the job. "Well, for one thing, we're pretty far off the beaten path."

She jerked on the hem of her jacket and rocked back on her heels. "Then it sounds like you don't have any choice, let alone a real reason not to take me on."

"Let's just say you aren't right for the job and leave it at that."

With Lane smack in the middle of one of his rebellious moods, Chase knew damn well he'd be foolish to hire someone who didn't look like she could handle the boy for more than twenty minutes. The hands had nicknamed their last housekeeper Old Hatchet Face—and she hadn't even lasted a full day. Chase knew he'd be out of his mind to hire a woman as beautiful as this to work on an isolated ranch populated by five grown men and a practicing adolescent. If he hired a looker like Miss Eva Edwards, he'd be asking for more trouble than he needed. He had already had enough trouble to last him a lifetime.

She took a deep breath and then dropped her gaze to stare at the crumpled ad, then down at the tips of the barely soiled dove gray shoes that peeked out from the hem of her skirt. Old Curly, the stray dog who had refused to leave the place, was sprawled out at her feet with his nose hidden beneath the hem of her gown.

Chase began to regret his curt manner, but there was little else to be done if he wanted to send her back with Carberry. He hated to have to spare one of the men to drive her all the way into town.

Slowly, she began to refold the ad. "I was afraid you'd say that," he heard her say softly.

For a moment he didn't know how to respond. "Say what?"

"That I wasn't right for the job."

A knot formed and twisted in his stomach when she looked up at him again. Instantly her green eyes filled with wavering, unshed tears. As if on cue, one lone droplet spilled over the edge of her lower lashes and trickled down her smooth cheek.

"Aw, lady, don't do that here." He reached into his back pocket for his bandanna and pulled it out. He thought twice about handing it to her—it was limp as a rag and worn thin from long use—but her tears were suddenly streaming unchecked, marring her perfect complexion. His gut clenched as tight as a banker's fist with a dollar in it.

Lane moved up behind him. "Who is it?"

Chase looked over his shoulder, and somewhere in the back of his mind he registered the fact that Lane had grown tall enough to look him in the eye.

"It's a woman come to ask about the housekeeper job."

"Just what we *don't* need." Lane's surly reaction was exactly what Chase expected of him. Turning back to face the young woman on the doorstep, Chase found her listening intently to the exchange. He was thankful, though, she had stopped crying.

When Lane stepped up beside Chase and got a good look at the woman, he went still as a post—but not for long. "I think she's just what we're looking for," he told Chase.

The gleam in Lane's eye was warning enough.

"And I think she should be on her way back to town."

The redhead wouldn't be put off. "Perhaps, Mr. . . ."

"Cassidy."

"Mr. Cassidy. Perhaps if I could just come in—" she suggested.

Lane shoved the door open wider. "Why don't you at least talk to her? Show some of those manners you're always harping on, Uncle Chase. Would you like to come in for a cold glass of water, ma'am? Or a cup of very bad coffee?"

Chase shot his nephew a warning glance but Lane ignored it.

To Chase Cassidy's dismay, the lady nodded, quickly swiped at the tears on her cheeks, and bestowed a glorious smile on Lane.

"I'd like that very much. It was a long ride out from town."

When Lane stepped aside, she brushed past Chase and entered. As he watched his nephew usher her in, Chase could only stare in amazement. Then, unable to ignore the sensual sway of the woman's hips as she moved farther into the front room, he shook his head.

He followed them through the sitting room to the kitchen, seeing the house through her eyes; the dimness of the place, the layer of dust on the crude, handmade furnishings upholstered in hides, and the odor of rancid grease in the air.

"She'll have to hurry if she's going to catch a ride back to town," he groused as he trailed behind them.

"With Carberry?" Lane paused long enough to turn to

Chase with a smirk on his lips. "That mama's boy couldn't find a cowbell up his—"

"That's enough," Chase warned, thankful that the young woman apparently hadn't heard Lane's rude comment.

"Thank you for letting me come in," she told them when they entered the kitchen.

Without comment, Chase reached for a crockery pitcher and looked for a clean glass amid the stack of dishes and pots and pans on the Hoosier. He found one near the back of the top shelf and poured out a generous glass of water.

As he handed it to her he said, "If you'll just wet your whistle and head back out before— "

"I'm Lane Cassidy. His nephew. Have a seat." Lane pulled up a chair and offered it to her despite Chase's execution of his best glower.

She looked up at Lane and said, "And I'm Eva Edwards." To both of them she explained, "I suppose I should outline my situation. You see, I'm all alone in the world now." This time a small sigh accompanied by a barely visible shudder escaped her. As Eva sat down, her gold-tinged curls bobbed around her cheeks, teasing the nape of her neck just below her hat brim.

Unable to take his eyes off the woman, Lane nodded in what appeared to be sincere sympathy. "That's too bad, ma'am."

Chase wanted to gag him. Before she could go on, he took a step closer, intent on ending the exchange. He didn't want to know anything about Eva Edwards. He just wanted her gone. Someone this young and pretty could get a job anywhere she wanted. She needn't be subjected to his own tarnished reputation or Lane's unpredictable behavior.

"Miss Edwards . . ."

"Please, Mr. Cassidy. This is so hard for me."

Her heartfelt admission stopped him as effectively as a slap in the face. He fell silent. Then, as if some memory pained her, she continued after another heavy sigh.

"I'm from Philadelphia, and I won't lie to you. I've never been a housekeeper before."

She stared up at Chase, her gaze riveted on his features, her concentration intent, as if her life depended on getting this job. "At least, I've never done housekeeping for hire—but I did take care of my family's home in Philadelphia."

Her voice took on a dreamy quality, as if she were weaving a fairy tale. "It was a beautiful place, two stories, with plenty of rooms and hardwood floors that had to be polished weekly . . . and there were linens to starch and . . . I have a collection of old family recipes—" She seemed to realize she might be going on too long and abruptly stopped.

"You talk to anyone in town about applying for this job?" Chase asked.

"Not hardly. I just stepped off the stage and barely had time to hitch a ride."

Just as he thought. She knew absolutely nothing about him, nor had she heard anything about her unsuccessful predecessors. She finished the water, handed Lane the empty glass, and concentrated on Chase.

"I can cook and clean and keep this house running right and tight." Her gaze flitted about the room and came back to him. "From the looks of this kitchen, you need me."

"I'm afraid—" Chase saw the hopeful look in Lane's eye and couldn't help noticing the way he had been reacting to Miss Eva Edwards. His abnormal show of control, not to mention decent manners, were a far cry from the sarcastic insults he had constantly heaped on the other women Chase had employed. True, it was early. But since Lane had taken a shine to her, maybe the boy would be less apt to throw a tantrum and run her off. Besides, she had been tenacious enough to badger Chase into listening to her tale of woe far longer than he would have imagined possible.

"You said yourself it wasn't all that much work, that even an older woman could do it," she reminded him.

Cassidy frowned. "This is a cattle ranch, ma'am. There are six men here, including my nephew. We're miles from town. If you're looking for a social life, there isn't any."

She seemed to be considering the ramifications of his

admission. Her hand went to the pearl button at the throat of her fitted jacket and she began twisting it back and forth. She drew a long shuddering sigh.

"My mother just passed away, Mr. Cassidy, rest her soul, after a long and harrowing illness. After months of nursing her, I found our savings were gone and I was forced to sell the house and the livery. There was barely enough to pay off the last of the doctor bills. All I want is a job and a little peace and quiet."

Chase shoved his hands into his pockets and leaned back against the kitchen cabinet, and noticed the way she was watching him from beneath half-lowered lashes.

"Your reputation might suffer if you stay," he warned her.

"You've had other housekeepers." Her hand fluttered to her throat again and she blushed prettily. "Did *their* reputations suffer?"

She appeared to be affronted—almost as if he had accused her of having a weak moral character. He was about to assure her that he meant no insult when Lane cut him off.

"If you'd seen those old hags you'd know why they weren't worried," the boy told her with a laugh.

The sound of Lane's spontaneous laughter drew his attention. The boy rarely even smiled. Chase realized that this was the way Lane might have been if his mother, Sally, hadn't died. It was a mark in Miss Edward's favor that the boy had even been civil to her. Chase had hoped he was making some headway with Lane and Lord knew he had tried as hard as he knew how to get the boy to trust him since his release from prison—but until a few moments ago, there had been only a few signs of progress. Now, after one look at Eva Edwards, Lane had offered the lady a cup of coffee, a chair, and he had actually laughed aloud.

As much as Lane accused him of the opposite, Chase did care about him and only wanted to see his nephew happy. And he had to admit, he was sorely in need of someone to look after the place and Lane so that he could leave on the spring roundup. If he hired the overeager Miss Edwards on the spot, he and the others could ride out as soon as tomorrow.

And Eva Edwards *was* insisting that she could handle the job.

As if she was afraid to call attention to herself while Chase was deciding her fate, she didn't move, but simply remained perched on the edge of her chair and looked around the kitchen. He watched her take in the table littered with the breakfast dishes, the stove dulled with spattered grease, the skillet with beans congealed in lard. Then, as if she had made a decision, Miss Eva Edwards abruptly stood up, brushed off her skirt and folded her hands at her waist.

Chase pulled his hands out of his pockets and straightened away from the cabinet. Certain she was not at a loss for words, he waited to hear what she had to say.

"Mr. Cassidy, you said earlier you didn't expect many applicants because this place was so isolated. Has *anyone* else applied?"

"Well—"

"Nobody," Lane smugly informed her.

"This ranch isn't all that far from town. Do you mind if I ask why no one wants this job but me?"

Chase looked over at Lane. The boy appeared dumbstruck. With a dark glance, Lane almost dared Chase to explain his recent behavior to this woman. He stood tense, visibly drawn inward, poised and waiting as if he expected Chase to embarrass him.

Chase Cassidy wondered if he could humiliate Lane by telling Miss Edwards that the boy had thrown a chair through a window during an argument—a chair that narrowly missed the first housekeeper's head? That he had threatened the second housekeeper by holding a knife to her throat?

Would it matter that Chase was finally seeing a *little* progress in the boy's behavior? Would Eva Edwards still be so anxious to have the job if he told her that he himself had only been out of territorial prison for a year? Chase looked from Eva to Lane and back again.

"Let's just say we're not the easiest family to work for and leave it at that." The relief on Lane's face made avoiding the truth worthwhile for the moment.

"I'm still willing to give it a try," she assured him. "Perhaps you could see your way into letting me have the job—on a trial basis, of course."

As he walked to a side window overlooking the paddock area, Chase noticed that Lane was watching him with a look of grudgingly given gratitude. Eva Edwards was also watching, expectantly waiting for an answer.

He had wasted half the afternoon arguing with Lane about school attendance and now this. Outside, Ramon was looking for orders. He knew how sick the men were of a steady diet of half-cooked beans and gluey rice and the woman *did* say she had some old family recipes with her.

He turned around and found himself still the focus of both Lane and Eva Edwards's attention. Lane appeared certain that Chase would send her away just to spite him. The woman's devastating green eyes silently begged him to give her a chance.

Life didn't give many chances.

Chase took a deep breath. He'd never met a more persistent woman in his life. If hiring her was going to prove to be a mistake, it was as much her fault as his.

"You can stay—"

Eva's cry of thanks nearly drowned out the rest of what he said.

"—until we see if this is going to work out."

He stiffened when he thought she was actually going to reach up and throw her arms around his neck, but she caught herself in time and simply clasped her hands in front of her breasts.

"Thank you *so* much, Mr. Cassidy. I know you won't regret this."

Chase shrugged.

He already did.

*   *   *

She did it.

She had actually won her first respectable position in a normal household. Well, almost normal. Obviously there were more reasons than he had let on why Chase Cassidy couldn't keep a housekeeper, and she knew men well enough to know that he was hiding something, but after her experiences at the Palace of Venus, she doubted very seriously that it was something she couldn't handle.

It was just a matter of time until she found out what that something was—for now Eva had a job to do and she intended to do it so well that Chase Cassidy would have no room for complaint.

"I'll get your bags and show you to your room, ma'am," Lane volunteered, cutting into her thoughts.

Eva smiled at the handsome youth who was a younger version of his uncle. She knew that more than a few hearts would be broken when Lane Cassidy discovered the ladies.

"That would be wonderful. Thank you, Lane." She turned back to Chase and caught him watching Lane closely, almost as if he were seeing him for the first time. There was something going on between these two that was deeper than the eye could see.

"What time do you want supper?" She was well aware that the afternoon was nearly gone and there was much to be done before she could get a meal on the table.

"Dusk." Chase reached up and took a tall, buff-colored Stetson from a hat rack made of deer antlers that hung above the wood box. When he paused in the open doorway, she noticed how much his wide shoulders diminished the width of the open portal.

Almost grudgingly he added, "As I said, there'll be six of us counting Lane. Seven with you. The men eat here in the kitchen, but they sleep in the bunkhouse. You'll find what you need in the pantry and out in the cabinet on the back porch. Make a list of anything else you want, and we'll see about getting it next time somebody goes into town. All you have to do is cook, clean, and stay out of the bunkhouse.''

It sounded easy enough.

"And where do I eat?"

He bit back a smile, as if her question amused him. "I've only got one table, so I guess you'd best eat with us."

"Don't worry about a thing," she smiled, mentally beginning to run through all there was to accomplish in a little under two and a half hours. As he nodded and bid her goodbye, Eva felt a wave of guilt for having manufactured her tale of woe as well as her tears. She offered up a silent prayer that her robust, flamboyant mother would forgive her for claiming she had died. Especially when at the moment, Esther Eberhart was somewhere in Topeka starring as Henriette's blind sister Louise in *The Two Orphans*.

Eva had won the job. All that mattered now was that she do a competent job and keep her former life a secret. Chase Cassidy had hired a lady from Philadelphia and that was what he was going to get, and she hoped with luck, none of his cowhands would recognize her. Most cowboys drifted around so much that there was no telling whether she might ever have crossed paths with one of Cassidy's hired hands or not. She would just have to wait and see.

The worst skirmish of the battle was over as far as she was concerned. By the time Cassidy did, if ever, learn who she really was, she would have proved that she was serious about making more of her life than serving up beers and kicking up her heels in a dance hall or starring in two-bit melodramas.

For now, she had a house to run. Eva watched Chase leave without another word, then she hurried after Lane. She was anxious to change into something more suitable to attacking one of the dirtiest kitchens she had seen since the Entertaining Eberharts played a tumble-down theater on the San Francisco Bowery.

She was determined to give the performance of her life.

Chapter Three

Eva wiped her brow with the back of her wrist and blew a wayward curl out of her eyes, then reached out to straighten a knife in the place setting at the end of the long kitchen table. As she stood back to survey her work, she knew a deep sense of satisfaction. It was almost dusk and she had accomplished every task.

Dinner might not be a triumph of culinary delight, but it would be edible. It had taken her a while and a bit of reading in the household hints section of her recipe book to get the stove working. Locating the fire chamber, ash pit, grates, and damper had all proved simple enough. It was helpful that Chase Cassidy had purchased a model complete with a separate warming oven and water reservoir.

Lighting the stove had been harder than she expected. When the fire was finally going, she again referred to the cookbook and used a time-tested method of sprinkling a spoonful of flour into a bowl and placing it in the oven. The flour turned brown in one minute, indicating the temperature was right for baking her biscuits.

Just now the drop biscuits were still browning while beef fricassee—made from a recipe she once begged from a chef in a St. Louis hotel—was simmering in a deep Dutch oven atop the stove. The potatoes were mashed and waiting in the upper warming oven.

She pulled off the makeshift apron, a dishtowel tied around her waist, and hurried into the small bedroom just off the kitchen. The tiny room assigned to her looked like she had stirred her belongings with a stick. Earlier, when she pawed through her things to find her copy of *Mrs. Applebee's Famous American Cookbook,* she poured out the contents of her satchel atop her bed. A colorful rainbow of frilly underclothes were strewn about the floor and, with a glance toward the door, she kicked them beneath the bed. Her gray gown still lay where she had tossed it before she changed into a simple dress of candy striped cotton.

The spartan room contained nothing more than a narrow bed with a utilitarian, dirt-brown bedspread, a small dresser with a mirror above it, a washbowl, and an oil lamp with a cracked chimney. There wasn't even a rag rug on the floor to relieve the chill that would surely permeate the place on cold nights. Her new abode made her shabby little room at Quincy's seem like a palace. She wished she had been brazen enough to take the floral bedspread.

Eva stood before the mirror, finger-combed and fluffed her shoulder length curls, and brushed a spot of flour off the tip of her nose. She was tempted to rub a bit of rouge on her lips, but decided against it. She was supposed to be a proper lady now.

Footsteps sounded on the back porch. She tried to still her excitement as she hurried through the door into the kitchen again. Lane came in first, his mood obviously darkened. The boy nodded in her direction, but didn't smile.

"Everything's ready. You can take a seat." Eva indicated the table with a wave of her hand and silently admitted to herself that everything looked wonderful. She had washed the dishes—the mismatched glasses and cutlery were sparkling. In lieu of a centerpiece, she had filled a crockery pitcher with drinking water and set it in the middle of the table. She could hear the deep sound of men's voices on the back porch as they spoke boisterously among themselves.

Eva watched as Chase Cassidy stepped over the threshold before his men. He walked up to Lane and casually laid a hand on the boy's shoulder and then reminded him, "Be sure to mind your manners. Did you wash up?"

Immediately, Lane stiffened and shrugged off Chase's touch. His glance slid over to Eva, then his expression darkened even more, and he glared back at Chase.

"Yeah," Lane said, his tone barely audible, "I did." He refused to meet Eva's eyes as he slunk to his place at the table.

Busying herself at the stove, Eva pretended not to notice the tension between the Cassidys. One by one the ranch hands filed in through the back door. She didn't spare them a glance as she reached for a heavy oval platter, carefully lined it with mashed potatoes to create a fluffy border, then began filling the center with beef cooked in thick, rich brown gravy. At long last she was finally doing what she had always wanted to do, and she was so tickled by her first success that she had to remind herself to stop smiling like a fool.

The shuffling and scraping of chair legs against the floor abruptly ceased. As if on cue, Eva whirled around with the platter in her hands and stopped short when she found four cowhands standing around the table staring at her as if they had never seen a housekeeper before.

"Please, all of you, do sit down," she told them.

They sat.

Eva carried the platter to Chase, seated at the head of the table. As he began heaping a portion on his own plate, Eva stood at his elbow, smiling at the colorful assortment of men gathered around the table, hoping beyond hope that none of them recognized her. They were a motley crew, much like the men she was used to entertaining at the dance hall. The Mexican she had seen earlier looked less sinister without his broad brimmed sombrero shading his face. His eyes were rich and brown with deep creases crinkling out from the corners. He watched her closely, then nodded, but did not smile or speak.

She waited a moment, giving Chase the opportunity to introduce her. Finally, worried that her drop biscuits would cool before he spoke up, she decided to take matters into her own hands.

"I'm Eva Edwards, your new cook and housekeeper," she announced. "I'm pleased to meet you all."

The Mexican stood. "I am Ramon Valenzuela Ortega Alvarado. I am *segundo,* second in command. Welcome, Señorita."

The foreman's unexpected gallantry, executed so coolly, surprised her. When she smiled in acknowledgment of his introduction, the three other cowhands at the table jumped to their feet.

"I'm Ned Delmont, ma'am." The fair-haired man was nearly bug-eyed, staring at her as if he were afraid to blink and have her disappear. Of medium height, he had sun-toughened skin and a crooked smile half-hidden beneath a blond moustache.

"And I'm Jethro Adams," said another young man in his twenties who was seated beside Ned. He was of the same height, bowlegged, with sandy brown hair. Despite a broken nose, he was ruggedly handsome and whipcord thin, and just like Ned, he couldn't take his eyes off of her.

Eva concentrated on the last cowboy. He appeared to be ancient, his skin even darker than Ramon Alvarado's sun-weathered brown.

"I'm Orvil Brown," he said, his voice gravelly as a salt shaker full of pebbles, "an' I'm here to say it's nice to have somethin' on the plates 'sides beans, rice, and flies . . . and it sure is a pure pleasure to have a real purty lady around the place."

He had a slow Southern drawl that she envied for she had never quite learned to imitate a Southern dialect on stage. With the majesty of a seasoned thespian at the end of a soliloquy, he bowed and then slowly lowered himself into his chair. Orvil moved as if every joint pained him. The older man's eyes were bloodshot, his shoulders stooped, his nappy hair streaked with gray. She wondered how much work the aged black man actually did around the place. He looked to be a likely candidate for the weathered rocking chair that sat out on the covered porch.

Eva clasped her hands at her waist. "I'm so happy to

meet you all. And I'm thankful to Mr. Cassidy for giving me the opportu—''

''Miss Edwards, we'd like to start. Could you please sit down so everybody will stop bobbing up and down?''

A study in impatience, Chase Cassidy was staring up at her, tapping his thumb against the tabletop. The gravy on his plate was beginning to congeal. The platter was still being passed from cowhand to cowhand. Lane had taken a helping, but stared silently at his plate, his lips drawn into a firm line.

''You go right ahead, before it gets cold. I'll just get the string beans and biscuits.'' She hurried to the stove, started to grab the pan of drop biscuits, burned her hand and let go. It fell back onto the oven rack with a clatter. Luckily, none of the golden biscuits were ruined. Eva grabbed a wadded dishtowel and retrieved them, tossed them in to a bowl, and hurried the fragrant bread to the table before she raced back for the pot of canned string beans. She began to ladle out beans onto each plate with a slotted spoon.

Taking her at her word, no one waited for her to be seated. Instead, they hunched over their plates, intent on shoveling food into their mouths. When Eva finally walked over and stood behind her chair, knives and forks clattered onto the plates, and every man at the table stood again.

When Chase Cassidy moved to seat her, the others immediately sat down. Eva smiled up at him, smoothed her skirt close, and held it out of the way as she lowered herself to her chair.

The dinner plate before her contained only the green beans she had placed there herself. She reached for a biscuit from the bowl, waited half a second, and then asked, ''Would someone please pass the beef and potatoes?''

The cowboys looked at each other sheepishly. Hand to hand, the platter was passed around to her. When it arrived, it was empty except for a few traces of brown gravy, a thread of beef, and a morsel of potato.

Eva looked up and caught Chase watching her. She didn't know if the frown imprinted across his brow showed irritation at her for not providing enough or at his men's lack of foresight.

Eva mentally reminded herself to make twice as much for the next meal. She made due with biscuits and green beans and took delight in the fact that all the plates were soon licked clean. No one spoke. The absence of conversation in the small room was deafening. Eva sought to relieve the tension as she stood to refill the coffee cups.

"I've made orange marmalade bread pudding," she announced from the stove. "I didn't know if you gentlemen took your coffee and dessert in the parlor or—"

"Right here is fine," Chase said.

She walked toward him with the tall enamel coffeepot in her hands.

"And then afterward?" She pressed.

"There's still work to be done. We get up before dawn." He was watching her intently.

She could feel the coolness in his stare and wondered if he had expected her to balk at his pronouncement. What Chase Cassidy didn't realize was that she had withstood catcalls, tomatoes, and various other objects hurled at her on stage. It would take more than rising at daybreak to get her to quit.

"What time would you like breakfast served?" She asked cheerfully as she circulated the table and poured steaming hot coffee into the cups.

"Five-thirty," he said.

She turned away so that no one would see her expression as she rolled her eyes heavenward. Dawn was a natural wonder she had probably only witnessed five or six times in her entire life.

The bread pudding was a success. Like the beef fricassee, the men wolfed it down, but this time there was a tablespoonful left for her when the dish came around.

Nearly all the men had finished when Lane shoved his chair away from the table. Chase stopped him with a curt, "Tell Miss Edwards thank you."

Lane spoke to Eva without looking her way. "Thanks,"

he mumbled grudgingly before he stalked out of the room.

Chase visibly relaxed, obviously relieved when the boy left. He settled back in his chair and picked up his coffee cup. One by one, the other men finished their meals, thanked her and left. All but Orvil Brown refused a second cup. "I'll just take mine along with me, ma'am. I like to drink it outside, if that's all right with you."

She glanced over at Chase who made no comment or sign that he had even heard. "Of course, it's all right with me, Mr. Brown." Eva watched the old man slowly get to his feet and was tempted to carry the cup to the door for him. As soon as Orvil shuffled outside, Chase stood and shoved back his chair. He stood there watching her closely, as if he wanted to say something to her but was weighing the consequences. It was a moment or two before he finally spoke.

"Miss Edwards?"

"Yes?" Eva waited expectantly.

"You were right," he said as he shoved his thumbs into his back pockets.

"About what?"

"You *can* cook."

Eva smiled. "Thank you."

He hesitated again as if he wanted to say something more. Eva walked over to the table and began stacking the plates. "Was there something else?"

"I should warn you that Lane's not always as easy going as he was when he met you this afternoon. He's so temperamental that the least thing can set him off."

Eva turned back to him and wiped her hands on her apron. "What do you mean?"

"He's got quite a temper."

"Should I fear for my life?" She was teasing, her tone laced with a laugh.

"I don't think so." Chase Cassidy was not smiling. In fact, he was frowning.

"You're serious—"

"Lane seemed to take to you this afternoon. That's the

main reason I let you talk me into giving you this job. I'm taking the men and leaving on a roundup in the morning, which means you'll have to look after Lane while I'm gone.''

"I see." He had not only hired her to do the house-keeping, but to mind his nephew. Eva couldn't remember seeing a single chapter in Mrs. Applebee's book of hints that detailed the care and feeding of a sixteen-year-old trou-blemaker who stood a good head and shoulders above her.

Chase sighed, his frown erased by an expression of frus-tration. "He shouldn't be as much of a problem once I'm gone. I seem to set him off more than anyone or anything else.''

She glanced toward the sitting room, dried her hands on a dishtowel, and closed the distance between them so that Lane would not hear what she had to say.

"I hope you don't mind my sticking my nose in where it doesn't belong, but maybe you shouldn't be correcting Lane in front of the other men. It embarrasses him, I'm sure. Boys his age don't like to be told what to do, let alone told in front of an audience.''

He looked her up and down and then folded his arms across his chest. "How would you know, Miss Edwards? What makes you think you're an expert on sixteen-year-old boys?''

Eva flushed. She wondered what he would say if she told him she had dealt with more young men at the Palace than he could count, young men just like Lane, out on their own for their first drink and their first woman? Boys who were fighting to prove they were men. Some even younger than Lane.

"I'm not an expert," she told him, "but I haven't lived in a cocoon, either. Would *you* want to be corrected in front of the other men?''

The corner of his mouth turned up a bit. "Is that why you waited until now, while we're all alone, to correct me?''

"I didn't intend to offend you, Mr. Cassidy." She linked

her fingers together and held them at her waist but did not look away. "I was only trying to help."

"No offense taken, but I'll decide how to handle Lane. While I'm gone, just see that he goes to school and does his chores."

"I couldn't help but overhear you two arguing about school when I first arrived this afternoon."

"For a woman who promised to mind her own business, you're sure interested in mine."

"I wasn't eavesdropping. Folks probably heard you in the next county."

Chase almost smiled. "He wants to go on the roundup. I told him he couldn't."

"Maybe he needs some help with his studies. Would you mind if I tutor him?"

"Not at all." He rubbed his hand across the back of his neck before he added, "If he'll let you."

She began to gather up the rest of the dishes and flatware. "When do you leave? Is there anything special I need to prepare?"

"We'll leave in the morning. We carry what we need."

"How long will you be gone?"

"Three, four days at the most. We're gathering all the cattle off the open range. When we get back we'll start the branding." He started out the door, making a grab for his hat at the last second. "I'll be out in the barn if you need me."

"I'll see that Lane stays in school while you're gone," she promised.

Standing on the threshold, Chase Cassidy eyed her skeptically. "Good luck, Miss Edwards. Don't forget you all but insisted that I hire you."

Chase stepped out onto the darkened porch and almost fell over Orvil. He spat out a curse under his breath, caught his balance, and landed with both feet on the ground.

"Best watch your step there, Cassidy," the aged cowboy said with a chuckle. "Don't want to be leavin' before my time."

"Sorry."

"Guess I know where your mind is tonight, that's for sure." Orvil laughed again and lifted the coffee cup to his lips.

"Yeah." Rather than get into a discussion about his new housekeeper, Chase walked toward the barn, thankful to be outdoors. He could only stand being cooped up for so long. As relieved as he was to be outside again, his thoughts were still mired in a hopeless tangle.

Chase paused beside the near corral, hooked his arms over the upper fence rail and watched a mare with her new foal. With one foot propped against the bottom rail, he let his eyes grow accustomed to the dark and relaxed with the familiar sights and sounds around him. Tonight, even the scent of the rich loam churned by horses hooves, the pungent, eye smarting smell of manure, and the cool night breeze did not soothe him. Not while all he could think of was Eva Edwards and the way she had looked standing in his kitchen tonight.

When he had walked in for supper, she was waiting there with a smile as wide as the Montana sky and her hair vibrant with the colors of sunset. She had changed into a pink and white striped gown that reminded him of a piece of peppermint penny candy. It was unadorned, but soft and feminine without trying, just like her. The colors highlighted her glowing complexion. Her cheeks were flushed from the heat of the stove, her thick copper curls encouraged by the steam from the bubbling pots.

When he saw his men standing there staring at her with their tongues hanging down to their toes, he had an uneasy feeling in his gut that hiring Eva was going to lead to trouble that wouldn't even be of her making.

She couldn't help that she was beautiful.

And she was definitely a lady.

Sooner or later, she was bound to go into town, and when she did, she was sure to hear all about the infamous Cassidys. It was hard to believe Millie Carberry had not had a chance to give her an earful already. If the storekeeper had gotten to her first, Eva probably would never have applied for the job. What would Miss Eva Edwards think when she discovered her employer had ridden with one of the most notorious gangs in the West and spent nine years in prison?

As if that wasn't enough to send her packing, how long would it be before she somehow set Lane off and he exploded at her the way he had at the other housekeepers? She didn't look to be any match for the boy. The former housekeepers all appeared to be made of much sterner stuff than the young Miss Edwards and they hadn't been able to withstand Lane's threats.

Chase heard the sound of chiming spurs and glanced over his shoulder. Ramon was moving toward him through the darkness.

"The horses are ready," he told Chase in his softly accented Spanish.

"Do we have enough?"

"Each man will have five in his *remuda*," he said, referring to a string of replacement horses.

"Good. We could use one more man, though."

Chase felt Ramon go silent and knew his foreman never wasted words. He used them like precious coins. "Why not take the boy? He is willing."

"I already told him no. Besides, I want him in school."

"You need to loosen your hold on him, amigo. He will fight the bit and wound himself."

"That seems to be quite the consensus around here tonight."

First Eva and now Ramon. Chase thought of times gone by, of the many years that he and Ramon had shared a cell in prison. It was their habit to talk long into the night. If it had not been for Ramon, Chase might have lost his mind. He knew his friend was merely trying to ease the tension that existed between him and Lane, but if there was one point Chase refused to waver on, it was his need to discipline the boy and keep him in school.

While he was in prison, his nephew's education had been sorely neglected. Now that Chase was back, he was determined to see that Lane attended school every day and stayed out of trouble. There was no way Chase wanted his sister's son to follow in his footsteps. He wanted to help Lane in every way he could, but he didn't know where to begin. Ever since he brought Lane back home a year ago, the boy had rejected every effort he made to get close to him. He balked at authority, especially at any rules that the former housekeepers had tried to impose upon him.

Finally Chase nodded to Ramon in the darkness. "I need to keep him on a short rope, at least for now. He doesn't respond to anything else."

He heard Ramon slip his tobacco pouch out of his vest pocket. The man could roll a cigarette as well in the darkness as he could in broad daylight. "The woman is *muy hermosa*," Ramon commented.

Chase agreed. "She *is* beautiful."

Ramon exhaled smoke and said, "She is not what she seems."

There was no moon. Chase could not make out the foreman's expression, only the outline of his features. From high in the rafters of the darkened barn behind them, an owl hooted and ruffled its feathers.

"What do you mean?"

"Why is she here?" the Mexican asked.

"She's from back East. Told me her mother died, that she needed a job."

"And she was convincing?"

Chase nodded, thinking of the slow tears that had streaked Eva's face that afternoon. "Very. What are you getting at?"

"Exactly what is she doing here? Perhaps she has been sent by one of your enemies to get close to you. To make you vulnerable."

Chase snorted, disbelieving. "Why would anyone go to all that trouble when they know where I am? They could ride in and get me themselves. Besides, the Hunt brothers are still in prison and will be for ten more years. I wouldn't worry about Miss Edwards, if I were you. Besides, once she finds out about me, she probably won't be around long.''

They stood in companionable silence for a while longer. Finally, Ramon told him, "I'm going in." The foreman flicked his cigarette butt in the air.

Chase watched the glowing red tip arc, hit the churned ground in the middle of the corral, and die.

"Buenas noches," Chase said, absently. His thoughts and his gaze drifted toward the kitchen. He saw the glow of the lamplight dim in the window in the back door and then go out.

Chase shifted uncomfortably, wondering what Eva was doing in her room off the kitchen. The few beautiful women he had ever spent time with had been bought and paid for, and now, suddenly one was living beneath his roof. His thoughts ran down a forbidden path as fast as an ornery bull on the loose, and there was little he could do to corral them.

It was all too easy to picture Eva standing haloed by the muted light from a single lamp, the highlights of her hair flaming. Alone, in the privacy of her room, would she free the buttons along the bodice of her gown and pause, perhaps listen for a moment, and then, certain that she would not be caught unawares, slide the gown off her shoulders?

It did not take much of an imagination to envision her bare ivory shoulders, the smooth gentle slope of her breasts where they rose beneath her chemise. She would lazily slip off the gown and step out of it. Shapely hips and legs would slowly be exposed to the cool night air. Would she cover herself from neck to ankle in a modest white nightgown or stand unclothed before the mirror while she combed her hair?

He would be the last one to know what a real lady did before she went to bed at night.

Just thinking about it made him hard. Chase wiped his palms along his thighs and shoved his hands into his back pockets, swearing softly under his breath.

He might need a housekeeper, but he sure as hell didn't need one that had him thinking about her constantly.

He was halfway into the sitting room, headed toward his own bedroom door when a slight movement made him tense like a coiled spring. His hand instinctively went to his hip but it came away empty. He hadn't worn a gun in years, but old habits die hard.

The low fire in the fireplace cast a glow that highlighted Eva in silhouette.

"What are you doing?" The words came out rougher than he had intended. He saw her flinch, her green eyes widen. Despite his fantasies, she had not changed clothes, but was still wearing her striped dress. She appeared tired, her flawless complexion marred by lavender shadows beneath her eyes.

"I'm sorry, I . . ." she stepped closer, lowering her voice with a glance toward the door to Lane's room. "I was going to light the lamp for you, so that you wouldn't have to walk through the dark—"

The other women he had hired had tread very carefully around him. They had all needed employment badly enough to apply despite what they knew of his reputation. Two of them had been somewhat efficient, but not one of them had taken the time to show any effort beyond their duties. Eva Edwards didn't have to see to it that there was a light left burning for him, yet here she was, doing just that.

Something compelling shot through him, a forbidden warmth he had not let himself feel in years. How long had it been since anyone had taken his needs into consideration? Now this woman, this virtual stranger, did not want him to walk into a darkened house.

Frightened by the faint stirring in his hardened heart, Chase didn't allow himself to think about her act of kindness. Nor would he let himself relax around her or get to know her well. He didn't dare. They were from two different worlds.

"Mr. Cassidy?"

"Don't bother next time," he said coolly.

She came closer, watched him intently, as if she were trying to figure out what sort of a man he really was. He almost told her the truth, then realized if he did—if she quit on the spot—it would mean leaving Lane at home alone during the roundup.

Her voice was soft, barely above a whisper. "For some reason you don't like me much, Mr. Cassidy, and I'd like to know why, when you don't even know me."

"It's not that I don't like you. I just don't think you belong here," he said bluntly. "I'm not all that comfortable with leaving you here alone with Lane, but I can't leave him on his own and I can't put off the roundup any longer. I didn't have much choice when I hired you and now I'm hoping it wasn't a mistake."

"Why? You admitted yourself that I can cook. I can clean. I can mend clothes. I can tutor your nephew for you. You've already agreed to give me a chance. And if you're still worried about my reputation—"

"I'm sure your reputation is spotless."

Her perfect features were marred by a sudden frown, but she turned away so quickly that he thought he might have imagined it.

"If you don't think I can handle Lane, perhaps you are judging me by the way I look, Mr. Cassidy. Believe me, looks can be deceiving."

"You're right about that." Who knew better than he?

She walked to the small organ against the side wall and her fingers stroked the oak lid closed over the keyboard.

"Do you play?" she asked, looking over her shoulder at him.

He shook his head and then realized she might not be able to see him clearly in the semidarkness. "No. It was my sister, Sally's."

"Oh." Eva rested one hand on the instrument. "Lane's mother?"

"Yes."

"What happened to her?"

Somehow he knew she was going to ask. He started to speak, felt his throat close and tried to swallow. Eva waited. Finally he was able to say, "She died."

"I'm sorry."

"So am I." He knew it would be best if he said good night, but seeing her backed by the firelight, with her attention focused on him, her willingness to talk arrested him. Her presence held him there.

"It must have been hard on Lane."

"It was."

He saw her brow wrinkle slightly and knew she was thinking of Lane, of his loss. "I'll do my best, Mr. Cassidy. You don't have to worry about Lane while you're gone. Just concentrate on rounding up all those little dogies out there."

Unable to keep himself from smiling, Chase closed his eyes for a second and shook his head. "I'll try, Miss Edwards," he assured her, "I'll try."

Back against the wall, still fully dressed, Lane sat on his bed in the dark and cradled the gun in his lap. Loading and unloading the Smith & Wesson double-action revolver in the darkness was a nightly ritual he never tired of. Holding the gun gave him a sense of power and control. As long as he had the revolver and was willing to use it, he knew that no one could hurt him, no one could take advantage of him.

He gave the cylinder a spin and then took aim at the shadowed outline of the door. Slowly, carefully, he lowered the revolver to the bed and let go of it. Then, pretending to hear a noise at the window, his hand snaked out. In an instant he palmed the gun and aimed toward the imaginary sound.

He was as fast as Chase was ever reputed to be. He knew it without ever having tested his skill. He practiced every time he had a chance. The gun easily slipped in and out of the holster with a rose embossed on the worn leather. He had never had the chance to use the weapon for other than target practice, but he knew for certain the gun could maim and kill. Hands other than his had proved that already.

Lane reached out in the darkness and felt for the holster and then slid the gun back inside. He lay the gun belt on the bed beside him and crossed his feet at the ankles. It was a wonder his uncle was still talking to Eva Edwards. The man rarely had a civil word for anyone, but even now he heard them talking softly beyond the door. He couldn't quite make out the words.

What would Miss Eva think if she saw his talent with the gun? A fine eastern lady like herself would probably swoon.

He let himself fantasize for a moment, imagined Eva gasping at the speed and dexterity with which he drew and fired against an imaginary adversary. With the same lightning-fast movement, he would holster the gun and catch her before she hit the ground in a dead faint. He would cradle her against him, gently lower her until he held her across his lap.

What would it be like to kiss her? Lane felt the blood flow hot and heavy through his veins and closed his eyes. Power coupled with a dark and forbidden feeling crept over him. His head started to pound, so he laid the gun aside and began to massage his temples. Unbidden fear welled up inside him, the same dark fright he always felt whenever he remembered his mother's death and the years immediately following it.

And where had Chase been when he had needed him the most?

Behind bars.

To his uncle's way of thinking, it had been time well worth sacrificing because, although Chase Cassidy had to pay for riding with one of the most notorious gangs of outlaws in the West, he felt he had avenged his sister's death.

But those same years had robbed Lane of both his mother and his uncle. Just as Chase could never give back those years nor erase what had happened while he was gone, neither could Lane forgive him for leaving.

Now Chase was back and insisted on treating him like a child. The humiliation was almost more than he could bear. This afternoon his uncle had embarrassed him in front of the men by telling him that he might as well stop whining about going on the roundup. Then, in front of Miss Eva, Chase ordered him to wash his hands before supper like some wet-behind-the-ears toddler.

The sound of his uncle's bedroom door closing went through him like a shot. Lane curled into a fetal position on the bed and stared at the wall that separated their rooms. The fear he had felt earlier began to creep back to the dark crevice of his soul from whence it had come.

He continued to concentrate on Chase, sick to death of his only living kin treating him like a child. Besides, Chase Cassidy didn't have the right, not after all this time.

Lane got up and reached under his bed, unerringly grasping the saddlebag he kept hidden there. He wrapped the gun belt around the holster and shoved it into the bag, then tied the rawhide that held it closed. Morning would come sooner than later, and Chase wasn't one to let him shirk his chores any more than he would let him miss school.

He peeled off his cambric shirt, then shucked off his boots and pants and crawled under the covers. There was one consolation in having to stay back while Chase and the others were gone—Miss Eva would be the only one here to keep an eye on him.

Chapter Four

The off-key notes of the organ music died on the still, warm air in the sitting room. Eva reached up to close the music book, then leaned back and sighed. It was harder to put the excitement of her old life behind her than she had expected, especially on late afternoons, when the hollowness of an empty house began to wear on her. She found herself looking forward to Lane's return from school.

Chase and the others had been gone a week, and in that time Lane had not given her any problems. He had been cooperative, if not downright talkative. She had grown used to his ability to turn his smile off and on without ever showing his true feelings. They spent hours working together, and in all that time he had yet to volunteer anything personal. He talked about the ranch, but said nothing about school, his uncle, or any mention of friends he might have made.

She stood up, stretched, and paced to the window. There had been plenty to do at the beginning of the week, but now that the house had been put in order and with only Lane and herself to cook for, Eva found herself with time on her hands.

She and Lane had fallen into an easy routine together. He rose early to see to the stock, and as he left the house he would knock on her door to wake her. Eva would then dress, make his breakfast, pack a meal for him to carry to school, and after he left she would start the bread, straighten the house, and make the beds. So far she had not tackled

51

the laundry, but she was dutifully reading up on the process.

Pushing aside one of the frayed blankets at the window, she stared out across acres of grazing land. It was a moment or two before she spotted a lone rider in the distance. When Curly barked and jumped up off the porch and eagerly ran to meet him, she was certain it was Lane. Eva found herself looking forward to the time she spent tutoring him, for it wasn't until they were alone at the kitchen table that the boy would let down his guard. She found she had even been able to make him smile on occasion.

Hurrying off to the kitchen, she took a plate of sugar cookies out of a pie safe near the door and set them on the table. Lane rode into the yard and took time to unsaddle his horse and feed and water it before he came in. Finally, he strode through the back door, his saddlebags over his shoulder, a half-smile barely curving his lips.

"How was school?"

His smile faded immediately. "Fine." He went straight through the kitchen and headed toward his room.

He was back within minutes with his composition book, pen and ink in hand. He set the items on the table and pulled out his chair.

"I thought Mr. Cassidy would be back before now," she said as she sat down across the table from him.

Lane shrugged and gazed at her with the uncommunicative stare that had become effortless. His coal-black eyes showed no emotion.

He slid down in the chair and reached for a cookie. "I guess they went further north than they counted on. They'll probably be home by tomorrow night at the latest."

"Are you worried?" She wondered aloud.

He paused with a cookie halfway to his lips, for a moment appearing confused by her question. "No. Why should I be?"

"Isn't herding cattle dangerous?"

"I don't think my uncle would consider it dangerous."

"I've heard it is. I just wondered if you were worried

about him, that's all." She thought perhaps she had given him the opening he needed to communicate. She thought wrong.

"I never worry about Uncle Chase. He can take care of himself."

She looked at the cookie plate, reached out and straightened a cookie balanced on the rim and then looked up at him. "You know, Lane, I couldn't help noticing that things are a bit strained between the two of you—"

"Shouldn't we get started?" he asked in an obvious bid to change the subject.

Eva knew from his surly tone there was no use questioning him further about his feelings. She did have a request of another sort. "There is one more thing. Do you think you could drive me into town tomorrow?"

Since Chase had been away longer than she expected, Eva had decided Saturday was as good a day as any to go into town for a few supplies. The trip would give her a chance to look around, perhaps meet some new people, shop for a few staples.

"Town?"

She laughed. "You know. Last Chance? I need to go to Carberry's to pick up some things for my recipes. I'm afraid your uncle's pantry lacks imagination, and it would be nice to get out and look around a bit. This would be the best time to do it, with the men away."

He didn't look very pleased at the prospect but agreed with a shrug. "I guess I can take you in tomorrow morning."

"Wonderful. Now, what should we work on?"

"Math. I figure that's what I need help with the most," he said without looking up.

She leaned forward, rested her elbows on the table and smiled. "I thought that today I'd give you a writing assignment so that I can see how your grammar and spelling are coming along. You've chosen math every day."

"You want me to *write* something?"

Eva nodded. She reached out and opened his composition book for him, laid it on the table, and turned it so that it was facing his direction. "How about . . . " she drummed her fingers on the table as she stared up at the ceiling, "one of your favorite childhood memories? You can choose the title."

The look he gave her was blank, devoid of all emotion. Eva smiled encouragement. "Go ahead. Take as long as you want. Write about something you remember, something that happened when you were a little boy. I'm going to start supper."

She puttered around the kitchen, digging into the barrel of pickled beef in the pantry, then collecting a few potatoes from a sack. The most personal thing she had learned about the Cassidys was that potatoes were a favorite vegetable of both.

As she contented herself with peeling potatoes, Eva spent the next few minutes thinking up a series of topics that might give her insight into the boy's problems. After a long stretch of silence, she glanced over her shoulder and found Lane had not moved since she had given him the assignment.

His shoulders were rigid, his back pressed against the rungs of the chair, his eyes hooded by the frown that creased his dark brow. Both of his hands rested palms down on the table. He had not attempted to pick up his pen, but continued to glower down at the page.

"Lane?"

He started, called out of his thoughts as sharply as if she had struck him. When he looked up at her, Eva almost flinched at the dark anger reflected in his eyes.

"Lane, what is it?" She whispered. The swift change in him was so dramatic, she was momentarily shaken.

"I'm not doing this!"

The violent explosion came just as suddenly. He shot up out of his chair so quickly, it toppled over behind him and clattered against the floor. His hands were balled into fists at his sides. His chest heaved. Swinging wildly at the table, he sent the ink bottle flying. It sailed across the room and hit the wall. The glass container shattered, splattering ink everywhere.

"Lane," Eva said softly, one hand extended to him in a silent entreaty for him to calm down. "That's all right, Lane. We'll clean up the ink and then try something else."

"No. Nothing else. Not today."

Eva found herself trembling. What in the world had set him off? Was this sudden outburst what Chase had been afraid of?

"All right," she said slowly, keeping her tone even, her voice low as she tried to appear cool and collected. "If you're not up to it, we won't do any studying today. Pick up the chair and put your book away. Supper will be ready in a while. You can clean up the ink while I set the table."

She could see him struggling to calm down, making an effort to breathe normally again. He continued to stare down at the composition book as if it were a snake, then he kicked aside the chair and stalked out of the room.

Determined not to let him get away with such impossibly rude behavior, Eva followed close on his heels. He stepped into his room and grabbed the edge of the door, intent on slamming it in her face.

"Hold it right there, young man," she told him with as much force as she could muster, determined not to go the way of the former Cassidy housekeepers. She wasn't about to let a sixteen-year-old push her around, no matter how much taller, stronger, or uncontrollable he seemed.

"Leave me alone, Eva. I'm warning you."

She shook her finger in his face. "And I'm warning you. Your uncle left me in charge here, and if I say you're going to be civil and clean up that mess in the kitchen, then that's exactly what you'll do."

He took a step toward her, his hands once more balled into fists at his side. Tightly leashed fury caused him to tremble. She could read the anger in his stance and on his face. The dark hostility in his eyes frightened her, but she had stood up to older, tougher men than Lane Cassidy and she refused to back down now.

Eva took a deep breath to calm herself, certain that one of them had to stay calm. "Listen," she began, lowering her voice but not cajoling, "I need this job. If you want to run me out of here, I'm here to tell you it's going to take a lot more than a little temper tantrum."

Lane was watching her intently, almost as if she had surprised him by standing up to his anger. He said nothing.

"Now, do you intend to tell me what caused that outburst in the kitchen?"

"No."

"Fine. But I still expect you to clean up the mess."

"That's your job."

She shook her head, mad enough to spit nails. "Not the way I see it. You did that purposely, and I want it cleaned up."

A war was raging within him. She could see it in his eyes. Eva decided to give him a chance to think things through on his own. "I'm going in the kitchen to prepare dinner. I expect you to have that ink cleaned up before you sit down to eat." Eva headed toward the kitchen.

"Are you quitting when Uncle Chase gets back?"

She spun around to face him again. Worry had replaced anger on his dark features. "I told you it would take more than a tantrum to get rid of me."

"Will you tell him?"

"Not if things get settled to my satisfaction," she said and started to walk away again.

"Eva?"

She could tell by the hesitant tone in his voice that she had won the skirmish.

"What?"

"I'm sorry."

Pausing in the door to the kitchen and looking across the sitting room at him, Eva smiled. "That's a start. Get a pail of water and I'll have some rags ready for you when you get back."

*   *   *

Silently thankful that she had not once mentioned his outburst of the day before, Lane drove Eva into Last Chance on Saturday. True to her sunny nature, she chatted all the way, and although he wanted to answer her many questions about the landscape and the birds and whether or not he had ever thought of learning to play his mother's organ, Lane retreated inside himself the closer they came to town.

Aside from the incident with the spilled ink, he had tried to be on his best behavior around Eva, and amazingly enough, it hadn't been as hard as he had thought it might. Other than gently reminding him to do his daily chores, she never tried to boss him around the way the other house-keepers had done. While sharing their quiet suppers, he even found he enjoyed her company. That, coupled with the fact that she treated him kindly, and for the most part, just as she would an adult, is what had kept him from lash-ing out at her when she stood up to him yesterday.

After getting to know her and being on his best behavior while Chase was gone, Lane found himself hoping Eva wouldn't quit on the spot if anyone happened to tell her about his uncle's past. Lane even wondered if maybe he shouldn't tell her right now and get it over with. Until now he had been content to fantasize that Eva might never leave the ranch, never find out that his uncle was a jailbird. Maybe it had been a crazy kid's dream to think that a kind-hearted lady like Eva would stay on at the ranch for a while, but it had been the only dream he'd had in a long while.

They came up over a rise that put them at the edge of town. The buildings stood together, lined up along Main Street like wooden soldiers on parade. Because it was Sat-urday, there was more street traffic than usual, but he suc-cessfully negotiated his way through. They passed a buggy driven by a man he recognized as one of his schoolmate's father, a man in baggy overalls sporting a long, graying beard. The man looked their way, recognized Lane, and immediately turned back to his team of mules without so much as a nod of acknowledgment.

Lane snuck a glance at Eva. If she noticed that the passersby on the boardwalks were giving them sly glances, she didn't let on. He let his mind wander and tried to imagine himself ten years older. He vowed that by then, he wouldn't be whispered about or snubbed anymore. Ten years from now he would have made a name for himself. Her words drew him out of his thoughts, shattering the silence. "I need to stop at Carberry's first."

Lane looked over and found her smiling up at him and felt like someone had reached into his chest and squeezed his heart. He couldn't answer.

It was wrong to have hoped that she would stay on very long. He should have let Chase talk her out of the job before he had come to know her, before she had spent time tutoring him, treating him fairly and with kindness. When she looked at him, it had never been with fear or disgust, only concern.

It was too late to think of any of that now. Lane pulled the wagon up before Carberry's store, set the break, and leaned back against the seat.

For a moment he considered not even helping her out of the wagon, but that wouldn't keep Eva from her self-appointed mission. He jumped down, went around to help her down, and stepped back to let her pass.

"I'll wait here," he said, tipping his hat brim down to shade his eyes. He crossed his arms, leaned back against the wagon wheel and watched Eva prepare to walk away.

Eva shook the trail dust out of her candy-striped skirt, straightened her very fashionable little hat, and ignored Lane's sullen demeanor. He had seemed fine when they left the ranch, but his temper was so mercurial that it could change like the weather.

As she walked down the sidewalk toward Carberry's store, she looked around what appeared to be a thriving, if not overly populated little town. Main Street was crowded with all sorts of conveyances, buggies, wagons, and men on horseback. Miners and farmers walked alongside cowhands and dust-covered drifters on the wooden sidewalks that fronted the stores.

Across the way, she noticed a garishly painted sign of red, blue, and yellow hanging above a corner building. It all but shouted to passersby the name of the Last Chance Saloon. Eva glimpsed a tall blonde standing just inside the swinging doors. The girl appeared to be not much older than Lane. Outfitted in black lace and emerald feathers, the barmaid leaned against the door frame, watching the townsfolk pass by. A shiver ran down Eva's spine as she experienced a feeling of déjà vu and wondered if the girl longed to leave her life behind as much as she had herself.

Concentrating on the task at hand, Eva stepped inside the general store. The place was packed with goods, the aisles narrowed by barrels and sacks full of produce. Farm implements and hams hung from the ceiling like last winter's icicles. She paused in the open doorway, drew her shopping list out of her bag, and stepped farther into the room. The store was well lit near the front windows, but grew dim farther back.

An old man with an equally ancient, cloudy-eyed spaniel sat on a crooked stool in the center of the room, one arm resting on the counter beside him. As Eva walked toward him, he grinned, bestowing a toothless smile on her. His beard was only shaved in spots, which left his chin covered with silver stubble. Broken, spiderweb veins lined his cheeks.

In a tone just below a shout he asked, "Looking for anything in particular, Missy?"

Eva smiled back at the cheerful old man. "I'm afraid I need quite a few things, sir."

Without warning, the old man hollered, "Millie! Get out here, woman, and come ready to work."

The harried, splinter-thin woman Eva had met briefly the day she arrived hurried out of a door at the back of the room, wiping her hands on her apron. Millie Carberry stopped short when she recognized Eva and quickly dropped the hem of her dampened apron.

"What can I do for you?"

Eva noticed a hint of suspicion in the woman's eyes, took a deep breath and tried to hide her concern. "I need quite a few things—" She paused long enough to see if Mrs. Carberry would refuse to serve her, but the woman simply stood there and made no response. Eva cleared her throat. "I need some cinnamon, some cloves if you have them. Some tea, vinegar, and some black ink. Oh, and if you have any honey—"

"We do. Is that all?"

"For now," Eva said, then added quickly, "but I'd like to look around, if I may."

"It's all right with me. Do as you please." Mrs. Carberry turned away, hurrying off to gather Eva's order while the old man reached down and scratched the spaniel behind the ears.

"You new here?" he yelled.

Before Eva could answer, a movement in the open doorway caught her eye. She looked up and saw a young woman step inside. Eva smiled, arrested by the newcomer's eyes. They were of a deep, royal blue, a beautiful contrast to her shining brown hair and rich, clear complexion. Modestly dressed in a gingham-checked gown with a navy shawl thrown over her shoulders, the newcomer looked to be but a few years younger than Eva. She remained on the threshold, paused long enough to glance over her shoulder at something outside and then continued into the store.

"I said, *you new here?*" The old codger on the stool chortled in glee when Eva jumped at his shout.

She smiled an apology to the young woman who was concentrating on a row of jellies. "I'm the housekeeper at the Cassidy ranch, Trail's End."

Millie Carberry's head popped up behind the edge of the counter. Her eyes were full-moon wide. "You took the job? You really plan on stayin' out there?"

Eva's smile wavered. "I had hoped to keep this job as long as Mr. Cassidy needs me—"

Millie Carberry snorted. "Mister, indeed."

"Excuse me." The brunette with brilliant blue eyes moved up to Eva and had touched her arm to gain her attention. Eva couldn't decide if the girl was shy or merely soft spoken. Her entire manner was hesitant.

"If you're from the Trail's End, I'd like to talk to you for a moment, if you don't mind."

"Of course not, Miss—?"

"Albright. Rachel Albright. I'm Lane's teacher."

Eva was speechless for a moment. Miss Rachel Albright didn't appear to be much older than Lane. She glanced over at the counter and noted that Millie Carberry had moved to the back of the room, climbed a ladder and was reaching up for a dust-coated bottle of ink on the top shelf.

"I'm Eva Edwards, the Cassidys' new housekeeper. What can I do for you?"

As she waited to hear what Miss Albright had to say, Eva marveled that less than two weeks ago she had been dancing three shows a night at the Palace of Venus Saloon, and now, here she stood in the middle of a general store like any well-respected citizen talking to the local school-marm while the store clerk filled her grocery order. She almost pinched herself, wishing John was there to share her elation.

"I really need to talk to someone about Lane," Miss Albright said.

"Is there a problem?"

The young teacher's eyes were wide and sincere. She nodded. "I'm afraid so, you see—"

Outside, two shots rang out. Reacting instantly, Eva grabbed the teacher and shoved her to the floor. She dove after her, and they lay side by side until the shooting stopped and someone shouted.

"Lane is out there," Eva suddenly remembered, panicked to think that he might have been wounded by a stray bullet. She was on her feet in an instant. As she headed toward the door, she could feel Rachel Albright on her heels.

Eva skidded to a halt at the edge of the boardwalk. The

wagon Lane had left hitched to the post in front of the store was unoccupied. As her heart began to hammer in her throat, Eva ran over to where a crowd had formed in front of a saloon.

"What is it?" she heard Rachel call out behind her.

Eva kept running. When she reached the crowd, she pushed her way between two burly male onlookers. Miss Albright collided into her. Eva watched as a tall, auburn haired, broad-shouldered man with a star pinned to his leather vest helped a wounded young cowboy in a canvas duster up off the ground. The injured man had his hand pressed to his upper arm, but that did not stop the slow trickle of blood seeping from his shoulder. A gun lay on the ground near the spot where he had landed.

Eva gasped when she recognized Lane. He stood opposite the sheriff and the wounded cowboy inside the circle of onlookers. His eyes were shadowed by his hat, his mouth held steady in a grim, determined line. She instantly became aware of the holster strapped to his hip. In his right hand, he held a gun.

"Just like his uncle," someone whispered beside her.

"Bad blood, that's what it is." Another hushed comment filtered to Eva's ears.

Behind her, Rachel Albright gasped, "Oh, my God."

The waver in her voice made Eva give pause and turn away from the scene, away from Lane who was belligerently eyeing the sheriff as the lawman moved toward him. She found Miss Albright as white as a freshly laundered hankie. Eva grabbed the teacher's hand and led her to the sidewalk, afraid the young woman was going to faint dead away at the edge of the crowd.

"Sit down," Eva demanded, frantic to get back to Lane. "Put your head between your knees."

"I'm all right," the schoolmarm protested. "Please, Lane needs you—"

Eva knew she was right. "You stay here. I don't know if we'll be able to have that talk today, I—"

Miss Albright shook her head. Her eyes pleading with

Eva as eloquently as words never could. "Please, go help Lane. Don't leave him standing there all alone."

Eva squeezed her hand, spun around and hurried back over to the circle of bystanders. "Let me through," she said, shoving her way in again, thankful for hours of experience on a crowded barroom floor. Jostled forward, she shouldered her way in, sensed a boot about to land dangerously close to her toes and pulled her foot back in time.

The sheriff was still holding the wounded young man by the arm as he lead both boys back to the shady side of the street. Lane had holstered his gun. Eva stepped out into the center of the crowd and hurried after them and followed them through the door into the sheriff's office. As he turned around to close the door on the crowd, he stopped short to stare down at her.

"Sorry ma'am, I've got business to attend to." A shock of auburn hair fell over the deep creases in his freckled forehead. Eva had to crick her neck to look up at him and guessed he was close to six foot four. His voice was so low, it seemed to come from the heels of his boots.

"I'm afraid this is my business, too, Sheriff," she told him, "as long as it has anything to do with Lane."

"What business is he of yours?"

"I'm the new housekeeper at the Trail's End. His uncle left me in charge."

Slowly, as if he might be looking over a good grade of stock, the sheriff dropped his eyes to her feet, swept them up to her waist, her bodice, all the way to her hat and then met her gaze.

"You're Chase Cassidy's *housekeeper?*"

She read the insinuation in his eyes. She had not left the Palace to have to put up with any gossip in this one-horse town and decided to put an end to it before it got started.

"Indeed I am, Sheriff. I am Miss Eva Edwards, formerly of Pennsylvania. I have been at the Cassidy ranch for six days, three of which Mr. Cassidy has been gone. I cook, I clean, I mend and wash clothing. I also tutor his nephew after school. If you have anything more to say on the matter, I ask you to say it to me now.''

''Well, ma'am, I guess I don't have a damn thing to say, since you put it that way. Did you just give me what some folks might call a set down?''

She wondered if he was making fun of her and decided to overlook his barb to get to the heart of the matter, which was Lane. ''What's going on here?'' She thought she already knew the answer but hoped she might be mistaken.

''Little matter of a shoot-out on Main Street, ma'am. I don't take kindly to any sort of hostile activity here in my town.''

''I'm sure Lane wouldn't—''

''Lane Cassidy would and did. By his own admission.''

Eva took a step forward and waited, refusing to believe Lane capable of trying to murder someone in cold blood. She turned to him.

''Lane?''

''What?''

His face was so sullen, his eyes so hopelessly blank, that Eva wanted to shake him. ''Lane, did you do this? Why?''

His shoulders were hunched protectively. He shifted his weight to one foot. ''What's all the fuss? I didn't kill him.''

The wounded cowboy lunged away from the sheriff and ended up toe to toe with Lane. ''You couldn't hit the side of a barn with a barrel. You couldn't—''

''Hold it right there, son.'' The sheriff reached out and as if Lane's adversary was nothing more than a spitting kitten, he picked him up by the collar and shook him, then set him down on his feet again, this time a yard away from Lane.

''He drew on me first,'' Lane argued.

''Did you, son?'' the sheriff asked the other boy.

The cowboy glared at Lane. Lane stared back without so much as a flicker of emotion on his face.

Finally, the young cowboy with blond peach fuzz on his chin wilted under Lane's stare. ''I did.''

''Thought you'd make a name for yourself outdrawin' Chase Cassidy's relation. Is that it?''

Eva wondered what the sheriff was driving at, but she was too concerned watching Lane to pay close attention.

The sheriff turned to Lane. "You fired in self-defense?"

Lane looked the man in the eye. It was a second before he nodded nearly imperceptibly.

"I want you to take off that gun and holster and give it to your housekeeper, son."

Lane's gaze shot to Eva and then back to the sheriff. She held her breath, certain he was going to refuse, wondering how she was going to tell Chase about this afternoon's incident and what he would do to Lane when she did.

"Give it to me, Lane," she whispered. "It'll be all right."

He made no comment. Nor did he move to obey, either.

"Do it, Cassidy, or I lock you up," the sheriff warned him quietly.

"What about me? He *shot* me," whined the cowboy. "You just going to let him walk out of here?"

"Shut up," the sheriff said over his shoulder. "*Now*, Cassidy."

Lane's hand moved to the buckle of his gun belt. He slowly unfastened it and handed it over to Eva. Her hand shook when she accepted the piece and wound the leather belt around her fist.

"Go wait in the wagon," she ordered Lane.

When he left the room, she sighed with relief and then turned back to the sheriff. "Thank you. I'll be sure Lane's uncle is told. I'm sure he'll see that this never happens again."

He handed her Lane's gun and watched while she slipped it into the holster.

"Are you, Miss Edwards? Are you sure?"

Eva realized she didn't know Chase Cassidy well enough to swear anything. "I'll try my best."

"My name's Stuart McKenna. You tell Chase I said I don't want to be slingin' that boy over a saddle and bringin' him home dead."

"I will," she managed to choke out, hating him for the

callous remark and the image it conjured. Turning in silent dismissal, she left the office.

There was no sign of pretty Miss Albright anywhere, but Lane was waiting outside, his back pressed against the wall of the jail with his hat brim pulled down low, shading his eyes. She recognized the stance. He was trying to appear uncaring, as nonchalant as he could be before the small gathering of onlookers who stood watching from across the street. His studied lack of remorse angered her more than the scene with the sheriff.

"Stand up and walk me to that wagon with your head up and your shoulders straight, Lane Cassidy, or you're going to have to answer to me *and* your uncle."

She waited until he was beside her and then she dropped her hand, trying to conceal the gun and holster in the folds of her skirt. She knew she could not succeed completely, but at least the weapon was no longer highly visible.

"Now, you will help me onto the wagon," she said in a low commanding tone that only Lane could hear.

He complied without argument, took her hand while she climbed up onto the seat and primly settled her skirt around her. Eva held her head high and kept her gaze straight ahead while Lane walked back around to the other side, climbed aboard, and took up the reins. She braced herself when the wagon lurched and began to roll.

She never once relaxed her posture, even after they left Last Chance behind them. Finally, although Lane had wrapped himself in his cloak of sullen silence again, Eva shattered the deafening stillness when she asked, "Where did you get this gun?"

He deftly adjusted the reins. "It's mine."

"Does your uncle know you have it?"

He continued to stare straight ahead, his shoulders hunched in on himself protectively. She knew from her own minor acts of adolescent rebellion that it was a hard age to go through. He was in a netherworld, not a boy, not yet a man. Lane was taller than average for his age. He shaved almost daily, his beard more than a shadow of fuzz as with other sixteen-year-olds. Where most young men were still gawky and angular, his body was already growing muscular and well defined.

Eva hated to think what Chase would do when she told him about his nephew's latest escapade.

"Lane, please. Talk to me about this."

He pulled back on the reins. The horses stopped, dust swirled around them. Lane turned to face her, his eyes stormy.

"Stay out of it."

"I can't stay out of it. Chase left me in charge."

"You don't know anything about me or Chase, and if you're smart you'll just stay the hell out of it. Don't ask me anything else about that gun or where I got it. It's mine. That's all you need to know."

She expected a harsher response. Lost in thought, she sat staring straight ahead, reminding herself that the Cassidys' problems were not hers even as she wondered how she could ignore the young man's obvious need of friendship and support.

Instead of starting up the team, he said, "Look, I'm sorry, Eva, but a lady like you just wouldn't understand. Stay out of this."

A lady like you.

If he only knew how far that was from the truth. Finally, she collected herself enough to look at him again. "You realize this is far more serious than throwing a bottle of ink. I have to tell Chase what happened today, Lane. If I don't, he'll find out soon enough, and I don't want him to think I was trying to hide anything from him."

She paused and drew a deep breath. "I told you before, I need this job."

She caught him studying her closely, and she watched his Adam's apple bob as he swallowed.

When he finally spoke, she had to strain to hear his next words.

"Do what you have to do. He already hates me anyway."

The wagon wheel hit a rut in the road and Eva reached up to hold on to her hat. "I'm sure he doesn't hate you—"

"I'm always in trouble."

"Do you always bring it on yourself?"

"No. It finds me."

Since he seemed willing to talk more than ever, she asked him for the answer to the question that had been on her mind since she took the job at the Trail's End.

"What happened to the other housekeepers?"

His hands were competent on the reins looped through his fingers. He waited so long to respond that she thought he had chosen to ignore her query, then he said, "The first one thought she had leave to whup me when I sassed her."

"Did she? What did your uncle say?"

"He couldn't say anything to her. She was already gone by the time he came in that first night." He glanced over at her from beneath his hat brim and admitted with a cocky half-smile, "I threw a chair at her head."

"Good lord."

"It didn't hit her. But it went through the sitting room window."

She had seen too many barroom brawls to let the thought of a chair flying across the room upset her.

"And the others?"

"I guess I was too hard on the second one, seein' as how she only meant to help, but one night I was takin' a bath on the back porch and damn, if she didn't come waddling out to see if I'd washed behind the ears."

Eva waited, certain there had to be more.

"Nobody touches me," he said, issuing a warning she couldn't pretend not to hear. "I can't stand to be touched— and that cow tried to hold me down and wash my hair and neck."

"Probably had experience as a mother," Eva said, musing.

"I went after her as soon as I was dressed. Held a butcher knife to her throat and told her I was going to kill her in her sleep some night if she didn't clear out."

Swiftly, her gaze cut in his direction. Eva found him watching her closely, waiting for her reaction. She hadn't found anything amusing in the least in his tale and let him know it. "Lane Cassidy, that's abominable. What did your uncle do?"

"Made me sit in my room for two weeks straight, but that didn't bother me a bit. I don't mind bein' alone. In fact, I prefer it." Lane shrugged. "Finally, he gave up and let me out."

She made another mental note. Almost afraid to hear the rest, she asked, "And the others?"

"The third lady crossed me and I threw all her clothes out into the corral. And the one before you, hell, all I did was lose my temper and begin swearin' at her. She backed up against the wall and started screamin', 'Don't kill me! Don't kill me!' Said she'd heard all about me in town and that she had been an idiot to take the job. I guess my reputation precedes me."

"Don't look so smug about it," she told him. "Your incorrigible behavior is nothing to brag about."

"Especially not to housekeeper number five, you mean?"

"I'm serious, Lane." Realizing that she was frowning, she pressed her fingertips to the point between her brows and slowly massaged her forehead. Thinking back over all he had just told her, she knew what control it had cost him to keep from violently lashing out at her when she demanded he clean up after his eruption yesterday.

"Thanks, Eva."

"For what? I still have to tell your uncle about what happened."

"For listening."

"That's easy enough to do."

"Not for everyone," he mumbled.

As they rode through the broad valley of the upper Missouri, she stared at the distant mountains, brown and purple against an aqua sky. Sagebrush and sparse grass were all that dotted the open range. There were few signs of spring, the colors of the landscape still of brown and sepia tones.

"You're teacher certainly seemed concerned," she said without preamble.

Lane nearly dropped the reins. "You met her? What did she say?"

Eva shrugged and shifted on the hard bench seat. "We didn't really have time to converse, not with having to hit the floor when the shots rang out. Then naturally, we both ran out to see what had happened. She was gone when we came out of the sheriff's office."

He relaxed somewhat, but didn't take his eyes off the road. "She's not all that bad. It's not her fault she just happens to work at the one place I don't want to be."

Watching him closely, Eva asked, "You've never blown up at her? Never thrown a book at her or held her up by the ankles or threatened to burn down the schoolhouse?"

He hunched over, put his elbows on his knees until his coat collar nearly reached his ears. Just when she thought he wasn't going to answer her jibe, he turned to her with a perturbed scowl. "No. I haven't. I told you Miss Rachel doesn't get under my skin."

"She's pretty, too."

"I never noticed."

"I'll bet."

He flicked the reins and grumbled, "What are you getting at?"

"Nothing. It's just nervous chatter. This has been quite an outing. I guess I'm just trying to keep my mind off of what your uncle is going to say when I tell him what happened today."

"You and me both."

"I suppose he'll be mad. He has every right to be, you know. You could have been killed."

"Mad ain't the word for what he'll be."

Eva knew he most likely spoke the truth. She hated to be the one to tell Chase Cassidy what had happened, but it was her responsibility. She *had* been the one left to look after Lane and besides, she had promised the sheriff to give Chase a full report.

Eva sighed. Dealing with Lane Cassidy was becoming a full-time occupation in itself.

Chapter Five

The house was quiet when Chase stepped through the back door. He pulled off his hat and tossed it over the antler hat rack, then dropped his saddlebags on a kitchen chair and walked over to the stove. He placed his hand on the iron stove and his touch met cold metal. Along with it came a wave of disappointment.

Eva Edwards was gone.

He was not surprised that she had already left, but he felt a wave of disappointment all the same. No doubt Lane had erupted and had said or done something to drive her away.

Then again, maybe it hadn't been Lane at all.

Maybe she went into Last Chance and found out all about his own past.

He had allowed himself to look forward to the end of the round up, let himself imagine that by some chance things had worked out with Lane and she might still be there when he came home.

There were cattle out in the pens smarter than he was.

Chase glanced around the kitchen. If she was gone, it hadn't been for very long. Everything was still tidy. The door to her room was partially open, tempting him to look inside.

Chase walked across the kitchen and stepped into the small bedroom. He felt confined by the meager space and wondered how Eva stood it after living in a fine home in Philadelphia. He saw it through her eyes; a drab and shabby little room, the bed taking up nearly all the floor space.

There was barely enough room to turn around. He would never have been able to sleep in this room. It reminded him too much of a cell.

Chase was nearly out the door again when his glance caught a flash of crimson, and he turned his attention to the three-drawer bureau.

Her things were still there.

Atop the dresser lay an ivory-backed brush, a comb, and a mirror, all yellowed with age. Beside them stood a small glass vial of perfume. He gently picked it up, raised it to his nose and closed his eyes, deeply inhaling the subtle, lilac scent. He set it down on the distressed surface of the old bureau, careful to turn the bottle exactly the way he thought it had been placed.

Like a snake to a warm rock, he was drawn to the top drawer. He found himself reaching out, touching the handle, and opening the drawer all the way to expose the entire piece of red satin that had tempted him toward the dresser in the first place.

The drawer was full of frilly, frothy undergarments, so full that when opened, the lace-edged ruffles sprang to life and brushed against his hand. He drew back as if burned, then glanced into the deserted kitchen. Like a thief, he reached down slowly and let his fingertips trace the frills at the hem of a bright red petticoat.

Shocked by the blood-red material, he wondered if all ladies as refined as Miss Edwards wore such daring under things.

Who could have guessed what was under those prim dresses of hers?

Chase glanced up and caught sight of himself in the mirror above the dresser and noticed his expression. It held only a trace of a smile, one that didn't even reach his eyes, but it was more than usual. But not even picturing Miss Eva Edwards in her red petticoat could erase the shadows that lurked behind his eyes.

He leaned toward the mirror. His eyes were bloodshot from trail dust. The sweatband in his hat had made an imprint on his forehead. He was dogtired and dirty, muddy from the trail, sweaty from working cattle. He needed a bath in the worst way and found he wanted to get cleaned up before he ran into Eva Edwards again.

With that in mind, he strode back through the kitchen. He paused to pick up a wooden bucket from beside the back door and stepped out onto the porch. Across the yard, Ned was feeding the stock. Curly leapt off the porch, barking and racing across the open range with more enthusiasm than usual. It was a moment or two before Chase recognized Lane and Eva driving in from the direction of Last Chance.

He set the bucket down and waited at the edge of the porch to watch Lane expertly maneuver the wagon across an open range due to sprout new spring grass. The wagon bounced along the rutted trail in front of the setting sun, which silhouetted them against a sky streaked with the colors of fire.

Lane drew the wagon up in the yard and held the reins while Eva climbed down. She had on the striped dress Chase had last seen her in. It made her appear younger, more frivolous, and less reserved than her charcoal gray suit. The carnation pink set off her copper curls.

He quickly noticed that she wasn't smiling as she crossed the yard. He could only guess at the cool reception she must have received in town.

Lane pulled the wagon around to the barn. Eva continued toward the house alone, her arms drawn back, hands behind her, when she looked up and found him watching. Chase saw her attempt to smile but could tell that she was having a hard time of it. He leaned his shoulder against a support post and waited for her to draw closer before he spoke. She paused at the step and tipped her face up to him.

Such natural loveliness caught him unawares, and he realized the picture of her that he held in his memory all week long had been incomplete. She was stunning, her skin clear and radiant. This afternoon there was a high blush riding across her cheeks.

"You're back," she said, watching him closely.

"So are you." He was almost afraid to ask, "Been to town?"

"I needed some—" She started to explain and then stopped.

"You needed what?"

Her eyes searched his face, dropped to his boots, and she lifted her lashes again. "I didn't find what I needed. I'll have to go back next week." She made no attempt to walk up to the porch and join him, instead she stood gazing up at him with her hands behind her. "How was your roundup?"

"Fine." There was no explanation for the tightness in his chest. For the first time in his life he wished he knew how to make polite conversation.

"Well," she said, looking past him toward the back door. "I'd better go in and start dinner."

He nodded. "Whenever you're ready."

She took a step forward and then another and when she came up beside him, Chase recognized the scent of lilacs and knew it was perfume from the little bottle he had examined in her room.

Chase did not move. His inaction forced her to brush past him. He closed his eyes so that his other senses might gambol in the essence of her nearness. The brush of her skirt against his pant leg, the hushed whisper of cotton, the lilac perfume and the hint of breeze ruffling her curls were all elements foreign to the self-imposed isolation he assumed here on the ranch.

Even with his eyes closed, he could feel the tension in her as she attempted to slip past. Chase opened his eyes and caught the flash of sunlight on steel against her skirt. Instinctively, he reached out, grabbed her arm and forced her hand away from the deep folds of the striped fabric. She whirled on him and tried to jerk her arm away.

"Let me go."

"A gun?"

"I—"

He lifted her hand and took the gun belt and holster from her. "Yours?"

"Of course not!"

Chase turned his hand over and froze when he saw the rose in full bloom tooled on the leather holster. His fingers tightened on the cursed object to keep his hand from trembling. Rage roiled inside him.

"Where did you get this?"

"Can we please go inside and talk about it?" She headed toward the door.

With his free hand he reached out and clasped his fingers tightly around her upper arm.

She turned on him again. "Let go of me, Mr. Cassidy."

He watched myriad expressions cross her face—confusion, fear, then anger. His own rage was nearly all consuming. He wanted to shake her—anything—to get at the truth.

"Where did you get this gun?"

"Come inside and I'll tell you."

Her eyes turned a darker shade of green. Her complexion paled. He could see she was determined not to say anything until she had her way and they were inside. He glanced over his shoulder. There was no sign of Lane coming in from the barn. Chase released her with what amounted to a slight shove in the direction of the door.

Once inside, Eva paused beside the kitchen table. He felt a second of regret when he saw her reach out and rest her hand against it for support. Then, still ignoring him, she, slowly and very carefully, reached up and unpinned her hat. She deliberately measured every move as if warning him not to rush her. She set the curious little hat with its long feathers and stuffed sparrow on the table beside her. Slowly, she ran her fingers through the curls at her temples and pushed them back off her face.

Chase waited, his insides coiled as tight as a rattler. He saw her gaze dart to the back door before she finally met his eyes.

"It's Lane's." She said the words softly and without further explanation.

The air went out of him in a rush. *This* revolver had not always been Lane's. Chase knew damn well where it had come from, but what he wanted to know was what *she* was doing with it and how Lane had come by it.

"Lane."

He spoke his nephew's name aloud as if to reaffirm what she had said. He stared down at the leather and cold steel in his hand; his thoughts traveled back over the months and years to the day he had come home and found his sister, Sally, lying dead in a pool of her own blood on the sitting-room floor. Not far away lay the body of one of her attackers, a hole blown through his chest.

At least she had taken one of them with her.

He had seen the gun and holster that day, would have recognized it anywhere because of the rose embossed on the leather holster. The Smith & Wesson revolver had been on the floor beside his sister. Lane had been there, too, hiding in the corner near the organ. Four years old at the time, the boy had witnessed his mother's attack and the brutal dual killing. He had been unable to tell Chase much, only that three men had ridden up to the house demanding food and drink and more than Sally Cassidy had been willing to give.

On that day, so long ago, Chase had not paused to think. He buried Sally, picked up the boy and took Lane to the nearest ranch. He left him there with a neighbor woman he knew only by name and rode away, hell-bent on revenge. He did not know he would not return to the valley or to Lane for eleven years.

Nor did he know how Lane had ended up with this gun after all this time.

"Mr. Cassidy?"

Her hand was on his forearm, a timid touch, nothing like the hold he had on her arm. Chase stared down at Eva's fingers, wondering for a moment how they got there.

"Chase?"

He met her eyes.

"Are you all right?" she asked.

Chase managed to nod. He barely got the words out. "How did you get this?"

She sighed and walked over to the stove. He heard her mutter under her breath when she noticed the fire had gone out.

Eva turned to him, again forcing a smile. "I think we could both use some coffee right now."

"What *I* need right now is to know exactly what happened."

"I don't know exactly. I was in the general store placing an order—and by the way, I was going to use my own money for the new ingredients I wanted, some ink, spices and things, and then tell you later. If you were willing to compensate me for—"

"The gun, Eva."

"I was in the store talking to Lane's teacher—who just happened to walk in—and we heard a gunshot outside. We ran out and found Lane and another young man about his age, maybe a year or two older, I couldn't tell exactly, but he looked to be a cowboy—"

"Lane drew first?"

She shook her head. "No. No it wasn't that way at all. The other boy challenged Lane. That's why Sheriff McKenna let me bring Lane home. He gave me the gun for safekeeping. I really don't think there was anything else Lane could have done, given the circumstances."

Chase closed his eyes and set the offending weapon on the table. When he opened them he caught her watching him very closely.

"Did he kill the other boy?"

"Who? The sheriff?"

At the end of his patience, Chase mumbled a word that wasn't really fit for a lady's ears. "Lane. Did he *kill* the other boy?"

She waved her hand in a gesture of dismissal. "Of course not. He merely wounded the scoundrel in the arm. If you want my opinion, I think Lane purposely aimed to miss him. Sheriff McKenna was very fair about the whole issue.

He told me to bring Lane home." She paused, her face paling somewhat before she spoke again. "And he told me to tell you to keep an eye on him."

"Just *when* were you going to tell me?"

"Tonight, after you had supper and time to relax. After Lane had calmed down."

As twilight wrapped itself around them, Chase felt removed from the scene. Someone really ought to light a lamp, he thought, but he didn't move to remedy the situation. He tried to face the truth. Lane had shot a man in the street today. Lane, his sister's kid, the child he swore he would raise as his own. All he had ever done for Sally and Lane was let them down. He hadn't been there to protect Sally, and now, because he had deserted Lane for so long, the boy was beyond his control.

Chase thought that at times he could almost hear God laughing.

He left the revolver on the table and walked out the door. He heard Eva behind him, felt her latch onto a handful of his shirtsleeve. He kept walking. She made another grab and this time held on to his arm. He was forced to either stop or rudely shake her off. He could tell by the grip she had on him that it would cost him his shirt if he tried.

"What are you going to do to him?"

"*Do* to him?"

"Please don't hurt him. I'm sure if you only talked to him, told him how dangerous it is to wear a gun, that he would listen. He's a bit hotheaded, but probably no more than a lot of other young men his age. I'm sure you can explain the hazards of gunfighting to him."

"The *hazards of gunfighting?*" He couldn't help himself. He laughed.

Instead of the anger he expected of her, he could see that his reaction had embarrassed and hurt her.

"What *should* I do to him, Miss Edwards? I could beat the living daylights out of him, but do you think that would help? I could lock him in his room for a week, but do you

think he would care? I try talking to him but he doesn't
listen.''

She took a step back away from him and found herself
pressed up against the table. ''I've been looking after him
all week and I have no problem talking to him. Do you
really talk, or do you just yell the way you're yelling at me
right now?''

''*Yelling* at you?'' He stepped closer, using his height to
force her to lean back to look up at him. ''Miss Edwards,
when I *yell* at you, you'll know it. What goes on between
Lane and me is our business, so just stay the hell out of
it.''

He turned and headed toward the barn, his spurs and boot
heels ringing against the porch.

Eva watched him go, her temper so riled that what was
left of her ladylike facade fell away like a discarded cloak.
She could feel the heat blazing across her cheeks. In a voice
trained to reach the back row of an opera house filled with
rowdy patrons, she yelled out into a yard now shadowed
with dusk.

''Chase Cassidy, if this is the way you treated all your
housekeepers, it's no wonder they up and quit!''

Somewhere out in the corral, a horse whinnied in response. She sagged against the door frame, afraid for Lane.
She couldn't recall ever seeing such a look of black anger
on a man's face. Chase's long, determined strides soon carried him across the yard and through the barn door. When
he had disappeared from sight, Eva turned around and
headed for the stove.

Tempted to remove the offending gun and holster from
the table, she realized she wasn't sure what to do with it.
She certainly couldn't put it Lane's room and she was not
about to enter Chase's. Listening for the sound of voices
raised in argument, she tried to calm herself enough to light
the stove.

After the kindling was laid, she added some wood shav-
ings from the nearby bucket, lit the fire, and watched the
splintered pieces of wood catch and flare to life. She chided

herself for not having built up the fire before she went to town, and then she berated herself for taking Lane on the outing in the first place.

Now that she thought back on it, he had been hesitant to go. She had insisted. Maybe he had known the young cowboy was gunning for him.

Once the fire caught, she added larger pieces of wood and closed the dampers. It would be a while yet before the stove was hot enough to boil water. The respite would give her time to comb her hair and freshen up from the ride to town. She also needed to decide what to cook for the men.

A shuffling sound at the back door arrested her, and she paused, half expecting to see Lane come dragging in, head down, temper up. Instead, after a quick knock, it was Orvil who stuck his head around the door.

"Miss Eva? Cassidy said to tell you don't make anything fancy and that it ought to be ready as soon as you can make it. And he said don't make as much as usual, 'cause Lane done run off."

Too stunned to respond, she stood there a moment going over what he had said. *"Lane done run off?"*

She hurried after him, opened the door and nearly ran into Orvil Brown. He would have fallen off the porch if she hadn't reached out and grabbed the wizened old man by the back of his flannel shirt.

The ancient cowhand reached up and straightened his high-crowned hat. "Lately every time I get on this old porch I nearly wind up gettin' myself kilt."

"I'm sorry, Orvil. Where's Mr. Cassidy now?" If Chase was going after Lane, she wanted to be there when he caught up with the boy. There was no telling what either of them would do.

"He's over to the barn, ma'am."

Eva lifted her skirt up away from her ankles and raced across the yard. The big hound, his tongue lolling, joined her, leaping and yelping. Eva ignored him and skidded to a halt as she cleared the door. The soft glow from a lantern hanging on a nail near the back of the barn signaled Chase's whereabouts. She could hear him moving around in the last stall, no doubt readying his horse for pursuit of Lane.

She hurried down the center aisle between the stalls, her shoes whispering over the clean straw spread on the floor. She found Chase in the end stall, but instead of saddling his horse as she expected, he stood currying a huge, well-muscled bay as if he had all the time in the world.

"I'd like to go with you."

He turned around, brush in hand, surprised to see her. "Go where?"

Eva swallowed. His face was impassive. He appeared emotionless, and yet she could feel the tension emanating from him. He glanced down at her hands as she lifted her skirt away from the littered floor. A brilliant fuchsia petticoat peeked from beneath the hemline, so she quickly let go of the cotton striped material and let her skirt fall back over her ankles and down to the top of her shoes.

His gaze flicked back up to meet hers.

"Aren't you going after Lane?" she asked.

He turned back to the bay and began moving the brush in long sure strokes again. "No. But I'm sure wild horses couldn't keep you from telling me why I should."

"Because he's only a boy, that's why. Because he's probably terrified of you and that's why he took off."

"If he's old enough to try and shoot down a man in the street, he's old enough to pay the consequences."

"But—" Slowly and very deliberately, Chase set the brush on the narrow shelf at the end of the stall. He spoke as he slowly closed the space between them. "I've tried every way I can to reason with Lane. He's fought me every step of the way for a year. You've only been here a week, Miss Edwards, and since you are still here, he was obviously on his best behavior until today. I'd appreciate it if you could keep from sticking your nose where it doesn't belong. We're not looking for anyone to fix our lives for us—just supper."

She stepped past the end of the stall, carefully negotiating her way around the horse until she and Chase were sandwiched between the wall and the animal's bulk. Her life in the theater had not lent itself to developing any real skill as a rider, nor had she been around horses for any stretch of time. Eva eyed the tail end of the big animal with some trepidation.

"Aren't you just the least bit worried about him? Has he run away before?"

Chase shook his head. "He's never run off, but he's threatened to. Maybe he'll learn he hasn't got it so bad around here after all."

"But what if something happens to him? He's young and impressionable. He could meet up with the wrong sort. He could fall in with some drifters, or gamblers. Why, he might even meet a gang of desperados."

Chase rested his forearm on the horse's flank and looked her in the eye. "Would you know a desperado if you saw one, Miss Edwards?"

"Of course I . . . wouldn't." Eva caught herself in time and blushed. He would never know the number of desperados she had encouraged to indulge in whiskey at the Palace—or the numerous drifters and wanted men who had thrown coins on the stage after her performance. "I know they're out there. I've read about them in newspaper accounts and Beadles dime novels."

His cool, unfathomable smile chilled her as much as his silence.

"Do you think he'll come back tonight?" she asked.

He frowned, as if weighing his answer. "I'm not sure. Maybe. He doesn't have anything but the clothes on his back and his horse to his name. I do know the men are hungry and tired and that if you want to keep your job you'll get in there and get supper on the table."

"Of all the nerve," she mumbled.

He leaned down until his face was close to hers. "Make it simple and have it on the table pronto."

Eva was tempted to tell him exactly who she was and where she had been and everything she had seen and done in her twenty-three years and then walk out. Instead, she thought of the life she had determined to leave behind, thought of Lane and how she cared enough about him to stay and help him make peace with Chase.

"I'll make your supper, Mr. Cassidy, but if Lane isn't back by morning I'll find a way to go after him myself."

"This isn't your responsibility, Miss Edwards. Why do you care?"

"He's a sixteen-year-old boy out in the cold. As far as I know, he has no place to go, that's why. Right now he thinks you hate him and probably is very certain you'll never find it in your heart to forgive him for what he did today."

He folded his arms across his chest. "How do you know that?"

She took a deep breath. "Because he told me so, that's how."

"And just how did *you* get him to talk to you about what he thinks?"

"I *listened*. Maybe you should try it sometime."

"And I suppose he told you I *don't* listen to him."

"He did."

"Did you ever stop to think there were two sides to every tale?"

She cocked her head and planted a hand on her hip, hating to admit she had not thought about his side.

"You haven't known me very long," he said softly.

"No, I haven't."

"Which means you don't know me very well."

"No, I don't, Mr. Cassidy."

He stepped closer. He was less than a foot away. "In fact, you barely know me at all, Miss Edwards."

She found herself unable to move, staring up into the fathomless depths of his black eyes. Until now she had been so caught up in arguing Lane's cause that she had failed to notice how close to one another they were standing. Less than a few inches separated them.

"That's true. But I have gotten to know Lane better while you were away, and he trusted me enough to tell me why your other housekeepers left.''

She could see that he was truly shocked by her revelation. ''He did?''

''He most certainly did. After hearing the sordid details, I concluded he must have been on his very best behavior since I arrived.''

''Until today.''

''Will you go after Lane if he doesn't come back tonight?''

He focused on a point above her head. It was a moment before he answered. When he did, he admitted grudgingly, ''Probably.''

It was enough for now. She could tell that his initial anger had waned, and she didn't think it wise to push him any further. He seemed to have suddenly withdrawn, as if he were struggling not to give in to any emotion whatsoever. He looked worn out, thoroughly exhausted from long hours in the saddle. Eva was tempted to reach up and touch his cheek where the dark stubble of his beard had begun to show.

She was tempted but did not dare.

A lady would never be so very forward.

''Miss Edwards?'' he said softly, still gazing down at her intently.

Embarrassed at having been caught staring up at him she said, ''Yes?''

''Go cook dinner.''

Chase watched her walk out of the stall, his turmoil over Lane's departure momentarily forgotten as he concentrated on the hypnotic sway of her hips and the determined set of her shoulders as she marched off toward the house. She had surprised him tonight, standing up for Lane the way she had, almost as much as the news that Lane had told her all about his previous run-ins with the parade of housekeepers.

He was too bone-tired and disappointed to give into the anxiety he felt when Ramon had told him Lane had ridden off as soon as he unhitched the wagon. Once Eva was out of sight, Chase rested his forearm on the bay and leaned his head against it. Seven long days in the saddle and sleeping on the trail had worn them all out. He had come home expecting Eva to be gone. Instead he was met with the news that Lane had faced down a would-be gunman looking for glory on Main Street. What shocked and alarmed him most was discovering his nephew carried a gun and obviously knew how to use it.

He straightened and left the stall, checked the rest of the horses in the barn while he moved toward the door, still hesitant to go inside the house. There had been a fleeting moment while Eva was with him when he had an overwhelming desire to reach out to her, to hold her and take comfort in her warmth and sweet innocence. The fact that she actually cared about what happened to Lane had moved him more than the sight of her full, ripe lips and startling green eyes.

But Eva Edwards was not some two-bit whore. She was a lady. To touch her without invitation would have been an insult. All during the roundup he had tried to convince himself that she couldn't be as lovely as he remembered. He had only been fooling himself. He knew it as soon as he saw her face to face. In the close quarters with the lamplight shining in her deep green eyes and on the red-gold highlights in her hair—it became startlingly clear that his memory had not done her justice.

She was a lady down on her luck, but still a lady born and bred.

He was Chase Cassidy, gunman, thief, felon.

He didn't deserve her. But that couldn't keep him from wanting her.

Chapter Six

She had wanted him to kiss her.

The realization struck her swift as lightning and hit her at the same time she burned the back of her hand on the frying pan. Eva swore under her breath and then glanced over her shoulder to be sure no one had overheard. She pressed the back of her hand against the apron at her waist and continued to fry potatoes.

Grabbing a long-handled strainer spoon, she began to lift the thickly sliced potatoes out of the hot grease and transfer them to a bowl. The men would be in any minute.

He would be in any minute, and she would have to go on as if she hadn't just realized that in the middle of discussing his nephew, she wanted Chase Cassidy to kiss her.

She tried to convince herself it was crazy. She had known him little more than a week, and most of that time he hadn't even been around. Still, there was something about the man that intrigued her, something beyond his good looks—his midnight eyes and rugged jawline. There was something silent, dark, and mysterious about him which piqued more than her curiosity. A lot more.

A warm current of air escaped the warming oven as she opened the door and lifted the heavy bowl to set it inside, so the potatoes would keep warm while she finished up a shredded beef, tomato, and onion dish. Eva wiped her brow with the back of her sleeve and wondered if perhaps she wasn't cut out to be respectable after all. Surely no well-bred lady would be so attracted to a man she barely knew.

Uneasy with the gun and holster still lying in the kitchen,

Eva carried the weapon into the sitting room and set it on the mantle before she began to arrange the bowls and platters full of food on the table. She wiped her hands on a dishtowel and stepped out the back door to ring the bell to call the men inside. Quickly, before any of them had time to cross the yard from the corrals and bunkhouse, she hurried into her room and ran her comb through her hair. She picked up her perfume bottle, stared at it for a moment, and then talked herself out of daubing on extra scent.

The men filed in after washing up and took their places. It seemed only Ned felt like talking. Although the others nodded and listened, no one added to the conversation. Eva joined them and noticed that, although they were not as obvious as they had been that first night, she still caught the two younger men staring at her appreciatively. Ramon Alvarado watched her too, but with a closed expression she could not quite define. She tried not to let her gaze wander to Chase, but even without looking at him, she was overly sensitive to his every move. She knew whenever he shifted in his chair or took another helping of food. She was at his shoulder when his coffee mug needed to be refilled and there to pass him the biscuits before he even asked.

She was thankful Chase had hardly looked at her since he walked through the door. He ate without comment, concentrating on his plate. She could tell that all of them were tired, but she suspected the silence that had descended over the table was due mostly to Lane's obvious absence and Chase's ominous mood.

When the men finished and walked out, Chase disappeared into his room without comment, and then came out with a clean shirt and a towel draped over one shoulder. Eva turned away from him and continued to scrape the leavings into a pie tin as he passed through the kitchen and mumbled something to her before he walked out about taking a bath down at the creek. Not until she heard the door slam shut behind him did she turn to watch him walk across the barnyard until he was swallowed up by the darkness.

Once the dishes were finished Eva tossed the soapy water

off the end of the porch. She went back inside, shoved the dented dish pan back under the dry sink and went to get her wool coat before she walked outside to deliver the dinner scraps to Curly, who had been whining impatiently outside the back door.

She set the scraps down and then walked to the edge of the porch, smoothed her coat and skirt behind her, and sat down. With her feet resting on the top step, she stared up at the night sky and wondered where Lane was and if he would ever come back. Eva tried to convince herself that his safety wasn't really any of her concern and he was old enough to take care of himself. She couldn't dismiss him from her mind that easily, anymore than she could his uncle.

As she sat there staring at a tapestry of stars that seemed to go on and on forever, the night song of crickets and cicadas filled the air. A shooting star streaked across the inky darkness, shining brilliantly, then fading from view. Eva thought of how little time mere mortals had to shine.

She found herself missing her cousin, wondering how John was getting along without her. Just fine, she reckoned. Probably sharing an upstairs room with one of the Palace dancers by now. All the girls had a soft spot in their hearts for him. She could easily see why. He was big enough to be an intimidating bouncer, but women found him gentle as a lamb. She smiled into the darkness and wished him well.

It was a night for making wishes on stars. She decided then and there to write John to let him know she was safe and had taken the position as housekeeper. She wondered what, if anything, he had told Quincy.

Quincy.

She thought it odd that she had no feelings left for him whatsoever. But she had decided long ago that she probably had not loved him as much as she had been infatuated with him. Her heart was tarnished and a bit hardened. She had hoped the lesson would keep her from making the same mistake again.

What happened to her resolve tonight when she found herself close enough to Chase Cassidy to reach out and feel his heartbeat if she had only dared?

She sighed and rested her arm across her knees, lowered her head and sat there, exhausted emotionally and physically. She had been up before dawn as usual and baked three loaves of bread before they left for town. The scene with Lane and her confrontation with Chase had worn her out more than performing three shows a night.

Eva didn't hear his footsteps until he was almost upon her. She lifted her head and found Chase standing a few feet away, outside the puddle of lamplight that spilled through the open back door. The limp towel hung casually around his neck. He was fumbling with the buttons of his shirt in the dark.

"I didn't expect you to be out here," he said, explaining away his half-open shirtfront.

She shrugged, the movement lost in the darkness. "I wasn't sleepy."

"The day starts early around here."

"That it does."

"I've been thinking," he began.

She expected him to say he was thinking about Lane, about where he might have gone or when he was going after the boy. Instead, he finished, "I think you should teach Orvil how to cook. He's really getting too old for much else. I noticed that on the roundup."

"Teach Orvil to cook?"

"If you think you can."

Eva rubbed her eyes. "I suppose I can. But if he learns to cook, then what am I supposed to do?"

He shifted his weight from one foot to the other and reached up to rub the back of his neck. "You won't be here forever."

As she sat there staring up at him in the darkness, thinking about what he had just said, she realized since the day she found the advertisement and decided to apply for this job that she knew it would not be a permanent position.

Life was too full of changes. But when she knocked at the door she hadn't planned on meeting a man like Chase Cassidy.

He waited a few feet from the porch, as if unwilling to squeeze past her. Eva straightened her spine and stretched. It was long past time to go in.

He took a step closer, hesitated a moment, and, without a word, reached down to help her up. She looked at his outstretched hand and reached up to take it.

It was a mistake to touch him. She knew it the minute his fingers clasped hers. Chase pulled her up. She went with the movement and once on her feet, she knew she should let go of his hand, but she didn't. She couldn't. Nor did he make a move to release her, and yet there was no demand in his touch.

They stood together in the darkness, her hand resting so very naturally in his. Eva closed her eyes, aware of the contrast of the warmth of his skin and the cool night air on her face. His shirtfront was still partially open. She wondered what it would be like to press her hand, palm open, against his damp chest and feel his heart beat. Was it as wild and erratic as her own?

He held her hand so gently it surprised her, for by looking at him one did not see gentleness. Not in a man like Chase Cassidy. There was nothing gentle about him, no sign of weakness in him at all.

Across the barnyard, Curly started barking and chasing the calves around in their pens. The louder the calves started to bawl, the more frantic the dog's bark became.

The sound shattered the silent communion between them as effectively as a gunshot in the night. Chase dropped her hand and broke the connection. Shaken, Eva clutched her fingers together, not only to fill the void but to still their trembling, and realized her heart was beating so hard that she could hear the blood rushing in her ears. For a moment, Chase stared down at her as if he had never seen her before, then raised his head and whistled sharply to call off the dog.

She took a deep breath and tried to calm herself in much

the same way as she did before she stepped out on stage to perform. Keeping her wits about her under stress had never been a challenge before, and she was not about to lose them now, not in front of Chase Cassidy.

"If you'll excuse me, Mr. Cassidy, I'm going in. It's past time I did."

Curly raced over, ran around them in a circle, then sat at Chase's feet, watching him expectantly, his long tail scraping back and forth across the dusty ground. Chase didn't move, but continued to stare down at her. Finally he said, "Since it looks like we haven't run you off yet, why don't you call me Chase?"

Eva nodded, wishing for all the world that she could think of something other than the way he looked standing there against the night sky. "Fine. Chase it is. Perhaps you should call me Eva."

"Good night then . . . Eva. I'll be in later."

"I'll leave a light burning in the kitchen for you." Eva lifted her skirt and hurried away, her thoughts in such a jumble that she forgot about exposing her fuchsia petticoat until she nearly tripped over the hound who jumped about her heels all the way into the house.

When she was out of earshot, Chase let out a pent up breath and closed his eyes.

What in the hell were you thinking, Cassidy?

The last clear thought he remembered before he took her hand was of how forlorn she had appeared sitting alone on the back steps with her head down on her arm. He had not taken time today to think of what the scene in town must have cost her. He was used to violence, but what would a purebred lady like her know about gunfights and sheriffs' offices and six-shooters? When he had reached down for her hand, it was a purely instinctive move, but then when their fingers touched, when he felt her smooth skin against his calloused fingers, when she stood before him so trustingly and moved easily within reach—he stopped thinking about anything but what she would feel like in his arms and what her lips would taste like beneath his.

Chase reached up to rub the back of his neck again and caught sight of the starry sky. He tried to force himself to think of something else, anything else but the way his body involuntarily responded to Eva Edwards. It was Lane he should be worrying over, but here he was, standing in the dark, as hard as a gun barrel, staring at the house like a sinner left out of a church social as he waited for Eva to turn out the light in her room so he could go inside without running into her in the kitchen.

"Aw, hell," he grumbled to himself.

With one last glance at the house, Chase headed off in the direction of the creek again. Maybe another dunking in the chilly water would be good for what ailed him.

Except for a dog barking somewhere at the far end of Main Street, there wasn't a sound or the sight of anything moving anywhere in Last Chance. Lane figured it was near nine, but without a timepiece, he couldn't be sure.

He did know he was hungrier than a bear after a spring thaw. He nudged his horse forward, holding the spirited young pinto to a walk as he approached the back of Miss Rachel Albright's two-story house at the far end of Main Street. She had pulled the shades, but he knew she was home because there was light showing behind one of them.

He didn't expect her to have anyone with her. It was too late for a caller, and she had told the class that she lived alone since her father had died six months ago.

Lane hated to have to turn to the soft-spoken schoolmarm for help, but he'd be damned if he went back to the ranch with his tail between his legs tonight. Let his uncle worry about him for a few hours. Hell, he was probably a fool to think that Chase Cassidy would lose a minute's sleep over him. Like as not, it would be kind-hearted Miss Eva who was the only one worried about whether he lived or died.

Almost to the back door, he dismounted, careful not to let the bridle jingle. His pinto was a good one. One of the best cow ponies they had. He had trained her himself. Lane tied the horse to a pump and crept closer to the door. He pulled his collar up and his hat low and knocked as loud as he dared.

For a moment he thought she might not have heard, then he recognized the sound of footsteps on the other side of the door.

"Who's there?"

She sounded scared. He answered quickly to allay her fear. "It's Lane."

The light inside bobbed and flickered. The shade over the window moved aside. He could see Miss Albright, her rich brown hair pulled back off her face, her blue eyes wide as she peered out into the darkness.

Recognizing him, she opened the door a crack and held up a lamp to see him more clearly. "What are you doing here Lane? Are you all right?"

"I'm fine, just hungry is all. You wouldn't happen to have anything I could eat to tide me over until morning, would you?"

The door opened a bit wider. "Have you run away from home, Lane Cassidy?"

He tried to look apologetic. "I'm afraid I have, ma'am."

She appeared concerned. "For how long?"

"How long will I stay here? Or how long ago did I run away?"

"Both, I guess," she said.

He thought he caught a hint of a smile and knew food was forthcoming. He could always talk her out of scolding him. It was the only good thing about having a teacher who wasn't much older than himself. "I'll take off as soon as my stomach stops rumblin' like a mine cave-in. And you'll be happy to know I've only been gone a few hours."

"Where are you headed?"

He shrugged. "No place. I'm going home in the morning. I won't get far without money in my pocket." *Or my gun.*

She opened the door, moving to step behind it, using it like a shield. "Come on in, then. I've got some cold chicken and biscuits, but that's about all.''

Before he stepped over the threshold, Lane glanced back to make certain his pinto was still tied to the pump. Rachel Albright closed the door and set the oil lamp in the center of the table. She was wearing a faded, sky-blue flannel robe over her nightgown. As he expected of a schoolmarm, the white cotton gown was buttoned up to her throat.

As she moved to set out the meal, her thick brunette braid swayed against her back. "There," she said, standing back, "chicken, biscuits, and milk. You go right ahead and eat, and I'll just go in and get the book I was reading.''

Lane waited until she had left the kitchen before he pulled out a chair and sat down. His mouth watered as he looked down at the crisp, golden-fried chicken and evenly-browned biscuits. He broke a biscuit in two. It was so rich it crumbled onto the plate. He polished off three biscuits in the short time it took her to walk into the parlor and return.

Rachel sat across from him, opened her book, and began to read silently while he alternately watched her and cleaned off his plate. Never having read a book himself, he didn't know what she found so fascinating. He tried to make out the title on the spine but the letters made little sense. When there was nothing left on his plate but a pile of chicken bones, Lane downed the milk and carefully set the empty glass beside his plate.

"Thanks, Miss Albright. That was some of the best chicken I've had in a coon's age.''

Almost reverently, she closed the book and laid it aside, folded her hands and stared across the table at him. He could feel one of her lectures coming and knew he would have to suffer it in exchange for the meal. In the time he had been going to the one-room schoolhouse in Last Chance, Lane had lost count of the number of lectures on his behavior that Miss Albright felt it her Christian duty to deliver. Lane eased himself back in the chair and sighed.

"I know what you're thinking, Lane Cassidy, and you're just going to have to realize I'm not about to give up on any of my students, you included.''

"No, ma'am. I don't reckon you aren't."

She leaned forward, pushed his plate aside, and watched him carefully for a moment before she went on. "I can't help but feel that I'm partly to blame for this latest fiasco of yours."

He frowned. "You mean the shoot-out?"

"You needn't smile like it was a great accomplishment, young man."

He hooked his arm over the top rung and rocked the chair back on two legs. "How do you figure you're to blame? You tried to keep me in school, an' you didn't take to yelling about it either, like Uncle Chase."

"Perhaps I should have. And I should have gone to your uncle the minute I learned you had that gun."

Lane dropped the chair to the floor. "Who told you?" Lane demanded. "I'll bet it was that little goody-two-shoes Freddy Wilson, wasn't it?"

Freddy "The Ferret" Wilson, was the freckle-faced son of the local preacher. A busier body had never lived. Two weeks ago Freddy had discovered Lane in the act of showing off his revolver to two of the older boys behind the schoolhouse. It seemed threats and arm twisting had done little to keep The Ferret from snitching on him.

"I was about to confide in your new housekeeper—"

"Miss Eva?"

She nodded. "I thought perhaps if she had a chance to talk to you before your uncle found out—"

"You thought things might go easier for me?"

"Yes." Rachel stood up and picked up the plate and glass and took them over to the dish pan on the cabinet. She set them aside, then turned back to face him, leaning against the edge of the cabinet, her arms crossed over her breasts. Lane stood up and walked toward the door.

She seemed startled to find he was leaving. "Where are you going?"

Lane shrugged, not knowing the answer himself. "I'll spend the night someplace, then head home in the morning."

"So you are going back?"

"For now."

Rachel was silent for a moment, watching him intently as if weighing her thoughts. Finally she suggested, "If you like, you can stay here tonight. I'll go back with you in the morning."

In imitation of one of his uncle's more sardonic looks, he arched a brow. "Why? You think I need your protection, teacher?"

"No, I think you need a friend."

He didn't have a ready quip to issue in reply. He was fairly certain Eva was his ally, especially after the talk they had had on the way home from town. She had promised to tell Chase about it when the time was right, and he expected she would keep her word. But his courage failed him and he hadn't waited around to take a chance to see how Chase would react. Flight seemed the right decision at the time.

Now he was out in the cold without a dollar in his pocket, his gun, or even a spare shirt.

He studied the woman standing across from him. She was armed with an education, the respect of the townsfolk, her position as schoolteacher. He knew she was no more than five years older than he, maybe less, but she obviously viewed him as nothing more than a child or she would never have asked him to stay the night.

What would Miss Albright think if she knew how many hours he sat hunched over in a too-small desk at the back of the stuffy school wondering what she looked like under her modest calico dresses?

"You can sleep on the settee," she added.

Were her cheeks a bit pinker than usual? Lane shrugged and shoved his hands in his pockets. His choices were limited to sleeping at the back of one of the shops along Main, taking his chances out in the open, or to head back home and try to slip into the barn unnoticed.

The sheriff might stumble over him on the street.

And he wasn't partial to sleeping in the middle of the open range without a gun.

He picked his hat up off the table, straightened the crown, and wiped off the trail dust with his sleeve. "I reckon I'll sleep on your floor, ma'am, if you don't mind."

She shook her head. "Not at all. I don't think I'd sleep a wink knowing one of my students had nowhere to go on a dark night. Tomorrow I'll ride out to the ranch with you and tell your uncle that you were here and perfectly safe."

Suddenly, he found it hard to look her in the eye.

Rachel did not notice. "I'd like a chance to talk to your housekeeper anyway. Miss . . ."

"Eva Edwards."

"Yes, Miss Edwards. She seemed like such a nice person. I'd like to welcome her to town."

He finally looked up and smiled. "That would be real kindly of you, ma'am. Miss Eva's a real lady. She's been more than fair to me, too. I doubt if anybody else'll be out to call on her, things being the way they are."

"No," she agreed softly, "I don't imagine they will."

He waited for her to pick up the lamp and lead the way into the parlor. She crossed the room and paused in the doorway to the narrow entry hall. "You know I'll have to tell them you missed school all last week, don't you?"

Lane nodded. "I expect you will, but with the shoot-out fresh on his mind, Uncle Chase can't get any madder, can he?"

A knock on the door startled them both. Lane put on his hat and began to move toward the kitchen.

"Wait," she said. "Don't run off again, Lane. That won't solve anything."

Undecided, he stood in the doorway between the sitting room and the kitchen and waited while she walked to the front door. She brushed aside the lace curtain and peered out the window, then turned to glance over her shoulder at him. She mouthed, "Don't move," and barely cracked the door open.

When he recognized Sheriff McKenna's voice, Lane tensed and stepped back into the interior of the dark kitchen.

"I saw young Cassidy's horse out back, Miss Rachel, as I was making a last pass down the street. You all right?"

"Perfectly fine, Sheriff. It seems Lane had a little run-in with his uncle, understandably, after what happened today, and he had nowhere to go. I'll be taking him back home in the morning."

"I can let him sleep in the jailhouse tonight, ma'am, if you'd feel better about it. I know I would. You never know what might happen with a Cassidy around."

Lane silently cursed Stuart McKenna and everyone else in town except Miss Rachel.

"He's my student, Sheriff. He'll be fine. In fact, the boy's already sound asleep."

The boy. When would they all know he had never been a boy? That his childhood had ended when he was four?

He listened as she reassured McKenna that she was fine and that she had nothing to fear from him. Finally, grudgingly convinced, the sheriff moved on. Lane stepped out of the shadows and watched Rachel close the door. With a heavy sigh, she leaned against it, then seemed to gather up her strength before she turned to him.

"You really aren't afraid of me, are you?" he asked.

"No." There was no hesitancy in her voice. "Of course not."

He wanted to thank her for that, but the words stuck in his throat. Instead, he said, "I'll see you in the morning."

"Promise not to leave without me," she said, holding the front of her wrapper closed with one hand.

"I won't," he promised. And meant it.

He could sure use a friend when he faced his uncle in the morning.

Chapter Seven

No one should have to eat breakfast before the sun comes up.

Half-awake, Eva sat at the kitchen table leafing through the April copy of *Ladies' Home Companion* she purchased for five cents before she left Cheyenne. She had hoped concentrating on the advertisements that filled the columns would take her mind off the incessant bawling of calves penned up in the corral awaiting their turn at the branding iron. As she listlessly turned a page, she wondered who decided that ranch work had to commence before the last star had faded from the sky. It was one particular feature of life at the Trail's End that would probably never appeal to her.

She shifted on the hard chair, elbows on the table, the open magazine lying between them. With her head propped on one hand, she studied an advertisement for Durkee's salad dressing and wondered if the Carberry's stocked it in their store. On the same page she eyed a silver-plated fruit dish with envy. She looked around the kitchen. Even if she had the money to order the dish, the piece would look incongruous in the crude log house with its handmade tables and chairs upholstered in cowhide.

Eva closed the periodical and stood up, intent on pouring herself a cup of coffee before going in to dust the sitting room. She had just taken a cup from the shelf when she heard the sound of panicked shouting outside.

She raced to the door and across the back porch. In the far corral, beside the barn, she saw the men huddled in a group around someone on the ground. Her heart racing, Eva hiked up her skirt and ran toward them. The ground was so churned by the animals' hooves that she nearly tripped on a dirt clod. A gate blocked her entrance to the corral, and she was forced to strain to lift the rail that held it shut and then take the time to close it again once inside.

Her anxiety lessened when she recognized Chase in his tall buff Stetson and dark shirt. He stood over Ned, who lay writhing on the ground, trying not to cry out. Orvil was on his knees beside the wounded man, despair imprinted on his wrinkled features. Jethro was trying to corner Ned's horse as it shied toward the far side of the corral. Half a dozen calves hugged the fence, confused and bawling for their mamas. As it had all morning, the scent of singed hide tainted the air.

Half hidden beneath the brim of his huge sombrero, Ramon was hunkered down beside Ned, fighting to hold him still.

"What happened?" Eva tugged on Chase's sleeve.

He looked down as if he couldn't place her for a moment. "He got burned with the branding iron."

As Ned turned his head, Eva gasped and pressed her hand against her mouth. The wound along the side of his head was raw and red, the Trail's End TE brand was partially burnt into the side of his jaw, across his ear and into his hairline. His skin had already blistered and had begun to ooze.

She swallowed. Her fingers clenched Chase's arm.

"Why don't you go back inside?" Worry shadowed his eyes.

After taking a deep breath, Eva shook her head. She was in his employ now and intended to help out wherever she could. Unmindful of her gown, she knelt in the dirt and manure beside Ned and took his hand. In a voice as calm and soothing as she could manage, Eva tried to be heard over the ruckus the calves were making.

"Ned, you just hold on." She swallowed and tried to keep her eyes averted from the angry wound. "I've got a book full of potions that are guaranteed to take away the pain as quick as lightning.''

Ned was squeezing her fingers unmercifully, but Eva ignored the discomfort. "Is it bad, Miss Eva? Does it look too bad?''

She smiled down at the handsome young cowboy, knowing full well the burn would leave a scar no matter what concoction she applied. With a bright, cheerful smile, she lied, "It's not bad at all. I'm sure it feels much worse than it looks.''

Eva felt Chase lay his hand on her shoulder. She glanced up at him, but he was addressing Ramon. "Get him into the bunkhouse.''

Ramon nodded. Jethro had joined them and brushed Orvil aside so that he could help. "Can you walk?'' Jethro asked the other cowboy.

Ned, who was sitting up now, nodded. "I'm feeling a might woozy, but if you can get me on my feet, I'll try.''

While the others struggled to lift Ned, Chase drew Eva aside. "Did you mean what you said about that burn potion?''

She knew her book of recipes and household hints told how to make more than one salve for burns. "I've never made one, but I have the recipes. I'll come up with something.''

As Ramon and Jethro moved off with Ned shuffling between them, she glanced over at Orvil, who stood by watching forlornly as the men walked away. Eva turned to Chase knowing Orvil was somehow responsible for Ned's accident.

He frowned, then directed the old man. "Orvil, take Miss Eva back to the house. She's going to need some help getting things together, I imagine.''

Listless, his shoulders drooping, Orvil faced them. Eva couldn't help but notice the unshed tears in his eyes.

"Do you mind helping, Orvil?''

He glanced down at the branding iron that lay in the dirt near his feet. He nodded silently. "Not at all, ma'am.''

Dropping his gaze to the ground, the old cowhand shuffled toward the house.

"What happened?" Eva turned to Chase, who remained beside her as he watched the old man leave.

"Orvil was working the branding iron and Ned was holding the calf when it kicked out and knocked him off balance. Orvil didn't react fast enough and he ended up planting the red-hot iron alongside Ned's head."

"Poor Orvil."

"Poor Ned," he added. "He's got to be in a hell of a lot of pain."

His reminder shook Eva out of her commiseration for the old cowhand. "I'll go right in and—" She paused, arrested by the hard look that had returned to Chase's eye. Turning to see what might be amiss now, Eva recognized Lane's pinto. The boy and a woman on a dappled gray horse were riding side by side toward the outbuildings.

Eva felt the tension in his arm as she reached out to Chase. "Chase—"

"Go in the house, Eva."

She wasn't about to leave without reminding him, "Don't forget, he's just a boy." She watched the riders as they drew near. "Why, that's his teacher, Miss Albright."

"Go *in*, Eva."

Torn between rushing to help Ned and protecting Lane from Chase's obvious anger, she clasped her hands together at her waist and didn't move.

"Give him a chance to explain," she urged. Chase's fury was visible in his stance—his feet spread wide, his dark eyes never leaving Lane.

Lane and Rachel Albright entered the barnyard. They hitched their horses to a fence rail and began to cross the corral. Eva glanced up at Chase and knew it didn't matter what she tried to say for he was no longer listening to her.

Behind them, Ramon called out from the bunkhouse, "Ned is in much pain, Señorita."

With a furtive glance at Lane and the teacher, she lifted the hem of her skirt in both hands and ran toward the house.

*   *   *

Chase watched her go, hoping Eva did have something that would help ease Ned's pain. He bent down to pick up the cool branding iron and held it tight in both hands while Lane walked toward him. In his wake came the young woman Eva had identified as the boy's teacher. Chase guessed Miss Albright could not be much over twenty years old.

Lane stood before him, smudges beneath his dark eyes, his expression unrepentant. Chase recognized his nephew's defiant stance—it was one he had assumed himself on many occasions. Chase fought for the right words, wished he knew what to say. He suspected any overture he made would further alienate Lane.

He had heard what Eva told him, although he had not acknowleged her. He knew Lane was only a boy. It was one of the reasons he was having so much trouble dealing with him. He had no idea how to go about it.

Chase took the coward's way out and said nothing.

Lane didn't say anything either.

When Rachel Albright caught up with Lane, she reached up to straighten the chin strap on the oversized man's hat she wore and said to Chase, "Mr. Cassidy, we haven't met, but I'm Lane's teacher. I came along with him to tell you—"

Lane cut her off. "You don't have to talk for me, teacher."

The teacher had more mettle than Chase would have guessed. The young woman gave Lane a cool stare and went on as if he had not interrupted at all.

"He spent the night at my house where he was perfectly safe. Given what happened in town yesterday, he didn't know what kind of a reception he would get from you, so he panicked and took off."

When she paused for breath, Chase handed the branding iron to Lane. All he said was, "You'll take Orvil's place on the iron. I'll talk to you later."

By now Ramon had saddled up and so had Jethro. The two well-seasoned men were ready to rope calves for branding. Chase waited for Rachel Albright to notice she was keeping them from their work. Lane walked toward the fire that was still burning in the center of the corral.

"Mr. Cassidy, I feel it is of the utmost importance that we talk about—"

Chase's relief at seeing Lane safe didn't help to stem his anger. He dismissed the teacher out of hand. When she spoke, he paused and looked back over his shoulder. "Miss Albright, I appreciate your coming out here, but this is between Lane and me and I don't intend to waste time talking to you about it."

"But I'd like to talk to you about school—"

"I told him that he has to be there every day. Right now, we've got work to do here, ma'am." He tipped the brim of his hat in her direction, hoping she would take the hint and leave. He started to walk away again.

"Do you mind if I go inside and talk to your house-keeper?" She called out.

Chase froze. There was every possibility that Miss Albright would tell Eva all about him. It might just be a blessing to have the threat out in the open. He rested his fists at his waist and shot her a glance over his shoulder.

"Be my guest."

"His bite isn't as bad as his bark," Eva said, glancing up from the copious cookbook in her hands. Before Rachel Albright had walked in the back door, Eva had skimmed over the various entries for treating burns. Many called for beeswax, and since she had none, she quickly read through the rest, dismissing immediately one remedy that called for spreading cow dung on the affected area.

Finally she settled on common wheat flour. Now, as she poured two cups full of flour into a bowl, she gave up trying to convince the teacher that Chase Cassidy wasn't as overbearing and pigheaded as he seemed. She wondered briefly how she could convince someone else when she didn't completely believe it herself.

"Miss Albright, I would really like to talk to you, but

right now I have a man out in the bunkhouse who's been burned very badly and needs my help. Why don't you pour a cup of coffee and I'll be back as soon as he's settled?''

"I'd be happy to," Rachel said, appearing relieved to have a task to accomplish.

Eva picked up the flour, two clean, folded dish towels, and a bottle of laudanum she found at the back of medicine shelf in the pantry. As she pushed the back door open, Eva remembered to slow down so she wouldn't trip over Orvil, who was seated on the edge of the porch, staring at the ground.

"Orvil, I need you."

Still forlorn, he looked up at her. Eva's heart went out to the old man. "I need to bathe Ned's burn in some milk and I know there's plenty of that around. Bring some to the bunkhouse as fast as you can."

She hurried to the bunkhouse that stood not far away beside a slow-moving creek. On the way across the yard, Eva glanced over to the corral where Lane was working with the other cowboys. Chase had mounted up and was taking his turn roping and throwing unmarked calves so that Lane and Ramon could brand them. She smiled when he looked up. If he saw her, he gave no sign.

The inside of the small, crowded log cabin was much as Eva anticipated it would be. Bunks lined the walls. A lopsided table took up the center of the room. A tin lamp hung from the ceiling above it. The place smelled of tobacco and unwashed men and needed a thorough cleaning. Eva tried not to pay attention to unsavory details as she focused on the man shivering in a lower bunk.

"Ned?"

He opened his eyes at the sound of her voice. He lay curled on his side, his hands wedged between his knees. He rocked back and forth fighting the pain. She knelt down and touched his shoulder. "Ned, I've got something that will help."

She drew his wool blanket from beneath him and pulled

it up to his shoulders. Then she felt his forehead. He was clammy to the touch.

Orvil walked in with a bucket of fresh milk. "Here you go, Miss Eva." He set the bucket down beside her. Eva left one towel folded, dipped it in the milk and then pressed the wet compress against Ned's burn. He closed his eyes.

"Better?"

"Yes, ma'am." His voice broke on the words.

She didn't believe him. Carefully, she bathed the burned area, his hair, his jawline, his ear, in milk. All the while, Orvil hovered behind her.

"I'm sorry, Ned," Orvil drawled.

"I know you are, Orvil," the wounded man assured him. "It was just a slip, that's all." His teeth chattered as he tried to talk.

Eva heard Orvil shifting around behind her. She glanced up to find Chase standing in his place.

"Do you need help?"

She smiled up at him. "We're doing fine. After I bathe the wound I'll sprinkle it with flour."

"You know what you're doing?"

Forcing a smile, she turned away from Ned and said between her teeth, "Do you have a better idea?"

He shrugged.

"Fine. Then I'm spreading flour on it. It's supposed to absorb the moisture from the blisters and it's easy to rinse off. Once it forms a paste, it'll keep the air out."

"It feels better already," Ned tried to assure them both as Eva pressed the milky cloth to the side of his head.

Chase leaned closer. "You find the laudanum?"

She nodded. They didn't speak for a time.

Finally, Chase asked her, "The teacher bothering you?"

She shook her head. "No. Of course not. We're having coffee together when I have Ned all tucked in."

When he didn't comment, Eva turned around to look up at Chase and found him watching her intently. He appeared to be struggling with something he wanted to say.

"What is it?" As she knelt beside the bunk, Eva kept

her hand on Ned's compress, but gave Chase her full attention.

"Nothing. Have a nice chat."

She wondered at his strange behavior, but with Ned's wounds to see to, she couldn't wonder long.

Eva sat at the table peeling potatoes for the midday meal as if there was nothing unusual about carrying on polite conversation with a schoolmarm. Rachel Albright appeared cool and collected, even after her ride out from town. Without looking, Eva could tell that her own hair was a mess. At least two escaped curls were dangling before her eyes. She tried to remain composed, striking what she hoped was a most ladylike pose, even as she tossed potato parings into a bowl on the table.

"I don't mean to be rude, Miss Albright, but the men will be expecting their noon meal. I hope you don't mind if I work while we talk?"

Rachel smiled. "Please, I know I'm interrupting, but I had to speak to someone about Lane—"

"Did you talk to Mr. Cassidy?"

"Yes, but he's so upset right now, not to mention busy. There seemed to be men and cattle everywhere and all that noise." She glanced at the door and scooted up to the edge of her chair. "May I speak frankly?"

Eva could tell that the woman was waiting for an answer. When she glanced up, she found Rachel studying her carefully. "Certainly. Do go on."

"How much do you know about the Cassidys, Miss Edwards?"

"Please, call me Eva, won't you?" When Rachel nodded, Eva went on. "To tell you the truth, I still hardly know them at all. When I answered the advertisement for housekeeper, I didn't know what to expect. But I wanted a job so badly that I talked Mr. Cassidy into hiring me. He took off on a roundup last week, and left me to look after things, so the past couple of days is really all the occasion I've had to be around him. But from the minute I arrived, I could tell that something is definitely not right around here."

Rachel Albright leaned back and sighed. "There is a lot more wrong than meets the eye."

"Is it bad?"

Rachel nodded. "Was Lane on the roundup last week?"

Eva stopped, pausing with the knife just above the potato. "No. Chase insisted he go to school."

Rachel's smile faded. "That's what I was afraid of. He didn't show up all week."

Setting aside the slick potato, Eva shook her head in wonder. "Then where did he go? I sent him off every day. I even packed him a sandwich."

"I'm afraid he might have gone off to practice with that gun of his. One of the children told me he brought it to school week before last. It seems he even showed it to two of the older children."

"Chase will be furious when he finds out."

"No doubt. I didn't think I'd ever hear myself saying this about a student, but in Lane's case I think he would be better off learning out of school." Rachel folded her hands in her lap, her coffee ignored, her brows knit close above her stunning blue eyes.

Eva could see the woman was uncomfortable voicing her opinion. "What makes you think so?"

Rachel glanced up. "Because he's older than any of the other students by three years. Since he has never even been to school until a year ago, he's so far behind that some of the six-year-olds read better."

"Lane had *never* been to school before he was fifteen?"

Rachel hesitated. "No."

"Why ever not? Chase obviously thinks it's very important. I heard them arguing about it the afternoon I arrived."

"Chase Cassidy has only been back for a year."

"Back?"

"From prison."

Eva's gaze shot to the door then back to Rachel. *"Prison?"*

"He served eight years as an accomplice in a series of bank robberies in three states."

Eva shook her head. "I can't believe it," she whispered.

Rachel continued, speaking rapidly, her voice hushed. "He rode with a gang of outlaws. Then, after his prison term, he came back here and tried to pick up where he left off."

Trying to comprehend it all, Eva realized now why Chase was always so silent and withdrawn.

Feeling the need to move, she gathered the potatoes and piled them atop the peelings in the bowl and carried them to the dry sink. As she took out a cast iron pot to boil them in, she asked over her shoulder, "Where was Lane all the time Chase was in prison? What happened to his mother?"

Rachel sighed as she nervously traced the pattern on her floral skirt with her fingertip. "When Lane came to school, I asked my father to tell me everything he could recall about the Cassidys. It's not a pretty tale, I can tell you that much.

"Lane's mother was Chase's sister. She was murdered when Lane was about four, I think. Chase went after the men who killed her and left Lane with a woman who owned a tumbledown ranch a few miles away from here. She never sent Lane to school. In fact, no one in town ever saw Lane again until Chase got out of prison and brought him back to the ranch. When school opened in September, he rode into town just long enough to leave Lane at the schoolhouse."

Eva poured water over the potatoes, grabbed the pot handle and swung it on top the stove. Thinking aloud she mused, "If Lane's mother was Chase's sister, why does Lane go by the name Cassidy?"

The young woman blushed to the hairline. "Lane's mother never married. His father was a drifter, a cowboy who left her when she became pregnant. At least that's the story around town."

Eva thought back to the day she arrived in Last Chance. There had been no time to speak to Millie Carberry about the Cassidys. When she mentioned needing a ride to the Trail's End, the woman had eyed her speculatively. Insecure about her own identity, Eva had been concerned only that Mrs. Carberry might have seen through her.

What irony, she thought. Here she had hoped to change her life and gain some respectability by working for a respected rancher, when in reality, she was employed by a former felon who was raising an illegitimate nephew.

Just then Rachel added, "Mr. Cassidy has quite a reputation as a gunslinger, too."

Eva rolled her eyes. "Do you have any other surprises in store for me?"

Rachel stood up and crossed the room. She brushed back a long tendril of hair that had escaped her thick braid. She paused beside Eva. "I hope I haven't offended or unduly alarmed you, but you seemed like such a nice person, and so truly concerned about Lane yesterday, that I thought . . . "

Reaching up to push her hair out of her eyes, Eva realized nothing ever changes, just the roles one plays in life. "I suppose the whole town's talking about me."

"Feeling sorry for you is more like it. Millie Carberry told everyone about you the day you came to town. It seems her boy explained about the advertisement you carried and how it was obvious you didn't know the situation out here. Nobody knew what to do, whether to come and tell you about Chase Cassidy and what Lane had supposedly done to the other housekeepers or let you find out for yourself."

"Lane has been headstrong, but not all that much trouble, really. I think he's trying to get along with me and mind his *p's* and *q's*."

Rachel nodded in agreement. "Aside from the fact that Lane has missed more school than he has actually attended this year—and dismissing that incident with the gun—I can't say he's really been any trouble for me, either. But folks tend to gossip. They like to see smoke where there's no fire and they're suspicious of both Lane and his uncle.

I just thought a lady like yourself deserved to know what you've gotten yourself into. If you ever need a friend, Eva, you can come to me. I'm a little more open-minded than most,'' she added. Her dark hair was enriched by the sunlight drifting in from the window behind her.

A lady like yourself. Eva smiled and on impulse, took Rachel's hand. ''Thank you, Rachel. I'll remember that, but I really don't think I need to worry. As I said, things seem to be working out.'' She wished she was truly as confident as she sounded.

''I have a question to ask before I leave,'' Rachel said.

''Go right ahead.'' Eva didn't think things could get any worse, not unless Rachel asked if she had ever danced at the Palace of Venus in Cheyenne. But Eva knew that was as likely as Rachel asking if she could fly.

''I couldn't help but notice the organ in the sitting room,'' Rachel said, with an abrupt change of subject. ''Do you play?''

Eva nodded. ''I do, when I have time and no one is around. But it's out of tune.''

Rachel smiled. ''I'll understand if you say no, but I'm putting on a short program for the last night of school, something I hope will draw everyone in town to celebrate the children's success this year. I'm finding it hard to direct, play the piano and keep an eye on the children, so I was hoping to find someone who could volunteer a few hours a week.'' She waited expectantly for Eva to agree.

Here I am, Eva thought, miles from the nearest theater, being asked to help with an amateur program. In a schoolhouse, no less.

''I have quite a bit of work here,'' she hesitated, thinking about how she had so far avoided the challenge of adding washing and ironing to her duties. ''I'm finding there's a lot more to housekeeping than meets the eye.''

''If you'd rather not. . .'' Rachel looked so disappointed that Eva changed her mind immediately.

''I'll have to ask, but I suppose Mr. Cassidy could spare me two afternoons a week. Would that be enough?'' She realized she found herself looking forward to excursions to town. They would help take her mind off of her growing attraction to Chase Cassidy. After what she had just learned, she knew she would appreciate the time to think things through away from the ranch.

"Plenty!" Rachel clapped her hands. For a moment, Eva thought the young teacher was going to embrace her, but then Chase walked in the back door unannounced and both women immediately spun around to face him.

"Chase—"

Myriad expressions cross his face, not the least of which was suspicion. He nodded to them both, but didn't move or speak.

"I have to be going," Rachel said as she took a step toward the door.

Once more, Rachel drew herself up before Chase and refused to be intimidated. "I spoke to Miss Edwards at length about Lane's situation at school. I'm sure she'll be happy to tell you what I said. I'm afraid I've taken up enough of her time." Then, to Eva, she added, "I'll see you Tuesday afternoon, if that's all right?"

"I'll be there," Eva said, unable to ignore Chase, whose very presence seemed to dwarf everything else in the room.

When Rachel Albright closed the door behind her, Eva turned back to the stove and lifted the lid on the potatoes. The water was just beginning to simmer, giving her enough time to get some pickled beef out of the barrel on the back porch.

"Have you ever thought of buying some chickens?" she asked Chase. "I would think you would be sick of beef every meal."

"This isn't a farm, it's a cattle ranch." He leaned one hip on the table and crossed his arms, intent on watching her bustle back and forth across the room. "What's wrong with beef?"

"For breakfast, lunch, and dinner?"

He was still frowning. "Where are you going Tuesday?"

"She needs someone to play the piano for a school program. I volunteered to help, that is, if you don't mind my taking the time to ride into town and back two days a week.'' Eva was so looking forward to the outings that she was willing to face the challenge of getting there on horseback if she had to.

He hesitated so long, she thought he would refuse. Then, as if silence meant permission granted, he went on. ''What else did she say?''

Eva wondered if she detected a note of worry in his tone. If so, it was so fleeting it was unrecognizable. She tried to sound offhand, ''Oh, just she wanted to tell me about Lane—''

''What about Lane?''

''She thinks he should quit school.''

He pushed himself from the table immediately. When Eva backed out of the pantry with two onions in her hands, she nearly collided with him.

''What? Why does she think he should quit school?''

''Because it's embarrassing for him. Although he's the oldest boy at school, he's behind everyone else, even the youngest kids. She thinks it would be better if he was tutored.''

He was quiet for so long, she found herself pausing to watch him as he concentrated on her announcement. Finally, when he spoke, his voice was so low she had to strain to hear him. ''Did she say *why* he was behind?''

Eva knew if she told him what Rachel had said about Lane starting school so late, he would also know that she had been told about his prison sentence. Until he chose to tell her himself about his past, she would respect his decision not to. Eva realized that had she not misrepresented herself to him, she might feel differently, but as it was, she couldn't exactly fault him for an omission of the truth.

Instead of telling him everything the teacher said, Eva only admitted, ''She told me Lane misses a lot of school because it's hard for him to fit in.'' Then, quickly changing the subject she asked, ''Did you get things settled about the gun?''

He was watching her too closely, perhaps weighing the truth, or, at least, the absence of it. Try as she might, it was still hard to believe Chase had been guilty of robbery and sentenced to jail for his crimes.

"Not yet. I put him right to work. He took over for Orvil."

Did he realize Lane might only be trying to live up to his own reputation? No doubt Chase knew better than she why Lane had done what he did. Unless she wanted to admit she knew all about the Cassidys and their dark past, she had to remain silent.

"Think about what Miss Albright said," Eva peeled off the tissue-thin outer layers of the onion and set them aside. "I'll be happy to continue to tutor Lane."

For the first time, she felt as if he were really thinking about what she said and weighing the proposition. He walked to the back door and rested one hand on the top of the frame as he looked out the window at the men still working in the corral.

"I do need another hand now that Ned's down," he admitted. "And Orvil's getting too old to work. If I'd have faced that sooner, then Ned might not have been burned this morning. How long do you think it will be before he's up and around?"

"I don't know. I'm not a doctor."

"No. I guess not."

As she chopped the onion, her eyes smarted. She reached up with the back of her wrist and swiped a tear off her cheek, sniffing as she did. "I'm sorry."

"Are you all right?"

She turned around and found herself nose to chest with him. "Onion," she sniffed.

He slipped his finger beneath her chin and tilted her face up. Gently, with his free hand, he wiped the tears from beneath her eyes. "A lady shouldn't ever have anything to cry over, Eva."

"I'm sure even ladies must cry on occasion," she said softly.

''You sure that schoolmarm didn't say anything to upset you?''

She nodded, afraid to speak and give voice to a lie.

His hands fell away from her face and he shoved them into his pockets. Turning away without a word, he opened the door and went back outside.

Eva watched him go, wondering how she managed to get herself out of one predicament and into another so very quickly.

Chapter Eight

It was a moonless night but the stars were out again, stretching across the horizon, up and away like paint spatters on a midnight quilt tucked over the land. Chase stood on the porch, leaning back against the house, knee bent, one foot propped on the log wall behind him. Familiar kitchen sounds drifted out to him as Eva put the dishes away. He didn't have to see her to know exactly how gracefully she moved, how her hips gently swayed as she walked, so subtly sensual, alluring, inviting. She was entirely innocent of the effect she had on him. He heard her begin humming a catchy, toe-tapping tune he thought he recognized but couldn't put to words.

The door opened and he felt himself tense, expectant, half-hoping to see her. Instead, it was Lane who walked out and stopped short when he spotted Chase in the shadows. Pushing himself away from the wall, Chase moved to the porch rail and took a long, deep breath. Now was as good a time as any to try and talk to the boy.

"I didn't know school was so hard on you," Chase began. He hoped Lane wouldn't ignore his overture outright and push for the usual argument instead.

"What did you expect?" Without looking over at Chase, Lane paced to the corner of the porch and stared out at the corral. "I couldn't even write my name that first day."

Chase wished he could reach out and hold Lane the way he did when he was a child. He closed his eyes against the starry sky and knew it was too late to bring back the past. Gone were the days when Lane would ask to ride on his

117

shoulders, climb up on his knee for a story, or beg to ride on his horse. Times like this, Chase wondered if their life before the pain had been nothing but a dream. Had he imagined those peaceful evenings, when he could come in after a hard day's work and listen while Sally played the organ and Lane sat on his lap and sang along?

The sullen fifteen-year-old he found living alone when he returned to Auggie Owens's deserted ranch house was nothing like the smiling, precocious four-year-old he had left behind. It had not taken Chase long to realize that he had made a terrible mistake to leave Lane with a virtual stranger. He had been so hell-bent on vengeance that nothing could have stopped him back then—and now he was twelve years too late to change anything.

"You don't have to go back to school." Lane reacted immediately by swinging around to face him. Chase couldn't see Lane's features clearly, but he knew by the hesitance in his stance that the boy remained skeptical.

"I don't?"

"No. But you'll have to work cattle everyday from now on. Ned will be out for a while, and I don't want Orvil doing too much anymore. Eva said she wouldn't mind tutoring you at night—"

Lane laughed. "I sure wouldn't mind that either."

Chase felt himself go cold. "How do you mean that?"

The teasing in Lane's tone instantly disappeared as he became immediately defensive. "Anyway you want to take it."

Chase silently cursed himself for pushing Lane to anger again when there was so much to discuss. He got right to the heart of it. "Where did you get that gun?"

The abrupt change of subject obviously caught Lane off guard. Shoving his hands in his pockets, he quickly turned away. Chase didn't think he was going to get an answer, but then Lane said, "While you were out burying Ma that day, I hid it. Back then, I figured if it killed my ma, it might kill you, too." He shrugged, shoulders drawn inward as if to protect himself from more hurt.

It was true Lane had ample opportunity to pick up the gun that day. Chase had been so distraught over Sally's death that he had wrapped up her broken body, mounted up with her in his arms and carried her off to the hills where he had buried her near a stand of pine. His blood ran cold when he pictured Lane as a four-year-old, still in shock, carrying the weapon through the house.

Lane went on. "Later on, when I was older, I figured I was entitled to it. That gun killed my ma. I ran away from Auggie's and came back here to get it when I was around twelve." He rubbed his temples as if his head ached. "I can't remember much about it all now. I was trying to get away from Auggie, but she found me. Didn't think to look for the gun though, so when I got back to her ranch, I kept it hid from her."

Reaching up, Chase ran his hand through his hair and tried to picture his sister. Pretty, loving, temperamental Sally. The responsibility of raising his dark-haired, dark-eyed sister had been his since she was eleven and he was eighteen. When she was barely older than Lane was now, she fell in love with the first cowboy who took a shine to her. A year later the cowboy was gone and Chase had Lane and Sally both to look after. He had not done any better with one than the other.

Chase stared at Lane for a moment. "Do you remember your ma?" The question left Chase's heart feeling as raw as Ned's burn.

Lane cleared his throat. "I remember the sound of her voice, the powdery way she smelled, the songs she played on the organ but not much more—" He stopped abruptly when the back door slammed.

"Must be Eva going out to look after Ned," Chase said. He wasn't sorry for the interruption. The little that Lane had said about Sally had him remembering each long forgotten memory of his own.

"Can I have my gun back?"

Chase knew the right answer was no, knew all the reason why he himself had sworn never to strap on a gun again. But Lane was still hot tempered and determined.

"I guess if I don't give it back you'll just go out and get another one, won't you?"

"Sooner or later." Lane admitted.

"I s'pose you've been out target shooting?"

Across the barnyard the marble-eyed hound barked and came running over to Lane. The boy walked to the edge of the porch to greet him. He bent down and scratched Curly behind the ears.

"You ought to be glad I've been practicing. I aimed to miss him or that cowboy would be dead now."

Chase recognized the bravado in Lane's tone. The tight rein on his own anger slipped a notch. "Or you might be looking at the underside of a grave."

"But I'm not, am I?"

"No, but if you keep this up, there'll always be someone out to get you, if not because of your own reputation, because of mine."

"I need that gun. You think it's easy to walk around wondering if somebody's going to shoot me in the back just to brag about killing Chase Cassidy's nephew?"

"If you're unarmed and someone draws on you they'll be facing the end of a rope."

"And I'd wind up dead anyway, so what difference does it make?"

Chase knew it was an argument he couldn't win. What ate at him most was the pure and simple fact that he was the only one responsible for Lane's attitude and predicament.

"You don't know what it's like to kill a man," Chase said.

"You think I'll be as cool as you are when it comes down to it, Uncle Chase? Is that why you don't wear a gun anymore, because you got to like killing too much?"

"Deep down a man always feels something when he kills another man. Some just learn to hide it so well that after a time it appears they don't care at all. When a man truly doesn't care, he has become nothing more than an animal."

Ramon's words came to him. *"Tarde o temprano, Dios da a cada uno su merecido."* Sooner or later God will give everybody what they deserve.

Chase was surprised Lane hadn't closed himself off already. As he stood there watching this boy who was almost a man, Chase knew there was much more that needed to be said between them. He wished he could come right out and tell Lane that he loved him, that he was sorry he had abandoned him, and that he would do anything to make those lost years up to him—but the words would not come. He had gone a lifetime without learning how to say them.

Lane's rigid stance, his defiant show of temper all masked the hurt he carried deep inside. Chase knew he was as much to blame for the injustice and pain in Lane's life as Sally's killer.

Curly whined and nudged Lane's hand, begging to be scratched. Lane bent down to oblige the dog. He looked over his shoulder at Chase. "Are you through preaching?"

Chase let the comment pass. He had opened a chink in the wall between him and his nephew tonight and he wasn't about to slam it shut no matter how hard Lane tried to provoke him.

"For now. I'm keeping your gun until the end of the week. When I give it back, I don't ever want to see or hear about you wearing it into town."

Lane straightened. He stared at Chase for a moment before he said, "You won't."

"You won't wear it, or I won't see you?"

"What do you think?" Lane shrugged and went back inside.

A bunkhouse was no place for a lady.

Chase knew that's exactly where Eva was because the sound of her laughter drifted across the barnyard, and for a moment an irrational surge of jealousy shot though him. Before he knew it, he was halfway across the yard.

She had not protested having to enter the cowboys' domain to care for Ned, but from what he knew of her already, lady or not, she wasn't one to let anything stand in the way of lending a hand where one was needed.

Admitting to himself he didn't know anything at all about how to treat a lady or what to expect from one, Chase slowed down when he turned a corner of the barn and drew near the bunkhouse. Two figures were seated shoulder to shoulder on the edge of the porch. The sight brought him up short. Eva was sitting there alone with one of the men.

As soon as he recognized Orvil's slow drawl, Chase relaxed. Unwilling to interrupt what was obviously a serious exchange between them, Chase leaned against the side of the barn to wait for Eva and walk her back to the house.

Chase heard her ask softly, "Have you always been a cowboy, Orvil?"

The old man chuckled. "No, ma'am. I was born a slave. Don't know the year. When I was around thirty, near as I can guess, the war started and I ran off. Fought with the Second Regiment West Tennessee Infantry of African Descent. It was the proudest day of my life when they gave me that blue uniform.

"By the time the war ended, the whole regiment was free. Some of us came west. Plenty of ranches needed cowhands, and nobody spent much time worrying about the color of a man's skin, with so much to be done. Got the same pay as the whites, too. Cowboyin' is still the best job in the world, far as I can see."

Chase didn't have to strain to hear the pride in the old man's voice.

"I can tell you love it," Eva said gently.

"I do. Same as I know Chase's been workin' way 'fore dawn until long after sundown to make ends meet around here. He's still got a long way to go." The was a pause before he asked, "Do you think he's going to turn me out, ma'am?"

Before Chase could step forward and put Orvil's fears to rest, Eva quickly gave the old man the assurance he sought.

"I would guess Mr. Cassidy needs every hand he can get. I'm sure there's still plenty for you to do around here, even if you aren't working cattle every day.''

"You think so?"

"I know so.'' She leaned over and nudged Orvil's shoulder with her own. "I could sure use some help around the kitchen. To tell you the truth,'' she lowered her voice conspiratorially, "all this work is wearing me out.''

"Even though you only been here a few days, you made a difference already, Miss Eva, and I don't just mean because you can cook. I seen the way that boy took to you. If anybody needs a friend, its Lane Cassidy.''

"Oh, Orvil, I haven't done anything special.''

"Why you think none of those other women worked out?''

"Actually, I was beginning to wonder if I've been interfering too much—''

The old man cut her off before she could go on. "Miss Eva, you got a good heart, and that's the one thing you brought to this ranch that it's been in need of for a long time.''

When Eva made no reply, Chase waited a moment and then stepped out of the shadows. She smiled up at the sight of him, her warm welcome dispelling the chill that had come with the darkness. Orvil had put into words what Chase had been thinking from that first night when he found her lighting a lamp for him. She was not just a lady, she had a good heart.

Orvil stood up. "I best be going in, Miss Eva. Night, Cassidy.''

They bid him good night simultaneously as he disappeared through the bunkhouse door. Eva didn't stand immediately. Instead, she sat there looking up at Chase with her forearms resting on her knees.

"You look tired,'' he told her. Without letting her know he had overheard what Orvil said he asked, "Is this job wearing you out?''

She shook her head. "No, of course not. I'm pretty tired, but I'm hoping this wasn't a typical day. Surely there isn't an accident every day, nor does the local schoolteacher show up for a chat in the middle of an emergency. Yesterday's trouble in town probably wasn't normal either. And you said yourself that Lane doesn't often run away, so I won't have that to worry about for a bit.''

"It *has* been a rough couple of days for you," he admitted.

"Did you talk to Lane yet?"

"We talked."

"I know it's none of my business but—"

He laughed. "When have you ever let that stop you? I told him that he wouldn't have to go back to school and that you would help him of an evening." As an afterthought he added, "Only if it's not too much for you."

"I'm sure all he'll need are a few basic skills. How to add and subtract enough to keep track of his accounts when he gets older. He can use some help with reading, I'm sure."

Chase nodded. "That'd be fine. Maybe some map reading," he said, thinking aloud.

"What about the gun?"

As much as he wanted to see the thing destroyed, he knew Lane would protest. He had to convince himself that it was only a gun, just like any other. Only the dark memory of what it had been used for made this weapon seem so very evil. He knew how concerned Eva was about Lane, so he tried to keep the worry out of his voice when he told her, "I'll give it back eventually. He'll be able to use it on the range. We run into snakes and porcupines, wolves sometimes."

"You don't wear one," she reminded him.

"No. I don't. I have my reasons."

Thankfully, she didn't push him into telling her what those reasons might be. Chase straightened. "You were good to Orvil tonight. You didn't have to be," he said.

She stood up and brushed off her skirt. It was still badly stained where she had knelt in the dirt to help Ned. "You aren't going to fire him, are you?"

Chase started back toward the house. Eva walked beside

him. "No. He'll never find another job cowboyin' at his age. I figure, if you teach him to cook, then if anything happens to me, he might be able to hire on as a cook for some other outfit."

She stopped in mid-stride. "What could happen to you?"

He shrugged and kept going. "You never know."

As they walked back to the house together, Chase thought of Eva's promise to help Rachel Albright. If she was going to be in town twice a week, how long would it be until the town gossips got to her? He hated to see someone as genuinely loving and innocent as Eva hurt because of him. If he had an ounce of the compassion she had shown his nephew and his men, he would tell her the truth.

All day long he had found himself thinking about her, listening for the sound of her voice and hoping for another chance meeting in the moonlight. Now, here they were, together again, and he was about to tell her the one thing that might cause her to walk away.

"Eva—"

"Where's Lane?" She asked before he could say anything more.

"He went to bed."

"I don't imagine he got much sleep last night." She crossed her arms and hugged herself to ward off the chill in the air.

It would have been hard to miss the way the movement drew the bodice of her gown tight and emphasized her breasts. He couldn't keep his eyes off her, nor could he bring himself to say the words that might replace the sparkle in her eyes with the same fear and suspicion he had seen plenty of times in others.

As she walked close beside him, he held his silence. The cattle penned nearby had finally settled down. Curly was stretched out in the corner of the porch. Chase stood there drinking in the tranquility of the moment with Eva while the scent of her lilac perfume drifted around them.

When they reached the porch, she made no move to leave him and go inside. Eva Edwards was courting danger and didn't even realize it. Chase wanted to reach for her, ached to pull her into his arms. What would she do if he touched her? How would she react? Her nearness was driving him crazy, reminding him of how very long he had been without a woman—but standing there beside her, Chase knew for certain that it wasn't just any woman he wanted—it was only Eva.

If it was merely release he craved, he could have swallowed his pride and ridden into town any night of the week to find solace. He might have been rejected by the God-fearing citizens of Last Chance, but whores couldn't be choosy when it came to earning their keep. Still, he had no intention of going into town when it was Eva who had moved him, Eva who had inspired this driving need. It was Eva with her copper curls, shining emerald eyes and tempting lips.

Chase almost reached for her again, then stopped himself.

He shoved his hands in his back pockets.

"Well, good night then, Chase." Her voice came to him softly, floating on the essence of lilacs that surrounded her like a whisper on the night breeze.

To make certain he did not reach for her, didn't swallow her up in a kiss that was driven by the frightening force of his need, Chase fisted his hands at his side and stepped back.

"Night, Eva." It was all he could manage.

He waited until she was well inside before he followed her and turned down the light.

Behind her own door, Eva paced as she wriggled out of her gown. She threw the filthy striped dress in the corner, determined to try and tackle the laundry as soon as she had breakfast cleaned up in the morning. She reached down to unfasten the petticoat buttoned to her lavender "combination," a one-piece undergarment which combined chemise and drawers. She continued to roam the tiny perimeter of her room, giving vent to her frustration.

Untying the ribbon woven through the trim around the neckline, she halted beside the bed, reached under her pillow and pulled out her folded nightgown. She threw the modest gown on the bed, slipped out of her combination, and tossed the gown's voluminous folds over her head. With a tug, she jerked the fabric down until the deep flounce around the hem swirled around her ankles.

Standing before the mirror over the dresser, Eva pulled the combs out of her hair and picked up the ivory brush her parents had given her on her tenth birthday. She attacked her hair vigorously, pulling the boar bristles through her copper curls until her scalp tingled.

"Damn it, Eva Eberhart," she whispered to the image in the mirror, "you're playing with fire." She couldn't imagine what had possessed her to stand there waiting for Chase Cassidy to kiss her. Even after everything she had learned about him today, even knowing the man had been convicted and sentenced for robbery, she was neither appalled nor frightened by him. In fact, she was just as attracted to him as she had been before she learned about his jail term. In the back of her mind, she kept telling herself that there was a very good reason for the crimes Chase had committed. There had to be.

All the way back from the bunkhouse she found excuses to walk as close to him as possible. Even he must have noticed there weren't *that* many piles of manure to avoid as they walked along. He attracted her like a beehive drew bees. She found herself listening for his voice above the others. She couldn't get enough of looking at him, at the way he stood, the way he moved, the way he sat his horse.

With far too much force, she slammed the brush down on the dresser and turned away from her traitorous image.

Maybe you're not cut out to be a lady.

She had quit the Palace because she was sick of men pawing at her. Yet she knew if Chase Cassidy—a man she had only known a short while—had attempted to kiss her, she wouldn't have minded it in the least.

Maybe she should go to him, knock on his door, and tell

him she knew the truth about his past and tell him she had quite a past of her own.

What if she told him the truth and he fired her on the spot? Chase Cassidy might have spent time in jail— but he had hired her under the assumption that she was a lady with a good reputation.

Certainly not an actress.

Definitely not a dancer.

Positively *not* a fallen woman who had already given herself to a no-account gambler, no matter how much she regretted having done so.

She blew out the lamp, whipped the rough-textured spread and blanket back, and climbed into bed. After yanking the covers up under her chin, Eva lay there fuming in the darkness.

Maybe it would be best if she left now, before she let her attraction to Chase Cassidy go any further. When she went into Last Chance to help Rachel Albright with the program she might even hear about another opening for a housekeeper.

But if that would be better for all of them, why did the thought of leaving so soon make her heart ache so?

As if her mind was dead set on worrying, her tumultuous thoughts turned to her parents. Where were the Eberharts now? The last time they had written to her at the Palace was months ago, but that was not unusual. Their letters came as infrequently as rain hit the Mojave desert.

What would they think of Chase? She couldn't even imagine what his reaction would be to her eccentric parents. Her mother would most likely burst into a song fitting the occasion of their meeting.

Eva groaned, rolled over, and beat her pillow into a wad.

Somewhere out in the barnyard, a calf separated from its mama bawled a loud complaint, so Eva pulled the pillow over her head.

Before she knew it, it would be time to get up and start the daily chores all over again.

Chapter Nine

Chase glanced up at the sky. There was no sign of blue, no hint that the sun existed behind the thick mass of heavy, bullet-gray clouds. Rain had threatened all morning but made little show except for a slight misting as the men rode to higher ground searching the brush and low pine forest for strays.

He forced his mount, an edgy dun-colored horse with the temperament of an ornery two-year-old, up a hillside mottled with tangled shadbush, thankful for the thick leather chaps that protected his legs from a profusion of twigs. The bushes were covered with clusters of buds that would open into long petaled flowers before the sawtoothed leaves appeared. In a few weeks, songbirds would pick off the small serviceberries and deer would graze on the twigs.

Before he reached the highest rise, he heard Ramon shout, and twisted in the saddle. After a minor tussle with his mount over who was boss, Chase kicked the horse in the side and rode toward his foreman. As he cleared a thin stand of pine, he spotted Ramon kneeling over what was left of the carcass of a calf.

He pulled up and dismounted, ground-tied his horse and walked up to Ramon. "Wolves?"

"*Sí.* Last night. Probably a pack." He straightened and pointed over his shoulder. The remains of a mother cow lay nearby.

Chase thumbed his hat brim back and found himself staring down at the carcass, his mind a few miles away. He couldn't shake the feeling that something was wrong at the ranch house. Ramon glanced up and Chase turned in the direction of an approaching rider. Lane, head low over his horse's neck, pushed the spirited young pinto toward them. He reined in with a flourish and fairly jumped out of the saddle as he dismounted. With a glance, he took in the dead mama and baby.

"I found another calf torn up like this over the ridge back there."

"Wolves," Chase told him.

"We going to do anything about them?" He walked over and jostled the calf's head with the toe of his boot. "It won't be safe to turn the herd out again until we clear some of them out."

"Have to do what the wolfers did in the old days. Poison the carcasses and leave them out here. Any scavengers will take the bait and die." Chase studied Lane for a moment as the boy stared down at the calf. "How would you like to collect the wolf pelts? A good pelt will still bring around three dollars."

Lane turned and watched him for so long that Chase thought he was about to refuse until a smile slowly tipped half his mouth. Lane nodded. "Sure."

"Ramon can show you how to take one without damaging it."

Ramon nodded in agreement. Lane made no further comment. Instead, he continued to watch Chase as if he were trying to figure out why he was being so beneficent.

Chase turned around and started back toward his horse. "I'll head back for the strychnine."

"I can send Orvil," Ramon volunteered.

Knowing how upset the old hand was over the accident with Ned, Chase let him ride along that morning, willing to wait a while before he assigned the aging cowboy to less strenuous chores.

Chase paused, one gloved hand on the saddlehorn as he turned to face Ramon and Lane. "Let him keep busy out here. I'll be back before noontime."

Lane merely shrugged, but Chase didn't miss the shake

of Ramon's head and his slight, knowing smile. Drawn by the image of Eva alone at the ranch house, Chase hid the turmoil roiling inside him and gave in to his desire to see her alone.

His outer clothing damp from the heavy mist, Chase paused beside the porch rail. "If fools were for sale you'd bring the highest bid," he mumbled to himself. He tied his horse and shrugged out of his canvas duster as he headed for the back door. His anticipation mounted as he used the boot scraper and stood on the back porch, listening to the sound of Eva moving around in the kitchen. He slung his wet coat over a peg outside the door and after one quick rap, pushed it open and stepped inside.

At the first sight of the homey kitchen, he failed to stop a rush of something warm and nearly forgotten that unfurled within him. The air was heavy with the smell of fresh baked bread. He was content to let it enfold him like a cozy quilt. He spied three loaves of bread lined up on the kitchen table, two of them a bit lopsided, the centers somewhat sunken, but their aroma still mouth-watering.

The two large, wooden wash tubs sat in the middle of the floor, one full of soapy water and the other somewhat clearer. A washboard straddled one. A scrub brush lay upside down on the floor in a puddle beside it. Wet clothing was piled on a kitchen chair. A tangle of shirt arms and pant legs dangled over the edge of the seat, each trailing steady, monotonous drips that commingled to form a narrow but determined stream of water that ran across the uneven floorboards and through the cracks between.

Eva was standing on tiptoe in front of the stove, stretching up to prod a stir-stick into a steaming copper boiler. Billows of steam floated over the rolling water and swept up into her face, the moisture dampening the loose curls that bordered her forehead and temples, forcing them to stick to her glowing skin like spun copper. She was stunning.

He stepped across the threshold. Immediately she sensed

someone's presence, for she stiffened and turned, her expression one of mingled surprise and trepidation. Her gaze flew to the shotgun behind the door, then up at him. When she realized it was only him, she visibly relaxed. Chase understood her reaction instantly, which made him unreasonably glad that she was not afraid of him.

Swiftly, she turned back to her task. He thought it odd she hadn't said a word in greeting—she'd been in an amiable mood at breakfast. At a complete loss for a moment, Chase wondered what might have happened in his absence and stood there watching her. Still she didn't turn around.

"Eva?"

When she made no response, he went to her. In two long strides he walked through the soapy water, muddied the floor in the process, and took her by the shoulders.

She let go of the stir-stick as he turned her to face him. Her face was so pink from the steam billowing off the top of the boiler that he had not noticed that she was crying. Now, just inches away from her, he couldn't miss the tears that misted her eyes and trailed down her cheeks.

"What's wrong?"

She took a deep, shuddering breath, gulped once, and said, *"Everything."*

Listlessly, she waved a hand over the mess on the floor. "I tried to do the laundry while I let the bread rise, but things got away from me somehow."

"Is that all?" He glanced down at the floor and tried to hide his relief. *She was upset about the stupid clothes.*

She shuddered after another deep breath. He wanted to pull her into his arms to comfort her, but, instead, he contented himself with staring down into her flushed, upturned face, drinking in the deep emerald shimmering through her tears and tried to concentrate on what she was telling him.

"First, the bread fell. Then I went out to take breakfast to Ned and change his dressing, and while I was gone, the wash water boiled over." She swiped at her cheek with the back of her hand. "And . . . and then . . . when Ned woke up from his nap, I heard him hollering all the way from the bunkhouse. I thought he was in pain, so I raced over there only to have him yell at me for . . . for taking his pants so . . . I could . . . wash them.''

That said, she burst into sobs and buried her face against his shirt front. Chase welcomed the excuse to hold her close. He smoothed his hand up and down her spine until she calmed down and her shuddering sobs subsided to mere sniffles.

''You don't wash a cowboy's work pants, Eva. Never. It's just not done,'' he told her softly.

''But, I thought . . .''

''They aren't even seasoned good until they can stand up by themselves.''

''But they were so *filthy*.''

''When the dirt gets too thick they can be scraped with a pocket knife, but never washed.''

''But that's . . . disgusting.''

He nodded over her head. ''That's just the way it is. I'll go have a talk with Ned later. It's not your fault. You didn't know any better.''

He turned her out of his embrace but kept hold of her elbow and began to guide her around the tubs and the mess on the floor, past the chair of sodden garments, over to her own place at the table.

''You sit right here,'' he directed, ''and I'm going to pour you a cup of coffee and then clean up this mess.''

She stared up at him until her lower lip began to quiver. Then she plopped her folded arms on the table and hid her face in them.

Perplexed, Chase didn't move. ''What'd I say?''

The words that issued from the well of her arms were muffled but comprehensible. ''You're being so *nice* to me.''

Her statement confirmed what he already knew. He clearly didn't understand anything at all about gently bred ladies. Ignoring her, he took off his hat and tossed it on the hat rack, rolled up his sleeves, and got to work toting the buckets of water out and tossing them off the back porch.

As he worked, he glanced over at her occasionally, relieved when she finally straightened, used her apron to mop up her tears, and even smoothed her hair back out of her eyes. When he hefted one of the near empty tubs and started for the door, she began to rise.

"Stay put. I'm almost done."

She sank back into the chair with a woebegone expression. "I'm all right now. I'm the housekeeper here. You really shouldn't be doing this. I'm sure you have other things—"

"Don't move."

She sighed.

He took the tub outside and came back for the other one. Between that and wiping up the floor, he poured her a cup of strong black coffee, which she ignored. Finally, when everything was back to normal, he poured his own coffee and cut a slice of bread from one of the lopsided loaves.

"Please," she said barely above a whisper. "You don't have to eat that just to make me feel better."

Chase smiled. "I know that." He stared down at the thick slice of bread in his hand. The center looked somewhat gummy, but not beyond eating. "I like soft bread."

"You like *dough*?"

He laughed and took a bite, quickly washing it down with coffee. Trying to smile, he said, "Mmmm."

"You're not a very good actor, Mr. Cassidy."

"No?"

She shook her head, showing the beginnings of a smile.

After a few seconds he said, "I imagine you've been to the theater, living back East and all?" Trying to make polite conversation made him feel as awkward as a new-born colt.

Her already heightened color darkened across her cheeks. Eva stared down into her coffee cup hiding her eyes. "Yes. I've been to the theater a few times."

"Always thought that might be something to see."

She watched him closely, hesitating as if she were weighing her words carefully. "Some plays are better than others. So are some actors."

"Do you have a favorite?"

She again found something interesting to stare at in her coffee cup. "Not really."

Sensing she found the topic somehow uncomfortable, he changed the subject. "Feeling better?"

She nodded and smiled over at him. "I feel ridiculous. I have a confession to make."

Chase found himself smiling. "And what terrible thing have you done, Miss Edwards?"

"I've never done laundry before, that's why the kitchen ended up in such a mess. Oh, I knew it wasn't going to be easy, not after I found three chapters devoted to it in Mrs. Applebee's book."

"Mrs. Applebee?"

"She wrote a book of recipes and household hints, and there are pages and pages of instructions on washing and ironing days. She suggested getting up earlier to get started." Eva sighed and set the empty cup down, then folded her hands in her lap as she looked across the table at him. "But I can't get up any earlier than I do, and I don't think it matters when I start, I'll never get the hang of this."

"You didn't have to do the laundry in Philadelphia?"

She looked at him oddly for a second, then rapidly shook her head. "We always sent them out." Reaching up to push a limp, wayward curl off her damp face, she asked, "What are you doing back so soon?"

Her question quickly brought him back to reality. As much as he would like to have tarried all day, he had more to do than sit around sipping coffee and making small talk.

He drained the cup. "I came home for some strychnine."

When he stood up to go, disappointment clouded her eyes and her hands closed tight around her coffee cup. "Poison? What for?"

"We found some cattle that had been attacked by wolves."

"Oh, how awful!" Her eyes grew round and her hand flew to her breast.

He couldn't help but smile at her dramatic reaction to the news. "These things happen sometimes. Every rancher expects to lose a few head every year. We'll rub strychnine into the carcasses and leave them out for the wolves to find. Usually they take the bait right away."

He went over to the pantry, walked inside, and came back out with a brown bottle in his hand. Eva stood up and carried their cups to the dish pan.

When she turned around to face him, she was frowning. "Can you afford to lose the cattle?"

He shrugged. "Not really, but it's part of the gamble. I put almost everything I had last spring into some new Hereford stock. We didn't lose any of them."

"Well, then that's a blessing," she told him.

Chase glanced out the window in the back door. The sky was still leaden. He wished it was raining. Pouring, for that matter. Then he would have an excuse to stay for the whole afternoon. There came unbidden images of the two of them alone together, the rain falling in an uneven tattoo on the roof. If she were his, he would welcome an idle afternoon. He'd light a fire, sit beside her for a time, enjoying the very nearness of her before he took her in his arms.

He already knew what she would feel like—soft and warm with the heady scent of lilacs wafting about her. She would be light as a feather in his arms as he carried her into his room. She would smile shyly as he laid her across his bed and carefully, slowly, tenderly undressed her. She would be warm and willing, yet unsure of herself as any untarnished virgin.

The images faded when he remembered he had never had a virgin in his life.

He would have to go slow, hold himself back.

It would be hell.

It would be heaven.

"Chase?"

He started, nearly jumped out of his skin when he realized she was standing inches away.

He had to clear his throat twice to get the words out.

"I've got to go."

She continued to stand there, her green eyes luminescent, shimmering with unshed tears.

"You're making more of a few soapsuds than you need to Eva," he said softly.

She shook her head, blinking furiously. "I know it. I don't know what's gotten into me, except that I just want to do a good job here."

"You do that already."

"You don't have to cheer me up, but I appreciate it, Chase."

Her admission made him feel ten feet tall and with a heart the size of Montana. "It wasn't any more than you would have done for one of us."

She reached up to straighten his collar and he froze, afraid to move, to breathe. He caught her wrist in his hand, felt her steady pulse beneath his fingers. He carried her hand to his lips and kissed her palm.

He expected her to shy away.

She reached up and slipped her free hand around his neck, raised herself on tiptoe and drew his head down, bringing his mouth close to hers. Chase obliged, let go of her wrist and pressed his lips to her sweet, pouting mouth. He pulled her closer, ran his fingers through her curls, and cupped his hands against the back of her head.

He deepened the kiss, tugged on her hair until her head tipped back and forced her to open her lips, to let him invade her mouth, to delve, to taste, to explore her with his tongue.

Everything went still around them. He no longer heard the cattle bawling in the corral outside or the lap of bubbles in the simmering boiler on the stove. Enfolded in the aroma of fresh bread, the warmth of the stove, the tang of strong soap and most of all the tempting scent of lilacs, Chase felt a moment of peace the likes of which he had never known.

When she arched closer, he reached around her and

cupped her buttocks, pressing her up against him. She returned his kiss full measure as he held her close, yielding to the need that drove him on. He tasted her hungrily, excitement throbbing through him as she trembled in his arms.

Eva was the first to end the kiss but she didn't try to move out of his embrace. Shaken, she clung to him and pressed her face against the hollow of his shoulder. They stood there, breathless, clutching each other close. Chase's heart was beating wildly, out of control. His instant, overwhelming response to the woman in his arms scared him more than any gunman he had ever faced down.

Outside, Curly started barking and she stepped away from him, her face aflame. Shock and dismay alternated across her lovely features. As he dropped his arms and let go of her, she stepped back, clasped her hands together, and stared at him in shocked silence.

Chase cleared his throat and glanced out the window.

"Looks like he's just barking at the wind," he said awkwardly.

She didn't move, nor did she respond.

Chase turned around and took his hat off the rack and shoved it on his head. He opened the door and, never having been one to run from a confrontation, paused on the threshold and turned around again. Eva was still staring at him as if trying to comprehend everything that had just passed between them. Her eyes were wide, filled with confusion.

"I'm sorry, Eva," he said, taking her silence for outrage.

She opened her mouth as if to speak, closed it again, and then looked down at her hands. "It's . . . all right. It's just . . . I'm sure . . . " A frustrated sigh escaped her. "Please, it was my fault as much as yours. I don't know what came over me. I just wanted to thank you for your . . . your kindness."

He turned around and walked out.

Once he had put on his oilskin slicker and mounted up, Chase allowed himself another glance at the back door. He thought he could see Eva through the shimmering window pane. She was standing right where he left her.

The homey scene—the warm bread, the coffee, the two of them chatting at the table—was nothing more than make-believe, a pretty scene from one of the plays Eva had seen back East. It was a pretty picture, but just like his rainy-day fantasy, it wasn't real and would never be real as long as his past stood in the way.

He might have been a gunfighter who had served time in the territorial prison, but he was too big a coward to tell her the truth about himself.

Eva stared at the door and watched Chase disappear from sight. Unsteady on her feet, she walked back to the table and slowly lowered herself into his empty chair. The seat was still warm from his body heat. Her fingers trembled as she raised her hand and touched her lips. She still tasted his kiss.

Every nerve ending was aflame, every inch of her had come alive. She had never been more aware of a man in her life—the warmth of his breath and the rain-dampened coolness of his skin, the scent of the open range, of pine and leather. Gunfighting wasn't Chase Cassidy's only accomplishment—his kiss was more exciting than she could have imagined. As if she had sampled a heady drug, she was still intoxicated, but lucid enough to know for certain that his kiss only made her lust for more.

You're playing with fire, Eva Eberhart.

She had set out to change her life for the better and here she was, already falling head over heels in love with a man she barely knew. A blush spread across her cheeks when she recalled how very forward she had acted a moment ago. What she had intended as an innocent peck, a thank you for what he had done for her, had somehow stampeded out of control.

She glanced over at the boiler and jumped to her feet. The water had nearly simmered away and if she didn't rescue it, her striped dress would be scorched. Thankful for a chance to take her mind off of Chase Cassidy for a moment, she stared at the copper pot with a frown and decided then and there that as soon as she went into Last Chance to help Rachel, she was going to find someone who did laundry and use her own savings to cover the cost.

As she dipped the stir-stick into the pot and lifted the sopping wet dress out, she wondered what Chase Cassidy might be thinking about the respectable Miss Eva Edwards right about now.

Lane hunkered down beneath the spreading limbs of an alder and hunched over the sandwich in his hands in an attempt to keep it dry. Ramon, Jethro, and Orvil were nearby, all huddled around the low campfire they had coaxed to life in the light mist. It was not a cowboy's habit to ever stop for a midday meal, but this morning, Eva had wrapped sandwiches for each of them, insisting, as she pressed them into their hands, that they needed nourishment on a cold day. No one wanted to hurt her feelings.

Cowboying wasn't easy on the best day, and the weather made this one of the worst, but still, Lane felt more at ease than he ever did in the one-room school in Last Chance. Every time he remembered that he would never again have to slide his oversized frame into one of the undersized desks at the back of the schoolroom, he wanted to whoop with joy.

He had to admit he would miss staring at Rachel Albright's breasts when she wasn't looking or watching the way her little behind would wiggle when she stretched up to write at the top of the chalkboard.

He would miss it, but he could do without the temptation.

Like Eva, Rachel Albright had been kind to him, but she had always treated him the way she did the other children. Miss Eva was another matter.

"Your thoughts are far away, amigo," Ramon said.

"I was just wondering what was keeping Chase."

"Something redheaded, I'd imagine," Jethro said around a mouthful of roast beef and wheat bread.

Lane immediately felt his blood run cold. "Don't ever let me hear you say anything like that about Miss Eva again." No one missed the threat in his tone, least of all Jethro.

"Jezuz, don't be so touchy, kid. Didn't mean anything by it," he mumbled, averting his eyes.

"Miss Eva's a real good sort. Like an angel," Orvil said to no one in particular. He was the only one who had chosen to sit on the damp ground. His wrinkled hands were locked about his knees.

They fell into silence again. Lane stared out across the gray landscape. *Chase and Eva.* Never. What would a woman like Miss Eva ever see in his uncle? The man was old. He was thirty-four. Lane wondered if a man that age even got excited anymore around a beautiful woman. Lane looked at the circle of men. Only Jethro was still in his twenties.

Lane sized him up. Some might say Jethro was handsome, with his sandy blond hair and ready smile. He was wiry and bowlegged but at end-of-the-roundup dances he never missed a chance to swing the local girls around with the fanciest of steps, even though he had an aversion to bathing.

"What are you starin' at?" Jethro demanded.

Lane realized he had been frowning at the man and shrugged it off. "Nothin' worth anything."

Jethro threw down his tin cup and stood up. "You want to fight?"

When Lane started to accept, Ramon reached out and put a hand on his forearm. *"Sientate."* Sit down.

Lane shook him off. Over Jethro's shoulder, he caught a glimpse of Chase riding over the rise. "Go ahead and hit me, Adams."

Jethro followed the direction of Lane's gaze, recognized Chase and then shook his head. "You'd like that wouldn't you? You'd like to get me tossed out."

Ramon stood up. "Shut up, Adams, and let it go. We have work to do."

Jethro pulled his gloves out of his back pocket and began working them on. "You think you're something, boy, just because you're Chase Cassidy's nephew? You still got a lot to learn."

"Yeah?" Lane stepped up to Jethro until they were nose to nose.

His uncle rode up to the campfire and dismounted. Reins in hand, he forced himself between the two. "Break it up. Adams, mount up and start those heifers moving down the hillside. Some of them have scattered again."

He turned to Lane, his temper barely contained. "Do I have to keep an eye on you every minute?"

Lane almost told Chase what Jethro had said about Eva, but decided not to bother. Refusing to drop his gaze, he returned Chase's stare full measure.

Lane knew he could hold out all day. So did Chase, apparently, for he finally gave in and said, "Get moving."

Lane walked away.

Chase watched him until he was out of earshot. "You think I'll ever know the right thing to say to him?" Chase asked Ramon.

The big Mexican pulled up the chin strap beneath his sombrero that kept his head and shoulders dry. *"Para saber hablar, hay que saber escuchar."*

To know how to speak, you must know how to listen.

Chase watched his nephew ride off. The youngster already sat as tall as he did in the saddle and handled his horse like a well-seasoned hand. Chase suspected there wasn't anything Lane couldn't do well if given the time and inclination to do it. He would be happy to listen to Lane. But first he would have to find a way to get the boy to talk about what was ailing him.

Because he needed time alone, Chase indicated that he would take the high ground to search for any more downed cattle. He mounted up and headed west, along the tree line, able to keep his eye on the low lying brush as he let his mind wander back to the kiss he had shared with Eva.

To say she had surprised him by initiating a kiss was an

understatement. Unwilling to relegate the moment to his memory, he went over every movement, every nuance and detail of it in his mind in order to understand exactly how it came about that Miss Eva Edwards had ended up in his arms.

In what seemed an innocent move, she had reached up to straighten his collar. He recalled grabbing her wrist and kissing her palm. Then, it was as if the moment had ignited as suddenly and inexplicably as a prairie wildfire. She had meant to give him a kiss of thanks, a peck no doubt, but he had not been able to resist, and forced her into more. It had been a mistake on his part to take such liberties with a lady.

Mistake or not, no woman had ever felt so good, so right in his arms—and no woman had ever been so wrong for him. If he lived to be one hundred he would never forget the crimson blush or the look of shocked bewilderment he had last seen on her face. She had been dumbstruck, unable to say anything at first, and then she had ended up apologizing to *him*.

His mind still on Eva, Chase rode past a weather-beaten, long-abandoned line shack nestled in the pines. He planned to make it serviceable again when he had saved enough money, but that day still seemed a long way off. Reining in his horse, he stared out over the valley below. From here, the ranch house was hidden behind a bend in the creek, one of the many that led to the Missouri. In the distance, the mountains stood almost entirely shrouded in low-lying clouds.

He usually took pleasure in something that most men took for granted. Ever since prison, the simple act of staring out across open land had sustained him, buoyed his spirit, and gave him the will to go on. But not today. Today the leaden skies weighed down upon the land as heavy as the thoughts that drifted like thunderheads through his mind. Only one thing seemed clear to him after mulling over all the possibilities— from now on, he would have to keep his distance from Eva and try to forget what had passed between them today.

He was fairly certain serving his prison term had been a hell of a lot easier.

Chapter Ten

The small schoolroom was stuffy, the air heavy with the smell of chalk dust, moldy papier-mâché, and sweaty children. After nine visits, Eva had begun to recognize the scents as peculiar to the place. Today was no different as she waited at the piano near the front of the room. She watched Rachel with mingled awe and respect, wondering how the young woman kept her patience while the twenty-three children surrounding her wriggled and giggled and poked and prodded each other. Eva was certain that if she were in charge, she would have thrown up her hands and sent them home an hour ago.

"Do you think we could try 'Listen to the Mockingbird' one last time?" Rachel asked in a voice meant to be heard over the hubbub.

Eva met her eyes over the bobbing heads of the children and responded by booming out a few minor chords. Some of the older students giggled, but the mournful sound caught the attention of the younger ones who immediately took their places and snapped to attention.

"That's more like it," Eva mumbled to herself, thankful she had not decided to take up education as her newly chosen profession.

Just as the introduction began, a ten-year-old girl in the back row shoved one of the smallest boys forward and whined, "Teacher, he bit me!"

Eva paused, hands hovering over the keys while Rachel took the offender in baggy overalls by the shoulder and, without a word, marched him to the nearest desk where he

145

was forced to sit in isolation, head down, face hidden in the crook of his arm.

"Harold Higgens, when you think you can behave like the gentleman I know you are, you may join us again." Rachel swept dramatically back to the front of the room.

As this was the freckle-spattered little imp's third or fourth attack in as many days, Eva wondered why none of the others simply didn't bite Harold Higgens back.

"Maybe he's hungry," Eva mused aloud.

Rachel turned so that only Eva could see her face. She rolled her eyes and mouthed, "He's a beast." Eva stifled a giggle and concentrated on the sheet music again.

The motley chorus snapped to attention. She played as the reedy voices trilled their way through the song to the last line, "Listen to the mockingbird, Still singing where the weeping willows wave."

As the final notes drifted away, Eva swiveled around on the piano stool and smiled at the children. "I think you're finally ready for tomorrow night. Don't you Miss Rachel?"

Rachel Albright nodded. "I do indeed. Which just goes to show that practice makes perfect, doesn't it?"

Eva began to close the sheet music when Rachel snapped out, "George Riley, stand still!" Then to Eva, "You don't think we need one more number do you? Something a bit livelier?"

Of the opinion that what she needed now was a good stiff drink, Eva merely smiled and began to play "Little Brown Jug." A few of the students who recognized the tune began to sing along.

"Ha, Ha, Ha, you and me—"

Rachel clapped her hands and called out, "Stop everyone! Immediately."

Eva stopped. The children, a study in mended pinafores, faded overalls, scuffed, ankle-high shoes, and sagging stockings, quieted down to eavesdrop as Rachel approached the piano with a very distressed look on her face.

In a hush she whispered, "Eva, I don't think that one would be appropriate, do you?"

"Well, I—"

"The chorus isn't so bad, but the verse! ..." She twisted her hands at her waist, obviously worried about offending Eva by rejecting her choice of songs.

Frowning as she hummed and ran through the words of the verse, Eva soon found herself blushing. "My wife and I lived all alone, in a little log hut we called our own; She loved gin and I loved rum—I tell you what, we'd lots of fun."

She recognized her mistake immediately. Of course, the song was inappropriate for a school program.

A lady would have never suggested it.

"I'm ... I'm sorry Rachel. I don't know what came over me."

Rachel put her hand on Eva's shoulder. "Don't worry. Obviously it's something the children have all heard at home, but I'm sure some of their parents would be offended to hear it here."

As Rachel moved to dismiss the students, Eva jumped when something brushed the hem of her dress. She pulled back her full skirt, careful to keep her frothy red petticoat hidden beneath it, only to discover Harold Higgens—the biter—on his back on the floor, wriggling into a position where he might get a look up her skirt.

"Why, you little stinker!"

She reached down and grabbed the offender by the ear and forced him to stand beside the piano stool. He didn't appear nearly as threatening on his feet—he barely came to her waist. As she gazed down into the wide blue eyes and dirt-streaked face, Eva was hard pressed not to laugh. Instead, she maintained a stern expression and brought her nose as close to his as she dared. It wouldn't do to have the end of her nose bitten off, especially if housekeeping didn't work out and she had to go back to the stage.

"Didn't anyone ever tell you that it isn't polite to look up a lady's dress?"

"Yeth," he lisped through the space where his two front

teeth should have been. "Thath what my mom alwath sayth."

"Maybe you should listen to her."

"But my dad alwath sayth, if you're gonna look Harold, be thure you don't get caught."

Sound advice. Eva shook her head and turned the tyke by his suspenders and gently pushed him toward the door. "Wash your face for the program tomorrow night, Harold. And please eat something before you get here."

She watched him meander through an unnecessarily intricate course between the desks and stop a few feet from the door. He turned and smiled an impish, toothless smile and waved as if she had not reprimanded him at all. "Thee you tomorrow, Mith Eva. You thure do play the beth muthic!" With that he scampered after the others.

Aware of the blessed silence, Eva shook her head, unable to keep from laughing.

"Do you really think they're ready?" Rachel asked.

Eva stood and picked up the sheet music, intending to practice that night at the ranch. "I think they're as ready as they'll ever be. I have to hand it to you, Rachel, you are a saint. I'm afraid I'd have thrown half of them out of here long before now."

Rachel smiled as she bustled about the room straightening papers, stopping to erase the chalk board and talking at the same time. "You get used to them. And once you see them with their families, you begin to realize why they act the way they do."

Eva was reminded of Lane. She had watched him at home with Chase, but still could not decide why he was so difficult to get along with or what would anger him. A lack of maturity had to account for some of his behavior, but not all. She guessed that Chase's absence and imprisonment was behind Lane's rebellion. How long would it be until the boy could put the past behind him?

As Rachel bustled around the room making preparations for lessons for the following morning, Eva waited in silence, the sheet music on her lap, forgotten, as she thought about the past two weeks. Every other afternoon, one of the ranch hands drove her into town and waited while she rehearsed. At first she had protested, certain Chase couldn't spare a driver, but since Orvil was usually entrusted with her care, she finally consented.

Chase had never once volunteered to drive her into town. In fact, after the kiss she had given him that gray morning in the kitchen, he had maintained his distance. Ever since then, he had seemed so preoccupied that Eva was sure she had offended him with her boldness. She was bound and determined not to fall into his arms again, no matter how much she yearned for him.

Over the past few days she had reorganized the kitchen according to the suggestions in her *Household Hints* book, and even found time to plant flower seeds around the porch. She and Orvil had finally convinced Chase that chicken would be a welcome change from beef once in a while, and now Orvil was building a hen house of scrap wood. On the surface, life at the ranch was running smoothly, because she and Chase were behaving like players in a melodrama, carefully executing their lines as they acted out roles and avoided their attraction to each other.

Motion near the double doors at the back of the schoolroom caught Eva's eye and she glanced up. For a moment her breath caught in her throat when she thought that Chase had come after her, but she instantly realized it was Lane silhouetted in the opening. At a glance, it was hard to tell the difference between the two. Both were tall; Lane had inherited his uncle's cocky stance, wide shoulders, and narrow hips.

She could not exactly say the boy had been happy since Chase had allowed him to quit school, but he did seem calmer, and there had been no further problems with his gun.

As he sauntered into the schoolhouse, Eva stood up and smiled in greeting. "I was wondering when you would be back to get me," she told him.

"I waited until I saw all those kids leave."

Eva shook her head and laughed. "I think I know why." She was tempted to tell him about Harold before Rachel interrupted.

"Hello, Lane. How are you doing?"

"Howdy, ma'am." He nodded at Rachel and tugged at the brim of his black hat.

"Are you coming to the program tomorrow night?" Rachel asked.

Lane shook his head. "I don't think—"

Eva smiled at him reassuringly. "Of course he is. If Chase can spare him, that is. I've invited everyone at the ranch to come see the show." When she caught Rachel's thoughtful look, she added, "That's all right, isn't it?"

"Oh. Well. Of course it is. Quite all right."

Although Rachel didn't exactly sound very sure, Eva decided not to press her in front of Lane. "You can't believe how hard Miss Albright has been working on this program, Lane."

"Really." He glanced at the far window then at the chalkboard. Everywhere but at Rachel Albright. "Are you ready?" He asked Eva.

She nodded. So much for leading him into polite conversation. She supposed she should be thankful they had gotten in and out of town without him getting into a fight.

"Just let me get my hat."

She bid Rachel farewell and promised to arrive early the following evening so that she could help with the children before the program. Lane helped her onto the wagon seat, where she settled her skirt around her. Before he threaded the reins through his fingers, he reached into his shirt pocket and drew out an envelope.

"I stopped by Carberry's and checked the mail. This came for you," he told her, handing over a letter.

"Thank you." She immediately recognized John's handwriting and blessed her cousin for not putting his name above the return address. Eva held the letter along with the sheet music and rested them on her lap as Lane headed out of town.

They rode in silence for a quarter of an hour. Eva was curious about the contents of the letter, but decided to wait to read it until she had a moment alone. She studied the greening landscape as she rocked with the sway of the wagon, and realized she was beginning to treasure the familiar sight of the gently rolling hills and the mountain backdrop beyond. The snowcaps were thinning with the rush of warm spring days.

"Aren't you gonna read it?"

Eva glanced over at Lane and shoved a bobbing curl away from the corner of her eye. "I want to wait until I'm home."

He was silent for a few moments more and then, "Letter from a friend?"

"My cousin."

"She look like you?"

"She's a he. My cousin John. He works in Cheyenne."

"What's he do?"

The image of John barrelling through a rowdy crowd to restore order in the Palace of Venus came to mind. She smiled. "He's a manager, of sorts." Swiftly changing the subject she asked, "Do you think Chase will come to the school program?"

Lane laughed. "Not likely. He doesn't go to town."

Unwilling to let him know that she knew *why* Chase never went into Last Chance, Eva kept right on chatting. "I'd hoped all of you could attend. It would be a good way to get to know some of your neighbors." *And a way to let them get to know you.*

He turned to her, his hands still steady on the reins. "Don't count on it, Eva. We're not likely to go." Lane became so quiet that she thought he was through talking, until he glanced sideways at her and asked, "You had much chance to talk to anyone in town 'sides Miss Rachel?"

Eva shook her head. "Not at all. Except for the children, no one has stopped by after school, and I haven't had enough time to spare to visit in town before its time to head back and start supper. By the way, did you get the pepper I needed?''

"Yep."

"Thank you."

"Miss Eva?"

"Yes, Lane."

"Don't get your hopes up. Nobody but Orvil will be at the program. It isn't anything against you, either. We just don't go in for socializin', is all."

She wished she could drop all pretense and tell him she understood, that she knew why Chase didn't ever leave the ranch and why he wasn't accepted among the townsfolk; but she knew what Lane's admission had already cost him and didn't want to embarrass him further. Tightening her hold on the sheet music in her lap, Eva thought about the hardworking cowboys and their handsome employer at the Trail's End and decided it was about time they had a little enjoyment in their lives.

Chase sat at his usual place at the head of the long table in the kitchen and wondered if Eva was waiting for him to comment on the many changes she had made around the place. Instead of the usually bare, scarred wood, a length of bright calico fabric Rachel had given her now covered the table. She spent a morning pounding nails into the wall beside the stove to hang utensils within her reach. Chase didn't know he had owned so many gadgets. He figured he had the succession of housekeepers to thank for it.

Somehow Eva and Orvil had put their heads together and badgered Chase into agreeing to buy a dozen hens and a rooster. The damned feather-brained fowl had crowed every morning at three causing him to toss and turn until it was time to get out of bed. During the long dark hours before dawn, his mind was filled with thoughts of Eva.

"This sure is good, Miss Eva," Jethro told her as he wiped the last bit of brown gravy off his plate with the remains of a biscuit.

Ned, whose wound had become a bright red scar on his

head, ear, and lower jaw, chimed in, "Ain't nothin' you cook ever tastes bad, ma'am."

"Thank you gentlemen," Eva said, executing a half-curtsy and then pausing beside the stove to glance over her shoulder with a smile. When her eyes flashed in his direction, Chase tried to look away and failed miserably. He longed to go to her, to run his hands through her copper curls, to bend over her while she stood at the stove. He would nuzzle her ear with a kiss and whisper sweet words of . . .

"Do you still want someone to ride out to check the west pasture tonight?"

Chase looked up and found Ramon watching him intently from the opposite end of the table as he waited for an answer. His foreman's dark countenance was split by a slight smile. Chase didn't look away, but met Ramon's teasing stare head on and dead serious.

"I think it would be a good idea."

Eva crossed the room and paused beside him, waiting to see if he had anything more to say. When he fell silent, she said, "I was hoping everyone would be around. I have something special planned for tonight."

An uneasy feeling started between his shoulder blades. What was she up to? He glanced around the table. Lane was watching her with as much curiosity as everyone else. Almost afraid to know, he asked, "What were you thinking?"

He saw her take a deep breath, watched her breasts rise beneath the bodice of her unadorned pale blue gown. What tempting piece of underclothing was she wearing today? She clasped her hands at her waist and stood poised as if about to make a grand announcement.

"Since you all know I have been working with Miss Albright on the school program, I've decide to invite you to my final rehearsal."

Chase didn't give anyone a chance to answer. "We can't come."

Eyes still wide and hopeful, she insisted, "Oh, yes you

can. Because it happens to be tonight. In the sitting room.''

Lane's fork clattered to the table. "All those school kids are coming here tonight?"

Stunned, Chase shuddered at the possibility of Eva having invited strangers into his house without asking.

Eva laughed. "Of course not. It's *my* rehearsal. I'm going to play the songs and ask all of you to listen. And—" she paused theatrically, "I've made a wonderful chocolate cake which I'll serve after you've all found a place to sit in the other room."

No one moved, although the cowboys all looked to him for permission. None of them had ever been in any room but the kitchen. They waited in anticipation of his decision, as did Eva. There was no way he could deny her and not look like the villain in the little drama she had staged. Instead of speaking to her directly, he chose to focus on Ramon. "I'll ride out to the west pasture myself—after dessert."

Everyone moved at once. Spurs jangled in the crowded kitchen. Jethro and Ned bumped into each other in their haste to get into the sitting room. Orvil began to clear the dishes, quickly scraping the few scraps into the slop bucket. Lane shoved back from the table, shook his head with a half-smile, but followed behind the others. Finally, Chase found himself alone with Eva as she took down a stack of mismatched plates for the cake. Intending to help, he reached around her, using the opportunity to get close enough to inhale the delicate scent of lilacs as he brushed shoulders with her.

"What's this all about, Eva?"

"Why, nothing at all," she said quickly, blinking twice.

He watched her eyelashes as the thick fringes of copper and gold brushed her glowing skin. The dusting of freckles across the bridge of her nose tempted him to kiss her.

She licked her bottom lip and continued to stare up at him. "I really do need one final rehearsal. Besides, you all work so hard that I thought it would be nice if you could relax awhile together."

He hesitated so long that she dropped her gaze. "If you would rather I just do the dishes and not take the time away from my duties then I—

He sighed. No matter what he felt about the impromptu concert, it was getting so he could deny her nothing. "You might be right. The men could use a little entertainment."

"Maybe you'll all come to the show at the school tomorrow night, too?"

He backed up a step. "Now just a minute here—"

"I'm sorry," she said immediately. The door slammed as Orvil walked in after feeding Curly. She smiled at Chase. "We'll talk about that later. For now, just go on in with the others and Orvil and I will serve the cake."

Chase knew when he was bested and left her just as she was drawing a long knife through a mouth-watering chocolate cake.

Within minutes he and the others had inhaled the cake and even asked for second helpings. Now, as Chase glanced around the crowded room, he watched the men sitting on the few pieces of furniture and the floor as they balanced cups of steaming coffee. Ned and Jethro were enraptured by Eva, who sat at the organ playing tune after tune while Lane turned the pages of the sheet music when she nodded.

Even with Eva in the room, the walls soon closed in on him. He vacated his chair and paced to the open door. Once there, he leaned back against the door frame and stared out into the yard, drinking in the night air. It was a bright, moonlit spring night. The music swelled around him until it seemed even the cicadas were humming in accompaniment. He crossed his arms over his chest and watched as Eva smiled up at Lane, and the song ended before Chase expected. Unable to move, compelled not to look away, he found Eva watching him from across the room. Their gazes held. She was smiling into his eyes. Her open, trusting expression flooded him with warmth and a deep sense of belonging, the likes of which he had never known.

He wanted to respond, wanted to return her smile, to let her know how much he had come to care for her and about her. He couldn't look away any more than he could permit himself to do more than stare. His emotions were locked in a prison as strong as any with iron bars.

Seated at the organ with her sky-blue gown heightening the color of her eyes to turquoise, she was a joy to watch, at ease with herself and comfortable performing for the others. In that instant, he realized that if he had the power to do anything, he would fight to keep the light and love that sparkled in her eyes there forever.

The thought of being the one to extinguish that glow kept him from telling her about his past. He was amazed that she had not returned from one of her trips to town ready to confront him about his prison sentence. Perhaps God was laughing at him again, purposely hiding the truth from Eva until she became so entrenched in his heart that his pain would be even greater when she finally left.

Chase concentrated on the wondrous sight of her in the lamplight that gilded her shining hair. She held herself erect, her shoulders even; her full breasts high and proud. Her long, graceful hands moved rhythmically as her fingers stroked the piano keys. He wanted to feel those hands and fingers play over his body in the same sensual way they touched the keys. He wanted . . .

He wanted her.

And he wanted her bad.

Chase shoved away from the door frame and walked out before she noticed the desire burning in his eyes.

The cool, bluish cast of the moon's light offered little comfort.

When she watched Chase disappear across the porch, Eva felt her smile falter for the first time that evening. Trained to be a good trouper, she kept on smiling until the last verse of "Listen to the Mockingbird" ended. Lane closed the music and announced that he was going after more cake. Ned called out, "Do you know, 'Buffalo Gals' Miss Eva?"

Preoccupied with Chase's sudden departure, she heard

only the last half of the question, but realized what Ned had said. She struck up a rousing rendition of the tune that she had kicked up her heels to three times a night. The men broke into song. After they had repeated all the verses four times, she finished with a flourish and gently reminded them again of the program tomorrow night—if Chase gave them leave to attend, she added.

Anxious to slip out after Chase, she was surprised when the usually taciturn Ramon paused beside the organ. When she gathered her skirt to stand, he reached down and took her hand, helping her to her feet.

"Gracias, Señorita, for a most enjoyable evening."

She had never had occasion to speak to the man alone. "Thank you for saying so Ramon."

He nodded.

She continued. "Sometimes I get the feeling you don't care for me very much. Do you have a reason?"

One of his dark brows rose slightly. She sensed he was choosing his words carefully. "Let me just say there are reasons I distrusted you in the beginning, Señorita."

Did he know who she was? Eva fought to hide her fear. "And now?"

"I am reminded of an old saying."

"Which is?"

"*Caras vemos, pero corazones no sabemos.*"

Eva crossed her arms beneath her breasts and glanced toward the door. Chase had not yet reappeared. "I'm afraid I speak very few words in your language, Ramon." *And most of those should not be used in polite company.*

"Faces we see, but hearts we do not know, Señorita."

"How very true," she said softly. "Hearts we do not know."

He left the room without further comment, and Eva walked across the bare pine floor, her heels ringing out in the stillness. She stepped onto the porch and spotted Chase by the corral. He was standing inside the fence, saddling the big bay horse he seemed to favor most.

He was not that far away. Eva knew if she hurried she

could catch him before he left, but she lingered to ask herself why she was in such an all-fired hurry to be alone in the dark with Chase Cassidy. She knew the answer, just as she knew she could not control her growing need for him. She sighed and nervously ran her palms down the front of her skirt. Frustrated, unwilling to go beyond the bounds of propriety and perhaps make a complete fool of herself, Eva went back inside.

Once she was in her room, she let her hair down and brushed out her tangled curls as best she could, changed into her night dress, then opened the top drawer where her letter from John lay hidden beneath her undergarments.

Earlier, she had tucked the letter away as a gift to give herself later. She waited all evening and now the moment had come. She climbed into bed and carefully opened the envelope.

> *Dear Eva,*
> *All the girls miss you, but not as much as me. Quincy is steaming mad about the damages and says you owe him two hundred dollars. I know you don't have the money but I think you better send along anything you can spare. He's been threatening to come after it himself but I won't tell him where you are. I'll be sending your things on to you soon.*

Eva glanced up and crushed the letter to her breast. Someone was walking through the kitchen and stopped just outside her door. She held her breath. Was it Chase? Would he knock? She hoped not, certain that whatever he asked of her tonight, she would be more than willing to give.

The footsteps moved on. Her heart was still beating at double time, but she returned to her letter.

I'll be sending your things on to you soon. She read the line again with dismay. What would she do if John sent anything incriminating? She hit her forehead with the heel of one hand. Good lord, what if he sent Chester? How in the world would she explain away a mummy?

"Oh, John, please don't," she whispered.

The letter crackled as she smoothed it over her lap and read on.

> *Your mother wrote. She wants to know where you are, too. I'll write again soon. Until then I remain your loving cousin, John.*

Eva got up and returned the brief letter to the envelope and shoved it into her top drawer beneath her underclothes. Her mother wanted to know where she was? Did that mean John had written to tell Esther that she was no longer working with him?

She groaned aloud and continued to pace. Dear, dear, big hearted, pea-brained John. By now he had probably told the elder entertaining Eberharts everything they wanted to know. If she was lucky, they would only write to her. She could always explain away a letter from very distant relations.

But what if they should show up at the ranch? How was she going to explain the resurrection of her dearly departed mother?

Chapter Eleven

Cantering toward the sunset, Chase squinted at the setting sun, a perfect glowing orb that was about to slide behind the mountains. In a few hours, Miss Albright's school program would begin and Eva would realize neither he nor any of the others were going to show up. He knew she would be disappointed.

He didn't like the way knowing that made him feel.

Silhouetted a few yards away, Ramon knelt beside the carcass of another dead calf. Not far away, Ned had roped and tied the mama cow to a tree and had begun milking her distended udder to ease her pain. Chase reined in near Ramon and dismounted.

Ramon stood up. He was as tall as Chase, his skin tanned to a deep nut brown. "Does it seem to you, amigo, that these wolves are the smartest around?"

Chase stared down at the dead calf, the seventh killed in as many days. The carcass was torn and bloody. Ravens chided them from nearby pines, angry at the men who had disrupted their macabre dining.

"Yesterday they found three calves dead in the north pasture. Today, this one. We've poisoned all the carcasses—"

"And taken only one timberwolf."

Chase let out a long, exhausted sigh. He was sick to death of all the never-ending, back-breaking work with nothing to show for it. It was bad enough the Trail's End was hemmed in by some of the biggest cattle outfits in Montana. Nearly all the money he had left had gone into new Hereford stock, and now seven calves had been lost. He felt worn out as an old bull that had been mired in a bog too long.

"Whoever did this does a hell of a job making it look like a wolf attack. I think it's time we faced the fact that somebody's trying to ruin us." The admission hurt like hell, but what hurt worse was that there wasn't all that much to lose. It wasn't that he wanted or needed much— the small spread would provide enough to live on, but he had hoped to build up the place up for Lane.

"Who do you think is responsible?"

Chase laughed, but the sound was not one of mirth. "It could be anyone in town who up and decided they don't want a jailbird for a neighbor anymore."

"You're nearest neighbor is six miles away, amigo. Perhaps one of the cattle barons wants your land."

Slapping the ends of his reins against his gloved palm, Chase watched what was left of the sun shrink to a mere flash on the horizon. He turned back to Ramon and shoved his hat onto the crown of his head. "Be sure to tell the men to stay armed and alert when they're away from the ranch house."

"The boy?"

Chase nodded. "Lane, too, but I want him to wear his gun only when he's at the ranch, not in town. I have a feeling whoever is up to something isn't going to leave it at this." He thought of Eva and her many trips back and forth into town the past two weeks. Orvil was to drive her into town tonight. They may have already left the ranch.

"And what of you?" Ramon asked.

A shake of his head answered the foreman's question. "I swore the day I walked out of the penitentiary that I would never strap on a gun again and I meant it."

"Even to protect yourself?"

"It'll only give some idiot an excuse to start something the way that boy did with Lane." Chase frowned, staring around him. In the gathering gloom, it was easy to imagine danger lurking behind every tree or crop of scrub brush.

As if reading his mind, Ramon reminded him, "The Señorita kept us all at the ranch last night."

"You still think that her showing up here was more than a coincidence?"

Ramon shrugged. "I was beginning to change my mind, but your problems arrived when she did."

More than you know. Chase shook his head. The image of Eva's bright eyes and sweet smile came to him, a startling reminder of the intense need he felt in her presence. They called him a thief, and yet Eva Edwards had easily worked her way into his life and stolen his heart.

"You, more than anyone, should know better than to convict someone without proof," Chase said. "You served five years in prison for a crime you never committed."

"There is no need to remind me," Ramon told him. "I was beginning to believe she had nothing to do with this, but—"

"Hold on to that belief a while longer, my friend. I'll find out if she's connected to anyone from my past." If indeed Eva was not what she seemed, if she was somehow connected to any of the men he had helped to convict, it was his responsibility to discover the truth.

"How?"

Chase pulled a faded blue bandanna out of his pocket and rubbed the back of his neck. "If I have to, I'll come right out and ask her."

The one-room schoolhouse, with its open-beamed, high-pitched roof, was filling up fast. Eva watched the townsfolk file in and noticed immediately the crowd was nothing like her usual audience. These were not drunken miners and cowboys out for a night on the town—they were farmers, ranchers, merchants, and their wives. Last Chance was not a wealthy town, but tonight everyone was dressed in their finest, from simple calico to silk gowns adorned with a few touches of elegance—a broach here, a bit of fine lace there.

Extra benches had been constructed and donated for the program by Harold Higgens's father, owner of the Last

Chance Lumber and Feed Store. His generosity was proclaimed by a handlettered sign tacked above the chalkboard. As the townsfolk gathered and squeezed into every available space, his handiwork was much appreciated.

Rachel had directed Eva to take a seat in the front row the minute she arrived. In a glance, she realized that if Lane or anyone from the ranch did not appear soon, they would have nowhere to sit. The storekeeper, Millie Carberry, greeted her with a slight nod, then shifted to whisper to a stern-faced woman beside her. Eva looked away.

She recognized Stuart McKenna as he moved through the crowd. The sheriff was a good four inches taller than anyone in the room. He was wearing the same leather vest and striped woolen trousers he had on the day of Lane's altercation in the middle of Main Street. He was headed in her direction.

McKenna paused at the end of the bench. "Miss Edwards." Hat in hand, he tipped his head in her direction and then smiled over at Rachel. "Miss Albright."

Eva watched Rachel blush a deep crimson as she returned the sheriff's smile. If she was to guess, Eva would say he was in his early thirties, probably around Chase Cassidy's age. It wasn't altogether impossible that he might be smitten with the pretty school teacher.

"Would you like to sit down, Sheriff?" Eva asked, offering to give up her seat so that he might sit close to where Rachel directed.

"No, thanks. I'm going to stand by the door, in case I need to get out of here in a hurry."

She frowned. "Are you expecting some kind of trouble?"

"Not at all, ma'am. It's just an old habit." He paused quite a while, then lowered his voice and asked, "How are things out at the Cassidy place?"

She felt her spine stiffen involuntarily and wondered at the newfound protectiveness in her that flared when the Cassidys were mentioned. "Things are going just fine, Sheriff. In fact, we had a little sing-along last night. It was most enjoyable." She folded her hands on her lap as prim as a preacher's wife at a prayer meeting.

"A sing-along, you say?"

"Exactly."

"I would have like to have seen that," he said in a slow drawl.

"Next time I'll have to invite you."

"See that you do." He tipped his hat and moved on.

Eva looked up and caught Rachel watching him as he walked away.

Five minutes before the start of the show she resigned herself to the fact that no one from Trail's End except Orvil would be in attendance, and no matter how much she encouraged him, he refused to budge from a standing position near the back door.

Not only was the room full, but the transformation in the students was amazing. Dressed in their Sunday go-to-meeting best, yesterday's motley gathering of bedraggled urchins had been primped, combed, and spit-shined into a chorus of apple-cheeked cherubs. An overabundance of hair tonic flattened cowlicks and plastered down parts. And, although most of the parents had avoided any show of welcome toward Eva, each of the children had greeted her as warmly as they did Rachel.

Lulabelle Thompson, one of the oldest girls, looked prim and proper in a ruffled gingham dress. She had even curtsied, then kissed Eva on the cheek.

"Aren't you excited, Miss Eva?" the girl asked, her long brown hair wound into tight bobbing ringlets. "I feel like I have a whole netful of butterflies trapped in my stomach."

Paralyzing stage fright was something Eva had never experienced in her life, but a feeling of excitement did send her blood racing before every show. "I think I know what you mean," she commiserated. "I have to play the piano without a mistake tonight."

Lulabelle grabbed her hand and squeezed. "Oh, I just *know* you'll do it perfectly."

As Eva thanked her, the girl noticed the empty seat Eva

had vacated. "Is anyone from *your* family coming to watch you?"

Eva's heart sank. She knew better than hope Chase would come to town; it was impossible to forget the brooding expression she saw in his dark eyes when he watched her play the organ last night.

She sighed and shook her head. "No, my family is far away," she explained. "But my friend Orvil drove me into town, and he's watching from the back of the room."

They broke apart as Rachel gathered the students and herded them into formation at the front of the room. The taller children stood in the back row, and the shortest, which included the six- and seven-year-olds, stood on a small riser in front so that they could be seen over the heads of the first few rows of the audience.

"I think we should start," Rachel whispered to Eva as she gave her charges a final once over. "Where's Harold?"

Eva swiveled around on the piano stool and noticed the empty space in the front row of the chorus. It gaped as wide as the space between Harold's two front teeth.

"He was here a minute ago," Eva whispered back. "I saw him come in with his family."

Sure enough, the elder Higgens along with an assortment of grandparents and aunts and uncles were all seated in the second row waiting for their precious Harold to perform. Eva drew back her skirt and glanced down at the floor beside the piano, but there was no sign of him.

Rachel began to wring her hands. She stepped close to the assembled chorus and whispered, "Has anyone seen Harold?"

"Harold peed his pants. He's hidin' in the coat room," little Nancy Jenkins volunteered in a piping squeak that carried over the noise in the room.

Titters and chuckles swept through the gathering, as those who had heard, whispered in explanation to those who had not. Mrs. Higgens, whose brassy, carrot-red hair identified her as Harold's mother, arose with all the aplomb she could muster under the circumstances and worked her

way to the aisle. She left the room like a ship under full
steam. Everyone continued to whisper and talk among
themselves until she returned a few moments later with
Harold in tow. She deposited him in the front row of the
chorus and returned to her seat. Eva noticed the angelic
way he posed with his hands clasped over the front of his
pants. She bit her cheeks to keep from laughing and, with
a last glance at Orvil who stood near the open double doors,
she turned back to the piano.

It wasn't until she was into the chorus of the first song
that her excitement deflated to true disappointment. She had
so wanted Chase to appear tonight, so hoped that with her
help he might begin to mingle with the townsfolk again.
He had paid for his crimes and shouldn't have to hide forever.

She had not even seen him before she and Orvil left that
afternoon. Feeling guilty about not being there to serve supper to the men, she left a huge pot of stew in the warming
oven along with biscuits and two apple pies. As Orvil drove
over the last rise, Eva kept glancing back to see if perhaps
Jethro, Ned, or Lane would catch up and accompany them
into town.

Eva hammered out a chorus of "Go Tell Aunt Rhody."
Most of the children managed to appear appropriately sad
while they warbled, "She died in the mill pond, she died
in the mill pond, she died in the mill pond, standing on her
head."

In midsong, she sensed a movement that translated itself
as nervous rustling and whispers. Eva glanced around. Her
fingers faltered on the keys, but she recovered, missing only
a beat, which was a miracle with her heart beating so hard
it nearly drowned out the music. Chase hovered just inside
the open doorway with a small bouquet of red, pink, and
blue wildflowers in his hand. Unexpected tears stung her
eyes. She looked away.

Forced to change the tune, she concentrated on finding
the correct piece before she glanced up. Chase hadn't
moved. Sheriff McKenna leaned back against the wall,

arms folded, not two paces to Chase's right. The lawman was watching him intently. Orvil was smiling from ear to ear.

Longing to run to Chase, greet him, usher him in and help put him at ease, Eva could do nothing but wait while Rachel announced the next song, ''Down in the Valley.''

She did not begin until she caught Chase's eyes, then nodded, nearly imperceptibly so, to her empty seat in the front row. Millie Carberry's head snapped around like a flag when the wind changes direction. One or two others followed suit and soon a low hush of whispers filled the schoolroom.

Eva played louder, hoping to drown out the whispers and draw attention back to the children. Puzzled, Rachel glanced over her shoulder at Eva. She followed Eva's glance to the back door and recognizing Chase Cassidy, whipped around and led the chorus with renewed vigor.

Within seconds, nearly everyone in the room was aware of Chase Cassidy's presence. They turned back and forth, alternately listening to the children and craning their necks to see what he would do next. Finally, when Eva felt so tense, she thought she might scream, she looked up. Her heart lodged in her throat. Chase was slowly making his way up the aisle to the front of the room.

Instead of the usual trail-weary clothing he most often wore, he had donned gentlemanly apparel that she had never seen on him. A clean white shirt accented his suntanned face and raven black hair. A slim, black bow tie closed the shirt collar at his throat and, instead of his usual denims, he wore black wool pants and a vest. A tall black hat replaced his familiar buff Stetson.

Once he started down the center aisle between the crowded desks and benches, Chase never halted. Nor did he look anywhere but at Eva. As if her gaze was a lifeline guiding him through troubled waters, she never once looked down, but finished the song without glancing at the music. She was afraid to look away from him, afraid that to do so would leave him unprotected and vulnerable.

She would not abandon him.

Not when closing such a short distance between them meant he would have to travel so very far.

Finally, he slipped into the place she had vacated at the end of the bench and awkwardly held the flowers in his lap. Like the other men in the room, he took off his hat and set it on his knee. Once seated, he broke his connection with Eva's gaze and concentrated on the front wall at a point just above the children's heads. His tan had deepened nearly three shades.

Eva dropped her gaze, but minutes later again found Chase watching her intently. She blushed furiously and smiled down at him. She wanted the crowd to disappear, wanted to be alone with him, to thank him and let him know that she would never forget what he had done for her that night. She wanted to apologize, too. She never guessed what it would cost him to walk into the crowded schoolhouse.

The crowd began to break up after the final song. Members of the audience stood together in small groups congratulating each other on their children's success. Others tried to work their way forward to thank Rachel. One weary-eyed young mother with faded blond hair, a babe in arms and a toddler clinging to her worn calico skirt, talked to Rachel and then complimented Eva. No one else spoke to her.

One by one, the well wishers began to single out Rachel, obviously snubbing Eva. She waited a moment more, until it was apparent that everyone was actually avoiding her. She searched the room for Chase. When she spotted him, he was moving through the crowd, headed for the door. A path spontaneously cleared for him, but no one said a word. Nor did anyone make eye contact with him.

Eva started after him and noticed the forgotten bouquet lying on the bench. She snatched the flowers up and hugged them tight. Working her way through the crowd, she moved faster when she saw him disappear through the door. Millie Carberry efficiently stopped Eva by stepping into her path.

Millie smiled, but there was little warmth behind it. "That was a real good show, Miss Edwards."

Distracted, Eva tried to see which way Chase had gone once he stepped outside. "Thank you so much but—"

"I don't think anybody in these parts has seen Chase Cassidy but once or twice since he came back. You must have some kind of influence on him, gettin' him to show his face here tonight." The pinch-faced woman leaned closer, inspecting Eva as if she were a strange new strain of bug.

"Makes one wonder what she had to do to get a man like that to follow her around like a pup," someone behind Millie whispered.

Eva nudged the storekeeper aside. A tall, buxom woman in her forties stood there, staring snootily down at Eva.

Weighing everything she wanted to say, censoring the saloon-tested vocabulary she could have used, Eva clutched the flowers and coolly smiled back. "Where I come from, Mrs. Carberry, a true lady would never even entertain such thoughts."

"Well, I never—"

"Excuse me." Shaking with anger, Eva walked past the gaping women.

Sheriff McKenna stopped her at the door. "What's Cassidy doing here?"

"It seems he just can't resist a school program, Sheriff. He told me so this morning."

"If Chase even looks like he's going to cause any trouble tonight, I'll lock him up faster than you can sneeze, little lady."

"I'm quite certain he only came here to see the program and escort us home."

McKenna glanced knowingly at Orvil, who had protectively moved up behind her. "I hope so."

She walked out without another word and with Orvil on her heels. Eva stopped short at the top of the stairs and tried to spot Chase in the darkness. Near a picket line between two trees, she recognized his white shirt front, luminous in the moonlight. He was untying his horse.

Eva glanced over her shoulder. "I'm going to get Chase. I'll meet you by the wagon, Orvil."

She picked up her skirt and began to run toward the man standing alone in the shadows. Eva couldn't see his face but she felt him watching as she hurried across the school yard. When she reached him, she had to stop to catch her breath. She moved as near as she dared, longing to touch him, to comfort him, to make up for every single person in the school room who had turned away, or worse yet, stared at him with open contempt.

He didn't speak, nor did he move. Chase stood beside his horse, head down, reins in hand, wishing he had mounted up and rode out before she ever caught up to him. The charade was over. He should feel relieved, he told himself. He should be glad she saw for herself what a pariah he had become. He wasn't good enough to wipe her shoes, let alone have her living on his ranch.

"Chase?" Eva kept perfectly still, fighting to find the right words. She reached out, almost touched his shoulder, but then let her hand drop.

With his back to her, he stared up at the moon through the spring buds on the branches of the oak tree. "I'm so sorry, Eva." It was all he knew how to say, all he could say.

His apology was so softly spoken she barely heard it. It tore at her heartstrings. "*You're sorry?* I'm the one who should be sorry. After all, I badgered you into coming. I should have known—" Aware of what she had admitted without meaning to, she cut her words off abruptly. He turned on her, whipped around to stare down at her. His expressive dark eyes were hidden beneath the shadow of his hat brim, but she could feel them piercing her all the same.

"What do you mean, you *should* have known? Known what?"

"I—"

He stepped closer, bearing down on her. His heart was thundering. He fought to keep his hands from visibly shaking.

"*What*, Eva? What did you know?"

She glanced around to see if anyone could hear them. There was still a knot of well-wishers near the door, but no one had crossed the school yard yet. Unable to meet his eyes, she stared down at the flowers in her hand. The stems were as bruised as her heart felt.

Eva said, "I know that you've only been out of prison a year." She heard him sigh, saw his shoulders slump as if he were bearing a great weight on them.

Chase felt as old as dirt and as worn as an old shoe. "How long have you known?"

She stalled. "How long?"

He nodded.

"Since the day Rachel brought Lane home after he ran away."

"*That* long? And you didn't let on? You went right on pretending you didn't know?" It galled him to think that he had been walking around trying to decide when and how to tell her about his prison sentence while she had known about it all along.

She took offense at the anger laced through his tone. "Don't you think *not* telling me *yourself* was just as much of a pretense?"

"I don't need this." He was never one to explain his actions to another living soul, let alone a woman whose very nearness was slowly driving him crazy. He turned around, put his hand on the pommel of his saddle.

She reached out and grabbed his shoulder. "Chase, stop."

He could have shaken her off as easily as he might a mosquito, but her touch was so gentle, yet so insistent, that he turned around. When he stared down at her hand where it rested on his sleeve, she let go.

"I guess there's nothing left to say, is there, Eva?"

"What do you mean?"

"It's pretty obvious. You've seen what the good folk of Last Chance think of me," he waved a hand in the direction of the school. "Maybe you can stay with Miss Albright until you find another job."

She tried to comprehend what he was, saying. "But, I don't want another job."

"Then you must be crazy. No decent woman in her right mind would want to work for a man like me."

No decent woman? She almost laughed aloud. "Chase, listen. I know enough about you to believe that you must have had good reason for what you did years ago."

Her trust frightened him. He didn't deserve it.

"A *good* reason? Can you think of a *good* reason for riding with a gang of murderers, thieves, and cutthroats? Can you think of a *good* reason for shooting men down in the street? Wake up, Eva. If you're waiting for me to tell you I'm some sort of hero like Robin Hood, forget it."

Years ago he thought he had reason enough, but since then he had plenty of time in territorial prison to think things through. It was easy to look back and see what an idiot he had been. Hell, if he was one of the good citizens of Last Chance, he would probably have snubbed himself tonight.

She sensed his trembling from a foot away, felt his pent up rage and wished to God there was something she could do or say to make everything all right. Eva glanced over her shoulder. The crowd was breaking up. Children were squealing, racing about playing tag in the moonlight while their parents made their way to the wagons and other conveyances drawn up around the school yard.

He had a sudden urge to hurt her, to show her he didn't deserve her trust, her caring. "What is it, Eva? Is this the closest you've ever come to the wrong side of the law? Does it intrigue you to know that I've spent time behind bars? Do you find that appealing?"

"Stop it."

"Does danger excite you?" He reached out and grabbed her by the shoulders. "Is that why you kissed me the other day? Did you decide you wanted to do something daring before you hightail it off to work on some other ranch with a more *respectable* employer?''

He was tempted to push harder, to go all the way and kiss her right here in front of God and everybody, to frighten and humiliate her so badly that she would run for safety.

''No . . . Chase, please. Can't we talk about this like two civilized people? Please. Drive me home.''

Hands fisted at his sides, he weighed her proposal as he fought to calm his temper. Not two steps away, Eva waited for an answer. She had been nothing but kind to Lane, to Orvil, and the others, and certainly to him, even after she knew the truth. She didn't deserve to have him take his anger out on her.

''Come on.'' Without a backward glance, he started across the school yard, leading his horse toward the spot where Orvil waited beside the open wagon.

Eva realized what he was doing. She hurried to catch up, nearly tripped, and dropped the flowers. After scooping them up, she hurried to fall into step beside him. Deciding that silence was the better part of valor, she said nothing while he turned his horse over to Orvil and instructed him to be careful in the dark.

The elderly cowboy was happy to oblige and mounted up.

Eva stood beside the wagon, waiting for a hand up. Chase started around to the other side, realized she was still standing there, and stopped. He stared at her a second, then returned to her side. With a quick glance around, he took her hand to steady her while she climbed aboard.

Eva waited, clutching the weary bouquet, while he climbed up and took the reins. It was enough just to sit beside him, to ride in silence, shoulder to shoulder as he expertly headed the team in the direction of the ranch. Under other circumstances she would have been content to take pleasure in the ride, to study the moonlight and shadows as they played across the land, to let the gentle breeze, scented with spring blossoms, ruffle her hair. But not to-night. Tonight she intended to find out as much about Chase Cassidy as he would share.

They had gone at least half a mile before she said, "Tell me how you ended up in prison."

"I rode with Hank Reynolds's gang for two years."

"His name means nothing to me."

He turned on her, unable to curb his anger any longer. "No, but then, you're not from around these parts, are you Miss Edwards?"

She was glad she couldn't see his shadowed eyes. It was enough to feel the angry tension radiating from him. She left the Palace, because she wouldn't allow herself to be man-handled. She wasn't willing to allow Chase to intim-idate her now.

"No, I'm *not* from around here, so you'll have to ex-plain—from the beginning."

"There's nothing to explain. After you get your things together, I'll have Orvil drive you into town tomorrow."

"Does this mean I'm *fired?*"

"It means your free to go. I'll pay you for the work you've done this month." *Don't argue. Take the money and go, Eva. Get out while there's still time to save your reputation.*

He was so anxious to be rid of her that for a moment she was afraid he might have heard something about her own hidden identity. "Are you letting me go because of something I've done?"

Ramon's suspicions came back to Chase in a rush. What was she getting at? What was she afraid of? Could she be working for someone who was out to ruin him? Chase pulled back on the reins and the team stopped. "What do you mean, something *you've* done?"

She shrugged and fiddled with the flower petals. "You're certainly anxious to see the last of me."

She was so open, so giving that he was ashamed to even hint that he suspected her of anything. In his heart, Chase wanted to believe she would never do anything to harm him. Nor could he her. He sighed.

"I'm trying to make it easy on you, Eva. I didn't think you would want to stay on after what happened back there."

"Who gives a fig for what anyone thinks?"

"I do . . . where you're concerned. And I'd think you would be, too."

"Don't worry about me, Chase Cassidy. You should be thinking about yourself and Lane."

"You're crazy."

"So my mother used to say."

Eva wondered if it wouldn't be better to just come right out and tell him that she was not the respectable lady down on her luck from Philadelphia that she pretended to be. But the longer she watched him sit there in the middle of the open plain stewing over the fact that she had not told him that she knew about his past, the more she became convinced that to tell him the truth about herself now would only compound the situation.

He was angry, not to mention humiliated. This was no time to tell him she had duped him into feeling sorry for her with a few tears and a bit of melodramatic overacting.

She didn't want to push him over the edge.

His hand rested on his thigh. Eva reached out and put her hand atop his. He looked down at her hand as if it were a rattler, but he didn't move to break the connection. The feel of his flesh beneath her touch was warm, tantalizing.

"Chase, tell me about it. Please. I want to understand."

He looked over at Eva, so innocent, so concerned as she primly sat there with his pitiful little offering of flowers on her lap. When he spoke, he sounded emotionless—even to himself—as if someone else was telling the story.

"I wasn't much older than Lane when my parents died. I had to work the ranch and look after my sister, Sally. Trouble was, Sally wasn't like you. She was wild and headstrong. She fancied men from the time she knew the difference between boys and girls.

"One summer, when she was fifteen, she got pregnant

by one of the cowhands. He rode off and left her behind, and after a time, I had both Sally and Lane to look after.''

Eva felt that he had relaxed somewhat. She lifted her hand, breaking contact, but continued to sit shoulder to shoulder. Chase lifted the reins and set the horses walking at a slow pace while he continued.

"One day I was out working the far range when three men rode up to the ranch house. They raped and murdered Sally. She managed to kill one of them before she was shot in the head.''

"Oh, my God, Chase.'' Suddenly, a vision of Lane as a child came to mind. "What about Lane?''

Chase swallowed hard, then cleared his throat. "He saw it all, but he closed up and couldn't tell me what the men looked like, or anything about them.''

Eva gasped. No wonder Lane was so troubled—and so very volatile.

Chase nodded. "I buried Sally, picked up the boy and took him to a nearby ranch that was owned by a widow named Auggie Owens. I told her what had happened, asked her to notify the law and to watch Lane for me. I set out to track them down and intended to come right back.''

"And being a friend of yours, she agreed.'' Eva finished for him.

He shook his head. It was as hard to tell this part as it was to talk about Sally's murder. "We weren't friends.'' The wagon lurched as it hit a pothole in the road. Their shoulders bumped together. Eva righted herself. "I was so bent on revenge that I left Lane with a stranger.''

"But I'm sure she—''

His words were whip-quick and they stung. "Not everybody's like you, Eva. Not everyone is good, and kind, and caring. As far as I can tell, she must have been terrible to Lane. He's never talked about it, but the boy I found when I finally came home wasn't the child I left behind.''

"He had witnessed his mother's murder,'' she reminded him.

Her childhood had been hectic, far from normal, but

there was one thing she had always been sure of—she had been loved. Eva shivered. "Do you think there's more, could this . . . Auggie have been cruel to him?"

"I don't know. She never once took him to town. When they built the school in Last Chance, Auggie Owens kept him home. When I showed up to get him, I found him living out there all alone, filthy, hungry, and little more civilized than an animal. Auggie up and disappeared the minute she got word I was out of prison."

"She moved out and left everything behind?"

"She didn't have anything but the clothes on her back and a tumbledown ranch house. Occasionally, she hired drifters to work a few head of cattle or put in a garden. She had nothing to leave behind but a run-down ranch house . . . and Lane. Sold the land to one of the big cattle outfits and took off." He fell into contemplative silence.

Eva was afraid Chase had closed himself off again and would refuse to go on. "You're lucky she didn't take Lane with her. And you can't blame yourself. You couldn't have known what would happen to him."

"That's exactly why I should never have left him in the first place. I dropped him off like some abandoned puppy. I'll never forgive myself for it and I don't think Lane will, either. And I can't blame him."

"Did you ever find the men who killed your sister?"

He shifted on the hard seat and tried to stretch one leg. "I picked up their tracks right off, followed them into Wyoming. I barely missed them at the first stop. Town folks told me two brothers name of Hunt rode through, raising Cain. I lost the trail but kept searching."

A cruel note of self-loathing he couldn't disguise entered his tone. "I was young and stupid, bent on avenging Sally's death single-handedly. I should have given up and come home, but I was obsessed with watching them die. I picked up work. I was always good with a gun. A man alone, an angry man with a chip on his shoulder is a sure target for anybody out to prove himself. I gained a reputation as a gunfighter."

Eva stared off into the distance. He talked without emotion, as if he had been swatting flies, not killing men in cold blood. Her mind swam with the implications. He was a gunfighter who had killed in order to survive. The picture was incongruous with what she knew of him.

"But you don't even wear a gun at all now. Out of all the men on the ranch, you never put one on, nor do you carry a rifle with you."

Chase thought of the long, empty years he had spent in the Territorial Prison, the countless hours thinking about what he had done, remembering what it had been like to pull a trigger and watch a man die by his hand, even if it had been in self-defense. "I made a promise to myself in prison," he confessed, "I swore I'd never wear a gun again."

"No matter what?"

"That's right. No matter what. Nothing good can come of it."

"How did you end up in prison?"

"While I was trying to find the Hunts, I ran into a man named Hank Reynolds. He had his own run in with them a few months before. I rode along with him and his gang."

Eva tried to absorb all he was telling her. She knew he must have been distraught, that he had acted beyond reason because of what had happened to his sister.

"On my own, I wasn't getting anywhere near the Hunts. Hank knew what they looked like, I didn't. We headed into the southern half of the territory to track them down."

She could make out the long, low shape of the ranch house ahead of them. They were almost home. "What happened?"

"Reynolds set up a bank robbery on the way. His gang was supposed to be damn good at it, but I guess bad luck was still with me. Since Hank didn't know me well enough to trust me on the inside, I was posted as lookout and held the horses. Something went wrong inside the bank. A teller slipped out the back to call the law. There was a lot of confusion. On the way out of town, my horse went down as the posse was chasing us. I was arrested. Since no one inside the bank could identify me, all I was convicted of was being an accomplice.''

Eva shuddered, but not from the slight chill which had invaded the night air. ''You're lucky you even had a trial. You could have been hung by vigilantes.''

''Sometimes I think maybe—''

''Don't even say it.'' She cut him off, hoping he was not about to tell her he thought he'd be better off dead. ''What ever happened to the Hunt brothers?''

''While I was in jail, Reynolds and his men split up. Eventually, he and the Hunts shot it out one day in the middle of Coulson. They were all brought in for trial, and I was allowed to send written testimony against the Hunts. I told the court what I knew of Sally's murder. The Hunts claimed they were innocent, that she killed herself. I had no hard proof. Besides, how many people are willing to believe the testimony of a convicted man? They went to prison for lesser crimes, but didn't hang for Sally's murder.''

So much was clear to her now. Chase had been motivated by revenge. Lane's anger and hostility toward Chase stemmed from his desertion and the neglect of his guardian in his uncle's absence. The boy wanted to prove himself a man by living up to his uncle's reputation.

In silence, they drove into the yard and Chase pulled the team up before the barn. Orvil stepped out of the dark interior and immediately began to unharness the horse. He told them Ramon and the others were not in the bunkhouse yet, but still out on the range.

Eva let Chase help her down. She had collected herself enough to bid Orvil good night. As they walked toward the dark house, Chase slowed his steps and she matched hers to suit.

She rubbed her arms more from nervousness than any chill. ''Where do you suppose everyone is? I left supper for them.''

Thankful for a change of focus, Chase took a deep

breath; somehow telling Eva everything had served as a release. By the time they reached the edge of the porch, he was able to look her in the eye again.

"They're out riding the perimeter in twos."

"Searching for the wolves?"

"Wolves of sorts."

Eva paused with one foot on the step when she reached the low porch.

"Rustlers?" She had been around cowboys long enough to know all about the sneak thieves who stole cattle and altered brands until they built up their own herds.

Chase shook his head. "I wish they were rustlers. Whoever's been hitting us is bent on one thing and one thing only—running me out."

Chapter Twelve

Eva stepped up to the back door and paused with her hand on the knob. Scroungy old Curly came running across the yard with a welcoming yelp and stood panting and drooling beside her skirt hem. She scratched his head and then looked up at Chase.

"Who would want to ruin you?" she asked

"Any number of people from what I saw tonight."

She reached down and gave the spotted dog one last, absentminded pat and then turned the door knob. "What makes you think it's not really wolves?"

He followed her into the dark kitchen, took three steps to the stove and found a match in the cast-iron matchbox hanging on the wall. Chase struck a match and the flame flared to life He cupped his hand around it as he moved to the table, lifted the chimney of the oil lamp and lit the wick.

"We poisoned the last few carcasses and no more than one wolf has taken the bait. The dead calves have been sliced up, shredded to appear to have been clawed and torn by an animal, but Ramon agrees it looks more like they were killed by some two-footed snake, not wolves."

As Chase replaced the chimney, Eva laid her bouquet on the table and thought of what Ramon said to her last night. He had been suspicious of her at first, but she thought he might have changed his opinion. She reached up and slipped the long hat pin out of her hat and carefully lifted it off her hair.

"Did *you* think I might have something to do with this?"

Chase shifted uneasily in the middle of the kitchen floor.

He watched her in profile as she studied the hat in her hands. Eva reached out and straightened a feather, then a shining silk leaf. She looked up at him, waiting for an answer.

He told her the truth. "When you showed up out of nowhere, and being the type of woman you are—"

Eva nearly dropped the hat. "What type of woman is that, Mr. Cassidy?"

"You're not exactly a typical housekeeper."

"Just what is a *typical* housekeeper?"

Chase wondered how he had been backed into this discussion and how he was going to get out of it. "I can only judge by the four I've had, but they all ran pretty much the same. All I can say is, you're nothing like them."

"Don't I do as good a job?"

He glanced out the back window at the empty barnyard. They were alone in the honeyed lamplight, once more sheltered from the world in the confines of the small kitchen. Her hair appeared dark bronze in the semidarkness except where the lamplight painted the ends shining copper and gold.

Chase lowered his voice. "You do a fine job. Better than I expected from what little experience you've had cooking for a crew of men."

"Then I can stay?"

"Do you still *want* to stay?"

Staring up into his dark eyes, she knew for her own sake, and for his, that if she possessed one shred of common sense she would tell him no. But she couldn't do it.

"Yes. I want to stay."

"But you don't belong here, Eva. A woman like you would have no trouble getting a good man to marry her."

What if I don't want a good man? The thought struck her unaware. *What if the man I want is you?*

Eva clutched her hat to her breast and took a deep breath. "I didn't come here looking for a husband, Chase. I came here looking for a job, some experience working as a housekeeper. You were kind enough to oblige."

"Between you and Lane both, I didn't have much choice in the matter."

She smiled in remembrance. Their earlier discussion came back to her. "You don't suspect me of being an accomplice in all this, do you?"

Hooking his hands in his back pockets, Chase answered without pause. "No."

"Why not?"

"Because of the way you've been with Lane. The kindness you've shown Orvil and Ned. Someone who was in the house just to spy on us wouldn't have taken the time to show she cared about anyone. If your attitude around here hadn't convinced me, seeing you with those children at the schoolhouse tonight would have done it. You were so beautiful, so innocent and angelic sitting there at the piano—"

He took a step toward her, his hands still in his pockets, afraid he would reach for her, take her in his arms and never let her go.

"You glow, Eva. You shine like the sun."

His compliments embarrassed her. So did his lofty opinion of her character. She shook her head in silent protest.

"You're the one good thing that's come along in our lives in years and I don't doubt that for a moment. You're as honest as the day is long and I'd horsewhip any man who tried to tell me different, Ramon included."

Every compliment fell like a hammer blow on her heart. She had never thought her scheme would succeed so grandly. Nor had she ever played a role as well as the one she was cast in now.

She couldn't go on letting him think of her as a something she definitely wasn't. She opened her mouth to tell him the truth, then snapped it shut again. What would he do when he found out everything he thought about her was a bald-faced lie? How could she tell him and make him feel like a fool after he had just poured his heart out to her? Before she decided what course to follow, Chase abruptly turned and walked away.

"I have to go," was all the explanation he gave. The walls were closing in on him again. He could no longer stand this close and not touch her. He had to get out. Now. He paused at the back door long enough to add, "I'm going out to see about the stock."

Dumbstruck, Eva watched him make his hasty exit. She let out a long pent-up sigh, reached up to unpin her hair and shook it free. Remembering to take along her hat and flowers, she went into the bedroom and lit the lamp. Unbuttoning her jacket, Eva tossed it on the bed and began to unfasten the long row of buttons down the front of her dove-gray gown. She nearly jumped out of her skin when a knock sounded on her bedroom door.

"Eva?"

It was Chase.

Still startled by the unexpected interruption, Eva realized he had never once knocked on her door during the entire time she had been at the Trail's End. She hurried to open it. Had he changed his mind and returned to convince her to leave? Or was God tempting her with another opportunity to tell him the truth?

As she opened the door wide enough to reveal his tall, broad-shouldered frame, she remembered that the front of her gown was partially open. Her hand flew to her throat. When her fingers made contact with her bare skin, she realized she was unbuttoned all the way down to the top of her frilly saffron corset.

"Chase—"

He reached out for her with one hand and grabbed her by the nape of the neck. With the other, he shoved the door all the way open with so much force that it hit the wall. She was in his arms before she knew what was happening. Chase drew her full up against him, dipped his head and covered her lips with his. She gave him access to her mouth, felt his tongue taste and tease hers. His arms locked around her and pulled her closer. His hands traveled the length of her spine and then up to cup the back of her head. He held her immobile while his mouth slanted across hers.

Eva was lost in a heady swirl of sensation. Feeling adrift, all she could do was grab hold of his black vest and hang on. She had been kissed before, but never like this. She could feel her pulse racing. Every inch of her was tingling with need. She pressed closer, wanting him desperately, needing him more than she had ever needed anything in her life. She heard him groan low in his throat, and for a split second she was terrified that he was about to pull away.

His hands left her hair, circled her waist, then slowly slid up toward her rib cage. Eva moaned when he cupped her breasts. She slipped her arms around his neck. Still kissing her, he took two steps into the room. She didn't know what had made him come back, or why, but right now she didn't care. Chase was here, in her arms, kissing her as if his life depended on it.

The least she could do was kiss him back.

Two more steps back and Eva felt the mattress hit the backs of her knees. She gave in to the heady weakness his taste evoked and let her knees buckle. Chase's strong arms took up the slack and lowered her to the narrow bed. He pulled back, breathing as hard as if he'd just run all the way from the west pasture. Eva reached up and brushed an ebony lock of hair off his forehead. She gazed up into his equally dark eyes and read a hint of confusion overshadowed by a passion equal to her own.

Still, without a word between them, he lowered his head to kiss her again. She gave a little gasp as his fingertips brushed her skin where it rose above her corset. He traced the gentle swell of her breasts as slowly and tenderly as a blind man seeking to know her by touch. She felt her breasts swell with the rush of sensation, her nipples, already peaked, hardened until they ached for relief. She moaned again and clung to him so tightly that the movement raised her shoulders off the bed.

He slipped his hand lower. His fingertips brushed her nipple. The fact that his hand trembled slightly only added to her excitement. It gave her an intoxicating sense of power to think that merely touching her could cause Chase Cassidy, gunfighter and outlaw-turned-rancher, to lose control.

In one swift move he drew her even closer to him, her hips tight against his hard arousal. Seeking friction between them, she arched to press her mound against his hard shaft. Frustrated by the layers of skirt and petticoats, Eva made small noises of protest deep in her throat. She grabbed a handful of his shirt and began to tug at it where it disappeared beneath his waistband. She was beyond worrying that he would think she was too bold; all thought had fled when his lips left hers and he began to trail kisses along the column of her neck. He nipped her gently with his teeth as he kissed his way to her collarbone.

Eva held her breath and arched her back, offering her breast to him. He had his fingers hooked over the lace at the top of her saffron corset and was about to expose her nipple to his lips when she heard a sharp whistle and the sound of hoof beats in the yard.

She stared up at him. In a choked voice she wondered aloud, ''Who—?''

Chase raised his head and covered her mouth with the palm of his hand. ''Shh—''

He sprang up and off her before she could respond. Eva pushed herself up and yanked the bodice of her gown together, then ran her fingers through her tangled hair and shoved it back off her face. Her last glimpse of him revealed a familiar dark scowl across his features just as he closed the door.

With a glance in the direction of Eva's room, Chase grabbed his hat off the kitchen table. He walked to the back door and paused. Resting his forehead against the frame, he took a deep breath and tried to forget the image of Eva lying warm and willing across her bed. Outside he heard Ned and Jethro talking as they turned their horses into the corral. His hand shook as he reached for the doorknob.

It would be a while before he could get himself under control. His arousal slowly subsided, but his heart still raced like a wild mustang loose in his chest. He whipped the door open and stepped out into the night, gulping fresh air as he jammed his hat on his head.

Damn it, Chase Cassidy, you're like an old drunkard where that woman is concerned.

He knew he had made some stupid decisions in his lifetime. He admitted it to himself on many occasions. He had years in prison to dwell on his mistakes—but he had never lost control of his mind until he had met Eva Edwards. Because of her, he had ridden into Last Chance. Because of her, he had walked into the crowded schoolroom and faced humiliation head-on.

Because she asked it of him, he had opened up his heart and told her the secrets of his dark past—all of it—Sally's murder, his life as an outlaw, the killings, Lane. Only Ramón knew as much about him. Others could only speculate. Determined to keep his hands off of her, he had ended their earlier conversation simply by walking out of the kitchen.

He had only made it halfway to the barn when, like a man who had lost his will, he returned to the house—to Eva. When she opened the bedroom door, he could not quite believe the sight of her standing there with her dress open so far that it revealed the rise and fall of her perfect breasts above the touch of bright orange-yellow lace that teased them. Her riot of copper curls had shone like a nimbus around her radiant face. Every good intention was thrown to the wind. He had been driven, as if by a force outside himself, to take her in his arms.

Now here he was, standing on the porch in the dark, trying to collect himself enough to go find out about the danger that threatened his very existence. He was so consumed, he was obsessed. How was going to get her out of his blood?

Within minutes he saw Ned and Jethro walk out of the barn and head toward the bunkhouse. He forced himself to leave the porch, but couldn't keep from looking back at Eva's window. It was dark inside now. She had blown out the lamp.

He wondered how he was going to carry on a civil conversation with his men while his mind contemplated the way Eva must look right now tucked in bed.

Eva lay in the darkness staring at the ceiling. She reached up and traced the seam of her lips, her fingers still shaking, as she fought to memorize the taste of Chase's kiss. Her lips still felt full and slightly bruised from his passionate assault. She closed her eyes and imagined him leaning over her, remembered the feel of him as he crushed his length against her. She didn't need a mirror to know her face flamed with embarrassment; she could still feel it burning. Good heavens, he had almost kissed her breast. If not for the interruption, he would have taken her nipple into his mouth and suckled it—

As a surge of need radiated through her, Eva groaned aloud and crossed her arms over her breasts. She closed her eyes and took a deep breath.

Come morning she would have to face Chase over breakfast, both of them all too aware of what almost happened, what surely would have happened, if the men hadn't returned when they did. She might have been able to rationalize away the innocent kisses they had shared before, but not this. No. Not this. Tonight they had gone beyond mere kissing. Tonight they had been force to stop at the brink of outright lovemaking.

She reminded herself of her brief affair with Quincy Powell. The dashing gentleman gambler was beyond handsome. He was smooth, his practiced assault on a woman's senses polished to a high gloss shine by vast experience. Quincy had the look of a naughty schoolboy about him— he had no doubt been the teacher's pet. He had the ability to make a woman feel as if she was the most special, most precious, most wonderful woman in the world—at least for a night. The trouble with Quincy Powell was that he had, unfortunately, made countless women feel that way.

Eva had held out as long as she could, trying to dismiss Quincy and his charm without falling into his arms or his bed, but he had eventually worn her down. For a good three months before he convinced her to let him make love to her, he had not taken a girl to his room—at least not any that Eva knew of then. Now, she was certain he could never have remained celibate that long.

"It will be magnificent, Eva," he whispered in her ear one moonlit night after closing. They stood alone in the dark interior of the saloon with the ghostly shapes of empty card tables and chairs all around them. The air was tainted with the smell of spilled liquor and stale cigar smoke.

"Let me be the one to teach you everything there is to know about making love to a man," Quincy tempted. "Let me make your body sing with pleasure."

For weeks he had been after her, trying to convince her that she meant more to him than all his other conquests combined. Hadn't he given them all up for her? Couldn't she see that the two of them were meant to be together?

Her mind equated his words with a marriage proposal.

His definition was an altogether different one.

Standing with him in the huge room, she listened to the sounds of the night—the call of a hoot owl in the eaves of a building across the alley, the increasing rhythm of the creak of bedsprings in one of the little rooms above the stairs, the whisper of his fingertips across the satin bodice of her costume. He had waged a long and valiant campaign to win her virginity and made his appeal when she was feeling alone and vulnerable. She was certain that she was destined for a lonely life on the road, a lifetime of entertaining drunken miners and unappreciative small-town audiences.

Finally, worn down by his lavish compliments and persistence, she had given in.

And in one respect, Quincy Powell kept his word. For three weeks she lived in a world of passionate, sensual experiences. For a brief time, it had been easy to move among the patrons of the Palace of Venus and suffer catcalls and whistles knowing she was working for the man she loved.

When she danced, she danced for Quincy. He would sit

at his favorite table near the stage and smile his perfect smile at her while she performed. He kept his promise and taught her everything there was to know about making love to a man. He had, indeed, made her body sing with passion.

But after three weeks of having been singled out by Quincy Powell, Eva lost favor to a newly arrived, diminutive blonde with breasts the local patrons dubbed the Grand Tetons. She went through myriad feelings—disbelief, humiliation, intense hurt, and finally, seething anger.

The argument with Quincy was glorious. There were still a few customers who loved to tell the tale. Eva had slapped Quincy so hard his teeth rattled. That night, John forced her to tell him what was wrong. If she hadn't intervened, her cousin would have broken a chair over the randy gambler's head. She and John both quit and were upstairs packing when Quincy came crawling in to apologize.

He offered Eva twice the pay she had been getting, still a paltry amount at best, and convinced them that they would be hard pressed to find jobs, where they were both needed, that paid as well. He admitted John was the best strong-arm he had ever hired and that it would be a long time before he could replace Eva as head dancer.

For a few hours, she was tempted to rejoin the Entertaining Eberharts, but John finally convinced her that she should put her experience with Quincy Powell behind her and stay on until spring. She told Quincy she would leave as soon as the thaw came and added, in no uncertain terms, that she would never go to bed with him again, so he need not waste his breath or his time trying to convince her otherwise.

It was the slowest winter she had experienced in years.

Now, as she found herself in another dilemma, Eva sat up in bed and tossed back the covers. Barefoot, she padded over to the window and pulled the curtain back slightly to stare out into the night. In the corral just outside her window lazed a few of the horses that hadn't been turned out to pasture. Here and there the white and gray animals stood out in the moonlight. The darker ones were mere shadows against the night.

She raised the window as quietly as she could so that the gentle breeze might stir the thin, uneven curtains. As she bent down to let the draft flow over her face and hair, she heard a door slam in the bunkhouse across the barnyard. She stepped back away from the window.

Returning to the edge of the bed, Eva sat down with a sigh. Quincy had taken her virginity, but had obviously not taken her heart. Now Chase Cassidy had gained possession of it. She wondered where he had gone and strained to hear his footsteps echo in the empty house.

What would you do if he walked in right this minute?

I would be strong, she lied to herself. I would tell him to leave, that what we were doing a few moments ago wasn't decent, it wasn't right.

Sure you would, Eva. You'd fall right into his arms the way you have each and every time he's come near enough.

I can stop myself. I have to. He thinks I'm a lady—at least he did before tonight.

Maybe you'll never change. Maybe you'll never be respectable after all.

Quincy had waged a campaign and finally sweet-talked her into his arms. Chase Cassidy hadn't even had to snap his fingers. All he had to do was show her his vulnerable side, open up and tell her the truth about himself, about his years before prison, and how he had been compelled to avenge his sister.

Before Chase, she thought she wanted security, a relationship that included marriage and children and a home with a flower garden and a white picket fence. Chase Cassidy could offer few of those, and still, he had attracted her from the moment she laid eyes on him. His dark, brooding nature had drawn her like the sight of an unexplored cave, and tonight she had taken more than a few steps inside.

Eva climbed back into bed, certain of nothing, her emotions in a knot, her thoughts in a tangle—her body craving release.

*   *   *

Lane reined in beside Ramon and tried to hide his surprise as the *segundo* handed a glowing cigarette to him. He took a long drag, fought to hold back a cough and succeeded, although his eyes watered intensely. He handed the cigarette back. The open range was as quiet as a down-filled pillow except for the occasional lowing of cattle. They had split up to ride in pairs, Ned with Jethro, Lane with Ramon, all slowly patrolling the perimeter of the ranch. It would be hours before they covered the lower, more easily accessible land. Up to now, they had not seen or heard anything out of the ordinary.

Ramon sat tall in the saddle. He leaned forward, resting his forearm across the huge silver disc that crowned his saddle-horn cap. Lane had always secretly admired Ramon's traditional Mexican saddle and trappings and planned to own a rig just like it as soon as he was out on his own and making good money. Silver inlay decorated the cantle, and the cinch was tooled with an intricately executed design. The same hand-carved design decorated the front of the *tapaderos,* leather shields attached to the stirrups to protect the rider's feet, much like chaps protected their legs from thorns and brambles.

Ramon Alvarado never said much to him as a rule, but then, Alvarado never said much to anyone except Chase, period. Lane often wondered how the Mexican and his uncle had become friends. All he knew was that Ramon had shown up with Chase when his uncle returned from prison. The day the two men rode onto Auggie Owens's ranch to find him, Lane wished he had been brave enough to spit in his uncle's eye and tell him he wanted nothing more to do with him. He didn't think he could ever forgive Chase for leaving him behind.

But when Chase arrived, Lane had been so hungry, felt so alone, that he would have ridden off with the devil. Even though right now, he couldn't claim anything but the gun that had killed his mother, his stash of savings would soon grow, little by little, from the money Chase owed him for his work as a regular hand. It wouldn't be long before he could move on. The way he had it figured, he didn't owe Chase Cassidy a thing. Especially his loyalty.

Lane shifted in the saddle and let his gaze rove over the landscape. "Things are mighty quiet tonight. You think whoever it was that killed those calves figures we're on to them?"

Ramon snuffed the butt of his cigarette on the heel of his boot and then flicked it over his horse's head where it was swallowed by the dark. "Perhaps. Maybe we just haven't come across them yet." He shrugged. *"Quién sabe?"*

"Yeah. Who knows?" Lane turned his horse in the direction Ramon had started walking his mount. He pulled up beside the Appaloosa that made his own pinto seem almost dainty next to it. It was going to be a long night. He voiced the question that had been on his mind a long while. "How did you and Chase meet up?"

Ramon looked at him for a while before he answered. "We shared the same cell in the prison."

Lane didn't know what to say except, "What'd you do?"

Alvarado laughed. *"Nada."*

Concentrating on circumventing an outcropping of rocks it was a few moments before Lane commented. "They don't put people in jail for nothing."

"Do not make a bet on that, amigo."

They reached the top of a rise, a good vantage point by day. Tonight they could see the mountains in the distance, the snowcaps reflecting the moonlight, and the trees casting ink-black shadows across the silvered land. There wasn't a sign of anything but cattle and low-growing brush on the hillsides. At times it was hard to tell the difference between the two.

"What happened?" Lane persisted.

"I was in the wrong place when a posse rode into Helena looking for a Mexican who had stolen a wagon load of supplies from a miner. To them, one Mexican was the same as another. I tried to tell them I had nothing to do with it, but when they took me back to town, the witnesses claimed it was definitely me that they saw."

"Didn't you have anyone to give you an alibi?"

"My horse. But unfortunately he could not talk."

Lane laughed. "So I guess you know Chase pretty well."

"I know him enough to know he will never forgive himself for leaving you for so long."

Stunned, Lane whipped his gaze over to Alvarado. Without hesitation the man had answered the one burning question Lane had carried inside him for so long. "How—"

"How did I know what was really on your mind?" Ramon shrugged. "Sometimes your thoughts are as clear as a mountain stream."

The idea that he was so easy to read frightened Lane. There were things about his past that troubled him greatly. Dark, frightening, inexplicable things that he could not recall in detail—things his mind refused to call up.

Ramon continued. "There is much inside you, amigo. And there is one thing you must learn. *El tiempo perdido no se recobra.* Lost time is never recovered. It is gone forever. Those years are gone. If your uncle could give them back to you, he would, but that is impossible. You need to forgive him—"

"I can't."

"Until you do, there will always be hard feelings between you. You will carry this pain until you forgive."

"Along with everything else, he treats me like a kid."

"You act the child and he will treat you accordingly."

Lane stared hard at the man who was watching him so intently. "You think you've got it all figured out, don't you, Alvarado? You think you can read my mind? Well, even I don't know what's inside it. Maybe if I did, I would know why I can't forgive Chase for leaving me behind." He kicked his horse into a trot without another word. He could hear Ramon's big black horse behind him.

Lane rode toward the full moon that rose above the

mountains. The flat, round, lunar face appeared to be laughing at him. It looked close enough to touch. Orvil told him once that the full moon was supposed to make people go crazy.

Tonight, Lane suspected the old man was right.

Chapter Thirteen

Dark clouds gathered against the mountains. Chase knew it was only a matter of time before they backed up over the valley and opened up to saturate the already damp soil with heavy rains. The wind was picking up, pushing the storm. He glanced up at the clouds as he walked from the corral to the back door, headed in to breakfast. To Eva.

Last night, after the scene in her room, he had ridden out to join Ramon and Lane without even taking time to change out of his dress clothes. He was feeling the effects of a night without sleep. Nervous exhaustion had driven him for hours. He had thought of a thousand things he could say to Eva this morning, but now, as he was about to face her, he couldn't think of anything at all. He took a deep breath and listened to the sound of the men talking inside and strained to hear her voice above the others.

Chase stepped into the kitchen. Disappointment mingled with relief hit him when he realized she wasn't in the room. All the cowhands were at the table, including Lane. None of them wanted to start a long, wet day on an empty stomach. Orvil was dishing up eggs and potatoes by the stove. Unconsciously, Chase tossed his hat on the rack beside the others and went to pour himself some coffee.

Ned looked up and paused with a biscuit halfway to his to mouth. "What's the occasion, Cassidy? We all gonna have to dude up from now on to ride the range?"

"Yeah, boss. You think whoever's killin' off the stock is gonna be so impressed when they get a look at you in those duds that they'll head out?" Jethro chimed in.

Everyone laughed as Chase unbuttoned his black leather vest and sat down at his usual place. For a moment he focused on the small, wilted bouquet in a water glass on the table and recalled the way Eva had clutched his pitiful offering all the way home last night. Some of the flowers had wilted the moment after he picked them, but then he hadn't been choosy as he picked the wild flowers, continually glancing over his shoulder to make sure no one caught him making a damn fool of himself. Blue lupins, violets, Indian paintbrush, penstemons, and shooting stars. He had learned their names as a young man. A thousand years ago.

His white dress shirt was covered with dust, the cuffs dirt-streaked. Chase took the plain onyx studs out of the cuffs, pocketed them and rolled up his sleeves. He leaned back, fighting to maintain a casual, nonchalant air, expecting Eva to waltz into the room at any moment. Would she meet his gaze or shy away? Would she still be speaking to him?

He shook himself out of his thoughts and found the others waiting for an explanation as to why he was so dressed up.

"I didn't change after the program at the schoolhouse—"

"Couldn't wait to get to work?" Ned shook his head with another laugh.

Chase took a long swig of coffee. "Yeah. Couldn't wait."

He leaned over his plate after Orvil set it down in front of him, thinking that he'd be damned before he asked after Eva. Try as he might not to, he kept glancing toward her bedroom door then toward the sitting room, expecting to see her appear at any moment. Maybe she was stalling. Maybe she didn't know how to face him anymore than he knew how to face her.

Orvil shuffled over to the table with his own plate and sat down with a heavy sigh. "Anybody else want more coffee, you got to get it yourself." He picked up his fork and attacked the mound of half-cooked, watery scrambled eggs, and under-fried potatoes.

They settled into silence. If anyone felt like complaining about the meal, they held their tongues. Chase was about to come out of his skin.

Where in the hell is she?

Orvil stood up, fork in hand, and reached into his back pocket. "Forgot to give you this," he said, holding a folded envelope toward Chase. "Miss Eva left it for you."

"She's not in her room?" Chase was certain that the fear snaking around his heart was evident in his tone.

Orvil shook his head.

Lane exploded. "Where in the hell is she? What happened in town last night?" He sent a fierce scowl in Chase's direction.

More than willing to shoulder the blame, Chase said truthfully, "The good people of Last Chance made it very clear I wasn't welcome."

Lane persisted. "What about Eva?"

"They didn't look like they were going to stone her for associating with me, but they didn't go out of their way to thank her for helping the Albright woman."

"Damn it, Chase." Lane shoved his chair back from the table and stood. "Why couldn't you leave well enough alone and stay away from town last night? Eva's worked hard with those little brats and Miss Rachel. She never hurt anybody, she doesn't deserve—"

"Sit down, amigo," Ramon said softly to the boy. He put his hand on Lane's wrist.

Still glaring at Chase, Lane tried to shake off Ramon's hold. "Now she's gone and it's all your—"

"Let him go," Chase ordered.

Ramon let go. Orvil set down his coffee cup and said, "Why don't somebody read the letter?"

Chase stared down at the forgotten envelope that he was clutching the life out of in his closed fist. Wishing he could read the letter in private, Chase laid it on the table and smoothed out the wrinkles before he carefully tore open the envelope. He glanced up. They were all watching him intently. Orvil scratched his head and leaned back in his chair. Lane was still standing. He looked like he wanted to hit something. Hard. Ramon's dark expression shouted, I told you so.

Her handwriting surprised him. It was bold, decorative, almost flamboyant, more like her red petticoat than the side of herself she showed the world. He skimmed the page. Key phrases jumped out at him. *Going to town on an errand. . . . Need to apologize to Rachel. . . . Need some time to think about last night . . .*

"She went to town" was all he told them.

Lane tucked his shirttail into his waistband. "Is she coming back?"

"Sounds like it. Said she's on an errand, that she had to see Rachel." Chase quickly folded the page, leaned forward and shoved it into his back pocket. The battered envelope lay beside his empty plate.

"The Señorita has been going back and forth to town for two weeks," Ramon mused aloud.

"So?" Lane took his seat again. Ned pushed away from the table and got himself more coffee.

Chase stared at his foreman. To those who didn't know him well, Ramon's expression appeared closed, but Chase knew exactly what Ramon was aiming at with his comment. "You still think she has something to do with the dead cattle?" Chase asked.

"Miss Eva?" It was Ned who protested this time. "There's no way she had anything to do with that." His gaze swung from Ramon to Chase. "Did she?"

"Of course not," Lane mumbled. "You've gone plumb loco, Alvarado."

Ramon's voice revealed little emotion. Calmly, coolly, he asked, "Have I? How do you know for certain that she has not been meeting someone in town and telling them of our every move? How do the bastards know where we are every night?"

"They could be watching us from a hundred vantage points. We ride out, they go in the opposite direction," Chase argued in Eva's defense.

Ramon shrugged. "A storm is coming. Why did she go back to town today?"

"She probably felt bad about walking out last night and not telling the schoolmarm good-bye, just like the note says." Chase raked his hand through his hair. "Hell, I don't know."

In his heart, he suspected that she had fled the ranch because of him, because of what he had done to her last night. He couldn't tell them that the reason she left was to get away from him.

Lane headed for the door. He paused long enough to take down his hat. As he shoved it on and straightened the brim he announced, "You can all think what you want. I know Eva's not spying on us."

He slammed the door so hard, the glass in the window rattled.

Ned and Jethro stood up. Before they quit the room, Ned paused on the threshold and stared at a spot on the floor between his feet. He cleared his throat twice and finally worked up the courage to declare, "Except for her makin' a mistake about my pants, Miss Eva's just about the best lady I ever knowed. She seen me through a rough time and I owe her for that. Why would she care about me, or any of us, if she meant any harm?"

Behind him, Jethro lingered and then spoke up. "I don't hold to blamin' Miss Eva, either. 'Sides, she's got the biggest pair of—" Ned jammed his elbow into Jethro's ribs so hard he doubled over.

Jethro finished by coughing out, "—of green eyes I ever saw." Ned turned around and ran smack into Jethro, who was still doubled over. He cursed beneath his breath. The two hapless cowboys couldn't get through the doorway fast enough.

Chase shook his head and told Ramon, "Looks like you stand alone in your opinion of Eva, unless Orvil has anything different to say."

Orvil smiled. "Not me. I carried Miss Eva to town nearly every day and I never saw her leave the school house." He stood up and began to clear the breakfast dishes. "Folks went in and out though," he added as an afterthought.

Outside, Curly was whining and scratching at the back door, begging for the scraps.

"Looks like you're outvoted on this one, Ramon," Chase said.

"I can't help the way I feel, amigo."

"Then it'll be up to you to prove us all wrong."

Ramon nodded. The sun-shaped rowels of his silver spurs sang out on the marred floor as he headed for the door. When it closed behind him, Chase picked up his coffee and drained the cup. He set it down and then rubbed the back of his neck. What if Ramon was right? What if Eva *was* part of some scheme to ruin him? What if she wasn't what she appeared to be and had them all fooled?

"Sure looks like it's gonna pour later," Orvil told him.

Chase glanced out the window and agreed. He stood up, worn out from more than a long night in the saddle. As much as he longed to stretch out and nap for a couple of hours, he knew he couldn't take the time, not when there was a full day's worth of work waiting for him and the others.

Chase started out of the kitchen, intent on going to wash up, change, and read Eva's note once more. Before he was out of the room Orvil said, "Sure hope Miss Eva makes it back before the storm hits."

Chase glanced out the window. "So do I."

Riding astride a skitterish little piebald mare, Eva reached down to be certain the hem of her striped dress was modestly tucked around her knees and ankles before she rode into Last Chance. Never a very confident rider, she had fought for control of the stubborn animal all the way to town. The ride had taken longer than expected, and by now, the shops and stores were open, and people were moving along Main Street. Hoping to avoid meeting anyone, she would now be forced to ride down the busy street with her

hair in a hopeless tangle from the wind and a bundle of
dirty laundry tied behind her saddle.

She reached up to shove her hair out of her eyes and
glanced skyward. Dark clouds with bruised, blue-black un-
derbellies hung over the land. They looked about to rupture.
If the storm did hit, she hoped it passed quickly. If not,
there was no telling how long she would be forced to stay
in Last Chance and sit it out.

Rachel Albright's house was located at the far end of
town, just off Main Street. Although the mare shook her
head in protest, Eva slowed the horse to a walk. Here and
there, a passerby would stop to stare as she rode along the
street. Still irritated by the reception the town gave Chase
last night, she made certain she looked as many of them in
the eye as possible, and even nodded and waved to others.
Let them gawk and whisper, she thought. If they knew her
true identity, it would really give them something to talk
about.

She knew Rachel's house on sight. Once it was everything Eva had dreamed of for herself, a wood frame two-
story, painted creamy yellow with accents of dark green,
rust and brown. Millwork adorned the porch, and budding
roses flanked the short walk from the house to the little
gate in the low picket fence. Eva awkwardly dismounted,
hanging onto the saddle horn and dangling for a moment
before she dropped to the ground. She tied the horse to the
iron post outside the gate and rechecked the knot. There
was no sight of movement behind the dainty lace curtains
at the windows. She could only hope Rachel was at home.
If not, Eva decided she would wait on the porch rather than
go looking for her.

After opening the gate, she strolled along the path, enjoying the budding rosebushes. A spattering of raindrops
hit her cheeks and Eva looked up. It was sprinkling lightly,
but a strong breeze was still sweeping the clouds along.
Perhaps the storm would pass quickly. On the covered
porch, she knocked twice and waited for Rachel to respond.
It was a moment or two before the schoolmarm appeared

and pushed aside the lace curtain that covered the oval window in the door. She smiled instantly. Eva breathed a sigh of relief at her show of welcome.

Rachel looked past her, spotted the mare, and ushered Eva inside. "Did you ride into town alone?"

Eva nodded. "I left a note and took off before the men came in to breakfast. I knew Chase would insist someone ride with me, and I know he can't really spare anyone right now, not even Orvil."

"I'm so glad you did. I can use the company. When school ends I always feel lost for a few days, as if there is something I should be doing but can't figure out what it is." Rachel led Eva through the entry hall into the sitting room. The dining room was visible through the open archway between the rooms. Inside, the table was covered with an intricately crocheted cloth that had yellowed to ivory with age.

"What a beautiful piece," Eva said, wandering toward the dining table. She reached out to trace the pattern of the cloth with her fingertips.

"My grandmother made it," Rachel told her. "My mother brought it with her when she came to America."

Eva knew Rachel's parents had both died; her mother, years ago, her father, more recently. She looked around the well-appointed house which showed tasteful choices in furnishings and accessories. In the sitting room, a settee was placed near the slate-fronted fireplace, along with two cozy chairs. Although she had few opportunities to ever visit such a house, building plans for homes much like this were often featured in the periodicals Eva enjoyed. It was exactly the sort of place she had always wanted, the kind of house she had envisioned every time she moved into another cramped hotel room.

"Do you ever get lonely living here all alone?" Eva asked.

Rachel shook her head. "Sometimes, but there's a difference between being alone and being lonely. I'm used to being by myself. As a railroad representative, my father traveled a lot, so I learned to entertain myself. I like to read and work in my garden when the weather is nice. In the winter I like to putter. Time seems to fly by."

"I know what you mean. Since I've been working on the ranch, it seems like the days aren't long enough."

"Please, sit down," Rachel said, indicating the settee. "I'll make some tea. Or would you prefer coffee?"

"Tea would be lovely," Eva said. She wanted to pinch herself. Here she was having tea with one of the nicest women she had ever met, who also just happened to be the most respectable woman in Last Chance. She wished John could see her now. He was probably the only one who knew how much this moment meant to her. Quincy would probably laugh and tell her to stop pretending to be something she wasn't. The sour thoughts brought her back to reality and reminded her why she had come.

"Listen, Rachel I wanted to apologize for last night—"

"For what?"

Ignoring the invitation to sit, Eva walked over to the fireplace and stared down at the empty grate. "For leaving without saying good-bye and for not thanking you for letting me take part in the program. I really did enjoy it— even with Harold Higgens trying to look up my skirt occasionally."

Rachel laughed and walked up beside her. She reached out for Eva's hand. "I should be thanking you. And don't concern yourself over leaving so abruptly, because I understand. I think there are more than a few people in town who should be apologizing to you."

Eva moved to the settee and sat down. She folded her hands in her lap as a bittersweet sadness overwhelmed her. "If I had known the reception waiting for Chase, I would have never encouraged him to come last night."

"Was he angry?"

"It came out as anger, but I think he was very hurt, and anger was a way to hide it. He was upset about the way most folks ignored me after the show."

"So was I," Rachel assured her. "And some of them

have already heard about their rude behavior, believe you me."

Eva looked up quickly. "Oh, Rachel, I don't want to drag you into this. You have a reputation at stake in this town—"

"Oh, phooey. Speaking my mind won't tarnish my reputation. If it did, I'd have been ruined long ago." She laughed. "I'll go make the tea."

Eva jumped up and followed her to the kitchen. Like the others, this room was warm and cozy, nothing like the crude, make-do kitchen at the ranch house. There were tall, glass-fronted cabinets on the wall above the dry sink, and the oak floor, unscarred by spurs and boot marks, was polished to a high-gloss shine. As Rachel moved about with familiarity, setting water on to boil, pulling out a tea set spattered with morning glories, searching a drawer for silver, Eva pulled a kitchen chair away from the table and propped her elbows on her knees.

"You have everything I thought I ever wanted," Eva told her.

Rachel spun around and stared at Eva for a moment. "What do you mean?" She carried silver spoons to the table and hovered there, waiting for Eva to explain.

"All my life I've dreamed of living in a beautiful home like this one, of spending my days sewing and gardening and cooking and—"

"But, you're from the city. I thought—"

Momentarily caught in the lie, Eva felt herself flush. "I was, but my home was nothing like this one."

Rachel looked thoughtful. "You said I had everything you *thought* you ever wanted. What did you mean?" Wondering how much she should confide in Rachel, Eva paused to consider. She felt the need to voice her concerns but there was no one else she could talk to, and besides, from the moment she met Rachel in Carberry's store, she felt they could become close friends.

Eva sighed. "I hate to admit it, but I'm afraid I might be falling in love with Chase Cassidy."

The tea forgotten, Rachel sank into the chair beside her. "Oh, no."

"Oh, yes." When Eva looked up, she noticed that Rachel was blushing to her hairline.

An awkward few seconds of silence passed before Rachel said, "Do you mind if I ask how you know you might be falling in love?"

Eva almost laughed, but Rachel's discomfort and sincerity were all too apparent. What could she tell the town's highly respected, certainly virginal, schoolmarm? She couldn't say that whenever Chase walked into a room her heart started racing, nor could she admit that, lately, just being near him made her go all weak and mushy inside. The sound of his voice made her tingle. The touch of his hands made her tremble. His lips on her skin made her hot with need.

No, she could never admit those things aloud to someone like Rachel Albright.

"Oh," Eva said, staring down at her hands, "I just know." Suddenly curious, she wondered why Rachel was asking. "Do you think you might be getting sweet on someone? Is that why you asked?" She laughed. "Is it Sheriff McKenna?"

Rachel covered her pinkened cheeks with her hands. "Maybe. I just don't know. He and I have known each other for years."

"Really? He certainly had an eye for you last night."

"I just don't know if I might be falling in love with him."

Eva sighed. "When it happens, whether you want it to or not, you'll know."

The kettle was hissing. Rachel jumped up and hurried over to the cabinet. She took out a decorative, gold and red tin of tea and set it on the table. Eva reached out and opened it, then began to spoon tea into the teapot while Rachel went to get the kettle.

"Falling in love with Chase Cassidy would certainly complicate things," Rachel said as she slowly poured tea into the morning glory pot. "It would be difficult in such close quarters."

"It's already hard," Eva muttered.

Rachel returned the kettle to the stove. "He . . . he hasn't tried to take advantage of you has he?" Her eyes were wide as gold pieces.

"No." *It's more like I've tried to take advantage of him.*

"Oh, Eva, I hope I haven't offended you. I know you would never—"

"Please, I—" Eva felt like a charlatan. She couldn't let Rachel go on apologizing. "I know you're concerned because we're friends."

Rachel used a small, silver strainer as she poured out two cups of tea. While they let them cool, she asked, "Eva, why did you become the housekeeper at the Cassidy's ranch? It seems like such an unlikely place for you anyway."

Why had she taken the job? Looking back now, she realized that talking Chase Cassidy into hiring her had been a gamble. She could have been walking into a dangerous situation, for all she knew, and yet she had insisted that he hire her. As she wondered how to explain, she was forced to admit to herself that deep down inside, she had been afraid that the job at the Trail's End might be the only one she could get.

"When I arrived at Chase's ranch in answer to his ad, it wasn't exactly the type of place I'd imagined working. But it was the first time I had ever applied to be a housekeeper, and I thought that if I could prove myself there, then I would at least have a reference and some experience when I left to find a better position."

"And now you're falling in love with Chase Cassidy." Rachel picked up her cup and saucer. "I have to admit, he's handsome, but scares the life out of me."

Eva was amazed. "Why?"

"He looks so foreboding. Have you noticed how Lane glowers in exactly the same way? They both look like they would take a person's head off if you talked sideways to them.''

"They're both very troubled men," Eva said.

Rachel took a sip of tea, blew on the amber liquid and sipped again. "They have had their share of problems.''

"So have a lot of other people." Eva settled back in her chair, her cup and saucer beside her on the table. "I wish they could put the past behind them. But Chase has been through his sister's murder and the prison term, and Lane can't seem to forgive his uncle for abandoning him. The worst part is, Lane won't talk about it.''

"I wonder if they'll ever change?" Rachel pondered.

"Letting the past ruin the present is something I've thought about for a long time, even before I met the Cassidys." She finished her tea and stared into the bottom of the cup at the stray leaves that had escaped the strainer. "People tend to hang on to trouble from the past like so much unnecessary baggage. When you have too much baggage, you have three choices, you can struggle under the load forever, you can try to convince someone else to carry it with you (which only burdens them), or you can leave it at the station, forget about the contents and start over. Right now, the Cassidys seem to want to drag all their overstuffed trunks around with them.''

"Not everyone is strong enough to leave the past behind and just walk away from it.''

Eva nodded in agreement. "And sometimes other people won't *let* you walk away from it. The folks around Last Chance certainly won't let Chase and Lane forget.''

"What are you going to do?" Rachel poured Eva more tea.

"I don't know. Everything is such a jumble right now. Sometimes I think I should just pack up and get out of there before I make a big mistake, but Chase has so much trouble on the ranch right now . . . '' she let her thoughts drift away.

"What trouble?" Eva weighed telling her friend and decided that maybe Rachel might have heard something about the sabotage attempts at the Trail's End. "Someone's been killing off the stock."

"How terrible!"

Agreeing with a nod, Eva added, "Chase can't afford to lose one single head, and he's lost ten or more."

"I wonder who could be doing such a thing?"

"You haven't heard anything around town? Anything about someone trying to run the Cassidys out?"

Rachel looked thoughtful. "No. I haven't heard a thing, but you can bet I'll keep an ear open. Has Mr. Cassidy told Sheriff McKenna?"

"No. I'm sure Chase wants to keep this quiet and handle it himself. At this point he doesn't know who to trust." When Rachel offered more tea, Eva refused. "I really should be getting back. Is it still sprinkling?"

Rachel stood up and carried her cup and saucer with her. She paused beside the window and looked out toward the mountains. "It's stopped for now. So has the wind, but the sky is still threatening. It won't be long before the brunt of the storm hits. I think you should spend the night here."

The offer was tempting, but what would Chase think when she didn't come back? Then again, after last night, he might be thankful if she were to leave. She couldn't believe how forward she had been, what she had actually let him do, how she had encouraged it and fueled the fire. Eva shivered, wishing she was in the last act of a melodrama and the curtain about to come down. At least then she would have already read the script and would know the outcome.

She stood up, prepared to leave. "I hope I haven't burdened you with *my* baggage," she laughed.

Rachel smiled. "I'm glad you consider me enough of a friend to talk things over with me."

"I need one more piece of advice," Eva began.

"Anything."

She tried not to sound too desperate. "Is there a good laundry in Last Chance?"

Rachel laughed. "You really are a city girl, aren't you?

No, there's no laundry, but Hazel Pettibone is a young widow who lives not far from here. She takes in laundry to support herself and her five children. She was at the program last night.''

"I'm sure I met her. A pitifully thin little thing with lanky blond hair and two babies close in age?''

"That's her.''

"She was kind enough to actually speak to me after the program. I guess I won't have to worry about what sort of a reception she'll give me if I show up at her door with a couple of dresses and Chase Cassidy's shirts to launder.'' Eva stood up, intent on leaving but still regretting having to end the pleasant interlude.

They walked through the house to the front door together. "Do you have a coat?'' Rachel asked.

Eva shook her head. "No, I really thought it would warm up.''

Rachel reached over to a hook on the wall rack beside the door and took down a dark blue wool shawl. She pressed it into Eva's hands. "Take this. You can return it next time you come into town—which I hope will be soon.''

"If you're sure—''

A bright smile lit Rachel's blue eyes. "I'm sure. Come back soon, Eva.''

"I will. I promise.'' On impulse, Eva reached out and hugged Rachel. "Thank you,'' she whispered, "for being my friend.''

By the time she dropped the bundle of laundry at Mrs. Pettibone's and headed back to the ranch, thunder was echoing in the distance. Used to riding in buggies, stage coaches, and railroad cars, Eva was having trouble getting the piebald mare to do anything she commanded. Rather than a pleasant ride through the countryside, she was engaged in a battle of wills with a headstrong young horse accustomed to driving cattle. Eva was afraid if she gave the little mare her head, she might never get her back under control.

The clouds overhead were so low she felt she could reach up and touch them. Nearby, trees were lashing against the wind, the silvery undersides of the leaves faced skyward as if thirsting for the rain. Thunder boomed and the horse started to bolt. Eva was fighting for control when lightning flashed and thunder shattered the air around her a split-second later. The mare reared, Eva screamed, frightened by the thunder directly overhead and the lightning crackling around her. She hit the ground and the air left her lungs in a whoosh. Flat on her back, she lay there staring up at the roiling clouds as raindrops spattered her with ever-increasing force. When her ears stopped ringing, Eva sat up.

Her tailbone was throbbing. She was shaking nearly out of control. Not far away, the lightning strike had splintered a huge oak tree in half. She doubled over, hugged her knee to her chest and buried her face in her arms. Gasping in deep draughts of air, she tried to calm down and forced herself not to cry.

This was definitely no time to fall apart.

The electrical storm moved on swiftly. She chanced a glance over her shoulder, saw the blackened trunk of the tree smoldering nearby and shuddered again. There was no sign of the mare. Rachel's shawl lay in a sodden heap nearby. Eva tried to stand, but she was trembling too fiercely. She crawled over to the shawl and hugged it close.

She had to get away from the trees. Drawing a deep, shuddering breath, she glanced around, searching for a place to hide until the fury of the storm passed.

Nearby, the land sloped gently upward toward the east, and near the top of a rise sat a group of boulders. It was as good a place as any, and the only option she had other than sitting unprotected among the trees, which acted as lightning rods.

"Lightning never strikes twice. . . ."

Eva hoped the old adage was true as she mumbled to herself and pushed up to her knees, then her feet. Slowly, carefully, head bent against the rain and wind, she worked her way across the open range toward the protection of the boulders. It was slow going with her skirt sopping wet and tangled around her legs. When she made it to the boulders she reached out and stroked the cold rock, then laid her cheek against it and drew a shuddering breath.

A moment later, she slipped as far between the rocks as she could manage, desperately hoping nothing deadly had already taken refuge there. She wrung out the shawl as best she could and spread it over her head and shoulders. Thus protected, she huddled there, staring off in the direction of the ranch, and hoping that sooner or later someone would notice she hadn't returned and mention it to Chase.

Would he send someone to search for her or come himself?

To take her mind off the miserable conditions, Eva began to recite the dialogue from the last role she had starred in as the heroine in *Darling; or Woman and Her Master.* The reviews had been less than encouraging, one unfeeling critic dismissed her lead in Thomas De Walden's play set during the Civil War as "overwrought with melodrama and forced pathos." The review that had hurt her the most had read, "all this critic can say about Miss Eberhart's performance is that her hair is of the most stunning coppery hue. She would be better served in any other profession."

Just now, Eva didn't care a fig for the cruel words of some self-proclaimed critic whose name she had long ago forgotten. Shouting her lines, as well as those of all the other actors, yelling against the fury of the wind, she wondered if leaving Chester and the mummy case in Cheyenne might not have been her downfall. Maybe there *was* something to her mother's claim that the mummy brought them good fortune.

She had never been this far away from Chester before and her luck had definitely never been this bad.

Chapter Fourteen

Lightning forced the men back into the bunkhouse and Chase spent the afternoon pacing the back porch as the rain fell in sheets from the roof and collected in puddles in Eva's struggling flower garden. Supper came and went. Orvil opened six cans of beans and made half-baked biscuits for everyone. As if sensing Chase's black mood, the men ate in silence and then hurried back to the bunkhouse to recommence their card games and take advantage of the forced time off. When the worst of the electrical storm had passed, Lane volunteered to ride out with Ramon to check the stock and fences. No one dared speak to Chase unless he had to.

Curly hung around the back door, whining whenever Chase stepped outside and ignored him to scan the horizon. Chase tried to convince himself that Eva would be home as soon as the skies cleared and that the sensible thing for her to have done was to sit out the storm at the schoolmarm's house. Again and again he told himself that was exactly what she had done.

She had not left him for good.

Not yet anyway.

He was about to go inside and suffer confinement indoors when he recognized the piebald mare that raced toward the corral like the devil himself was on its heels. Once he saw the trailing reins and the flopping stirrups, he cleared the porch with a bound and splashed through the mud to stop the frightened animal.

The horse churned the muddy ground with its hooves,

shaking her head to keep Chase at bay, her eyes wild with fear. He tried to speak soothing words above the sound of the rain, held out his hands to calm the frightened animal and was eventually able to grasp the reins. He recognized the saddle, an old spare that was rarely used because each man owned his own. He noted how high the stirrups had been placed and knew this was the horse Eva had ridden to town.

He led the mare to the barn and whistled in the direction of the bunkhouse. Orvil walked out of the over-large shanty and stood there staring at him through the rain.

"Is this the horse Eva took this morning?"

Orvil cupped his hands around his mouth and yelled, "Must be." He stared at the riderless horse for a moment, then left the porch without bothering to go back inside for his hat. He headed toward Chase through the deepening muck in the yard at as fast a trot as he could manage.

Chase led the mare just inside the barn door and waited for Orvil. When the old man walked in, he began to run his hands over the mare's flanks and, like Chase, spoke soothingly to the quivering animal.

"Whoa there, Pie. Settle down, girl."

As Chase stood there staring at the empty saddle on the winded horse, something inside him snapped.

"Where in the hell is she?" He bellowed to no one in particular. "What gives her the right to think she can take off anytime she wants?"

The horse reared again and began to back away from him. Chase handed the reins to Orvil. "I'm going out to look for Eva. Rub this damn animal down. If anything happened to her because of this idiot mare, I'll shoot it myself."

He hurried to the stall where he kept his favorite mount and saddled the big bay. Already soaked to the skin, he was determined not to waste a second more. Rushing to the house, he returned wearing a slicker and carried another one rolled up under his arm for Eva. There was no doubt in his mind about finding her. He would not come back until he did.

Chase tied the slicker behind his saddle. He was about to mount up when Orvil grabbed his arm.

"Take a gun, Cassidy."

Chase frowned. He had promised himself and swore to God he would never wear a gun again. He did not bother to answer Orvil. The old man would not let him go.

"What if this is some kind of trap?" Orvil asked.

Chase turned on the old man and said sharply, "I didn't think you suspected Eva of trying to ruin me."

"I don't," Orvil said, squinting up through the pouring rain. His shoulders were soaked, the dark stain spreading down his shirt, forcing it to cling to his skin. He was still fit after a lifetime of hard work. "Somebody might be holdin' her until one of us goes lookin', just like you're about to do."

"No gun," Chase shouted over the rain. "Now get in out of the rain," he yelled. He turned the horse's head. The big bay pranced and shook its head, unwilling to settle down. Chase pulled on the reins again, forced the bay in the direction of the barn, rode inside and took a long, coiled whip off of a nail.

"Get back inside," he shouted to Orvil before he headed the bay down the rutted trail toward town. It would not be hard to find Eva if she had stayed on the trail. Praying she had not been knocked unconscious or set upon by wolves, he kept his head low and urged his horse on.

An hour later, he was still searching. The usual violet shades of twilight were dimmed by storm clouds. It was becoming harder to see as Chase reached the border of his land. Truly afraid of what he might find, he reined in when he recognized the ghostly shape of an old oak against the gathering gloom. The huge tree had been sheared in half by lightning. Its charred, twisted limbs lay on the ground beside the grim portion of the remaining trunk that clawed the sky.

Chase walked the bay, wiping rain out of his eyes as he

searched the sodden ground for any sign of Eva. On a rise not far away stood a group of boulders. Recognizing it as a perfect hiding place, Chase hoped to God Eva had thought to take refuge there. He spurred his horse into a canter and began to shout her name.

After crouching in the same position for nearly two hours, Eva thought she heard her name carried on the wind. She bit back a sob. Huddled there shivering in Rachel's shawl in the pouring rain and howling wind, she wondered if she was losing her mind. Her wet hair was stuck to her face, so she pushed it aside and peeked out from beneath the heavy, wet wool. For a moment she thought her eyes were playing tricks on her as she strained to see through the curtain of rain.

The wavering image of an approaching rider in an oilskin coat became clearer with every heartbeat. Wild with relief, Eva started to call out to him, but the words caught in her throat. There was someone out to ruin Chase, someone who might be bent on harming anyone connected with Trail's End. She strained to identify the rider, but the full-length oilskin covered him from neck to calf. He wore a black hat pulled low over his brow to shield him from the wind and rain.

Eva crouched lower, straining to identify the man. She saw him cup his hands around his mouth. Her name was carried to her on the wind.

It was Chase.

Sobbing with relief, Eva tried to stand, but her ankle throbbed and her legs, left so long in a cramped position, barely held her. Fighting for a hold on the slick granite surface, she felt her fingernails snag, but somehow she clung to the rock and levered herself to a standing position. She had to call out to him before it was too late and he rode on.

When she made it to her feet, Eva tried to step out beyond the rocks where he could see her, but her ankle wouldn't hold her weight. She cupped her hands in imitation of him and shouted his name.

He rode straight for the boulders. Eva began waving her arms and then tried to twirl the shawl above her, but it was so wet it kept falling over her head. Frustrated, she shoved the heavy shawl aside and let it fall into the mud.

"Chase!" she screamed again. Alerted by the sound, his head went up and he urged his horse closer.

She was afraid if she let go of the rock she would fall flat on her face.

Chase thought he saw movement against the granite, thought he had heard someone call his name. It wasn't until he was almost upon her that he saw her pink striped dress against the rock.

He was there an instant later, vaulting from the saddle, pulling her into his arms and then running his hands over her to be sure she was real and alive and unharmed.

Eva burrowed into him, hid her face against the chilly, slippery fabric of the oilcloth slicker. She was shaking so hard, her teeth chattered, not so much from cold but from relief and the heady excitement of having been found at last.

She raised her head. He looked down. Her face was sheltered by his hat brim. "There was lightning," she said, "it split a tree and the mare threw me."

"Are you all right?"

"I twisted my ankle."

He reached down and scooped her up into his arms as if she weighed no more than a dust mote and carried her to his horse.

"Can you stand?"

She nodded and he put her down. Eva grabbed his stirrup and hung on as he quickly loosened the leather ties behind the saddle and unrolled the extra slicker. She stared at the black whip coiled like a wet snake beside his saddle.

"I brought you a fish," he said, using the cowboys' name for the raincoat. "Put this on." He held it out for her, assisting as she slipped into it.

As soon as Eva had the slicker on, he mounted up, and then reached down and pulled her up behind him. She slipped her arms around his waist, thankful to press her face against his back to shield it from the rain and wind.

She thought she heard him call, "Hold on," over the rain, but she needed no warning. She clung to him like her own sodden clothes clung to her skin, hoping his warmth would soon penetrate the oilskin.

Eva closed her eyes as he urged his mount toward the ranch.

It was dark by the time they reached the house. Her teeth chattered. Eva shook so hard she knew he must feel it. Chase drew his horse up before the back porch and jumped down and reached for her; she went easily into his arms. Just as he opened the back door he heard a whistle and paused long enough to wave at Orvil, who stood across the yard beneath the bunkhouse eaves. The veteran cowboy was barely visible though the dizzle, but Eva saw him wave back, evidently satisfied that Chase had everything under control.

When Chase finally carried her over the threshold into the familiar warmth of the kitchen, Eva nearly burst into tears again. A fire was going in the stove, and the small, crude room was heavily scented with the heady aroma of hot coffee. Until this very moment she hadn't realized how much she had already come to think of the place as home.

Without a word, he tossed his hat on the table and set her down on the nearest chair before he knelt down beside her. "Let me see that foot," he said, reaching out toward her skirt.

"It's my ankle," she said through chattering teeth as she hugged herself, missing the warmth they had shared on horseback.

She wondered what he would do if she said, "Hang the ankle and hold me," but he looked so serious, so stern and darkly foreboding as he stared up at her, that she did not dare test him.

His thick, dark hair was damp, matted against his forehead by his hat. He gingerly held the hem of her gown for a moment as if debating with himself, then lifted it barely enough to expose the top of her muddy shoe where it graced her lower calf. Eva felt her cheeks flame when his move revealed her sodden red petticoat.

She thought she might die of embarrassment. She swallowed hard and realized after a moment or two that Chase was too much of a gentleman ever to comment on it. He held her foot gently in his hand as he began to flick open the buttons on her shoes. She couldn't take her eyes off his strong hands and fingers as he moved efficiently to gingerly free her from the miserable wet leather. Chase drew off the shoe and cradled her foot, carefully felt her ankle for any broken bones, then stripped off her wet sock.

He never looked up, never met her eyes.

As she stared down at the thick fringe of dark lashes hiding his eyes, she longed to reach out and touch his cheek and thank him for coming after her despite the fury of the storm.

As he began to unlace the other shoe, he took her by surprise when he asked, "Where did you go?"

Longing to see the expression in his ebony eyes, she wished he would look up at her. "Didn't you get my note? I went to see Rachel."

A long silence passed. He drew off her second shoe and her stocking and laid them beside their mates. The scarred plank floor beneath her chair was darkened by the water dripping from her wet gown. Despite the fact that he had been out in the storm, his hands were warm as he wrapped each one around her feet and simply held them. After a moment or two he let go, brushed his hands against his thighs and stood up. He did not meet her gaze, but turned immediately to the stove and paused to take two cups down off the narrow shelf.

He lifted the coffeepot, then set it down hard without pouring any. Chase turned away from the stove to face her at last.

Eva's heart stopped.

His dark fury was gone. The pain on his face was open and visible as a new wound.

"I . . ." he was forced to stop and clear his throat. "I thought after last night you had left for good."

Unmindful of her ankle, the wet floor, and of the punishing cold that had seeped into her bones, she stood up. Limping, she crossed the three feet that separated them. She kept her weight on her uninjured ankle.

Looking up into his eyes, she touched his cheek. "But I didn't leave, Chase. I'm still here," she told him softly.

He reached out to cup the edge of her jaw. She noticed that his hand shook slightly so she stepped closer. Her heart was pounding.

"Eva."

He didn't move, didn't do any more than touch her cheek and speak her name, a reaffirmation that she was home again.

Eva shivered, more from excitement than from fear or the cold. Chase didn't move. Eva stared at the front of his slicker, then met his dark eyes. She could no longer hide her powerful need of him.

"I'm so cold," she whispered. "I don't know if I'll ever be warm again. Hold me, Chase. Keep me warm."

Without hesitation, he reached out and enfolded her in his embrace.

Caught in a web of her own making, Eva took a deep, shuddering breath. Damn respectability. To hell with the house with the white picket fence. Rachel had a perfect home with all the trimmings, and yet she lived alone. All Eva wanted at this very moment was Chase Cassidy. Right now she cared about him more than she cared about seeing the sun rise tomorrow—but she knew he would never make the first move. For the first time in her life, she had succeeded as an actress, succeeded too well, and now, much to her dismay, Chase Cassidy saw her as a well-mannered, respectable miss from Philadelphia.

If anything was going to happen between them, it was up to her to make it happen.

Eva took a deep breath and wrapped her arms about his neck. "I want you, Chase."

He stood so still for so long that she thought perhaps he hadn't heard her. Then, in one fluid motion, Chase reached down and slipped his arm beneath her knees. When he lifted her against his chest, she thought for a moment he was going to carry her into her room. Instead, he glanced toward the back door and the darkened yard beyond, then headed through the unlit house, across the sitting room into his own bedroom.

He kicked the door shut behind him and left her standing in the center of the room. "Oh, God, Eva," he whispered as he peeled off his rain gear and tossed it over the one chair in the sparsely furnished room.

He reached for her and drew her near. His lips touched her forehead, her eyelids, her cheeks with light, feathery kisses. He kissed the tendrils of damp hair at her temple. "I've never wanted anything so bad in all my life."

She slipped her arms around his neck and welcomed his kiss when he bent his head and covered her mouth with his own. His lips moved against hers with a vengeance, as if he could not get close enough. He pressed her to him. His hands slid down to cup her buttocks and press her against his groin. She felt his hard arousal—it would have been difficult to ignore—and involuntarily moaned low in her throat, straining to get closer.

The kiss went on and on as his lips moved over hers. She thought she might drown in the heady sensations. His tongue dipped and delved. She answered by tasting him back. They were breathing hard and fast, clinging to one another, their need mounting, when Chase suddenly pulled back and held her at arms length.

"You don't know what you do to me, Eva. I want you so damn bad I—"

She reached for him, pulled him close again, her hands clutching the damp fabric of his shirt. All pretense forgotten, she whispered against his lips, "Then have me. Take me, Chase."

When she pressed full against him, he thought he might go mad with wanting. His aroused member strained full and heavy against the tightly fitted fly of his denim trousers. Chase could not stop the deep moan that escaped him.

Thankful for the blessed darkness, he let his fingertips play along the scooped neckline of her gown until he felt the beginning of the long row of buttons. His hand never shook when he held a gun, but tonight he couldn't seem to control the raw emotion raging through him. Chase warned himself that this was no back-room whore, but a lady, an untried virgin, a woman to be coddled, cherished, and adored.

She did not move as he slowly, carefully, opened the bodice of her gown button by button. In the darkness, her angelic profile was a mere, shadowy outline. Eva stood before him, her shivering subsided as she looked toward the one narrow window in his room and listened to the rain as it beat against the windowpane.

He eased the clinging, wet gown off her shoulders and helped her draw her arms out of the sleeves. Hooking his fingers into the gathered material at her waist, he pushed her gown and petticoat over her hips. The weight of the sodden cloth worked to aid him and the mass quickly pooled around her feet.

She shivered.

He reached out and placed his hands on her bare shoulders. Her skin was cold and damp to the touch.

"You're freezing," he whispered.

"I can't feel it," she said softly. "I can only feel you."

He let his hands slip down her arms to her wrists and led her to the bed that stood against the wall opposite the window. She made no protest, but followed him willingly. In the dim light he could barely see the fabric of her chemise and drawers against her skin. He wondered what whimsical color she had chosen.

At the bedside he paused, unwilling to push her too far, too fast. If she denied him now, Chase knew he would have to let her go, it was all he could do, no matter what it cost him. Taking her over protest, even to ease his own burning need, was not an option.

In silent invitation for her to enter his bed, he pulled back the covers. She hesitated.

He held his breath.

"I think perhaps I should take this off myself."

She had uttered the words so softly that he thought he might not have heard her correctly. With his heart hammering in his chest, Chase reached out to help her ease the clammy fabric off. It was not a chemise and drawers, he discovered, but a one piece affair that forced her to grab hold of his arm for balance as she stepped out of it.

He could hear her teeth chattering again. Despite her protests to the contrary, she was still cold. He bent and lifted the covers, and when she slipped nude beneath them, Chase drew the bedclothes up to her chin. He sat down on the edge of the bed and it sagged beneath his weight. His boots were so wet, it took more than a tug to get them off. They hit the floor with distinct thuds that could be heard over the rain pounding on the roof.

He shed the rest of his clothes and slipped in beside her, careful not to move too quickly and frighten her with his nearness. The bed was barely wide enough to accommodate two. Not touching her anywhere was a challenge. A moment ago, when he had held her in his arms, everything seemed right and natural. Now that they were lying side by side the situation had become awkward. He was no longer sure of himself or of what Eva actually wanted.

Have me. Take me, Chase. Had she meant what she had said? Did she even know what she was asking?

"Chase?"

Her soft, honey-laced tone reached out to warm and tantalize him in the darkness. He reached out and raked his fingers through the length of her hair. "What, Eva?"

"Hold me." Her request shattered his hesitation. In a heartbeat, he pulled her across the sheet and into his arms. She reached up and wrapped her arms around his neck. The movement lifted her breasts up full against him.

He held her tighter, his flesh pressed against hers. Her skin was still chilled from her ordeal. He felt like his was on fire.

There was no way she could be unaware of his throbbing member as it pressed against the velvet nest that covered her soft mound. He lay as still as possible, held her close to warm her and reveled in the feel of their hearts beating a tatoo against one another, loving the way their breath commingled as need and excitement vibrated through them. He buried his face in her hair, kissed her temple and then the pulse point at her throat.

"Eva." It was all he could say. Her name became a prayer that left his lips after each tender, worshiping kiss. "Eva. Eva. Eva."

She pressed closer, moving her hips against his arousal, teasing him with slow, circular, undulating motions. His mind shut down and ceased to question anything that happened. The rain hammered down as the wind blew it in sheets across the roof. The noise filled the room, surrounded them, matched the tempo of their heartbeats. The passion and mounting pitch of the storm outside could not outpace his own increasing need. As Eva moved against him, Chase was afraid he could not hold back any longer. What if he lost control and spilled his seed before he entered her?

She moaned low in her throat and opened her thighs. His turgid erection slipped between them. Chase rolled her onto her back and leaned on his elbows, poised above her, his staff pressing against the moist warmth at the apex of her thighs. Her eyes were open, he could see little more than the sheen of unshed tears in the darkness.

"Are you sure?" His hand captured her breast. It fit his cupped palm perfectly.

She moaned again and arched against him. Her words rushed out on a whispered sigh. "Oh, Chase. Please don't make me wait any longer."

Chapter Fifteen

Tonight she was his.

Certain he must be dreaming, afraid to hurt her, Chase pulled back. Lightning flashed overhead. The storm was building momentum again. The blue-white light gave him a brief glimpse of her face. Her eyes were moist and shining. The stunning green usually so brilliant was muted, nearly colorless in the dark.

"Are you crying?" he asked.

She kissed him, long and languorously, drawing out the pleasure, stoking his need. "Not because I'm sad," she whispered when the kiss ended. "I want you, Chase. I want you now."

On this night of nights, he didn't want to hurry but he didn't know if he could trust himself not to lose control.

On the morrow, when the storm cleared and the morning sun lit the eastern sky, Eva might choose to put this night behind her. If she chose to walk out forever, then so be it. He would have to learn to live with another sorrow in his life.

Tonight she was giving him a most precious gift. No matter what happened tomorrow, he wanted to make certain she would never forget tonight.

"You sure this is what you want, Eva?"

"Yes. Yes, I'm sure."

He shifted his weight to one side, ran his hand from her breast to the soft nest of curls and cupped her heated mound.

Eva gasped as he lifted her. She moved, arching against

his palm. Her scent filled the air, driving him wild. Chase slid his fingers along the slippery wetness coating her lush, ripe opening, dipped one and then another inside, stretching her, preparing the way for his entrance.

He prayed the final act would not hurt her, hoped he could hold back long enough to be gentle. Excitement mounted, fed by the memory of his years of celibacy and anger in prison, of the monotony and loneliness of life in a cold, bare cell. If not for Ramon's company, he would have lost his mind. He had paid whores to service him after his release, but until Eva, he had never allowed himself to dream he might have a decent woman in his life or in his arms.

Never, not once in all those years had he dared to dream a dream like Eva Edwards.

Now she was his.

Lightning struck again. Chase dipped his head and took her peaked nipple into his mouth, bit it teasingly and then suckled. Eva cried out. The sound was muted by thunder that reverberated in the small room. She grasped his shoulders. Her nails dug into his bare shoulders. The minute pain was pleasurable.

She was writhing beneath him now, her head moving from side to side on his single pillow. He withdrew his fingers and rolled over her again, grabbed her hips to stop her wild thrashing, and held her still. Suspended above her, he ached, throbbing and heavy, unable to keep from thrusting up and in.

Eva cried out, not in pain, but in ecstasy. She felt Chase go rigid, his breathing harsh and ragged. He rasped, ''I've hurt you. ''

''No—'' She kissed the side of his face, then his ear. ''No. Please. I'm . . . all right.'' Barely able to utter a coherent thought, she longed to tell him it didn't matter, that he need not be gentle, that she was not a virgin. She craved to urge him on. It was all she could do not to beg him for more, to push him to go deeper, faster, and begin the torrid thrusts that would bring them both to fulfillment. But even now, the voice of reason niggled in the back of her mind—if she seemed too eager, he would realize she was not a virgin.

Eva admitted to herself that she was not actress enough, or devious enough, to try to purposely play the part, to feign outright fear and the loss of a nonexistent maidenhead. Not now. Not at this magical moment when she wished there was no lie between them.

When he kissed her, a low groan escaped him. She knew the moment he lost control. He tore his lips from hers and began to plunge into her in earnest. Buried in her to the hilt, he thrust against her again and again and unleashed the power that had caused him to tremble when he held her so tenderly in the kitchen. Eva cried out at every lunge, lifted her hips and dug her nails into his shoulders.

The force of his movements carried her up and back until she reached out to grab the edge of the mattress. Rising up off the bed, she wrapped her legs around his waist and arched into him. Eva cried out his name until it became a chant that kept time to the rhythm of his forceful thrusts.

The fire inside her escalated until she knew she was about to explode. When there was no longer any means of holding back, she became frantic, forcing him to increase the speed and depth of his movement. She could hear him gasping for breath as he raced toward his own climax. A thunderclap shook the room. The sound drove him on. When the convulsive reaction started deep inside, when she felt her inner core tighten and throb around him Eva managed to gasp, "Now. *Please, now,* Chase!"

He rammed into her with one final thrust and threw back his head, stifling his own shout through clenched teeth. She let go of the mattress and threw her arms around him, felt him shudder out his seed as her own climax continued to wring more and more from him.

She buried her face in the hollow between his throat and his collarbone and drew a long, heaving sigh. She yearned to tell him that his lovemaking had brought her to new heights, that Quincy had never made her feel the way she did now. But afraid the truth would shatter his newfound trust in her, she held her silence. Besides, even thinking Quincy Powell's name during so precious a moment repulsed her.

Slowly, their breathing returned to normal. Still resting between her thighs, Chase kept most of his weight off her and held her close. She was afraid to speak and break the spell, and so she just lay there, content to watch the lightning flash and illuminate the now familiar line of his jaw and listen to the thunder as it rumbled angrily overhead. She wished they could stop time and stay locked away in the small room, forever protected by the curtain of rain outside.

The covers had twisted around his legs, but she didn't feel the cold any longer. Lightning flickered again, and Eva saw the long line of his muscular flesh against hers. The sight aroused her as much as the feel of his skin pressed to hers. She wondered if he had fallen asleep with his head on her breast until Chase began to trail his fingertips along her hip and then slipped them between her buttocks and the mattress. He cupped her, lifted her and gently rubbed her against him.

She could feel him hard and ready again and marveled. Unwilling to protest, for her own craving had returned, Eva nuzzled closer and began to kiss the vulnerable hollow of his throat. She dipped her tongue into it and then licked a path up the corded muscle along the side of his neck to his ear.

He shuddered against her, squeezing her buttock, lifting her up and grinding against her mound. "I want you again, Eva."

She answered him with a deep, stirring kiss, using her tongue to arouse him even more. He broke the kiss and drew back until he could take her nipple into his mouth again. He suckled first one and then the other, moving back and forth, the rough, day's end stubble of his dark beard teasing her until she found herself gasping and crying out again.

Each pull at her breast was like an electrical surge shooting through her to the throbbing bud between her legs. He nipped at her, pulled back and extended her nipple as he gently held it between his teeth, drew on her breast and then released it to worship the other.

In no time at all she was once more writhing beneath him, silently begging him to end the sweet torture and at the same time, hoping beyond hope that he might prolong the delicious agony forever.

This second time around he seemed more than willing to comply with the latter.

Lane wondered why the house was dark. After what he and Ramon had found between lightning storms, he prayed no one had slipped in to extinguish the lights and lie in waiting. He knew Chase had found Eva. Orvil told them all as much when he came in. Lane hadn't bothered to give up his winning poker hand to come in and hear what had happened to her on the way back from town. He figured she was probably cold and tired anyway. Besides, most likely, they would hear all the details at breakfast in the morning.

He left the back door open to the rain and moved stealthily through the dark kitchen. When there was no response to a quick knock at Eva's door, he tried the knob. The door swung open. In a flash of lightning, he could make out the unbroken surface of her empty bed.

Where in the hell was everybody?

He moved on, unreasonable fear gripped his entrails with icy fingers. The sitting room was empty, too. Between flashes of light and claps of thunder there was only the sound of the rain. Fear for Eva's safety mingled with murky thoughts that frightened the hell out of him. Once, long ago, he had stood small and helpless in this very room and listened while his mother was attacked. He had seen her die, the event so horrifying that he could not recall it in any detail.

He paused at the edge of the crowded sitting room and stared across at the two bedroom doors on the opposite wall. His palms were sweating. A sound that was undisguised by the rain filtered through to him. It was a cry. The sound held no threat of pain, but it frightened him nonetheless. He thought he heard a low groan follow close behind the first whimper. Bile rushed up into his throat. He choked it down.

What in the hell was wrong with him?

Lightning flared and he waited, held his breath until the thunder crashed seconds later. Lane took another step. His right hand rested on the damp leather of his holster as he forced himself to move forward without a sound.

There was a break in the lightning and thunder, and above the rain he heard the cry again, louder this time, more urgent. A shiver snaked through him. Lane found himself frozen to the spot as effectively as if someone had nailed his boots to the floor.

He closed his eyes. Pain was throbbing at his temples. He shook his head and tried to fight off the sounds and unwanted memories they invoked. His hands began to shake, not from the chill of damp clothes beneath his oilskin fish, but from long suppressed recollections buried deep inside.

He saw Auggie Owens as if in a nightmare, unwashed, meaty arms and thighs, her rank smell. She leaned over him, beckoning him with a sick smile and a piece of penny candy. Countless times he wished she would eat the candy herself, put it in her mouth and choke on it. But that never happened.

"Come here, boy. It's time to go to bed. . . ."

He shook his head but the vision didn't clear.

She grabbed him by the arm, twisted and pulled until he yelped, dragged him struggling and crying toward the sagging bed that took up most of her room.

"Stop your snivelin' and get under the covers with me."

She climbed in beside him, trapping him between her bulk and the wall.

Lane opened his eyes and forced the hideous memory back where it belonged. Haunted by the sounds issuing from his uncle's room, Lane was drawn toward the door like a sleepwalker. He paused with his hand on the latch, rested his forehead against the rough wooden planks and cursed silently. He could no more turn back than he could erase all that had happened to him so very long ago.

The sickness locked inside so long drove him forward. He had to see, had to know what was going on behind that door—even if the nightmare of it drove him insane.

Now. Now while the rain was beating on the shingled roof with a vengeance. He grasped the latch and pressed down. The door swung open just as another flash of lightning snaked down and lit the room as effectively as a hundred oil lamps.

In that brief moment, that eerie blue blaze of light, he saw them. Eva's red curls were unmistakable against the white pillowcase. Feet spread wide and braced flat on the mattress, knees bent, she arched up to take his uncle inside her, pressing him deeper with her hands on his buttocks. Lane suppressed a cry of his own when he saw Eva beneath his uncle.

Chase lunged above her like a stallion, his skin pale and ghostly in the searing blue flash of light.

Thunder claimed the silence. Unable to move, Lane watched.

Seconds seemed like hours as the scene quickly unfolded, dredging up hideous memories of other dark nights and far uglier scenes. He heard his mother's cries, not Eva's. He closed his eyes.

Eva cried out again—it was a sound that held no hint of pain—but was a sharp, searing cry nonetheless.

He heard his uncle grunting in rhythm to his frenzied thrusts as he moved with Eva. Moaning, whispering Chase's name over and over, she wrapped her legs around his waist and clung to him. The sight of her arms and legs locked around his uncle like that made Lane dizzy. His head was pounding. He had to get out before he threw up right there in the doorway.

Another burst of light filled the room. Lane heard Eva

cry out again, but this time the sound was a cry of warning. He stared at her across the room. In that one brief instant, that explosion of light, their eyes met.

Lane turned and ran.

"Eva? What is it?" Chase was slow to recover this time. He felt groggy, like a man swimming upstream in molasses—and with good reason. He had just finished making love with an angel for the second time that night.

Eva frantically tried to pull away from him. She grappled for the covers twisted beneath them.

He hoped he had not hurt her. She seemed desperate to get away. "Are you all right?"

"I don't know, I—"

Chase reached down for the sheet and blanket and drew them up, but Eva shoved past him and climbed out of the bed. She favored her injured ankle as she stood staring across the room. He glanced over his shoulder and for the first time noticed that the door was standing wide open. He swung his legs over the side of the bed and watched while she pawed through the pile of clothes on the ground.

As she held up the black shirt he had been wearing and shook it open, she explained. "Lane was here. He saw us. He was standing in the doorway."

Chase sighed, "Damn it to hell."

"We have to find him. He's still just a boy, Chase. He didn't know he'd find us in here like this. Think of what he must be going through right now—"

Reaching up, Chase ran his splayed fingers through his hair and watched as she shrugged into his shirt and began to button it up the front. Something wasn't right. He could feel it in his gut but he couldn't quite decide what was nagging at him.

"He'll get over it. How much could he have seen before you screamed like that?" He wondered aloud.

She swung on him. "Plenty." Barelegged, she limped across the room and shut the door again before she hobbled back.

Chase leaned toward the bedside table, fumbled for a match, struck it and lit the oil lamp. The wick was too high. It smoked when the light flared and fogged the chimney. He lowered the wick and watched Eva. She appeared disheveled, beautiful in her disarray, but far from embarrassed or as shocked as he expected under the circumstances.

"Just what do you plan on telling him when you find him?" Chase wanted to know.

"I don't know, but I hope you're coming with me. If not I'll go alone. I plan to apologize, certainly."

She was at it again, bent over, searching the floor for clothing. This time she grabbed one of her stockings. It was limp and still wet. She frowned and cast it aside.

"What are you sorry about, Eva?" She heard the tension in his voice, the unspoken question in his tone.

Eva crossed the room to stand before him. Chase sat there nude at the edge of the bed, hunched over, his fore-arms resting on his thighs. He looked up at her and a shock of midnight hair fell into his eyes.

"I'm sorry he had to see us like that, is all."

His stare was intense, suspicious. She was afraid of what he was thinking when she realized she was not reacting the way he expected. Had Chase come to the conclusion that she was not what she had pretended to be?

She had to escape his stare.

"I'll see if he's still in the house," she said, tugging the bedspread off the bed and quickly wrapping it around her hips. Eva wrenched open the door and stepped into the sitting room. The light from the oil lamp in Chase's room reached far enough to cast heavy shadows beyond the doorway.

The lamplight barely illuminated the tall silent figure standing near the fireplace.

"Ramon," she whispered. Her words lodged in her throat the minute she noticed the gun in his hand. Eva dropped her gaze and concentrated on the weapon. "What are you doing?"

"Where is Chase?"

She indicated the other room with a nod of her head. "In there. Where's Lane?"

"I saw him leave the house in a big hurry. Why, Señorita? What made him run?"

Chase came to the doorway and stood there bare to the waist. Half-buttoned, his pants gaped open. His *segundo* stared at him for a moment, then turned to Eva. Slowly Ramon holstered his gun.

"Where's Lane?" Chase asked Ramon.

The Mexican shrugged.

"We have to find him." Eva felt ridiculous issuing commands while dressed in Chase's damp shirt and the bedspread, but at this point she didn't care. She knew how sensitive Lane was, and the boy mattered most right now— more than any false modesty, more than what Ramon thought of her.

"We rode out between lightning storms," Ramon began. He shifted his weight. The slight motion set the ornate rowels of his spurs singing. "At the east water hole, we found twenty-seven head poisoned." He glanced at Eva and then back to Chase. "We came straight back to warn you."

Chase stared at Ramon for a moment as he took in the ramifications of what he had just heard. His hands tightened into fists. In an explosion of rage, he yelled, *"God damn it!"* and hit the door frame with his right fist.

Eva winced at the force and knew the blow had to hurt. Chase was oblivious to the pain. He stepped into the shadowed room, his obsidian eyes studying her intently. He walked up to her, reached out and brushed a lock of hair back off her face then grabbed her by the nape of the neck. It was all she could do not to flinch at the fury in his eyes.

"Well, lady, you really had me fooled. That was quite a performance."

At first, Eva couldn't find her voice. Then, she managed to whisper, "What do you mean?"

She knew what he would say before he said it, sensed what he was about to accuse her of.

"I knew there was something wrong the minute you jumped out of bed to run after Lane." He pressed closer, forcing her to look up. "It's been eating at me all night, stayed right there in the back of my mind since you let me take you into my room. You're no down-on-her-luck lady in need of a job, and you were no virgin when I took you to bed tonight, either."

"Chase, please let me explain—"

"You don't have to explain anything to me, Eva. I might be nothing but a big, dumb rancher, but once I get the point it's well taken."

She glanced over at Ramon and wished the man would leave them alone. She had to explain quickly or the damage would be irreparable.

"Who are you working for?" Chase demanded.

Eva stepped back, driven by the rage behind his words. "No one."

He grabbed her by the shoulders. His punishing grip tightened. "Don't lie to me. Was it Hank Reynolds or the Hunts that sent you out here to set me up?"

"No one, Chase. You have to believe me, I—"

He shoved her away and stalked past, rubbing the knuckles of his right hand on his thigh. He began to pace the room, glancing now and again at Eva. "I was such a blind fool, I fell right into your trap, didn't I? You reported to them, kept me preoccupied, and got me to let down my guard."

She was shaking so hard she nearly dropped the patterned blanket.

"No, please . . . " Eva reached out to him as he strode past, but he ignored her outstretched hand.

"Was it all an act? Did you deliberately hide out in that storm tonight knowing I'd be fool enough to go out looking for you? And then, to be certain whoever you're working for had time to kill off enough of my herd, you finally begged me to bed you." He laughed, a deep, throaty laugh laced with pain.

Eva's heart ached for him, for the misery he was going

through, for the raw pain she saw in his eyes.

He made another pass, but this time he paused when he reached her. "Does it feel good, Eva? Are you happy knowing that your part in this little scheme succeeded so very well?"

Tears welled up in her eyes to blind her. She blinked them away, and they rolled down her cheeks. "You aren't even going to allow me to tell my side of this, are you?"

"I don't feel like listening to any more lies." He turned on his heel and headed for his room. "Ramon, get the others saddled up. The storm's played out."

"We ride to patrol the herd?"

"Damn the herd. We'll stay together and try to ride down the men who did this to us."

"*Sí, patrón.*" The tall man paused long enough to stare at Eva for a moment. "What of her?"

Chase shot her a backward glance of dismissal. "If we're lucky, she'll be gone when we get back."

Ramon nodded and left the room.

Fear ripped through Eva. In the mood he was in, Chase wasn't thinking clearly. He could easily fall prey to whoever was out to ruin him. She limped after him to the door of his room. He stood rigid, his back to her, as he stared down at the rumpled bed.

"Chase, listen to me. I don't care what you think—"

"Obviously not."

"—I'm not working for anyone. I don't know who poisoned your stupid cattle and right now I don't care. I love you, Chase Cassidy and I—"

He turned on her, and in three strides was across the room looming over her. "Shut your vile mouth. Do you think for one minute I am ever going to believe anything that comes out of it again? Do you think those false tears of yours are ever going to move me again? Do you think I'd *let* you?"

"If you just listen I'll tell you everything. My real name is Eva Eber—"

"I don't care who you are. I should have known you were lying. I was a fool to let myself think that a *real* lady would ever see anything in me." He looked at her hair, let his gaze fall to her breasts hidden beneath his shirt, then lingered on her lips.

Silent beneath his angry perusal, Eva shifted uncomfortably. There was no use arguing with him anymore. She had been tried and condemned in a matter of seconds.

He turned around and walked away. "Get out of here. I need to change."

Her knuckles whitened as her hands tightened on the woven blanket. Eva spun around, headed for her own room. She heard the bedroom door slam.

As she limped through the darkened kitchen, she stubbed her toe on a chair and doubled over with the added pain. When she was safely in her room, Eva slammed her own door.

How could she have been so stupid as to let herself get carried away by passion? Quincy Powell had been forced to use all of his persuasion before she gave in to him, but the fiery need she experienced tonight with Chase had never entered into her former relationship.

Tonight she realized that despite his past, she had truly come to love Chase Cassidy. She was willing to spend the rest of her life making a home for him and Lane. Now he hated her with a vengeance and Lane, understandably shocked by what he had seen, had run off. She thought of Lane, alone in the storm, running from what he had seen. She could only pray that he had sense enough to go to Rachel's again.

Eva walked over to the dresser, rested her elbows atop it and buried her face in her hands. Dry, heaving sobs racked her body. Afraid Chase would hear, she hurried over to the bed, lay down, drew her knees up to her breasts and pressed her fists to her lips.

It wasn't long before the tears came.

* * *

Fully dressed in dry clothes, Chase sat on the edge of his bed and pulled on his boots. Rain still slapped the windows, but the intensity of the storm had lessened. The room was damp. Eva's lilac fragrance and the musky scent of their lovemaking lingered to haunt him.

He stared down at the discarded pink striped gown at his feet and the red petticoat that was visible beneath it. Chase rested his elbows on his knees and dropped his head onto the heels of his hands. How he could have been such a blind fool was beyond him.

Now, even the tenuous relationship he had established with Lane was in ruins.

"She is not what she appears to be."

He should have listened to Ramon from the very beginning. He'd been warned. This whole mess was of his own making.

Once more everything was his fault. He hadn't used his head, but his heart. He had acted from the gut just like he had when he ran off after Sally's killers, neglecting Lane and the ranch. Nothing but hatred had driven him then. Love for Eva Edwards had driven him tonight.

Love and hate. As far as he was concerned, they were one and the same, and both accomplished nothing. From now on, he decided, he wouldn't allow himself to succumb to either. It was far better to feel nothing at all.

Right now he had to rid the ranch of the culprits who had cost him so many head of cattle.

Chase walked to the crooked wardrobe that stood against one wall. He knelt down before it and opened a bottom drawer. Inside lay his gun and holster.

He stared at the worn, soft leather, at the inlaid handles. His palm itched to hold it. He rubbed his hand on his thigh.

Seconds ticked by.

Chase closed the drawer. He would depend on his men. The whip offered some protection. It could do some damage, but it wouldn't stop a bullet.

He didn't think it mattered much anymore anyway.

Chapter Sixteen

As he leaned his shoulder into the door of the abandoned line shack, Lane prayed to God his uncle would not come looking for him anytime soon. The rickety door gave under his weight and creaked inward. The smell of wet dirt, mice, and something rancid hit his nostrils. He left the door open and stared into the darkened interior of the one-room shack. The place had been deserted for years.

Although his uncle had talked of making plans to renovate the old cabin enough to house a line rider next winter, Lane knew that after the losses of the last few days, Chase would be lucky if he did not have to sell the whole place.

Lane walked in. The rain had stopped coming down in bucketfuls, but an insistent drizzle still fell outside. The roof leaked badly in places. Water pooled on the floor. He was soaked through, so he lit the fire in the small stone fireplace that had been set against one wall. Fumbling in the dark for matches and a few pieces of dry wood that remained in a lopsided wood box near the fireplace, he soon had a fire going and enough firelight to see by.

Lane hunkered down before the fire and scanned the room. On the far wall the remains of a supply shelf hung perpendicular to the floor. A few rusted bean tins, the tops sawed open and jagged, lay on the floor in a heap beneath the bed that had been built into the wall.

After one look at the straw-filled mattress full of holes, he figured he would be better off sitting up beside the fire than spending the night on top of a mouse hotel.

He leaned back against the wall, elbows resting on bent

knees, and pulled his hat down to his eyebrows. He did not dare sleep. Not tonight. Not when the new-old memories were so fresh, so horrifying and vivid in his mind's eye. It all seemed a jumble now; the nightmare he had lived since witnessing his mother's death, the subsequent years with Auggie Owens.

If anyone had asked him which experience had been worse, he couldn't say. *Wouldn't* say was more like it.

It took a while for him to realize he was shaking. Lane wondered if he would ever stop. Until he had walked in on Eva and Chase tonight, he had unconsciously blocked out the memory of the way his guardian had forced him to pet and fondle her when he was a little boy.

How long had it gone on? Certainly not those last few years, or his memory would have been much clearer. Lane rubbed his temples with his fingertips. He tried to recall when and why Auggie had finally stopped forcing him into her bed, but his head was throbbing too hard to dwell on any one memory too long. The old recollections fused with the sight of Eva and Chase making love; and somewhere in the back of his mind, they all twisted and blended into a confusing composite portrait of then and now.

What were Chase and Eva thinking now? She had definitely seen him standing there, frozen to the spot, staring at them. He thought he heard her cry out in alarm. And what of Chase?

Eva and Chase.

Eva in Chase's arms. Eva doing those things *with his uncle.*

He would have never pictured them together, not in a million years, and yet, on an instinctive level, he had known what was going on between them tonight from the moment he stepped into the darkened house and heard her whimper. He had never made love to a woman, yet he had instinctively recognized the sounds of passion.

Lane put his hands over his ears, afraid. The sounds had been both terrifying and disturbingly arousing as well.

On another level, it was almost impossible to believe

what he had seen. He might have expected it of Chase, but Eva?

Not Eva. Not the beautiful lady who had befriended him. Her stunning copper hair and fancy manners really had him fooled. When he thought of how kind she had always been toward him, how much she seemed to really care—the way she went out of her way to make him feel like a man. When he thought of those things, he grew so angry, all he could think of was hurting someone, hurting someone or something until they hurt as much as he did.

Eva. How many times had he wondered what she would feel like in his arms? He had even imagined kissing her. Hell, he had to admit to himself that at times he had wondered what it would be like to make love to her the way Chase had done. But after having seen his fantasy played out in the flesh, complete with sights, and scents, and sounds, all he felt was shaken and repulsed.

What if he never, ever wanted a woman in his life?

What if he never, ever let anyone touch him again?

What if he could never live a normal life because of the newly awakened memory of Auggie Owens and the little games she had made him play when he was a child?

He leaned away from the rough log wall, which had begun to press uncomfortably into his spine. The fire did little to take away the chills that racked his body.

No wonder he could barely tolerate the sight of his uncle. Until tonight, Lane never knew why he so resented Chase leaving him with Auggie Owens. And now, for the first time, he was able to recall the details of his mother's death. He reached up to wipe his face, shocked into the realization that his cheeks were wet from his own tears and not rain.

His mother had chosen to leave him. He knew that now. The memory was all too vivid, too raw, too unthinkable. After her death, when he should have been nurtured and coddled and cared for, Chase had thrust him into a hellish nightmare where he had been forced to submit to Auggie Owens's twisted demands. And then, just like his mother had done, Chase deserted him, too.

Lane shook his head and cursed.

The room was dark, the hour late, yet he wasn't about to doze off. He couldn't allow it, not with so many nightmarish scenes crowding one upon another in his mind.

Lane stared around the filthy line shack and wondered how long a body could exist without sleep.

For the first time since she had arrived at Trail's End, Eva was up and anxious to greet the dawn. Her ankle was much recovered, the slight swelling already gone. Still distrustful of it, she stepped carefully, keeping her weight on the other leg as she moved around the room. Outside the window, raindrops clung to the leaves of the low scrubberry bush beneath her window. A few slow drops still dripped from the eaves, but the night's storm had finally passed. Welcome sunshine broke across the sky. She wondered if anyone would come in for breakfast and glanced toward the bunkhouse. In need of a strong, black cup of coffee, she stoked the fire and made a full pot. By the time the coffee boiled, Orvil came in the back door, eyes downcast, shoulders slumped.

"Word travels fast," she mumbled.

He paused in the middle of the kitchen with hat in hand and stared at her, his mouth drooping, his forehead creased by a frown.

"Did you do it, Miss Eva? Did you trick Cassidy and help those devils kill off the stock?"

She was forced to set the coffeepot down because her hands had begun shaking.

"Is that what you really think, Orvil? That I'm guilty?"

"I don't want to, ma'am. I sure don't."

"Well then don't, because I'm innocent." She walked toward the back door, rubbing her upper arms as she did, pausing to stare out the window at the corrals and barn. "I don't know how I'm going to prove I'm innocent, but I will. First I have to find Lane. Do you know if anyone has seen him?"

Orvil stared down at his boots. "Not yet. But as far as I know, nobody's been looking for him. They're all aimin' to run down whoever it was poisoned the cattle last night. Chase and the rest came in and changed horses a couple hours before dawn."

Chase had been in and she had missed him. Eva turned away from the window. "Lane may have ridden into town hoping Rachel Albright would take him in again. Do you have any idea where he might be if he's not there?"

The veteran cowboy shook his head. "I sure don't, but I can tell you when he lit out of here last night, he weren't headed toward town. I saw him go west, toward the hills."

After life in various towns and cities across the country, she was still in awe of the wide-open landscape. Eva thought it would be an impossible task to find Lane, but she wasn't about to admit defeat before she even started.

"Do you think you could saddle up a horse for me, please, Orvil? I want to—"

He shook his head. "Miss Eva, after what happened last night, I don't think Cassidy wants you out ridin' around all alone, and I can't go with you because he told me to stay put in case trouble come ridin' up to the door."

"But—"

"I wish I could help, but I can't, ma'am. I work for Chase Cassidy and long as I'm takin' pay from him, I have to do what he asks."

Eva studied Orvil carefully. It would do no good to argue with him. After all, she had no desire to get the man into trouble, but she was determined to go after Lane. She would just have to do it without Orvil's help. If she did not confide in him, then he could honestly tell Chase he didn't know anything about it when they discovered she was missing.

She waited impatiently, puttering about the kitchen, trying to keep busy while he drank a cup of coffee and finally left. As soon as he was out the door, Eva hurried through the house to Lane's room and took his spare trousers off a nail beside the window. She rolled them up and tucked them beneath her arm as she hurried back through the house.

Once in her room, Eva closed the door and quickly changed. She pulled Lane's trousers over her combination and took the shirtwaist blouse that went with her traveling suit and slipped it on. She took a bright yellow ribbon out of her top drawer and tied it around her hair to keep it back off her face.

She waited near the back door, where she could see Orvil moving about, feeding his chickens. When he walked back toward the bunkhouse and then disappeared inside, she slipped out and ran across the yard in a crouch. The mud sucked at her shoes as she made her way carefully into the barn.

The building was cool and damp inside and smelled of hay and horses. She felt a moment of panic when she realized all the horses were out in the corral—even the piebald mare was not in her stall. Then, straining to see through the dim light, she recognized the big bay horse that Chase usually rode standing in the end stall. She walked the length of the barn and stared through the rails at the bay.

Eva sighed. Things would have been much easier if she had been raised on a ranch instead of out of a show trunk backstage. She searched for the old saddle she had used before, found it in the adjoining tack room, and after much tugging and careful prodding, she saddled the horse to her satisfaction.

Eva led the massive creature out a side door, thankful that he seemed willing to follow her silent commands. Once mounted, she walked the horse until she was no longer visible from the barn. It wasn't until she headed toward the hills that she finally let the horse run.

Riding four abreast, Chase and the others reached the south end of the ranch and reined in near the outcropping of boulders where he had found Eva. It seemed centuries ago, not mere hours, that he had ridden close to these very rocks shouting her name. He noticed the navy blue shawl lying in a crumpled, sodden wad on the ground beside the tallest boulder. He tried to ignore it, but Ned rode over, dismounted, and picked it up. The cowboy wrung it out, and then bundled the wrap and tied it behind his saddle.

The rain had battered down the wild flowers growing all around as effectively as the horses hooves were doing now. He closed his eyes for a second against the memory of the night at the school house, where he made such a fool of himself. A wave of heartache as intense as a physical wound tightened around his heart when he thought of Eva and what had passed between them last night. He had never experienced such boundless joy in the arms of a woman, nor had he ever felt so betrayed.

"There is no sign." Ramon fought the reins to keep his mount in line.

"Want to push on, boss?" Ned Delmont's crooked smile had disappeared when he was told about the lost stock.

An unusually silent Jethro Adams completed the quartet. None of Chase's men appeared eager to give up and go back to the ranch, even though they all could have used a hot meal and black coffee.

Chase looked out over the rolling landscape, past the outcropping of boulders, across the plain. Behind him the hills rose gradually to create a series of pockets and valleys that might hide any number of culprits. Last night, caught up in the shock of the raid on his stock and the realization that Eva had betrayed him, nothing could deter him from hunting down the men responsible. Now, in the bright light of day, Chase found he didn't care one way or the other. He didn't care about anything.

"We need to get back," he began. "We've still got the rest of the herd to worry about and I have a feeling that whoever is out there knows just where we are. We'll need to bring all the cattle in close to the ranch and keep an eye on them."

"That'll mean feeding them. What we had left of the

winter feed supply is near gone," Ramon reminded him.

"Right now I can't think of much else to do," Chase told him.

Ramon glanced back toward the hills. "Perhaps we should split up on the way back."

Chase felt a sense of foreboding and shook his head. "I think we should all stay together. We can't cover as much territory this way, but since we don't know how many men we're dealing with, we can't take the risk." He thought of Lane out there somewhere alone and prayed the boy was safe.

"Rider comin' from town." Jethro's excitement was clear.

Chase turned in the saddle and watched as a lone traveler rode toward them. The man appeared taller and more broad-shouldered than Lane. Chase waited, as did the others, for the rider to draw near. It wasn't long before he recognized Stuart McKenna.

The sheriff reined in before the men. Sunlight glinted off the star pinned to his vest. His quick gaze took in the hands, Ramon, and finally Chase. He nodded coolly. "Cassidy."

"What can we do for you, Sheriff?"

"You don't seem to be too hard at work today," he commented.

Chase rested his forearm across his thigh and stared at the man he had known since his youth. McKenna's family had been one of the first to settle the area, long before the town of Last Chance was established. Stuart McKenna was everything Chase wasn't—wealthy, respected, gifted with a sense of humor, always on the right side of the law. Chase had not been surprised to find out Stuart McKenna had been appointed sheriff.

Chase met the man's light blue eyes. "You ride all the way out here just to see if we were working, Stuart, or have you got something else on your mind?"

McKenna pushed his hat back off his forehead exposing the shock of bright red hair along his hairline. "Came to let you know I got a telegram from the capitol this morning.

Seems the Hunt brothers broke out of prison about three weeks ago and at last report were headed this way. Thought they might be out gunning for you, Cassidy. Thought you ought to at least have a fightin' chance.''

Chase went still, the only visible sign of alarm was the tightening of his hands upon the reins. He stared at McKenna for a long moment, his mind racing back over the years to the day he penned a letter implicating the Hunts in his sister's death. He knew that if given the chance, they would kill him for putting them away.

McKenna watched him closely. Finally he broke his stare and looked at the other riders. ''You don't look like you're pushin' any cattle right now. You haven't seen any sign of them have you?''

Chase shook his head. ''No, but you might have cleared up a little mystery we've had going on here lately.''

''Such as?''

''For the past few days somebody's been killing off my herd bit by bit. Last night during the storm, we found close to twenty-five head poisoned. Rain's washed away any tracks. We were about to head back to the house,'' Chase told him.

The house.

As far as he knew, if she hadn't packed up yet, Eva was alone with Orvil at the ranch house. Fear uncoiled with the speed of a whip in the pit of his stomach. If Eva had been telling the truth, if she wasn't acting as accomplice for the Hunt brothers or whoever it was that was out to ruin him, then she was as vulnerable as any of them to attack.

He straightened, anxious to head back and see that she was safe. He paused long enough to ask McKenna, ''Did you hear of anyone working with them?''

When could Eva have met up with the escaped convicts? Where did she meet them?

Stuart shook his head. ''Far as I know, they're alone, but they may have had help getting out of prison.''

Again, Chase thought of Eva. Had she gone so far as to provide the men with a means of escape from prison? Was she connected to them by old ties? Could she be a friend, a sister . . . a lover?

"Will you let me know if you see them, Cassidy?" McKenna looked doubtful. "I'd hate to have you go off half-cocked and end up like you did before."

Chase was so blind with fury he could barely see. He had to get back to the house and question Eva again. His words, when finally uttered, sounded stilted even to himself. "I'll let you know."

"You do that, hear?" McKenna turned his horse toward town. "I'll do the same."

Chase did not bid the man farewell, nor did he say a word to his own men. He simply headed in the direction of the ranch and started back, anxious to see if Eva's web of lies was as tangled as he suspected.

When they reached the ranch proper, the others went to the corral for fresh horses. Chase rode up to the back of the house. An unfamiliar horse and buggy stood in the yard not far from the porch.

Chase dismounted, whipped the reins around the hitching post, and was across the lopsided planks in three strides. He yanked the door open so hard it bounced back off the wall and slammed behind him.

"Eva?" He called her name as he walked through the empty kitchen, straight to her bedroom door. Without even the courtesy of a knock, he jerked the door open. The room was deserted. One of her dresses had been tossed across the bed, the dresser drawers gaped wide, revealing the jumbled contents. It was as if she had rustled through the contents of each drawer in a hurry, yet most of the items had been left behind. There appeared to be little, if anything, missing. Her lilac toilet water, as well as her comb and brush, were still atop the dresser.

Chase heard footsteps behind him. He whirled around. His hand instinctively went to his hip but came away empty. The man across from his lost all trace of color before he realized Chase was unarmed.

"You could have killed me," said the slick-haired blond

stranger, his tone one of realization rather than fear.

Chase eyed the stranger. They were of much the same height, but where he was dark, this man was light. His hair, although blond, was slicked down with hair tonic and appeared darker. He reached into his brocade vest pocket and withdrew a card, flicked it over in his fingers and extended it to Chase.

"My name's Quincy Powell. I came after Eva Eberhart, but she's not here."

Eberhart, not Edwards.

"I don't know any Eva Eberhart," Chase told him, biding his time. He forced himself to appear relaxed and leaned casually against the doorjamb between Eva's room and the kitchen.

The man stared over Chase's shoulder into the small bedroom. Even white teeth accented his perfect smile. "I've already seen her things in there. There isn't anybody but Eva who owns so many colored underclothes." He shoved his hands in his back pockets and rolled forward onto the balls of his feet and then back again as he boasted, "I ought to know, I've seen 'em all."

Chase wanted to rip the man's throat out. Instead he kept his voice as controlled as possible. "What do you want with her?"

Quincy Powell laughed. "I want her back, period."

His blood, running hot and cold, Chase was barely breathing now. "What gives you any claim to her? Far as I know she's never even mentioned your name." *There was a hell of a lot Miss Eva Edwards hadn't ever mentioned, it seemed.*

"She owes me big," Powell told him. "Besides, things haven't gone right at the Palace since she left. She ran out after starting a brawl that nearly shut me down for a week and besides that, she was the best dancer I ever hired."

Dancer? Chase fought to piece the story together. "She *danced* at your place?"

"You're damn right she did, even though she thought that after starring in two-bit theater productions all her life she was above dancing at the Palace. I've had a streak of bad luck at the tables since she walked out, and I aim to turn that around here and now. I'm taking her back to work off what she owes me.''

Quincy pulled a gold watch out of his pocket, flicked the lid open and noted the time, then snapped it closed. "So where is she?"

Chase watched the man pocket the watch. He knew Quincy Powell's type. He had encountered the same sort of smooth-talking gambler plenty of times in plenty of saloons and gambling halls during his search for his sister's killers. Powell might look the type who never dirtied his hands in a fight, but more than likely he carried a derringer in his pocket and a knife strapped to his ankle.

Pushing off from the wall, Chase stalled. "The lady that lives here is named Eva Edwards. Far as I know the only thing she had in common with the woman you want is that she's partial to colored underclothes. How do I know she's the one you're looking for?"

Quincy smirked. "Redhead. Good legs. Great butt." He held his hands out in front of his chest. "Tits out to here."

Chase dove for the man's throat. He grabbed his collar and drove Quincy Powell across the kitchen floor until he had him laid out flat across the table. The gambler tore the front of Chase's shirt in an attempt to grab hold and began to sputter. His eyes bulged, his fair skin quickly turned a mottled red.

"How long have you two been working for the Hunt brothers?" Chase loosened his hold on Quincy's throat barely long enough for the man to gasp a strangled response.

"I don't . . . know who . . . you're . . . talking about—"

Chase buried his fingers farther into Powell's windpipe. The man's lips began to purple. "You swear you know nothing about the Hunts?"

Quincy Powell tried to nod. All he accomplished was a slight movement of his head.

"Does Eva know them?"

Powell's eyes grew wide and he shrugged. "Don't . . . know," he croaked.

Chase let go and dragged the man to his feet. He shoved him down into a chair so hard the gambler winced. Quincy Powell's well-oiled blond hair was standing out around his head in matted, sticky bundles.

"If you have a lick of sense you'll get out of here and won't look back," Chase warned.

Still gasping, Powell shook his head. "Not . . . without . . . Eva. Nobody walks out on me. Besides, she still owes me money."

Chase flexed his hands and Quincy flinched. "How much?" Chase wanted to know. "*How much* does she still owe you?"

Quincy straightened the intricate tie around his neck, smoothing it back down inside his vest front. "Two hundred dollars."

Seconds ticked by while Chase stared down at the gambler who carefully avoided his gaze.

"Wait right here." Calling himself every kind of a fool under heaven, Chase walked to his room. Once there, he shoved his dresser away from the wall and took down the yellowed envelope he kept nailed to the back panel. He took out two hundred in bills, then replaced the nearly empty envelope and moved the dresser back. It was an inordinate amount of money, almost everything he had left. Chase tried to tell himself he was only getting rid of Quincy so that he would have the opportunity to personally see that Eva pay for what she had done to him. But deep inside, he was afraid to admit that despite everything, the thought of Eva owing a man like Quincy Powell turned his stomach.

The rowels on his spurs sang loud and clear as he recrossed the sitting room with determined strides and entered the kitchen. He found Powell still seated where he had left him with his forehead resting on his arm. When Chase entered the room, Quincy Powell looked up.

Chase held out the wad of bills. "Take this and get out."

Quincy stared suspiciously at the handful of money then

smiled slightly as realization slowly dawned on him.

"You're sweet on her—"

"Take it and get out. Now."

Powell stood up and grabbed the money from Chase. He bent to retrieve his brown hat and hurried to the back door. Chase followed him out. He walked him all the way to the hired buggy.

As if the man was not content with merely taking the money, Quincy paused, one foot on the step and straightened the frilly white cuffs of his right sleeve.

"You know," Powell said, staring Chase right in the eye, "I would have let her work it off in bed." That said, he turned away and started to climb aboard the rig.

"Powell?"

Quincy turned around.

Chase leveled him with a right to the jaw. Quincy Powell's spotless brown hat rolled under the buggy and came to rest beside a pile of horse manure.

Chapter Seventeen

"Lane?"

Eva stood back to survey the dilapidated line shack with its rotting eaves and split log walls with holes gaping in the chinks between them. She reached out and knocked again, certain Lane was inside. She recognized the pinto that was tied behind the shack.

"I'm not going away, so you might as well open this door."

Inside, a shuffling sound was followed by the creak of the door. When it opened, Lane stood there fully dressed but hatless, his eyes bleary, red rimmed, as he stared back at her.

"May I come in?" she asked.

He didn't move. He couldn't.

Lane never expected Eva to come after him herself. Now that he was staring her in the face, he didn't know where to look, what to say or what to do. He ran a hand through his hair and tried to concentrate. It was well after dawn before he finally allowed himself to fall asleep. Now, a few hours later, still groggy, at first he thought he had dreamed the sound of her voice, but here she stood in the flesh, her hair in wild disarray. She was dressed in a pair of baggy denim pants, the hems rolled into thick cuffs. It appeared she wasn't about to leave.

He shrugged and stepped aside, allowing her to enter.

"Thank you," she told him politely. Far too politely for the situation. Eva wished she knew what to say, but she had never found herself in such a predicament before. She decided not to sidestep the issue.

"I came to apologize for what happened last night and to ask you to come home."

He shoved his hands in his pockets and walked over to the nearly dead embers of the fire. He stood there, staring down into the ashes, unmoving, silent, wishing last night never happened, wishing away the last eleven years.

"Lane, please."

Eva watched him carefully. He seemed so despondent, so alone. She wished she could comfort him, but was afraid that would only make matters worse. He had trusted her, believed her to be something she obviously was not. Now he was hurt and angry, and worst of all, alienated from Chase again.

Staring at his rigid shoulders, she refused to be ignored. Eva crossed the floor until she was close enough to touch him.

"Lane, I want to talk about last night."

He cringed inwardly. He didn't want to talk at all, but there was one thing he had to ask, something that had bothered him all night long. "Did you want it, or did my uncle force you?"

"Oh, Lane." Eva's hand went to her lips. She took a deep breath to calm herself and then straightened. "I . . . we . . . we both wanted it."

He said nothing.

"Chase and I have strong feelings for each other and we couldn't . . . we didn't . . . oh, Lane this is so hard for me."

He turned on her and found her standing right behind him, wringing her hands.

"Hard for *you?* You'll never know what this has done to me. *Never.*"

Suddenly, she realized, or thought she realized, why he was so upset. "Lane, you didn't hold any *special* affection for me, did you?"

She prayed it wasn't true. All she had ever wanted was to be his friend, to support him, to help him.

He shook his head, determined never to tell her that before the memories of Auggie Owens came rushing back to him last night, that yes, he had nurtured a fanciful crush on her. He could never tell her that, just as he could never tell the truth of what Auggie had done to him. Not now. So he lied.

"No."

"Then why did you run?" The hopelessness she saw in his eyes made her want to flinch.

"I was in shock. Seeing you like that, seeing Chase," he rubbed his hand across his eyes. "It was like a bad dream."

She reached for his sleeve. "It must have been hard on you, and I'm so sorry for that, Lane. We should have both realized that you or one of the other men might have come looking for him. Maybe I shouldn't have given in to my feelings, but sometimes people don't think about consequences beforehand. Sometimes things just happen."

He could see the tears and turned away quickly so she wouldn't see his own. "We can't change the things that have already happened, can we, Eva? We can never make them go away."

Aware of the subtle nuances in his tone, she frowned and brushed away her tears. He was still upset. Far too upset for the circumstances. "Lane, is there something else you're not telling me? There is, isn't there?"

He shook his head and walked to the far end of the room. A broken shelf dangled just above the floor. She noticed a pile of tin cans and some shredded paper that looked like an animal's abandoned nest. The summer wind that had blown away the storm wafted through the open door.

"Finding all those dead cattle had to upset you, too. Chase is out now trying to find the men who were responsible. As soon as he finds out who's behind this, things will get back to normal."

Lane laughed. It was a cold, mirthless sound for someone so young. *"Normal?* Our lives have never been normal, Eva. Not Chase's and not mine."

She crossed the room, sidestepping the saddle on the

floor beside the shoddy mattress. She began slowly. "My life has never been what you would call normal either, because I'm not the lady I claimed to be. I didn't grow up wealthy, living in a big house in Philadelphia."

Dropping the barrier of lies between them might be the only way to reach him. She had failed with Chase because she had perpetuated a lie; she didn't want to leave without trying to salvage Lane's future.

She could tell she had his complete attention. "My real name is Eva Eberhart. I'm an actress and a dancer. My mother and father still make appearances across the country. I was on stage as soon as I could walk."

Eva glanced up and noticed that he was staring fixedly at her, listening intently. "My last job was in Cheyenne. I worked in a two-bit dance hall and gambling saloon until I read your uncle's ad in a Montana paper somebody left on a table. I decided to try to salvage what was left of the rest of my life. That's why I came here and that's why it was so important for me to convince Chase to hire me. I needed to start over and I needed a reference, so I lied to get the job."

"I always wondered why a lady like you wanted to work for us."

"To me, this was as good a place to start as any." She turned away from him, her hands knotted at her waist . "I didn't bargain on falling in love."

"So you really are in love with him?" Lane sat down on the edge of the bed. It sagged pitifully beneath his weight. He watched her carefully, tried to imagine Eva performing in a saloon. The image didn't come.

"Yes," she whispered. "I really did fall in love with Chase. Now he hates me."

"Why?"

She shrugged and walked to the open doorway, stared out at the land for a moment. Then, framed in the sunlight pouring through the door. She glanced over her shoulder as she spoke.

"Ramon suspected me of working with the men who are

trying to ruin your uncle. Then, last night, when you and he brought word that the cattle had been poisoned, Chase assumed I only made love with him to keep him occupied while the deed was done. Nothing I said could convince him any differently.''

''But, you didn't have anything to do with it, did you?''

It hurt her to think that he harbored any doubt at all. ''No.'' She shook her head. ''Sadly enough, I don't know anything about it. All I know is that Chase needs you, Lane. He needs all the help he can get to protect this place and what cattle he has left.''

Chase needs you.

Lane wanted to yell at her, to rant, to rave. Where was Chase when he had needed him? Where was Chase when he was only five, six, seven and eight? Where was Chase when Auggie Owens would force him to get into her bed and touch her, to let him touch her? Where was Chase when he, Lane, ran back to his pallet on the floor in the kitchen, pulled the filthy covers over his head and cried himself to sleep?

''Chase doesn't need anybody,'' he told her.

''He does, Lane. He needs you and he needs a way to heal from his years in prison. He needs to be loved as much as you do. We all need to be loved. Please, Lane. Please try to understand. He was only doing what he thought best for you at the time.''

''What if it's too late to heal, Eva? What if none of us can survive the past?''

''We have to *believe* we can,'' she insisted.

He wanted to believe, he really did want to believe her, but he was too afraid. When he was a little boy he used to dream that Chase would come back and save him from Auggie. Then, after he grew older and Auggie no longer forced him into her bed, he didn't want Chase to come home because he was afraid his uncle would find out what he had done. As he matured, Auggie left him alone. Instead, she treated him like a work animal, forced him to labor on her land, to plow, to snare and gut small animals for food.

The dark memories of the earlier years were shoved into a far corner of his mind. It was the safest thing to do when there had been no hope in his life, when there was nothing to believe in. Now, here was Eva asking him to try.

Just yesterday, Lane had believed Eva was an angel sent to help him through the rough places in his life. Now that he had lost faith even in her, how could she expect him to have any faith in himself or his ability to overcome the tragedy of his past?

Lane reached down for his saddle and hefted it to his shoulder. He retrieved his hat and put it on. Eva moved across the room. When he looked up, she was standing beside him again.

The woman refused to give up. "Will you go back with me?"

He shook his head. "I can't. There's no going back."

She had failed. Eva felt desperate enough to beg. "Please, Lane. Do this one thing for me. No matter what happens, Chase loves you. I know he does. I know at times he doesn't show it, but that's because he doesn't know how. I think he's afraid of you, Lane. He's afraid to hurt you any more than he already has and he just wants to make everything right—"

He shoved the saddle away from him. It fell to the edge of the bed, dragged down by its own weight until it hit the damp floor. "Give it up, Eva. I can't go back and I won't, not even for you—"

"But—"

He held up his hand. "There's too much you don't know, too much I can't and won't say. All I know is that after last night, I can't go back—"

She grabbed his hand. "I told you, I'm sorry. If I could take it back, if I could undo it all, I would."

She meant every word. She doubted if she would ever experience the joy she had felt in Chase's arms with any other man. She had lost his trust and his love, but right now, if she could only save Lane any more of the anguish she read in his eyes, she would feel as if she left something worthwhile behind.

For her, there would be no going back.

He shook off her hold. "You can't undo it all, Eva. Don't even try." He reached for the saddle again. When he moved to the door, she followed close at his heels.

"Where will you go?"

"I don't know."

"How will you live?" She glanced down at the holster on his hip, at the rose carefully hand tooled into the leather. The delicate floral artwork on the holster that held the deadly weapon was a chilling sight.

With his back to her, he shrugged.

"I'll survive."

He stepped out into the sunlight. Eva followed him. The sun was warm. It shone down on the wet ground, drying out the land, but its warmth didn't reach her. With nothing any more convincing left to say, she walked a little behind him as Lane headed for his horse. They rounded the corner of the line shack. When Lane halted abruptly, she walked into him.

Eva heard the click of a revolver and froze. She peered around Lane's shoulder and gasped. A short, older man, wearing thick eyeglasses, a pinstriped suit, and a bowler hat, was aiming a gun at Lane's heart. In any other circumstances, she would have thought the moustachioed little man an accountant or perhaps a salesclerk. The gun made him deadly.

His threat was clear. "Stand right where you are and don't even think about moving. You too, little lady."

He waved the gun in Lane's direction again. "Drop the saddle. After you do, the lady can reach around you and unfasten your gun belt. Do it slow like," he cautioned her, " 'cause it won't bother me none to have to shoot you both."

Eva's hands were shaking. She reached around Lane and finally managed to unfasten his gun belt and let it fall to the ground.

"Who are you, mister?" Lane asked.

Eva wondered how he could sound so calm.

"Byron Hunt. You might have heard of me."

Lane shook his head. "Nope."

"You haven't?"

"Nope."

Eva noted the acute disappointment on their abductor's face. "I never heard of you, either," she added.

"You should have. I'm one of the Hunt brothers." He smirked at Lane. "Remember me, boy? I haven't seen you since you were in a long nightshirt."

Mindless of the gun aimed square at him, Lane took a step forward. Eva grabbed the waistband of his pants as Hunt threatened to shoot.

"I'm going to kill you," Lane promised.

Eva whispered, "Lane, please—"

"Don't worry about me, ma'am. He's not gonna do any such thing, 'cause he's not gonna live long enough to get around to it."

"You mean to kill us both?" she asked.

"Whether or not I kill you depends on how cooperative you intend to be, little lady."

"Don't count on me doing you any favors," she mumbled.

"What's that?" Hunt asked.

"Nothing." Eva could feel the tension emanating from Lane and refused to let go of him. He was sweating, his ebony hair shining with blue highlights in the bright sun. Knowing his quicksilver temper, she couldn't depend on him to calm down enough to think about a plan of action. She decided their best defense was to keep Hunt talking.

"I thought you were in jail," she said.

Hunt laughed. The sunlight glinted off his thick lenses and distorted the beady eyes beneath them. "We busted out, and now we intend to see Chase Cassidy pay for what he done. We're gonna burn this place down and kill off his cattle. That bastard's sister killed our little brother and then he helped send us to jail."

"He should have killed you," Lane said.

Eva yanked on the fabric in her hands to send Lane a silent warning.

"Who's with you?" Eva asked Hunt. "You keep saying *we* but I don't see anybody else around."

"My brother's gone to deliver a message to Cassidy. Let's just say I expect they'll both be here before too long. Now why don't you and your lady friend turn around and head back into the cabin?"

Lane didn't move. He tried to conjure up Byron Hunt's image, tried to piece the details of his mother's death together. Three men had sweet-talked his mother into letting them in. She had served them supper while his uncle was out on the range.

The bespectacled Hunt had seemed bigger then, brawnier, rough and foreboding. This man looked more like a dry goods drummer than a killer.

"Why should I let you shoot me in the back?" Lane demanded to know.

Eva whispered, "Please, Lane."

"Listen to the little lady, son. Besides, I need you for a while longer yet." His cajoling tone switched to a terse command. "Get moving."

Eva let go and Lane turned around. She was amazed by the composure on his face. There was no emotion in his usually savage, dark eyes. Absolutely nothing gave away his feelings. His lack of emotion scared her more than his threats. He had the cold, merciless stare of a killer.

She knew if Chase were standing in his nephew's place, she would see the same frigid look in his eyes.

Hunt reached down and untied a long rope coiled on Lane's saddle. He motioned them toward the house. Eva led the way. Immediately upon stepping over the threshold, she looked for something to use to clobber Hunt.

She paused in the center of the room, like Lane, waiting for the felon to make a wrong move.

"Tie him up." Hunt tossed the rope to Eva.

She stalled. "Where?"

Hunt blinked owlishly and looked around. "To the bed-post."

Lane sat down on the floor and put his hands behind him. Silently, he stared into Eva's eyes.

She stared back, communicating silently as she slipped the rope behind him and around one leg of the bed.

"Make it good and tight, gal, 'cause I'm going to check it myself."

Afraid for Lane, she did as she was told and stepped back.

Hunt checked the rope, tightened it, and finally satisfied, waved the gun at her. She sat on the floor at the other end of the bed. Hunt made no move to bind her.

Eva glanced over at Lane. He was staring at the wall in front of him, ignoring them both. "What do we do now?" she asked Hunt.

"We wait." Hunt leaned up against the fireplace wall where he could see down the length of the valley through the open door. "We just sit here and stare at each other and wait—unless you can think of a way to amuse me."

Chase prodded his horse through the herd of bawling, drifting cattle. Whistling, shouting, and whirling his hat above his head, he forced the last few strays through the wide gate that closed off the pasture nearest the out build-ings. Still on horseback, he reached out for the gate, swung it closed and slid the wooden bar in place.

Orvil wasted no time in telling him that Eva was gone.

Chase left Ramon, Ned, and Jethro standing with Orvil in the middle of the yard and walked away. There was no way he could face them and conceal his hurt at the same time. Nearly half an hour of precious time passed while he stood behind the house, unable to do more than stare at the distant mountains, at the jagged peaks against the rain-washed sky and the foothills spread out before them.

He thought of last night's storm, of the intensity of its fury and likened it to his brief time with Eva. He had shared but one night with her, a night filled with passion and profound release.

And treachery. His soul had withered when Ramon told him about the poisoned cattle. The only thing left to believe was that Eva had been part of the scheme. Why else would she draw him away from the ranch, lead him to search for her, and then keep him occupied with her body? She had lied about who and what she was.

Still, after what McKenna had told him, after his confrontation with Quincy Powell, Chase wasn't sure what to believe about her. Had she somehow—unbeknownst to Powell—met the Hunt brothers sometime after she quit her job in Cheyenne? Did she need money so desperately that she had agreed to help them? Was it the only way she hoped to pay back Quincy Powell?

Hell, he didn't even *know* Eva Eberhart, so how could he hope to understand what motivated her?

Maybe she *was* innocent of everything except lying about her own past. If so, the only thing she was guilty of was wanting to start a new life.

After wrestling with his thoughts, he no more knew what to believe now than he had earlier. Determined to take on one problem at a time, he went back to mount up and join the others.

After learning from McKenna that the Hunts had escaped prison, there was no doubt in his mind that the brothers were out to get him—and they were far from finished.

When they were a few miles from the ranch house, Ramon and Jethro rode up beside him. The foreman paused to wipe his sleeve across his forehead. Jethro scowled into the midday sun. "It would have to heat up right away," he grumbled.

Neither Chase nor Ramon commented. "We got most of the cattle that were nearby," Chase told them. "We'll post Orvil as guard, then the three of us can go on up into the hills for more."

He was determined to work until he dropped. It kept him from thinking. Trouble had fallen on his doorstep, and he had to sweep it clean before he could do any more thinking about Eva.

"Anybody seen Ned?" Jethro was looking off in the direction of the creek. "He said he was gonna stop to water his horse and then meet us here."

Ramon asked. "When did you last see him?"

Jethro lifted his hat enough to reach beneath it and scratch his head. "Shoot, I don't know. Twenty, thirty minutes ago."

Chase tensed. His gaze swept the surrounding foothills. There was no sign of the missing hand. "There'll be no splitting up to look for him," he warned the others.

Jethro stared at Chase, his thick, blond moustache drooping. "You think something happened?"

"I hope not."

"Maybe we ought to get something to eat and wait a few minutes," Jethro suggested.

"We do not need to wait at all," Ramon said.

Chase knew the man well enough to recognize the foreboding sound in his tone. He braced his palm on the cantle of his saddle and turned to look over his shoulder. His heart sank when he saw Ned's riderless horse in the distance, lazily grazing beneath the warm sunshine.

Jethro was off and cursing, whipping the reins as he urged his horse across the open ground. Ramon shot a dark glance at Chase, and the two men followed in his wake. As they drew nearer, Chase could see the horse was not riderless at all. Ned's body had been draped across the saddle.

By the time they reached him, Jethro had already cut his friend loose and had Ned stretched out on the grass. Chase knew without Jethro saying a word that the young cowhand was dead. His neck was twisted at an impossible angle, the pink and withered scar where he had been burned was still visible.

As Jethro stood and swiped at his eyes with the back of his hand, Chase felt nothing but a swift, sure coldness that unfurled within him. It was almost pleasurable to feel the old, deep seated hatred again. It felt far better than hurt.

"Why?" Jethro wanted to know. "Ned never hurt anybody. I should have stayed back with him."

"Muerte que venga que achaque no tenga," Ramon said. There is no death that comes without an excuse.

"Because of me," Chase said, his voice devoid of emotion. "He died because of me." He spotted a piece of folded paper in Ned's shirt pocket and bent to retrieve it.

Slowly unfolding the smudged message, he read it quickly, then again, as if a second reading might change the words.

"They've got Lane at the line shack."

No one asked how the Hunts had found Lane. Staring down at Ned's lifeless form, they simply believed.

"What are you going to do?" Ramon stood at his right shoulder.

Chase looked over at his *segundo,* his friend, and wished there could be another answer. "I have to end this here and now. And this time I won't fail."

They put Ned back across his saddle. Jethro led the horse behind his own. Ramon remained silent, watchful.

Chase felt nothing. He couldn't afford to let emotion get in his way.

They rode up to the back of the house, and Orvil stepped out onto the porch. He saw the young cowhand's body draped across the saddle, shook his head and went to meet them.

"I'll take him in the barn and lay him out proper. If anybody feels like eatin', I kept some stew warm for you," he offered.

Chase looked at Ramon and then Jethro. "I don't care how you feel right now. I suggest you eat something. We won't be back until this is settled." He tied his reins to the hitching post and then directed Orvil, "As soon as you've seen to Ned, ride into town and get the undertaker and the sheriff. Tell McKenna the Hunts did show up. They have Lane at the old line shack. You lead him back there."

"Who's got Lane?"

"The men who killed his mother. I sent them to prison a few years back, but it seems they decided not to stay." He reached into his back pocket and took out the note they found on Ned. "Give that to McKenna, too. Ride the bay. He ought to be rested up by now."

Orvil nodded, hesitant to speak. "Cassidy?"

Chase was halfway to the door. Impatient, he snapped, "What is it?"

"Your horse ain't here. Miss Eva took him."

Chase had one hand on the door. Now that he was determined to wear his gun again, he wanted to feel it riding his hip.

Off the porch again in two strides, Chase towered over Orvil, forcing him to crane his neck to look up at him. "What are you saying, old man? When you told me she left earlier, I thought you meant for good."

"She asked me to saddle up a horse for her this morning, said that she had to go find Lane 'cause no one else was lookin' for him. I told her no. Later I noticed your horse was gone and so was Miss Eva, but she didn't take her things with her. I'm pretty sure she snuck off to find Lane—I told her I saw him head toward the hills, toward the ol' line shack—"

Chase didn't wait to hear more. He left Orvil talking while he strode off toward the house. The back door slammed behind him.

If Eva had gone after Lane, and if she had found him, then the Hunts were holding her hostage, too.

Chapter Eighteen

Byron Hunt looked down at Eva in disgust. "You're just a little jaybird, aren't you?"

Eva ignored his question and kept up her nervous stream of one-sided conversation. " . . . then one time, in Kansas City, my father decided it would be a real money maker if we added a magic act to the show. Well, naturally, being thirteen, I thought it sounded wonderful, so I insisted he let me do the magic. Instead of—"

"Aren't you the least bit worried?" Byron paced to the door, glanced around the corner of the shack, and ducked back in.

"Not at all," Eva lied, feigning a cheerfulness she certainly didn't feel as she acted her heart out, trying to convince the outlaw that she wasn't the least bit disturbed by her circumstances. "Are you?"

"Can't figure out what's keepin' Percy."

Percy, she had learned, was Byron's brother. Mrs. Hunt had obviously held greater aspirations for her sons than what they achieved.

"Chase probably killed him by now." It was the first comment Lane had uttered in nearly an hour.

Byron spun away from the door and paced over to the surly young man tied to the bed frame. He pressed the barrel of the gun to Lane's forehead and cocked the hammer.

"Want to say that again?"

Before Lane could oblige him, Eva drew Byron's attention by trying to stand. "My legs are killing me, all folded

267

up like this. You don't mind if I—''

Byron turned on her. "I do. Sit."

Eva stared back at the aging outlaw and realized the old proverb was true—you really couldn't tell a book by its cover. Twelve years ago Byron Hunt might have appeared more formidable, but without the gun in his hand, he wouldn't have seemed threatening in the least. His moustache was gray, as were the thin wisps of hair that showed beneath his bowler. His jowls had begun to droop. It was hard for her to imagine him attacking Sally Cassidy, or anyone else for that matter.

She let out a dramatic sigh and winced as if her legs pained her terribly. In truth, her ankle was still tender, but she no longer limped. "I told you I was a dancer, didn't I?"

"There hasn't been much you haven't told me in the last hour." Hunt uncocked his gun, but kept it ready at his side. He paced back to the door.

"I'm really surprised you haven't heard of me," Eva declared, hoping to appear genuinely disappointed.

Byron shot her a perturbed glance. "If I tell you I have heard of you, would you shut up?"

"You don't know what you've missed. Why," she glanced around as if a thought had just struck her, "you know, there's plenty of room here. I could go through a couple of the chorus numbers if you'd like. Might help to pass the time—''

The sound of an approaching rider drew their attention. Eva held her breath, willing to risk everything and shout a warning, certain Chase was about to ride into Byron's trap. Byron Hunt wasn't about to take the chance. He lunged for her, imprisoned her against him with his palm pressed tight against her mouth. She could feel the tension in him as he waited, poised to fire, until he heard his brother call out. "It's me, Byron. Don't shoot."

Relieved, Byron shoved Eva aside and stepped out the door. She glanced over at Lane the minute their captor was out of sight and whispered, "Quit goading him, Lane. He's liable to lose his temper and—''

"Kill me?" Lane looked as if he didn't care one way or another. "He might just be doing me a favor."

"Don't talk like that. You'll see once we're out of here—"

Eva fell silent when Byron walked back in, leading his brother, Percy Hunt. Percy was younger, taller, and far more formidable than Byron. His hair was grayed only slightly, his girth still narrow. He had a hard-eyed stare that was split by a hawkish nose. The way he was looking at her chilled her to the bone. The man glanced at Lane for barely a second and then concentrated on her again.

"I didn't bargain on this," he grumbled, throwing a scowl his brother's way. "But it looks like now we've got even more to entice Cassidy with." He moved closer, hunkered down in front of Eva and lifted her chin with his thumb and forefinger. "You got ties to Chase Cassidy?"

She shook her head, effectively breaking his hold. "No. In fact, the last time I saw him, he was hoping he would never have to lay eyes on me again. If you're thinking of using me as bait, well—"

"She's lyin'," Percy cut in. "I heard her talking to the boy when I came up on 'em. She was trying to convince him to go back to the house. She's in with them somehow. Did you give him the message?"

"I did. And the way I delivered it, Cassidy won't be ignoring us."

Byron laughed. Eva was forgotten for the moment. She glanced over at Lane. Their gazes met and held. She knew that despite his feigned disinterest, if the opportunity arose, he would try to escape.

As the Hunts took up positions near the door, Eva watched them carefully. Somewhere, somehow, they had found a way out of prison, obtained respectable clothing and horses. Dressed in tweed and plaid wool, starched collars and bowler hats, they would easily blend in among decent, hardworking townsfolk. Only their weapons and the suspicious glint in their eyes gave them away.

Eva knew that Chase wasn't likely to ignore their summons—especially when he found out they were holding Lane hostage. She had to do something to divert their attention long enough for Lane to work his way free.

"I was just telling Byron that I would be happy to perform one of the dance numbers I'm most famous for," she offered, focusing all her attention to the newly arrived Percy.

He glanced over his shoulder, eyeing her as if she had lost her mind. Eva was beginning to think she might have as she chattered on like a magpie while she faced the barrel of a gun.

"Well, Percy, how about it?"

"Lady, what are you talking about?"

"Dancing."

Byron tried to clarify. "She's a dancer. Famous one, she claims. Been at this jabbering for an hour."

His interest piqued, Percy turned his back on the door and concentrated on Eva. Incredibly, his hard stare softened. "You don't say? I used to know a little dancer down in Chihuahua. Always swore I'd get back down to Mexico to see her one day. You do any Mexican dancing?"

"Percy—" Byron's tone held a warning. Eva was on her feet in an instant. "Mexican dancing is one of my specialties." It was a lie, but she was confident she could feign enough steps to fool Percy.

Byron started to argue. "Percy, this ain't the time—"

The younger brother waved Bryon away. "Shut up. We got plenty of time. Cassidy won't come bustin' in here without thinkin' things through."

"All the more reason we got to be ready," Byron decided aloud. "What if he thinks of a way to—"

Before Byron could protest, Eva trilled a long, high note followed by a shout. She began whirling around the tight quarters of the little room, high-stepping, and kicking up her heels, careful to avoid putting too much pressure on her injured foot. She reached up and snapped her fingers above her head in imitation of castanets. She released the ribbon in her hair and began to swing her untamed curls around her shoulders.

Pitching her voice as high and as loud as she could, she bellowed out a tune using the only Spanish she knew. *"Aye, aye, no si, no no, no gracias, no mucho."* As she whirled, she pretended to wave an imaginary skirt and threw flirting glances at Percy Hunt. He stared in open-mouthed awe while Byron continued to fume and lean against the wall near the door.

Lane watched her with awe mingled with something akin to disbelief. When Eva started singing and dancing around the shack, an icy shiver of fear trickled down his spine. Not for one moment did he let the Hunts' appearance fool him. Despite their appearances, they were outlaws on the run. Unpredictable as rattlers, they could strike at any moment.

He knew Eva was trying to divert their attention away from him so that he could get free, but he had not been able to loosen the rope around his wrist. As he watched her throw her head back, singing at the top of her lungs, he was almost as shocked as he had been earlier when she first admitted that she was a dancer. If he were so amazed upon learning the truth, what must Chase be thinking? If his uncle still thought she was siding with the Hunt brothers, there was every chance that he might come bursting through the door intent on seeing Eva get what she deserved.

Lane yanked on the rope around his wrist and tried to work his fingertips between the knot. Eva kept moving his way, glancing down at him now and again, acting as if she expected him to spring up off the ground at any moment. He dropped his gaze, half-afraid he might give into a nervous urge to laugh at her outrageous performance. As he shifted his attention, he caught sight of the burning coals in the fireplace. If he could somehow communicate to her, get her to use the white hot coals to start a fire in the room, they might use the billowing smoke to cause enough commotion to escape.

Glancing up at her, Lane caught Eva's eye and whipped

his gaze back to the fire and stared pointedly at the embers. There was a slim chance she would understand—but it was better than no chance at all.

Flinging her head back, Eva whirled to the other end of the room and then, in order to create a false sense of trust, danced right back again. She continued to sing, to balance on her uninjured foot and point her opposite toe in the air while she practically shouted at the top of her lungs. If nothing else, she was keeping one of the Hunt brothers off guard, at the same time whooping loud enough to alert Chase.

She finally stopped for lack of breath and bent over, hands on her knees, pretending to be more exhausted than she really was. From that position, she glanced over at Lane, whose gaze jumped from her to the fireplace.

"You know any more songs?" Percy wanted to know.

"Do I know any more songs? Mr. Hunt," she gasped, fighting to catch her breath. She flicked open the top two buttons on her blouse and fanned the open edges. Percy Hunt's eyes were glued to the cleavage she had revealed. "You are looking at a woman of endless talent. I know more songs than a hen has feathers."

"I like Mexican dancing the best."

"And you can bet I'll be sure to do that little number again. Right now, how about a waltz?"

She began to hum "The Flying Trapeze" and waltz around, dancing with an imaginary partner. With a pained, somewhat bored expression, Lane stretched his legs toward the fireplace as if they had begun to cramp up. Without missing a beat, Eva stepped over him and twirled toward the back of the room, then moved forward once again.

Still hovering in front of the open door, Byron mumbled, "I think I see something moving on the far ridge—"

Acting as if she hadn't heard him at all, Eva sang a little louder. She bowed with a flourish as she ended the waltz in front of Percy.

"Would you care to dance, Mr. Hunt?"

The felon actually blushed, frowned, and then blustered, "I don't think I . . . that is I haven't ever. . . "

"Why, it's easy. And I am a professional. What kind of a dancer would I be if I couldn't teach you?" Eva swallowed her fear, took his free hand and glanced at Lane again when Percy holstered his gun and stepped forward. She tipped her head to the side and smiled up at Percy Hunt with her most beguiling smile. "You said you liked the Mexican dance the best, why don't we start with that one?"

Byron turned away from the door, his forehead creased with worry lines. "Percy, if I was you, I don't think—"

Percy turned on his brother with a snarl. "Well, you aren't me." He turned back to Eva, who was trying to ignore the savage side of the man that had surfaced so instantaneously and just as quickly disappeared.

"What do I do now?" He wanted to know.

"Hold your arms up until your hands are near your ears and then clap them together, like this." She demonstrated his part in the impromptu flamenco. "And you should stomp your heels at the same time."

"I feel kinda stupid," he said as he began stomping and clapping.

"You are stupid," Byron groused.

Lane pointedly ignored them all.

"You're doing just fine." Eva encouraged. "Don't pay him any mind, Percy, honey."

She held her breath, then burst out singing in stilted Spanish again and launched into her own dance steps. She spun, she twirled, she kicked, and snapped her fingers. Tossing her head back, she was able to watch Lane. All he did was stare intently into the low burning fire in the crumbling stone fireplace.

The *fireplace. Fire.* The only weapon at her disposal.

"*Si, si, no gracias fandango,*" Eva warbled, "*aye no, si gracias mucho! Muchas gracias, Lane-o.*" Suddenly inspired, she stripped the holey blanket off the bed and threw it over her shoulders like a cape. She used it to dip and twist, the musty wool blanket furling and unfurling about her. She glanced down at Lane. He nodded imperceptibly toward the fire.

Although she was beginning to get hoarse, Eva sang even louder. With a beguiling smile and a toss of her head, she tempted a clapping, stomping Percy Hunt closer to the fire.

Chase and Ramon dismounted and began to work their way nearer the line shack situated amid a stand of alders. Even from the distance of a hundred yards, they could hear Eva singing and laughing, her voice carried on the warm wind. Chase's hand tightened on the gun butt until his knuckles whitened.

"You hear that, Ramon? Ned's dead, Lane's a hostage, and she's got the nerve to sing."

Ramon was frowning in the direction of the cabin, listening intently. "She sings in Spanish."

"I hear."

"She told me she speaks no Spanish."

Chase felt his gut tense. "Just another of her lies."

"Perhaps, but what she's singing makes no sense."

Chase shook his head as he recalled his run-in with Quincy Powell. "Nothing about her makes any sense." He listened for a moment, wondered what Eva was up to now. "She might be trying to warn us off."

Ramon shrugged. "You still hope she's innocent?" Then he added, "Perhaps she is. If what the gambler said is true, she may have nothing to do with the Hunt brothers. If so, then I have falsely accused her."

Afraid to hope and then have to endure the pain of her betrayal all over again, Chase tried to dismiss Ramon's comment.

"Right now, all I care about is getting Lane out of there safely and taking care of the Hunt brothers once and for all."

"McKenna and his men will be here before too long," Ramon reminded him. "Perhaps we should wait for Jethro—"

"How do we know McKenna will back us up? I'm not

leaving Lane in there any longer than I have to. Would you listen to that? She's singing so loud she's starting to lose her voice.''

Ramon nodded. "It is very distracting."

"You have a point. I'll try and move closer, circle around the back." As he slipped up to the front of the cabin, Ramon would go around behind, where the trees were thickest.

"Get ready," Chase told him.

Ramon crouched low, gun at the ready, staring at the lush stand of trees behind the line shack. Chase zigzagged forward at a crouch until he was able to duck behind a fallen log, well within shouting distance. He took a deep breath and hollered, "You in there, Hunt?"

A shadowed figure in the doorway moved, but did not respond. Chase shook his head in frustration. It appeared no one could hear over Eva's boisterous song.

He glanced over at Ramon, cupped his hands around his mouth and tried again.

"You hear that?" Byron turned away from the door.

Eva's heart began to pound, not from overexertion, but from the fact that she, too, thought she had heard a shout and knew Chase and his men had to be close by.

She realized she had only seconds to act. Byron Hunt was no longer paying her close attention. He stood with his head cocked toward the door, listening intently. Lane was still staring at the fire, but she could see he had drawn in his feet. He appeared tense, ready to move.

Percy was wheezing, out of breath. If he heard his brother's question, he gave no sign. He lumbered after Eva.

She whirled the blanket about like a matador's cape and trailed one end near the fireplace, moving so close that one corner settled atop the coals. With part of the rough wool tightly in hand, she continued to sing. She was afraid to look behind her, terrified that the blanket might burst into flame quicker than she had calculated. An acrid scent began to drift about the confined space.

In a barely audible tone Lane whispered, "Now, Eva."

She flipped the fiercely smoldering blanket over her shoulder. It fanned out and then down over Percy Hunt's head, taking him by surprise. Furious, he cursed and inhaled a mouthful of smoke. He began to wheeze, like a cat with a hair ball, trapped in a burlap bag. Frantically, he tried to wrench himself out from beneath the burning blanket.

"What the—" Byron shoved away from the door and barrelled across the room, brandishing his gun as he tried to extricate his brother.

Eva lunged at Percy's calves and brought him to the ground. He fell backward. Byron went down with him. Both men hit the ground hard. Byron's gun went off. The bullet ricocheted off the wall.

Lane struggled against his bonds. He screamed, "Get out, Eva! Run!"

She struggled to extricate herself from the tangle of arms and legs. Bryon reached out to grab her wrist. She bit his hand, tasted blood. He flung her back so hard she hit the wall. The air left her lungs with a groan.

"Eva, go!"

She scrambled to her knees.

"I'm not leaving you," she yelled at Lane. The Hunt brothers writhed in a hopeless mass of blanket and smoke. She crawled to the woodbox and reached for a piece of damp firewood, then began to strike the undulating bundle as hard as she could. The men howled in pain.

Eva dropped the wood and raced over to Lane. She fought with the rope, struggling until she finally worked the knot free. Just then, Percy pushed himself to a standing position.

Lane shoved Eva aside. He crouched low before he sprang toward the two men and buried his head in Percy's midsection. Behind them, Byron struggled to his feet. Eva looked for the wooden club but couldn't locate it. She needed something to hurl at the older outlaw so she grabbed an open, rusted tin can with the jagged-edged lid jutting out. Beside it lay a perfectly round rock that had come loose from the fireplace. She dropped the rock into the can and hurled the weighted tin container toward Byron's head.

When the shot rang out inside the cabin, Chase froze. Crouched low, Ramon sprinted through the trees, pausing long enough to maintain cover, then darting off again. Chase threw caution to the wind and headed in a more direct line, straight toward the cabin. The shouting inside increased, but there were no more gunshots. When he heard Lane call out Eva's name, his gut tightened in a searing knot that nearly bent him double. He went cold and then instantly knew a blinding rage. He saw red.

He ducked and ran, zigzagging close to the ground while Ramon bore down on the place from behind. Chase reached the front wall unnoticed and pressed his back against the rough surface, sliding along until he was inches from the open front door. He could hear the sound of a scuffle inside.

A man growled, "Damn it! You cut me!"

Ramon met him on the opposite side of the door and signaled that he was ready to rush the room.

Chase took a deep breath and found himself unreasonably calm, totally in control of his emotions. He was an old hand at facing death. He had done it countless times. Today was no different.

Gun drawn, he stepped around the door frame, willing to face death, if need be, to save Lane. He felt Ramon at his back.

Chase took in the scene before him in an instant. Lane had a much larger man pinned to the floor. The boy appeared to be beating the life out of him. Crouched against the far wall, Eva looked like a wild woman, her hair in a mass of copper tangles that covered half her face. She squatted on her haunches, gasping for breath.

Byron Hunt stood over her, his back to Chase. One of the man's hands was pressed to his cheek. With the other, he aimed a gun directly at Eva. For the first time in his life, Chase experienced a split second of uncertainty. There was far more at stake here than his own life. One wrong move and Eva might wind up dead. His gun hand was steady.

"Drop it, Hunt!" he shouted.

"You won't do it, Cassidy," Hunt called over his shoulder. "I can kill her before I hit the ground."

Chase cocked his gun. He didn't dare look at Eva. "Shall we see?"

Byron Hunt didn't even twitch. He held out his arms and let his gun fall to the dirt floor.

On the other side of the room, Lane straddled Percy Hunt. He pulled back his fist and landed a right punch square on the heavier man's jaw. Hunt's eyes rolled back and he ceased to struggle. Chest heaving, Lane leaned back on his heels and sucked in great gulps of air. He wiped the cuff of his jacket across his bleeding lip.

It was all Chase could do to concentrate on Byron Hunt and not rush over to help Eva. "Turn around nice and slow and don't even think of making any unnecessary moves," he warned Hunt.

The outlaw turned around slowly. Chase noticed the jagged cut just below Hunt's right eye. Eva grabbed the wall for support. Her hands shaking nearly uncontrollably, she ducked forward to retrieve the gun Byron had dropped.

"If you're smart, you'll hand that over to Ramon," Chase told her. He barked an order over his shoulder. "Ramon, tie up the man on the ground. I'll take care of this one."

"You aren't going to kill me in cold blood, are you, Cassidy?" Byron Hunt swallowed hard, his eyes flicking over Chase and the gun barrel aimed at his gut. Sweat glistened across his upper lip.

It would be so easy, Chase thought, so very easy to pull the trigger. He could kill both Hunt brothers and still walk away a free man. They were wanted men, prison escapees. No one would question their deaths, not even at his hand. Justice would finally be served. Maybe then his nightmares of Sally's death would end along with the black need for revenge that had possessed him for a third of his life.

He could end it all here and now.

"Chase?"

He felt something warm come to rest on his arm. It was a tentative connection, a gentle touch with the weight of a butterfly, but heavy with calming influence. He felt her hesitancy and doubt, too. As if in a trance, Chase looked down and found Eva at his elbow. One of her small hands rested on his sleeve. She stared up at him with her clear, knowing green eyes. Her blouse was partially unbuttoned. He could see the furious beat of her pulse where it quivered against the soft, white flesh at the side of her throat. She pushed her hair back off her face. Her fingers, smudged with ashes, left a trail across her cheek.

His immediate reaction was to wrap his arms around her and hold her close, but the memory of her betrayal, her web of lies, and fear for his own battered heart kept him from doing so. He shrugged off her hold.

"Step away from me, Eva."

"Don't talk to her that way," Lane said from the opposite side of the room. The boy was on his feet again. In an instant, Chase noticed that his nephew was wearing his gun. He couldn't believe that Lane stood poised, ready to draw. On him.

"Don't be a fool," Chase told him in a tone barely above a whisper.

Byron Hunt shifted from foot to foot. "Can I wipe off my face?" Blood was dripping onto his stiff, once-white collar from a cut near his eye.

Without taking his eyes off Lane, Chase ground out the words, "Don't even think about moving, Hunt."

Ramon had succeeded in tying up Percy, who showed no signs of gaining consciousness anytime soon. The Mexican moved back to Chase's side, his own gun now trained on Byron Hunt. "Should I tie this one up, too?"

"No. This one I want to see outside. Alone."

Byron tried to appeal to Eva. "You can't let him kill me . . . it wouldn't be fair. I'm not even armed. Give me a chance, at least, Cassidy. Let me have my gun. You know you can outdraw me . . . you—"

"What chance did you give Sally that day, Hunt? Did my sister beg for mercy? Did you listen to her?"

Byron Hunt shook his head but his eyes never wavered from Chase's own. "She killed Billy. The way we figure it, you ought to pay, too. We been in prison for ten years—"

"You should have hung. If I had any proof that you killed my sister, you would have," Chase reminded him, "but there aren't too many juries willing to take the word of a prisoner."

"You couldn't prove we murdered her because we didn't do it. Billy paid with his life, but he didn't kill her. Ask your boy over there." He tipped his head in Lane's direction. "Go on and ask him."

"Leave him out of it," Chase said.

"Stopping here that day was all Billy's idea. He was hungry, he said. Hell, he was always a pain in the ass, but he was our little brother. Nobody was around but the woman—"

"Her name," Chase reminded him, "was Sally."

"Nobody was home but your sister. She didn't seem to mind at first. Welcomed the company. Hell, Billy was a good lookin' bastard. She even seemed to take a shine to him."

Chase raised the gunbarrel until it was aimed directly at Byron's heart.

The outlaw held out his hands. "Don't, Cassidy. Don't shoot—"

Oblivious to everyone else in the room, Chase concentrated on Byron Hunt. "Go on. Get on with it. What happened?"

"Billy started to get a little too friendly. She tried to push him off. Then," Byron ran the pointy tip of his tongue over his lips, his eyes darting left to right and back to Chase. "Then he pulled her out of the kitchen and into the next room. We heard her arguing, trying to fight him off—"

"But you didn't go to help her?"

"We figured she was Billy's business. He finally got her settled down, sounded like he was having some fun, too. 'Til the gun went off. We ran into the room. She was stand-

in' there staring down at Billy where he lay on the floor
shot, in the chest. Her clothes were torn, her face was
bruised, her nose bleedin'. She kept mumblin' something
about not meaning to kill him, about how he deserved it,
though. Percy went wild. Started to charge her. She took
one look at the two of us and before we could do anything
about it, she put Billy's gun to her head and blew her brains
out.''

Chase felt bile rise up in his throat. "You're lying. You
raped and killed her.''

"Hell, Cassidy, our little brother was layin' there bleedin' to death all over your floor. You think we had rape in
mind at the time?''

"She must have thought you did.''

"I can't be blamed for what she thought, nor for what
Billy did, for that matter.''

Eva shifted beside him. Chase closed his eyes against the
truth. His hand tightened on the gun. He opened his eyes
again and stared at one of the men he had hated for so long.
His mind rejected this "truth," this new version of the act
which changed his life forever.

Eva moved closer. He could feel her warmth at his elbow. She whispered, "Chase, it's over. Chase, please.''

He could feel the others, Ramon and Lane, watching,
waiting to see what he would do. His heart felt like an
unwanted stone that lay heavy in his breast. He had to know
the truth. Percy Hunt was still unconscious. He asked the
only other person in the room who knew exactly what took
place that day. "Is that how it was, Lane? Did it happen
like that?''

As if he knew Chase were judge and jury and his life
hung in the balance, Byron Hunt pleaded, "Tell him, kid.
Tell him it happened just the way I said.''

It was a moment before Lane answered. Eva glanced
over at him and found him nearly unrecognizable. His face
was twisted with pain. His usual dark complexion was
ashen. He was staring at Byron Hunt as if he didn't see the
man at all. She knew he was looking into his past instead.

When Lane did finally speak, his voice was thick with emotion. "Most of it's true." He spoke slowly, carefully, as if each word hurt as it passed his lips. "But Ma didn't want to go into the sitting room with Billy, the young one. He dragged her in there while these two sat at the table and ate and laughed about it. She told me to run, so I ran into my room and shut the door because I was afraid. Mama was crying. I could hear her through the door. She was begging the man to stop, to let her go. Then, for a while she quit shouting and just whimpered. I could hear him grunting. Right after that, she must have gotten his gun away from him, because I heard a shot. I was afraid she was dead, so I ran out to see. Ma was standing over him with a gun in her hand."

He took a deep breath, his gaze shifted from Byron Hunt to Chase. His words were uttered in a low, leaden tone. "She was standing there shaking really hard, looking down at the dead man. When the other two ran into the room, I thought she was going to shoot them, too. But she took one look at them, lifted the gun to her head," his voice dropped to a strangled hush, " . . . and shot herself."

Lane looked down at Eva, then back at Chase. His voice broke on the last words, but he did not cry. "She didn't think about me for a single minute . . . didn't even know I was there watching. She didn't stop to think that *I* might need her, that I might not want her to die. She killed herself, left me alone to wait with her until you came home and found us." His eyes were bleak as he looked directly at Chase.

"You went all quiet and mean. Never even asked me what happened. You picked me up and rode off to the Owens place . . . and then you left me too, Uncle Chase." His voice caught in his throat. "You walked out and left me, too."

Chase was barely aware of Eva's grip on his arm. For the most part he felt as if some greater, more powerful hand had a hold of his heart and was slowly squeezing the life out of it. He barely felt the pain. A heart of stone didn't ache. Nor did it bleed. Stunned by the reality of the truth, Chase slowly lowered his gun to his side.

Chase couldn't look at Eva. Nor could he face Lane any longer.

Ramon stepped up behind Byron Hunt, pulled the man's hands tight behind his back and began to tie them together. While his foreman led the first of the two men outside, Chase stared at the wall opposite him, let his gaze slide over the rough-hewn log wall, at the open spaces where the mud-daubed chinking was missing.

The truth hadn't set him free. If anything, it had made him even more aware of what a waste his life had been.

Sally had taken her own life.

All he could recall of that day was the silent, dark-eyed child who had been too shocked to say anything, let alone give him any details. Chase wondered if he would have listened even if Lane had been able to articulate.

Chase looked down at the gun in his hand, surprised to see it there. It was a symbol of the shambles he had made of his life. Looking back, it seemed as if his life had always been a disaster. The Hunts' deaths wouldn't free him from the past any more than the truth.

He collected himself enough to look down at Eva. She was still beside him. Tears were streaming down her cheeks. He wondered if she had manufactured the tears the way she had the day she begged him to hire her.

As if Lane could read his mind, he said, "She didn't have anything to do with these men, Chase. About the only thing Eva's guilty of is lying to you about who she is and where she came from. She's really—"

Chase finished for him, watching Eva intently as he spoke. "A dancer from a two-bit dance hall in Cheyenne that's owned by a gambler by the name of Quincy Powell."

Eva winced. She blinked back tears, shoved her hair away from her face and then straightened away from him. "That's right. That's who I am, Chase Cassidy. I might have lied to you to get a job, but I swear I never lied about anything else. I don't know these men. Lane can tell you that. I came here to ask him to go back and work things out with you. I knew sooner or later you would find out I never meant to harm you or anyone else. And then you would know that everything . . ." she looked down at her hands, brushed at the dirt on the front of Lane's borrowed pants and looked back up at Chase, her cheeks aflame, " . . . that everything I've done or said has been sincere."

Before Chase could respond, Ramon called out, "The sheriff's here."

On the floor at their feet, Percy Hunt groaned and curled himself into a fetal position on his side. Lane stepped over the man and walked out the door. Chase couldn't wait to get out of the close confines of the cabin. Eva trailed behind him out into the sunlight.

The fresh air was a relief after the wood smoke and stuffiness of the shack. The wind whipped her hair back from her face as she wiped off her tears with her shirt sleeve and willed herself not to cry anymore. Everything would be all right. Chase needed time to heal, to wrestle with the circumstances surrounding his sister's death.

She watched as Stuart McKenna and a posse of ten men drew up and dismounted. There was a noisy milling about as questions were shouted and answered. She spotted Jethro among the men, his smile down turned, his eyes shadowed with sorrow. Orvil was at the back of the group. He dismounted slowly as if his joints ached. Ned was nowhere to be seen. She became uneasy when she couldn't locate Chase's missing cowhand anywhere among the group.

Lane stood off to one side, detached as he watched the unfolding scene. McKenna talked to Chase first, and then Byron Hunt. Three other townsmen, two that Eva recognized from the night of the school program, went into the cabin and came out dragging Percy Hunt between them.

Reaching down, she grasped the belt around her borrowed pants and hiked them up above her waist. They slipped down as soon as she let go. Chase had dismissed her entirely. Not once did he even glance in her direction as he stood huddled with Stuart McKenna. She was tempted to slip off, collect her horse and go back to the ranch house alone, but as she watched Chase, she saw how aloof he remained, standing alone, watching the others mill around. She could no more walk away and leave him than she could fly. Not if he still needed her.

With her heart in one hand and the other securely on the waistband of her borrowed pants, she went to him.

Chapter Nineteen

Chase did not acknowledge her when she reached his side, but he was aware of her presence.

Eva hovered at his elbow, waiting, he supposed, to talk to him. He fought to focus his attention on Stuart McKenna while posse members milled around muttering to each other. Four men led the prisoners out of the shack and over to their horses. Most of the men were edgy, as if the two Hunts, both with their wrists securely tied behind them, might try to escape.

Ramon brought Eva and Lane's horses around from the back of the shack and moved up alongside her. She acknowledged him with a nod, but focused her attention on Chase, while she listened to Stuart McKenna in shock.

"You've got reward money coming, Cassidy. Dead or alive, two thousand each man. That ought to help you replace some of your stock."

Around them, men were mounting up. McKenna's deputy and four others kept the prisoners, now on horseback, surrounded. "We're ready to ride, McKenna," someone called out.

The sheriff glanced over at Eva and nodded, then held his hand out to Chase, who accepted the gesture and shook the lawman's hand.

"I don't want to see you in trouble again, Cassidy." McKenna looked pointedly at the gun strapped to Chase's thigh, then he turned to Lane who was still slouched against the door frame of the line shack. "You either, boy."

Lane remained silent. The only evidence that he had

heard was a nearly imperceptible jump of the muscle along his jaw.

McKenna walked away.

"Chase?"

"Not now, Eva."

Chase finally looked down at her. She was as innocent of the Hunts' scheme as she had claimed, and yet he could not easily dismiss the tender ache left behind by the hurt he had suffered. He was tormented by thoughts of Lane, of Sally's suicide, of Quincy Powell's revelations. He couldn't risk hurting her by speaking in anger, and just now, he couldn't deal with any more emotional upheaval.

Rebuffed, she crossed her arms beneath her breasts and watched the posse thunder out of the clearing. A hollow silence was all they left behind.

An awkward, unwanted feeling crept over her as the seconds ticked by. Chase remained unmoved. Rejection was a feeling she had never experienced in her life. Her mother and father had always doted on her. She had played to full houses of paying customers eager to be entertained despite the reviews. Even Quincy had wanted her for himself, on his terms, of course, right up to the day she walked out. She tried to think of a graceful way to exit and save face, then looked over at Ramon, who had tactfully moved a few paces away. He was busy checking the saddle cinches. The foreman seemed content to give Chase as long as he needed to collect his thoughts.

Eva looked up at Chase and found him watching her. The look in his eyes was still cold, void of any emotion, certainly without any hint of the passion he'd shown last night. He did not move to touch her. He seemed miles, or perhaps it was years, away. His words, when he finally spoke, were for Lane and his men.

"Let's mount up."

Ramon stepped forward to hand the pinto's reins to Lane. The boy shoved himself away from the open doorway but did not reach out to take them. His obsidian eyes were shadowed by his hat brim, his cheek darkened by a bruise.

"I'm not going back," he said softly.

Chase's expression never changed. "What will you do?"

Lane shrugged.

Eva wanted to step in, to say everything she knew Chase was incapable of telling the boy. She wished Chase could simply walk over to Lane, slip his arm around his shoulder and tell his nephew how much he loved him and how very much he wanted them to make something of the ranch together. She wanted to hear Chase tell him that they would put the past behind them, that they would *all* put the past behind them and begin anew.

She wanted a happy ending.

But no one else except Ramon knew how very headstrong the Cassidys were. The only thing the two shared was their name and a lifetime of misfortune. She knew whatever she tried to say now would only be seen as interference. Perhaps Lane was making the right choice. Perhaps only time and distance would heal their wounds. Once Lane found himself, he might be able to open his heart to Chase, and then to love.

She watched Lane. He was still tense, poised as if he expected Chase to argue his decision. Eva's breath caught in her throat when she noticed Lane's hand hovering just above his gun.

Would he be reckless enough to try and outdraw Chase? Did he hate his uncle so much that he wanted to kill him, or was he trying to prove that he could outdraw the legend?

Refusing to let them kill each other, Eva started forward. Ramon grabbed her arm before she could take more than half a step. She swung around and started to protest but the look on his face stopped her. Without words, he was asking her to wait, to let the drama before them unfold without interruption. Eva held her breath and swung around again. Ramon's hand dropped away from her sleeve.

"Let's settle this," Lane told to Chase. "Once and for all."

"Don't do it, boy," Chase warned. "You'll regret this all your life."

"Not much in my life I don't already regret."

Chase didn't comment. Nor did he move. He kept his hands loose, casually hanging at his sides. He didn't blink, nor did he seem to breathe. Eva knew with certainty that he would never draw on Lane, even if it meant losing his own life.

She wanted to scream. The silence became deafening. Her gaze flew from one to the other. Time that was too fleeting to be measured crept like hours. Finally, with lightning speed, Lane drew his gun and fired. Eva did scream. She covered her ears and screamed like a banshee.

The shot went wide.

Unharmed, Chase was still standing. He never even drew his gun.

Eva ran to him. She didn't know how long her legs would support her. She clutched the front of his shirt. He put his arm around her shoulder, but continued to stare over her head at Lane.

Lane holstered his gun without comment. Then, without any outward show of emotion, he took the reins from Ramon and mounted up. He straightened his hat, nodded to Eva, and rode away without a backward glance.

Eva's knees still felt like jellied consommé. Chase watched Lane until he disappeared through the trees.

"I knew you couldn't draw on him," Eva whispered.

"If I had, he'd be dead now. He purposely aimed wide." His arm dropped away from her shoulder.

Eva felt the loss as Chase stepped away from her.

"If you had drawn your gun?"

"He still wouldn't have defended himself."

Sudden realization shocked her. "He wanted you to kill him," she whispered.

Chase stared off through the trees, squinting at the bright sunshine in the valley below them. He walked away as if in a trance, went to his horse and mounted up. For one brief moment, he paused long enough to turn and stare back at her. Emptiness was the only emotion mirrored in his dark eyes.

His shoulders rigid with tension, Chase rode away.

Once more, Eva felt Ramon at her side. "Your Spanish is terrible, Señorita."

Still thinking of Chase, of Lane, and what had just happened between them, she turned to him and forced herself to comment. "You heard me singing?"

He gave her a half-smile. A grand concession on his part, she decided.

"I didn't want you to walk into a trap," she told him. "I was so afraid for Chase." Eva watched the distance between them widen and felt her heart sink to her toes. "Do you think he'll be all right?"

"Sooner or later, God gives everybody what they deserve. I think my friend is due much happiness."

She sighed. Happiness was something she would gladly wish for Chase. Obviously, she was no longer welcome to be part of that happiness. Eva reached out for the reins. "I suppose I'd best go collect my things so I can move on."

Ramon helped her mount up. If he had an opinion, he kept it to himself.

Chase knew, somewhere in the back of his thoughts, that Eva was riding in behind him with Ramon, but his mind was still reeling. *Lane was gone.*

Sally had killed herself.

His blithe-spirited sister had taken her own life after killing the man who raped her. Lane had proven that he no longer cared if he lived or died. He had ridden out of Chase's life as surely and finally as Sally had left them both.

Chase felt only emptiness and cursed. After years of harboring hatred founded on misconception, he thought he should at least feel something, some new sense of freedom, the relief of letting go of a heavy burden. But he felt absolutely nothing. No hatred, no sorrow, no pain. Nothing.

As he rode across the land that was all he had left, Chase looked around as if seeing it for the first time; the rolling hills dotted with brush, the cattle moving about in their slow, methodical way as they grazed. In the distance, the long, low house echoed his own hollow emptiness.

And Eva? Somewhere behind him, Eva rode with Ramon. Chase knew he was treating her badly, knew he had wronged her with his distrust. He had hurt her so deeply that he couldn't blame her if she never forgave him. He had taken the love she offered and thrown it back in her face when the only thing she had really lied to him about was her identity.

What crime was there in that? Hadn't he often wondered what it would be like to start over and to wipe the slate clean? How often had he wanted to become someone else, someone without a past, without a reputation?

He had hurt her far too deeply to expect her to forgive him now. No wonder she had not protested when he rode away from the clearing. Hell, he wished he could ride away from himself—from the truth, from everything—the way Lane had done.

As he neared the house, he noted clearly the dilapidated sag of the roofline, the rotting shingles, and simply stared at them. For the first time since his return, he failed to mentally tally up all he had to do to make the place a home again.

Someone moved in the shadows beneath the porch overhang. Chase wondered for a fleeting moment if it might be Lane and dismissed the notion when he recognized the dappled gray mare tied to the top rail of the side corral. The schoolmarm's horse.

As he cantered into the yard, she stepped off the low porch, her eyes shaded by the wide brim of a straw hat.

Careful to keep one hand on her hat, she looked up at him. "Mr. Cassidy, I hope you don't mind, but I heard there was trouble out here and I came to see if I could do anything to help Eva. Is she all right?"

"She's fine. They should be along any time now." Chase stayed mounted, resting his forearm on his saddle horn as he leaned toward her. He could tell that her concern for

Eva was genuine and silently thanked her for that.

"And Lane?"

Chase found himself unable to speak the words aloud. He merely stared at her.

"Oh my God," she whispered. Her royal-blue eyes grew as round as silver dollars and her hand flew to her throat. It fluttered nervously there. "He isn't—"

Able to shake his head in denial, Chase finally managed, "He took off on his own."

She collected herself immediately, straightening the cuff of her sleeve and smoothing her waistband. Finally, she looked at him directly, her brow furrowed in thought. "I wish there was more I could have done for Lane, Mr. Cassidy. I know I haven't been teaching all that long, but he was the first pupil I was never able to reach, no matter what I did. I pray he finds his way."

He straightened in the saddle and looked off toward the horizon. Eva and Ramon were within shouting distance. "Don't blame yourself, ma'am. I don't know if anyone can really help him." *Or any of us, for that matter.*

Rachel followed his gaze and gave a small cry as she recognized Eva riding beside Ramon. As she ran to meet them, the wide straw hat blew off and dangled from her neck by its shining navy ribbons.

Chase swung his leg over the saddle and stepped down as Eva and Ramon rode up. The foreman continued on to the barn. Eva jumped down and all but fell into Rachel's embrace. He could not see her face, and wasn't even certain he could bear it if he saw hatred there. He stayed where he was, waited until the two women finished speaking softly to each other.

On the way to the porch, Eva paused in front of him, her arm linked through Rachel's. Standing quietly beside Eva, the schoolmarm reminded him of a quiet brown wren who was lending strength to a wounded, more exotic bird. The smooth, unlined skin beneath Eva's red-rimmed eyes was shadowed, evidence that she had been crying. He wanted, more than anything, to take her in his arms and beg her to forgive him, but he was still too numb, the hurt still too raw. And her silence frightened him more than anything.

Eva wanted to rant and rave and shake Chase out of his silence, but she wasn't about to humiliate herself any more than she already had. If the man wanted her, he would say so. She had misjudged Quincy Powell and suffered for it. She left the Palace determined to gain some respect. If she groveled before Chase to the point where she could no longer respect herself, then she would lose all she had gained.

Eva wasn't sure what she would have done if Rachel had not been there offering quiet strength and friendship. Eva made up her mind to go on. She looked up at Chase, using the moment to memorize his lips, his eyes, the very essence of him, before she finally took a deep breath and softly said, "I'm going to pack a few things and move to Rachel's until I can find another position. I'll send for the rest as soon as I can."

She realized they were much the same words she had said to John when she left the Palace. If this kept up, her belongings would be scattered all over the territories.

"Fine." One terse word issued without feeling. It was all he offered.

It was enough to strengthen her resolve to go.

Chase watched Eva straighten her shoulders before she turned and walked away. He didn't take his eyes off her as she moved across the yard, up the step and over the porch.

How could she know she was taking what was left of his heart?

Ten days later, a black steamer trunk and a strange, short, oddly shaped wooden box arrived at Trail's End.

Chase tried to convince the driver of the delivery wagon that Eva Edwards no longer lived there, but the man said he'd only been paid to deliver the goods this far and it was where they were staying. He added that if Chase wanted the lady to have them, then he could damn well deliver them himself.

Chase had the items put in the barn where they sat against the back wall another two days. Finally, after a dismal supper of skillet cornbread, bean soup, and watery chocolate pudding, Chase fed Curly and found Orvil waiting for him at the back step.

The days had grown long as summer kissed the land to full bloom. They stood in the gathering twilight, the shorter, older man refusing to sit. Instead, he paced back and forth, his hands rammed in his hip pockets, his ebony features shadowed by the weak twilight. Chase sat on the edge of the porch, his elbows resting on his knees, his fingers locked.

"You antsy for some reason, Orvil, or are you just not ready to go back to the bunkhouse yet?"

Orvil cleared his throat. He shifted his weight and his worn boots scuffed the dry earth. In profile, he looked off toward the corral and asked, "You going to go after Miss Eva or not?"

"Not."

"You got a reason besides pure cussedness?"

"Nope."

"You sure?"

"No reason I feel like putting into words," Chase said.

"You're just going to let her go without trying to get her back?"

"I never had her in the first place, Orvil. She didn't even trust me enough to tell me her own name. Can't think of what she must think of me by now."

"She loved you enough to stay here after she found out what the name Chase Cassidy stood for, didn't she?"

Chase had no answer for that.

"You could tell her 'bout the stuff that was delivered to her. Good excuse to start up a conversation," Orvil suggested.

"Aren't you a little bit long in the tooth to play cupid?"

"Might be something in there she needs right away."

"She hasn't needed any of it before now. She probably doesn't need it at all." Chase took off his hat and set it on the porch beside him. He raked his fingers though his hair. It had been a long hot day, and what he wanted a lot more than a lecture was a swim in the creek. Curly summoned enough energy to walk over and lick his ear before he stretched out beside him.

Orvil persisted. "You going to tell me you're holding it against her because she wasn't everything you thought? Ain't that a bit like the pot calling the kettle black, Cassidy?"

"Why don't you go to bed, old man?" Chase glared up at the veteran cowhand.

Orvil pinned him with a rheumy-eyed stare. "Why don't you get up off your sorry ass and go after her?"

As the old man walked off toward the bunkhouse, Chase shook his head. "Ought to fire that old reprobate," he mumbled to himself. He stood up and stretched, reaching skyward. A horse whinnied in the distance. Another answered.

He looked back at the house. Darkness filled each and every window. There was nothing inside, no one to welcome him. He had prowled through the silent, shadowed rooms for nearly two weeks and knew there was no way he could ever pretend the place was a home.

He knew as sure as he drew his next breath that he wanted Eva beside him again, in his life and in his bed. And he knew that the only way he had a chance of getting her back was go into town and beg on bended knee if he had to. Maybe Orvil was right. The arrival of her trunk was as good an excuse as any to go talk to her.

He found himself drawn to the barn and before long, he was standing in the doorway. Chase lit the lantern hanging beside the door. The flame flared and he adjusted the wick. He could barely make out the outline of the trunk and wooden case against the far wall.

Recalling Orvil's words, he wondered if Eva might need the contents of the trunk. He figured that if it contained anything worthwhile, Eva would have locked it before she left Cheyenne. But it wasn't locked, so he lifted the lid. As Chase stared down at the jumbled contents inside, the scent of Eva's lilac perfume drifted out. He closed his eyes, tempted to shut the lid and walk away. But intrigued by the sight of the curious collection inside, he went down on one knee for a closer look.

Rolls of paper lay atop the pile. He lifted one and carefully unrolled it. After he studied the woodcut illustration, he read the fancy script; "Sinbad the Sailor, Performed by the Entertaining, Energetic Eberharts, Featuring Little Eva Eberhart as Sinbad, the Boy Sailor." He let the sheet roll up on itself, set the playbill aside and picked up another. "The Entertaining, Energetic Eberhart's Perform Ouida's Firefly." Chase lifted aside the rest of the posters and found some assorted costume pieces, a feather boa, a metal skullcap with antlers protruding from either side, a pair of elbow-length white gloves.

Beneath the objects he could identify at a glance lay a pile of folded gowns fashioned of shining emerald green, lemon yellow, fuchsia, and sky-blue materials. A cigar box was barely visible beneath the ruffles. Half-open, some of the carefully clipped, yellowed newspaper articles had spilled out of the box.

Chase lifted out the box and gathered the articles, intending to stack them and set them back inside. Instead, he unfolded some, curious as to why Eva might have been saving housekeeping advice and reviews of past theatre performances.

He skimmed the first review and found himself becoming angered by the words on the page:

> The Eberharts are in and of themselves so
> melodramatic that they do not bear
> watching. Their offspring, billed as "Miss
> Eva, the darling of the stage," shows every
> evidence of following closely in their
> footsteps.

There were more of the same, various reviews from performances held in a variety of cities and towns across the country. Keeping his anger at bay, Chase carefully folded them all, tempted to throw the offending pieces away. Why did Eva cling to the bad reviews as well as the good? He tried to imagine what she must have felt when she read them, and wished he had been there to share her pain. After smoothing the yellowed pages, he put them back into the cigar box and closed the lid.

He thought back to the day he had first laid eyes on Eva Eberhart. Passing herself off as Eva Edwards, relating the pitiful story of her mother's death and her loss of her childhood home must have inspired the best performance of her life. He had not doubted her for even one minute. Of course, he had been too occupied watching the crystal teardrops form in her green eyes to see through her act.

He closed the lid on the trunk. She didn't need any more bad memories. Nothing crucial was packed inside the trunk, but as Orvil said, telling her about its arrival would at least provide an excuse for a meeting.

Had he waited too long? Would she be willing to talk to him?

He started to stand, but his eye caught the glint of the remaining flecks of gold paint left on the strange wooden case beside the trunk. There seemed to be an image of sorts painted on the lid. In the lantern light, a wavering, barely visible face with wide-set eyes outlined in ebony stared back at him.

He tried to lift the lid and found it locked by some interior device. Rubbing his forehead, Chase stared at the strange object, pondering its purpose. He tapped it once. It made a hollow sound. He knocked along the length of the case and then down the edges. Finally something inside clicked.

Chase tried the lid and it opened easily.

What appeared to be a bundle of rags formed in the shape of the box was nestled inside. Chase reached down and carefully lifted out the bizarre bundle. It didn't fall apart as he expected. As he sat there with the strangely wrapped figure on his lap, he couldn't help but notice it was shaped like a child.

What in the hell did she have here?

Chase realized for the first time in days he was feeling *something*. More than something. He could put a name to it. He felt alive, curious, intrigued. Indirectly, it was Eva, through her things, who had brought him back to life.

He reached for the loose end of one of the ragged bandages and began to unravel it. Within three minutes, the floor surrounding him was covered with the yellowed gauze strips and in his hands he held an odd-looking wooden doll. The eyes were outlined with black paint in much the same design as on the lid. The arms and legs were jointed. The curious creation was dressed in a strange garment. When he lifted the doll to a sitting position on his knee, its mouth dropped open and hung there. Chase felt an opening in the doll's back. He stuck his hand inside and discovered that by working a lever hidden inside, he could make the doll's mouth move up and down.

He laughed. The sound of his own laughter shocked him into silence. He sat the unique creature on his knee, worked the mouth up and down and laughed again.

The mysterious doll appeared to be laughing back at him. "Who are you?"

He asked it.

He flapped the doll's mouth and raised his voice an octave. "Who are *you*?"

Leave it to Eva to have such a whimsical item in her possession. Deciding he had pried into her past quite enough, he began to carefully rewrap the doll. When his finger became caught in one of the bandages, the doll rolled out of his hands and hit the floor. As he reached for it, he noticed the shimmer of something brilliant in the dust beside the doll. He reached down and picked up a beautifully cut diamond and held it in the palm of his hand.

He turned the doll over and was astounded to discover another opening, this one a small square—so small he had not noticed it before—in the back of the doll's head. He was even more astonished when he opened it all the way and pulled out a black velvet bag that had been wedged inside. The letter E was embroidered on the bag in gold thread.

Chase opened the drawstring on the bag, shook the contents into his hand, and held his palm close to the lamplight. Gemstones of various sizes and colors reflected the light like a rainbow of fallen stars.

What was Eva doing begging a job as a housekeeper when she possessed a fortune in jewels? He sat there staring at the treasure in his hand. Finally, he concluded that the only reason she would hide the gems would be to safeguard them or because they were stolen.

He glanced over his shoulder and quickly sifted the stones back into the bag, pushed the bag into the secret compartment in the doll's head, and then hastily rewrapped the doll. He knew it was safe enough in the barn, but the sooner he handed the thing over to Eva, the better. A man in his position couldn't afford to have stolen goods on his property.

He walked to the barn door, blew out the lantern and hung it on the nail once again. Outside, darkness had etched its way across the land. Chase paused for a moment, outwardly calm. His discovery had raised questions only Eva could answer.

He could hardly wait until morning.

Chapter Twenty

Buttery sunshine spilled over the window sill into the corner room Eva occupied upstairs in Rachel Albright's frame house. Upon awakening, Eva stretched and fluffed her pillows, then leaned back. She was content to laze away a few minutes while she pondered her situation before she dressed to join Rachel downstairs.

As a warm breeze ruffled the organdy curtains at the window, Eva drew her knees to her chest and hugged them tight. The room was the loveliest place she had ever stayed, and yet her friend apologized profusely for the mess, which consisted of nothing more than a sewing machine covered with notions. There was a quilt rack that stood catty-corner to the windows. Three quilts were draped over it, one appeared quite old, its colors faded to dim pastels.

The cozy room in the well-appointed home, coupled with Rachel's unfeigned joy at having a live-in companion, had lulled Eva into a sense of complacency that kept her here for almost two weeks. The two women slipped into an easy routine, Eva gratefully embracing her old habit of sleeping in of a morning, while Rachel was content to read and putter about until her guest was up and ready to share conversation over a cup of coffee.

Upon Rachel's insistence, Eva accompanied her friend on her daily errands—trips to Carberry's store, the butcher shop, and the school house. Even though it was summer recess, Rachel insisted the school room be swept and dusted almost daily. As she ventured out among the townsfolk, Eva found people thought of her as a heroine of sorts. Sheriff McKenna's posse members wasted no time in spreading the tale of her part in the capture of the Hunt brothers far and wide. Now, whenever she walked along Main Street, she found herself treated as a celebrity—of the respectable kind.

Her first day out and about had been the most difficult. Although she had only revealed her true identity to Rachel, Eva moved uneasily among the citizens of Last Chance. Rachel had insisted no one need know the details of her life unless Eva felt it necessary to tell them. So far, there had been no reason to clarify the situation to anyone.

Now that Eva no longer worked for Chase Cassidy, she was accepted by one and all. For the first time in her life, she felt part of a greater community than the theater folk she had grown up around. Everyone nodded and waved to her, acknowledging her on the street. Miners, ranchers, and merchants alike tipped their hats in greetings that befitted a lady. Everything she had once dreamed of for herself had come true, and yet she took no real pleasure from the experience.

Nor would she until she was over Chase Cassidy.

The sound of Rachel's high button shoes moving briskly along the upper hallway drew Eva's attention to the door. Just as Rachel knocked softly, Eva called out, "I'm awake."

Rachel stuck her head and shoulders around the edge of the door and smiled. "Good morning, Miss Stay-a-bed. The coffee is on and there is fresh bread and butter, too. One of the children stopped by to tell me Tommy Fairchild broke his wrist climbing a tree, so I'm going to go and sit with him for a while. I'll be back after I've done the grocery shopping."

Eva climbed out of bed, padding softly across the multicolored Oriental rug, intent on giving Rachel part of what little cash she had left. "Let me get you some money," she said as she reached for the heart-shaped tin on the dresser.

"Absolutely not," Rachel insisted. "You'll need that to get started again."

Eva pulled out a bill and, as Rachel started to leave, pressed it in her hand. "Please. Take it," she insisted. "I don't want to be a burden."

Rachel hesitated, finally took the money and shoved it into her bag. "You aren't a burden. I should be paying you. Can you imagine what it's like to live in this empty house day after day? You're the first guest I've had since Father died and as far as I'm concerned, this is your home for as long as you want it."

Eva blinked back the tears that came so easily to her these days. "Oh, Rachel—"

Rachel stepped into the room and put her arm around Eva's shoulders. "I didn't mean to make you cry, Eva. Please don't do that, you know what happens. . . ." The schoolmarm's eyes filled with tears of sympathy. "This is all Chase Cassidy's fault," she blubbered.

"I know it is," Eva sniffed.

Suddenly both women began giggling through their tears.

"Just look at us," Eva said, pulling away as she began to scrub the tears off her cheeks with the cuff of the overly modest, long-sleeved night dress Rachel had loaned her. "We're like a couple of watering cans, ready to blame it all on a man."

Rachel hugged her quickly and dried her own eyes with a lace-edged hankie she pulled from her handbag. "Enough of this, young lady. No more moping. I'm going, but I promise to be back at noon, and you better be dressed and ready to help with dinner. This afternoon we'll go out riding. I'll borrow another horse from the Carberry's."

Eva tried to brighten, if only for Rachel's sake. "I'll be all right. You get going."

With a smile and a cheery good-bye, Rachel was gone. The house was once again as silent as an empty bird's nest.

Before she dressed, Eva made the bed and took pleasure in the routine of tidying up the already neat room. As she pulled the linen spread with its cutwork design up over the starched sheets, she thought she heard something downstairs and paused to listen. Certain she had been mistaken,

Eva walked to the closet to decide which of her few gowns she would wear.

She nearly jumped out of her skin when she heard a loud, determined pounding at the front door. Eva ran to the window and leaned out to see who might be there but the roof blocked her view of the porch.

"Hello?" she called.

The pounding continued.

"Who's there?"

"Eva, open this door." Chase Cassidy didn't have to yell. His deep voice carried to her window. She recognized it immediately.

Her hand flew to her breast. She gasped, whirled away from the window and grabbed her satin wrapper. Shrugging into the sleeves as she hurried down the hall, Eva pulled the lace-edged lapels closed and belted the sash. Careful not to trip as she raced down the oak-trimmed stairway, she paused at the top of the lower landing to catch her breath.

She could see Chase's profile silhouetted against the filmy curtain over the window in the front door. Her heart was thundering in her ears as she moved down the last few steps.

Chase had actually come to town.

Perhaps, she thought in those final fleeting seconds as her hand reached out for the knob, perhaps he had not come after her, but to finalize their relationship.

It was impossible to quiet her racing heart, nearly as hard to still her trembling, but she closed her eyes in much the same way she did before she stepped out on stage. She took a deep breath and opened the door.

"Hello, Chase."

She tried to appear at ease, tried to keep a friendly lilt to her tone without sounding overeager or desperate, but the moment she saw him standing there with his hat in his hand, she felt both. His dark eyes immediately found hers and latched on to them with the intense gaze she had come to know so very well. Rendered powerless by his unexpected presence, Eva did not move. Nor did she welcome him beyond that first hello.

Finally, when she was convinced that she would never collect herself enough to speak again and that he had probably already changed his mind about coming to call, a buggy rumbled past the house. The sound, a blunt reminder of where they were, seemed to break the spell. Chase broke his stare and quickly looked her over from head to toe.

"Don't make me stand out here all day."

She managed to find enough voice to speak. "Rachel's not home."

"I know. I saw her."

"Oh, well then. . . . ." She gathered the lace trim at her throat in her hand as if it might offer her some protection against his heated stare.

"I'm not leaving until we've talked. You can either come out here dressed like that, or I'm going to have to come in. What'll it be, Eva?"

"Come in, then." She stepped away from the door until he stood in the narrow entry hall.

Appearing awkward and ill at ease, Chase held his hat brim so tight that it began to curl in his hands. She was grateful that the well-appointed house gave him something to inspect besides her. As she closed the door and cinched the sash on her robe tighter, she watched Chase take note of the tasteful interior of Rachel's home.

She offered, "If you'd like to sit down—"

He cut her off. "I didn't come to sit down."

"Maybe a cup of coffee . . ."

"I don't want any coffee."

"I see."

He took a step toward her and stopped, looked down and noticed what he was doing to his hat brim and tried to smooth out the damage. "I came to let you know a trunk and some kind of a painted wooden box were delivered for you yesterday."

Chase watched her closely, waiting for some reaction to the news. Would she suspect him of searching through her things? Was she at all worried that he might have found the hidden jewels? If so, her face gave away nothing of her feelings.

"I'm sorry you had to be bothered with them," she said.

"I've never seen anything like that wooden box." Again, he paused, waiting for some response.

Eva wondered what he was getting at, for he stood there so expectantly. She reached out to toy with the head of a long cane in a tall brass umbrella stand near the door.

"It's a mummy case," she said absently, wondering how she was going to spend the rest of her life without him. "It belonged to my great-grandfather Eberhart."

"What's a mummy case?"

Eva finally worked up the courage to look him in the eye again. "A case for a mummy."

"That's very funny, Eva."

She smiled, but didn't feel at all humorous. "I'm sorry. Mummification is the way the Egyptians used to embalm their dead. They would wrap a body in cloth and let it dry out—I think—and then they put it in a wooden case and build a tomb around it."

"You have a body in there?" He knew damn well what was inside the case. He couldn't believe she would go to such lengths to lie about it.

Brushing her hair back, she looped it behind her ear. "Probably not much of one. No one's ever unwrapped Chester to see what's left of him, or what he was to begin with."

"Chester?"

"That's what Grandpa said Great-grandfather always called the mummy. He claimed Chester would always bring the family good luck. Mama swears he will, too."

"Do you know where he came from?"

His dark gaze distracted her. "Great-grandpa?" Eva asked.

Chase sighed. "No. Chester."

Frustrated, she dropped the cane into the umbrella stand and crossed her arms. "Why are you so curious about that old case? I didn't really even want it, to tell you the truth, but my mother insisted my cousin John and I take it with us when we went off on our own.''

''So you've never opened it?''

''Of course, I've opened the case. Some of the girls at the Palace asked about it once.''

She smiled as she remembered the dancers reactions to Eva's embellished and mostly fabricated tales of life in ancient Egypt. She delighted in ending with a flourish and opening the lid to reveal the wrapped mummy. Some of the girls would scream while others fell into gales of laughter. Somehow a three-foot-tall mummy didn't command much respect.

Hoping to end all discussion concerning the thing, she added, ''We might be a theatrical family, but no one ever considered unwrapping a dead body entertainment. Chester is just Chester. We didn't need to unwrap him to believe in his luck.''

Maybe mine will improve now that he's here, she thought.

She walked over to a round, marble-topped table that stood beside the stairs. With eyes downcast, Eva pretended to straighten a lacy doily beneath a hand-painted lamp, careful to keep her face averted so that he might not see the tears pooling in her eyes. It was truly over. He didn't want her possessions around any more than he wanted her.

She forced herself to ask, ''Is that what you came for? To tell me my things are piling up at the ranch?''

Chase felt like the proverbial bull in a china shop standing in the confines of the narrow entry hall. He had not expected her to welcome him with open arms, but now Eva turned her back on him, content to fuss with the arrangement of a lamp on a spool-legged table.

He had never seen such elegance. Not only were the furnishings waxed to a high-gloss shine, but the floor was in better condition than his supper table. This was the type of home Eva deserved. He certainly had nothing so grand to offer.

"I came to tell you there's no hurry picking them up. I'll keep them safe for you." He turned to show himself out.

"Are you leaving?" She knew it was over, but she did not want to live with the truth just yet. Once Chase walked out the door, he would be gone forever.

Please, she begged silently, *just a little longer.*

Chase stood before the door. He slapped his hat against his thigh and took a deep breath. What the hell? He was never going to see her again, so what did it matter how badly he humiliated himself?

His voice sounded strained, even to his own ears. "I don't expect you to forgive me, Eva. Not after everything I said to you the night that . . . well, that night."

She was taken aback and whirled around to face him again. "Forgive *you?*"

"I know I wronged you by not believing in you—"

Eva shook her head, trying to deny his words. "But, I lied to you, Chase. I was living a lie from the minute you opened your door to me that first day."

"And so was I. But you weren't guilty of all the horrible things I accused you of that night, Eva, and I never even apologized." He looked down at the hat in his hands and then back up at her again.

Eva couldn't bear the sorrowful sound in his voice. "How *could* you believe me? I lied about who I was, what I had done—"

"I lied about myself with my silence, didn't I?" Chase took a step forward, his hand extended in an open, pleading gesture. "I could have told you that first day that I had been in prison, that the last four housekeepers had quit on me because of Lane's surly behavior or the talk around town, but when I opened the door and laid eyes on you, I couldn't do it. I was afraid to tell you the truth, afraid you might leave."

She moved toward him until she was close enough to see the shimmer of tears in his eyes.

"I want you to come home with me, Eva."

Eva flung her arms around his neck. Chase let go of his hat. It fell to the floor as he gathered her up in his arms and held on to her as if his life depended on it. Without words they clung to each other, heart beating against heart, until Chase slipped his hands into her hair, pulled her head back so that he could look down into her eyes, then covered her lips with his.

With her fingers buried in the front of his shirt, she pulled him close and hung on as she became lost in the depth and passion of his kiss. His mouth slanted across hers, his tongue delving into the warm recesses, warring with hers as they fought to taste and savor each other. Eva moaned and leaned into him. She pressed herself against his throbbing arousal.

Shaken by her passionate response, he pulled away, breathing hard as a stallion racing toward home. "I was ready to grovel, Eva."

"You don't even have to beg," she told him with a smile and another kiss, this one brief as the flutter of a hummingbird's wings.

Chase hugged her close, unwilling to let her go. He rocked back and forth with his cheek resting on her hair. He remembered the jewels hidden in the doll's head. They belonged to the Eberharts, whether any of them knew of the treasure or not. He was determined to tell Eva about them, but not now, not when he finally had her in his arms again.

"I don't know if we'll ever have a place like this one, but I'll try my damnedest to give you all I can."

His honest vow brought tears to her eyes again. She knew she was getting the front of his shirt wet, but it didn't seem to matter. "I used to want a house exactly like this. That's why I left my parents' theater troupe. But do you know what I've found out?"

He stroked his hands up and down the back of her satin robe.

"No. What?"

She blinked away her tears. "Rachel is a wonderful soul,

but still, I can't help but feel sorry for her. She may have lots of nice friends and this pretty little house, but when I move out, she'll be all alone again. A house is empty without love, Chase.'' As soon as she put the thought into words, Eva realized how much she had gained in the last few weeks.

He smiled down at the top of her head, smoothing back her riotous copper curls. ''No matter what else I have, I want to know you'll be there waiting with that sparkle in your eyes when I come in from a hard day's ride. I want to know you'll always keep a light burning for me so that I'll never have to walk into a dark house again.''

He slipped his fingers beneath her chin and tilted her face up to his. With his lips hovering above hers he whispered, ''I want you to keep the darkness out of my life, Eva. Now and forever, I want you.''

He slipped his hand inside the opening of her satin robe and began to unbutton her nightgown. The tiny pearl buttons obliged. Chase's hand slid beneath the white lawn and he brushed the peak of her hardened nipple with his thumb. Eva's breath came quick and shallow. He kissed her, a slow and languorous kiss, while he kept up the exploration of her breast with his hand.

Her face flamed with color as memories and feelings came flooding back. Heat suffused her. She thought of the night of the storm and the bed they had already shared. ''Before we made love that night you thought I was a virgin,'' she whispered. ''Were you disappointed?''

He shook his head. ''A virgin would be a hell of a lot of trouble,'' he whispered. His head dipped to taste the bud that was exposed when he pushed her nightgown off her shoulder.

Her fingers tightened in his thick, dark hair. She gasped and pressed him closer. His teeth gently toyed with her nipple before he laved it with his hot tongue.

''What do you mean by trouble?'' she whispered.

His head came up and he smiled, his lips moist, too inviting to ignore. Eva took his lower lip between her teeth and gently tugged on it, teased it with her tongue and then drew back and smiled.

"I figure a virgin would never let me do this," he told her, pulling her nightgown to her waist before he cupped her buttocks in his hands. He lifted her until she was forced to lock her legs around his waist.

Eva let go of his hair and slipped her arms around his neck. "No, I don't suppose she would," she nibbled on his lower lip with a sigh of pleasure.

He reached behind him and slid the bolt on Miss Rachel's front door, then headed for the stairs. "Can you hold on until we get upstairs?"

"I'm a dancer, Mr. Cassidy. You might be quite surprised at what I can do."

Chase carried her upstairs and paused in the hallway, long enough for Eva to point the way to her room. Once inside, he shut the door with his foot and carried her to the bed.

He carefully lowered her onto the edge of the bed. He knelt down before her and stripped her of her robe. The ruffled hem of the white nightgown was bunched around her hips. Chase reached out and tenderly, almost worshipfully, ran his hands down the silken length of her thighs. His fingers tightened on her knees and he parted them. He moved up between them.

Eva bent close, took his face between her hands and kissed him full on the mouth. Chase cupped the mound between her legs and massaged her gently. Eva moaned with need.

"Do you think," he whispered, "that a virgin would let me take such liberties?"

"Only if she didn't intend to remain a virgin much longer." She sighed against his mouth as he parted her with his fingers and explored the warm, wet flesh at the apex of her thighs. Gradually, he delved further and increased the slow, sensual stimulation until she lay back on the bed and writhed beneath his hand.

"Oh, Chase!" Eva cried out as she climaxed against his

hand. Chase covered her with his body. Cradling her against him, he held her until she stopped shuddering and quieted beneath him.

Unable to stop touching her, his own need building ever higher, Chase kissed her ear, teased her earlobe with his teeth and nuzzled her neck. Eva slowly responded in kind and soon began running her hands up and down along his spine.

She had never felt so adored. Eva lay beneath him, within the protective circle of his arms and reveled in the honeyed warmth that spread through her.

She closed her eyes and whispered, "Mr. Cassidy, you have too many clothes on. I want to feel you against me."

She reached down and jerked the hem of Chase's linen shirt out of his striped wool trousers. He pulled back, giving her access to the front of his clothing. Eva wrestled with the buttons down his shirt until they were free. She peeled the fabric back off his shoulders. He shrugged out of the sleeves, and she tossed the shirt over the end of the bed.

Eva ran her fingers through the tight thatch of hair that covered his broad, well-defined chest. She rose to taste one of his nipples and was pleased by the harsh guttural sound he made deep in his throat when her lips touched him.

Desperate to feel him inside her, she fumbled with the buttons down the front of his pants. He pulled back to help her divest him of his Levi's and he laughed. The joyous sound brought joy to her heart. He drew her nightgown over her head and flung it toward the headboard. She spread her legs. He knelt between them.

Chase knew she was more than ready to receive him. Unwilling to prolong the sweet agony any longer, he rose to his knees, grasped her hips and pulled her toward him until she was impaled upon his turgid staff. He took her calves in his hands and placed them on his shoulders.

Eva cried out, her arms outstretched, hands clutching the bedspread. Her copper hair was as bright as a flame against the white spread. She responded to his carnal act with a raw cry that came from deep inside and let him fill her entirely. She arched away from the bed, her legs spread wide, her toes pointed as he rocked back and plunged into her again and again.

She tightened around him. Tensing, flexing, imprisoning him when he thrust forward, she moaned when he withdrew, only to cry out with the sheer, savage excitement of anticipation as he poised at her moist threshold. She begged him to enter her again, gasping out for more until the bed was rocking with the force of his thrusts.

He dove forward, pressed her back against the bed and covered her until they lay breast to breast, thigh to thigh. They came together. She called his name over and over again while Chase poured his seed, together with his soul, into her. Silent tears of joy streamed down her cheeks as she clung to him.

Eva listened to the sound of their breathing. It was ragged and wild. The warm summer breeze that filtered in felt cool against her overheated skin.

Chase raised his hand to brush back curls from her face and noticed that he was trembling. He curled his fingers into a tight fist and ran his knuckles along her cheek. She turned instinctively toward his hand and kissed him there.

"Sure glad you weren't a virgin," he whispered hoping to banish any lingering self-consciousness she might harbor.

"Too much trouble, I suppose," she murmured back.

"Way too much." He rolled to his side and pulled her against him. It felt right. Natural. It was where he wanted her forever. Chase realized that for the very first time in his life, everything seemed right. This was the way it was supposed to be, this is what all the hardship in his life had led him to—a new beginning with Eva.

"What are you thinking?" Eva watched him carefully. The usual deep shadows in his eyes were no longer lurking there. She lay content to study him, to wonder at the light of hope that had been kindled in his dark eyes.

"I was thinking about the way things have worked out. About you and me."

"What about us?"

"I like the sound of that," he smiled. "*Us.* I was thinking about how lucky I am to have you. What if that newspaper hadn't made its way to Wyoming and you had never seen my advertisement?"

She laughed. "What if I hadn't gotten mad enough to quit working at the Palace? I would have never found you."

His expression sobered. "Somehow I would have found you, Eva."

"Somehow we would have found each other." Her heart was near to bursting with love and pride. She felt herself blushing and kissed him quickly on the lips. "I think we ought to dress before Rachel comes home."

Unwilling to release her just yet Chase said, "She made certain I knew she wouldn't be back for a good long while, but I don't think she'd take to finding us like this. She probably has a virgin's sensibilities about such things."

"I'm sure she does."

He took her hand and brought her fingers to his lips. He kissed her fingertips and stared at the golden tips of her eyelashes. "Let's go home."

Eva took a deep breath. "Are you proposing, Mr. Cassidy, or am I to remain a fallen woman for the rest of my life?"

"I think it's about time we both tried to be a bit more respectable, don't you?"

Chapter Twenty-one

A week later they were married.

Two weeks later, her parents moved in.

Not to stay, they explained immediately after their surprise arrival, but merely to "spend a few idyllic weeks getting to know their new son-in-law."

Regretting Eva's sending a telegram to her parents so soon after the wedding, Chase managed to spend most of the first week of the Eberharts' visit in the saddle, in the barn, or otherwise occupied. Tonight he found himself missing Eva's company so much that he joined her and her parents on the porch. It had become their habit to sit outdoors each evening to enjoy the balmy summer nights and watch the fireflies flit around Eva's flower garden and count the stars as they appeared in the sky.

Eva had quickly recognized his aversion to close quarters and quickly tried to remedy the situation. She created what she called the summer parlor by arranging the sitting room chairs and two side tables on the porch.

Esther Eberhart was comfortably ensconced with her feet propped up on a table, not the least self-conscious of the way she showed her ankles and the underside of her skirt. The deep flounces on her purple petticoat gaily fanned open. She was lost in the midst of spinning yet another story of her trials and triumphs on stage.

Eva bore no resemblance to the tall, buxom woman with a wide mouth, luminous blue eyes, a broad nose, and a headful of hennaed hair. Incredibly, her exuberance far outpaced her daughter's. She spoke in such a loud voice that her side of every conversation could clearly be heard in the bunkhouse. Unwilling to "step in anything disgusting," she rarely ventured off the porch.

"What do you think, Endicott? Would you rather open in Topeka or California in March? For my money, I choose California. For one thing, the weather is far better. Well, actually, you can't compare the two in March. Not fair to Topeka at all. . . . "

As Esther went on and on, Chase glanced over at Endicott Eberhart. With his head resting on the back of a deep armchair, he appeared to be sound asleep, but that failed to keep his wife from addressing him. Although Chase found the man amiable, Endicott had little to say to him—not that anyone ever got a chance to say much of anything if Esther was in a talkative mood.

Eva's father was dressed in short leather trousers with colorfully embroidered suspenders and a white shirt with billowing sleeves. The actor claimed the outfit was quite the style in the mountains of Europe, and since Montana was as close as he was bound to get to an Alpine atmosphere, he would wear his *liederhosen* with pride. Each day he took his daily constitutional across the hills and valleys of the ranch, hiking with a tall walking stick Orvil had cut for him, shouting out the lines from all his favorite theatrical roles.

He was the talk of the bunkhouse.

Seated at the edge of the porch with his back resting against the railing, Chase looked down at Eva where she nestled beneath his arm. Curly lay on the step below them, snoring. The old dog's head rested on Chase's lap. Without thinking, Chase tightened his hold on Eva and pressed a kiss against the crown of her head.

He felt her gently lay her hand upon his thigh in acknowledgment of the tender gesture. He found it remarkable how they could communicate without words. Even with her parents around, he had never in his life known such peace. Except for the heartache he experienced whenever he thought of Lane, Chase was content.

"Mama." Eva tried to interrupt Esther's monologue. *"Mama."*

"What dear?" Esther took her feet off the rail, shook out her skirt and petticoat, and shifted until she found a more comfortable position in the chair. "Did you want to say something?"

Eva smiled up at Chase, then turned her attention back to her mother. "Chase was curious about Chester. Do you have any recollection of anything Grandpa Eberhart told you about him?"

Esther tapped her cheek. "Let me see—"

Endicott Eberhart sat straight up like a man risen from the dead. Chase tried not to laugh aloud. Obviously, Eva's father had been waiting for just such an opening. "Chester came to us from my side of the family, dear, so I'll tell this story if you don't mind. Where is he, by the way?"

"Out in the barn with some of my old things," Eva told him.

"In a very safe place," Chase added.

"*My* grandfather, Ellison Eberhart, obtained Chester long before my own father, Emerson, was born. I seem to recall the story my father passed on to me was that Grandfather once had a very dear friend he worked with in the East. Never was very successful. When he died, he willed Chester to my grandfather. I think I do recall that Chester was once referred to as Pharaoh. Yes, that's right. Pharaoh, an Egyptian king."

"A very *small* Egyptian king," Esther interjected with a snort. "At times I wish we could have asked Great-grandfather about how the mummy came to be in America. He didn't have much of his mind left when he died, poor old dear," she said with a wave of her hand. "Sang day and night. Opera. Top of his lungs. It was terrible. We had to give him lots of laudanum to get him to sleep so we could have some peace and quiet."

Chase cleared his throat. He wondered if the elder Eberharts knew how very eccentric they were. If so, they obviously didn't care. He looked over at Endicott. "Did your grandfather have much money?"

Eva glanced up at him quickly. He could see his bluntness shocked her, but the question didn't seem to bother Endicott in the least.

"At one time he did. Seems he had quite an inheritance, but when he became an actor he went through it all trying to support his family between bouts of steady work." Eva's father ran his thumbs up and down behind his suspenders and stared up at the night sky. "Didn't know there were so many stars."

Chase pulled away from Eva. "I'll be right back," he whispered against her ear. "Don't go anywhere."

She smiled into his eyes and watched him walk toward the barn. Just watching the way he moved caused her heart to beat faster and a heady rush of passion to warm her in places that made her blush to think of. As a husband, he was kind and gentle, loving and giving, still as stubborn as a mule when it came to convincing him to go into Last Chance.

Eva had vowed to love, honor, and obey him—up to a point—and she had also promised herself she would never give up trying to help Chase find a place in the community.

"You're in love, aren't you, dear?" Esther asked.

"Oh, yes, Mama. I'm in love."

"We like him." Her father said, as if she might have forgotten that he told her the same thing every time Chase left the house. "Good man. He'll take good care of you. Wouldn't want to cross him, though."

Eva looked across the barnyard and saw Chase walk out of the barn with Chester's mummy case in his arms. She couldn't get over his fascination with the thing.

She leaned toward her father and asked softly, "Do you still have your book on ancient Egypt among your things, Papa?"

Endicott scratched his head. "I don't recall off hand. Why?"

"I've never seen Chase so interested in anything beside the ranch . . . and me, of course," she laughed. "He might like to read more on the subject."

"On what subject?" Chase paused at the edge of the low porch and rested his foot on the step. He set Chester's case down beside him. Curly half-heartedly sniffed the box, and then flopped back down on his side.

Eva looked up at him. The glow in his eyes when he watched her was anything but warm, it was downright incinerating. She traced the outline of her lips with her tongue and nearly purred, "The subject of Egyptology. You seem very curious about Chester's origins."

He couldn't take his eyes off her lips. Wishing he hadn't brought up the subject just now, Chase wanted to thrust the mummy case aside, pick Eva up, and carry her to the nearest bedroom. Instead, he tore his gaze away from her before his arousal became obvious and he embarrassed himself in front of her parents.

"I think I might know more about Chester than any of you," he confessed, tapping the case on the head.

"How so, Chase?" Endicott leaned forward, his elbows on his knees. Sunlight had all but faded from the sky. As they talked, Eva rose and lit a lamp on the table between her parents' chairs. She slipped inside for a moment to light the lamp on the mantel, and joined them again.

Chase began to explain. "When Eva's cousin had her things delivered, she was staying in town at her friend Rachel's—"

"For propriety's sake, of course," her mother said.

Chase and Eva glanced at each other and smiled.

"Anyway," he continued, "I didn't know whether she needed her things right away or not—and the trunk was unlocked," he watched Eva as he spoke, "so I looked through it."

She encouraged him with a smile. "Not much to see, was there?"

He thought of the satins, the costumes, the recipes, and the reviews. "Some of it was pretty interesting. Our children will love the costumes someday." He silently promised himself that he would make sure the bad reviews disappeared.

Esther stood up. "Children? Oh, Eva! Are you—?"

"No, Mama. Please sit down."

Esther sat.

"About Chester," Endicott gently prodded.

Chase glanced at each of them in turn. He felt so awk-ward holding court that he couldn't help but admire the Eberharts' ability to perform in front of a crowd. Just the thought of standing up before a roomful of people made his blood run cold. "After I closed the trunk, I picked up the mummy case and opened it."

Eva ran her hand down the faded lid of the case. "You found the secret latch."

He nodded. "I was tapping the lid and found it by ac-cident. That's not all I found." He opened the case again. "I didn't know anything about mummy cases or Egyptians. I didn't know what Eva might have wrapped up in here. For all I knew, it was a body."

"A very *small* body," Esther snorted again.

"You *unwrapped* Chester?" Eva thought it was the most disgusting thing she had ever heard. "What was it like? Horrible?"

"Not at all."

"Nothing much left of him, I suppose." Endicott spec-ulated.

"Plenty." Chase hunkered down, laid the case on its back, and opened the lid. Chester lay just as Chase had left him, still rewrapped in the aged linen bandages. He lifted the doll out and began to unwind the cloths.

Eva covered her eyes. "Do you have to do that here?"

"Keep watching. I promise, Chester is not what you think."

The feet with sandals painted on them, and then the bare wooden legs, were unwrapped. Unable to wait any longer, Endicott stood up and knelt down to help Chase.

Eva's father said, "It looks like . . . "

Esther was hanging over her husband's shoulder by the time Chase removed the last of the bandages.

"A ventriloquist's dummy!" Esther shouted so loud that

the bunkhouse door slammed shortly afterward.

Eva glanced around and saw Orvil, Jethro, and Ramon hurrying across the yard.

"I don't believe it," she said, turning back to Chase, who had set the dummy on his knee and was using the mechanism inside to move the mouth up and down. He seemed so delightfully out of character holding the wooden Pharaoh that she hooked her arm around his neck and kissed him soundly on the cheek.

"He's wonderful," she laughed.

"Your husband or the dummy?" Esther barely got the question out before she began hooting with laughter and slapping her knees, tickled by her own wit.

"I'll let that comment go, Mother, but behave yourself," Eva warned with a smile.

"There's more," Chase told them. He flipped the dummy over and showed Endicott the small door in the back of Pharaoh Chester's head, then handed him over to Eva's father. "You had better open it yourself."

Orvil, Jethro, and Ramon were leaning over the porch rail. Endicott made much of the moment and the audience. He twirled his wrists and flexed his fingers. He pressed on the tiny door, using the same motion it took to open the mummy case, and the small, hinged square popped open.

The silence was deafening. Again Endicott engaged in the finger flexes and the wrist twists. Eva was sure he would have demanded a drumroll if there had been an orchestra present. Her father then reached into the secret compartment with thumb and forefinger and pulled out the small velvet bag. He smoothed it out, traced the elegant golden E embroidered on the bag, and handed Chester back to Chase.

The actor couldn't hide his excitement. He looked over at his wife, then his daughter, and finally at Chase. "You know what's in here?"

"I do." Chase admitted.

"Will it make me happy?"

"I don't know about happy," Chase told him truthfully,

"but it'll sure as hell make you rich."

"Open it, for heaven's sake, Endicott," Esther bellowed.

Eva leaned against Chase's knee. "Yes, open it, Papa."

Endicott opened the drawstrings and spilled the contents into his hand. He stared down at the sparkling jewels in disbelief. An assortment of sizes, most of the gems were the size of his thumbnail. For the first time in her life, Esther Eberhart was at a loss for words.

"Oh, my," Eva whispered.

"You can say that again," Orvil's deep, gravelly voice carried to them through the dark.

Eva looked up at Chase. "You knew these were inside Chester's head all the time?"

"Since the day I unwrapped him, the day before I went into town to ask you to come home. That's why I kept asking so many questions about Chester that day. I couldn't figure out why you wanted to hire on as a housekeeper if you knew you had these jewels. Then I wondered if maybe—" He halted abruptly and frowned.

"You wondered if I had come by them dishonestly, is that it?"

Even if it meant risking her anger, he vowed to tell her the truth for the rest of his life. "At first I wondered if you stole them. After questioning you, I could tell you obviously didn't know a thing about them. I decided to wait for a time when I could turn them over to all of you." His next question was for Eva alone. "Can you forgive me?"

Eva watched him for a long, silent moment. No one around them spoke. Endicott continued to examine the stones. She reached up and tenderly pushed a lock of hair back off Chase's forehead, then leaned forward and gently kissed his lips.

As she drew back, Eva told him, "If the boot had been on the other foot and I found something like this hidden around here, I'd probably have wondered the same thing about you."

Her comment broke the tension. Everyone around them began to laugh. Esther stood and burst into a chorus of

"The Battle Hymn of the Republic," shouting "Glory, Glory, Hallelujah," at the top of her lungs. Talking softly among themselves, Jethro and Ramon followed Orvil around to the kitchen for a cup of coffee.

Endicott finally silenced his wife. "Esther, a little more decorum, if you please. Think of the neighbors." He turned to Eva, who was still on her knees beside Chase at the edge of the porch. "Hold out your hand, Evie. You too, son."

"Oh, Papa, no—"

Endicott drew himself up as Eva had seen him do so many times in preparation for delivery of a soliloquy. He lifted the palm full of precious gems and began solemnly, "These are your great-grandfather Ellison Eberhart's family jewels. Since my own father never found them, Great-grandfather's inheritance is his legacy directly to us, by way of Chester, of course." He bowed to the dummy that was once again propped on Chase's lap. "I am certain that he would want you, Eva, and you, too, Chase, to have your share."

Chase shook his head. He wouldn't let them think he had married Eva because he knew she was not the penniless dancer she thought herself to be.

"Sir, I can't take anything from—"

"Enough nobility, son. You are a part of this family now. Did you not vow to love Eva through sickness and health, for richer, for poorer?"

"Yes, sir."

"Well," Endicott said as he took a quarter of the gems and lay them in his daughter's hand, "this is the 'richer' part. In my experience, it's best to enjoy it while you have it. Just look at Great-grandfather. He died penniless. Hid a fortune away, and when he needed it, he couldn't even remember that he had it in the first place."

He measured out an equal amount of gems for Chase. The remaining stones he poured back into the bag and handed it to his wife, who ecstatically clutched the black velvet to her bosom.

"Oh, Endicott," she gushed. "Should we *celebrate* tonight?"

"Of course, my dear." He waggled his eyebrows at her. When he crooked his elbow, she linked her arm through his. "Good night, children," Endicott announced grandly. "We are off to bed."

Together they made a sweeping bow and disappeared into the house. Chase watched them walk through the sitting room where Eva had a lamp burning on the mantel. He smiled. In two weeks she had never failed to light a lamp as soon as the sun began to fade. He knew that she would never forget her promise to leave a light burning for him, no matter how many years they spent together.

They were alone now except for Curly, who rarely left Eva's side when he was not working cattle with the men.

Chase could feel the gemstones in his fist. They had warmed to his body heat. He set Chester on the armchair and took Eva's hand. He poured the multicolored stones into her palm where they mingled with her own share.

"If I could," she said softly, "I would trade them all away to have Lane home again."

Chase sighed. Never a day went by when he didn't think of Lane. "He's got to find his own way, Eva. Maybe, when he does, he'll come back."

She stared down at the stones again, fascinated by the range of size and color. "What will we do with them?"

"Anything you want," he promised. He looked into her upturned face, at her green eyes that shone brighter than any emeralds, and wondered how a gunfighter and jailbird came to be the luckiest man in the world.

"I already have everything I want sitting here right beside me," she whispered. "I love you, Chase Cassidy."

"I love you, too, Eva. With all my heart."

She reached out and toyed with the button at the neck of his shirt. "So, do you think we should go celebrate a little ourselves?"

"I think a private celebration is definitely in order."

Chase helped his wife to her feet. She dusted off her

skirt with one hand, the jewels clenched tight in the other. He blew out the lamp on the table and waited for Eva in the open doorway.

The lavender scent of lilacs floated on the night breeze as Eva moved past him. Before Chase closed the door, he winked at the dummy on the chair.

Chester was smiling his gaping smile.

Chase was certain he saw the dummy wink back.